The Best Days

C. E. Knight

First published by Kindle Direct Publishing in the United Kingdom in 2024

Copyright © C. E. Knight 2024

All rights reserved.

No part of this publication may be reproduced, distributed, or transmitted in any form or by any means, including photocopying, recording, or other electronic or mechanical methods, without the prior written permission of the publisher or author.

All persons, places, incidents and actions in this novel are fictitious. Any similarity to real persons, living or dead, places, incidents or actions is coincidental.

Cover design © Alex Knight 2024

For Jenni Wyn Hyatt and Christopher Nash,
my mum and dad

"The fool doth think he is wise,

but the wise man knows himself to be a fool."

William Shakespeare, *As You Like It*

1: The End of Last Year

The traditional end-of-term summer ramble had been cancelled. Grey rain thrashed the empty playground with vicious, punishing strokes. It had poured without stopping for two days and the sky was bruised and swollen and heavy. Turning away from her computer, Liz Marshall looked out of her classroom window and up at the sky, where the clouds loured, threatening to ruin the glorious summer that was just one more day away.

She exhaled noisily and chewed her pen, resigned. It was true; they couldn't risk taking hundreds of teenagers (some of whom would have ignored advice and embarked upon the hike in flip-flops) along the eight miles of by now treacherous footpaths that traced the flanks and spine of the Bremeldon Hills, which rose behind the school. In fact, how they ever managed to get all the kids and march them in one ramshackle crocodile along the carefully planned route without killing or losing any of them in *fine* weather, let alone in this, was a mystery to Liz.

Still, the King Richard the Lionheart High School summer ramble was always a huge success. More than that, it was an institution. And even though many of the kids had cheered at its cancellation, in reality, they loved it—once they got started. Except for those who stayed at home. Or those who wore the wrong shoes and got blisters. Or that one who broke his ankle at the top of the hills, had an asthma attack and the air ambulance had to be called. But apart from that, they absolutely adored it.

The head's email to staff, however, had outlined the alternative arrangements he had put in place now that the whole school would be confined to the building, rather than free to walk on the hills. The next day—the last day of term—was to be a day of normal lessons with proper learning objectives and success criteria. With absolutely no watching of films or playing of games. The senior leadership team, he promised, would be patrolling the corridors and classrooms to make sure. Great.

How times had changed. Liz remembered how it used to be when she first started at King Richard's. The last day of any term was a day when teaching was suspended, when kids brought in films to watch, games to play and, if you were lucky, the odd present for the teachers. They were days to be looked forward to with excitement and back upon with fondness, days when hooligans stayed at home and bullies bunked off, days when both teachers and students let their guards down and enjoyed each other's company, days when they were on the same side.

Liz closed the email with a huff; this was inhumane.

Dave Bishop, Liz's head of department, stomped into the room, glasses flashing, cheeks, pink with indignation. "Have you seen Bob Woodfield's email about tomorrow?"

"I know," said Liz. "He's not usually such a bloody jobsworth. We wouldn't have been teaching if we'd been on the ramble, would we, so why can't we have a bit of fun?"

"I don't get it; he's retiring anyway so what difference does it make to him?" Dave sighed. "Oh well, bang goes leaving early; I'd better go and plan some lessons. The kids'll be on the ceiling tomorrow."

"You can't blame them," said Liz. "Oh, and don't forget your bloody learning objectives."

Now, she too had six lessons to plan and six objectives to think up. She'd have thought they could have made it out before five on the last-but-one day of term, for God's sake. It had been a long year and they were all on their knees. There was a bottle of red at home with her name on it.

Right, she thought, *if he wants an objective, I'll give him a bloody objective. Just one. For the whole day.*

The next day, it was still raining. Relentlessly. The hills loomed, scornful under slabs of sullen cloud.

"Look where you could be today," they seemed to say and more than once, as the morning dragged on, Liz's gaze lingered on them until her classroom windows became so smothered by steam that the hills disappeared from view completely.

Liz had written the mandatory learning objective on the board: *to review and consolidate last term's learning.* Every one of Liz's six classes was doing exactly the same thing and Liz vacillated, as always, between worrying *what if I get caught?* and resolving *let them catch me.* The kids didn't mind; Liz had produced a crate of colourful gel pens and highlighters to make their work seem a bit less like work and they chattered excitedly, tidying books, ready to take home; setting targets for the next year, and assessing one another's writing.

They didn't mind the rain, either, spending break and lunch tearing round the playground, kicking sheets of grit-filled puddle water at each other, howling and yelping, before shaking themselves like dogs and bounding back to lessons.

After lunch, Liz's year eights charged in with a cheerful, but unequivocal, lack of recognition of her attempts at control. It would have been useless to try and make them sit quietly for the register; she just had to hope that the head didn't choose that moment to check up on her, trust that they would settle themselves eventually. Her trust was reasonably well founded and their exuberance was subsiding, when a boy rushed in late and stood in the doorway, giggling, apparently waiting for everyone to notice him. He was grinning widely, his hair was plastered to his head, his clothes were dripping and a puddle was spreading around his feet. "I'm wet, Miss," he stated.

Liz looked in mock relief. "Oh, *that's* what it is—I thought you were melting!" at which the others screeched with laughter—kids were easily pleased—and a fresh cacophony arose as they hunted for books and fought over chairs, asking each other, "Did you hear what Miss said?" and generally winding themselves and each other back up.

Despite the head's warning about policing corridors and monitoring class rooms, not a single member of the senior leadership team had graced the English block, let alone Liz's room, with their presence all day, which was at once galling and a relief. Despite her natural inclination to rebelliousness, the scars of a horrendous first year in teaching—at another school—had never left her and she had spent the next fifteen years in perpetual terror of being thought incompetent. So, she stayed on her guard and her eyes flicked to the doorway every time she heard movement outside it. Some of the students noticed and called out, "Woody's coming," or, "Hello, Mr Woodfield," whenever Liz had her back to the door, causing her to whip her head round every time and then laugh and roll her eyes: "Got me again."

Finally, as Liz's most challenging class arrived for the last lesson of the school year, she breathed in, forced a smile onto her face and greeted them as they bounced, shoved and wrestled their way in, still damp and muddy from their lunch-time exertions. The last lesson of the last day. With lower band year nine. Wonderful. And just the sort of lesson Mr Woodfield might check up on.

They weren't bad kids really—just a bit feral—and Liz's clenched smile relaxed into something more genuine as they hailed her cheerily. They didn't even seem to mind too much when their chorus of, "Are we watching a film, Miss?"

was answered in the negative. Liz had put paper and coloured pens and pencils on each table so the students could work in groups and, when they had tidied their books and peer-assessed each other's latest piece of writing, they would be allowed to choose from a variety of *Macbeth*-related extension tasks: drawing and labelling the three witches, completing a word-search or crossword, or filling in missing words from soliloquies.

For once, Laylah (who struggled to read and write modern English, let alone Shakespearean and usually occupied herself with a—frankly astonishing—repertoire of gleefully executed nefariousness) was doing what she should have been. More than that, by half-way through the lesson, she had tidied her book, assessed her partner's writing skills and set her own targets for next year: *1. lern the storey off macbethe, 2. larn abot the carcter's of macBeth, and, 3. lerne the keye vocably off mack beth*.

"Can I have a sticker, Miss?" she said. "I've done all the work and I've been good today, ain't I?"

Liz pulled up a chair and sat down. "This is lovely work, Laylah," she said, as she adorned Laylah's book with ticks, stickers and stars.

"I've decided to be good for the rest of the year." Laylah wriggled in her seat and sat up straight in proof.

Liz smiled. "I noticed. Well done."

Whether she was saving her energy for a bit of 'twocking' later or she had already started on the 'wacky baccy', Liz wasn't sure, but hers was not to reason why and she just enjoyed it while it lasted. Laylah could be quite sweet—when she wasn't dismantling and smashing pens—or accusing other students of looking at her funny—or shouting obscenities into other classrooms. No, apart from that, she was all right. Her previous misdemeanours evaporated and Liz prompted, "Are you going to take it home with you?"

"I might do," she said, "after I've shown Miss Bosun. She always gives me a cup of tea and some toast in the morning. Anyway, my mum don't like school stuff. She chucked it away last time."

"Oh dear," Liz said, "Miss Bosun would love to see it, though."

Laylah's eyes widened, serious, hopeful. "Would she *really*, Miss?"

"Of course."

And she would. As head of year seven, Barbara Bosun kept an eye on all her 'sad little ones' throughout their whole time at school, and would be heartened by this half-hour improvement in Laylah's behaviour. Liz handed her a word-search containing *Macbeth* quotations and a pink highlighter and Laylah set about searching, whispering the letters to herself and frowning as she combed the grid.

"Got one!" she said: *something*."

"Keep reading along; there's more," Liz said.

Twenty minutes to go and then they would all be free. The class room felt jollier and more purposeful than it had in any last lesson of any Friday all year. Liz relaxed. It was fine.

Suddenly, the sound of footsteps in the corridor put her back on the alert. He wouldn't come now, would he? Anyway, what if he did? Everything was going well. *She* was *doing* well.

"*Wicked*," read Laylah, falteringly, highlighting the word-search as she read.

Liz laughed. "Keep going; you've nearly got it."

Laylah traced beyond the words, mouthing *something wicked* and found the next part. "*This—way—comes*!" she shouted in triumph.

All of a sudden, Liz stiffened, aware of a shadow in the doorway. Were her thumbs pricking? She froze and held her breath. Her day flashed before her eyes and, doubting herself, she peered wildly at the whiteboard to check: the learning objective was still there. She eyed the kids: still purposefully occupied. She glanced at the screen again: success criteria all in place. But she was still gripped by panic. There was bound to be something wrong.

When she saw who it was, however, she breathed again.

"Hi, Pam. Come in." It was the special needs coordinator, come to see some of her students one last time before she, too, retired. Pam just nodded curtly in response—a little strange, but she had always been rather on the formal side—and walked, noiselessly around the room, speaking in a low voice to each of the students on the special needs register, which was almost everyone in this class. It was touching that she had made this effort and Liz felt sorry for her when some of the students were less than enthusiastic in their responses. Pam finally sat down next to Laylah and listened, nodding, as she showed her how much work she had done in today's lesson and how many stickers 'Miss' had given her. She even spelled out *Macbeth* (correctly) without looking at the worksheet. Progress.

Liz wandered around, looking at the students' books and giving out stickers, frowning and putting a finger to her lips when one or two asked, "What's *she* doing here, Miss?" or commented, "I hate her; she's horrible."

Pam was strict, it was true, but that was so she could support her students and their over-stretched class teachers, so Liz shut any criticisms down and made absolutely sure their comments were not heard. Teachers had to have each others' backs.

Five minutes before the final bell of the school year, Pam stood up, nodded again and slipped out of the room without saying a word. Odd.

"Where did Miss Hooper go?" one of the students asked.

Liz shrugged, bemused. "I expect she didn't want you to make a fuss of her on her last day," she said. "Anyway, have you seen the time? It's nearly the holidays. Look! It's stopped raining. The sun's come out!"

The students squealed and launched into a frenzy of tidying before counting down the last ten seconds to the bell, which sounded its metallic blare—just a few seconds after the collective crescendo of *zero* (one of these days, they'd get it spot on), and a cheering chaos of teenagers surged through the door.

Golden sunlight crept through the windows. Golden silence settled on the classroom. Liz sighed happily as she straightened tables and chairs, picked up pens and empty water bottles and bits of paper. The year was over at last. At last, she could stop worrying. It was the beginning of the holidays. Summer was here.

She had thought too soon, though; there was a distant, low, menacing growl and, once again, rain spat at the window. She should have known.

Dave came in from his room next door.

"All right, Bish?" Liz grinned at him. "We made it, then. Pity that sun didn't last. You going over to the staffroom for the leaving speeches? Free Prosecco!"

Dave did not smile back. "Look what Pam just gave me." He paused. "Arsehole."

The room darkened and the thunder grew to a roar as the rain slashed down again.

Dread bloomed in Liz's throat and plunged to her stomach. She looked from the sheet of paper in Dave's hand to his grim expression.

"Oh God," she said and sank into a chair. She took the sheet from him, skimming past Pam's comments about

Laylah's work not being challenging enough and the learning objective not being aspirational enough to the verdict at the bottom of the page: *requires improvement*.

"She doesn't know what she's talking about, Liz," Dave said. "She's not even supposed to rate lessons any more. Everyone knows she's useless; that's why the head's been on at her all term to finish her observations. She must've had one more to fit in and you had the class with the most special needs kids in it."

Liz tried to swallow a sob. "But that's the best lesson I've ever had with them. They've never behaved that well or done that much work before. Laylah Brown stayed in her seat and even got onto extension tasks. She finally learned how to spell *Macbeth*, for fuck's sake. If that's not bloody good enough, I don't know what else I can do."

Dave sat down opposite her, shaking his head. "You don't *need* to do anything else. None of us could have done any better."

"No, but I'm the one she saw. I'm the one she wrote the report on. I'm the one who requires improvement." She stopped and sighed harshly. "Just when I was starting to get the hang of it. Oh God—" She put her head in her hands. "Next year, it'll be constant observations and book checks and more hoops to jump through. Not to mention worrying and planning all over the holidays."

He leaned towards her and patted her arm awkwardly. "Come on; don't be upset. It won't come to that; you're a great teacher."

Liz snorted. "Well, I was starting to think I was good *enough*."

"I'm going complain to the head," he said. "She shouldn't have watched you in the last lesson. She shouldn't have come in without warning. It's fucking outrageous." He stopped. "And I'm not clapping her leaving speech, either! I might even heckle." He stood up. "Come on. On your feet, soldier."

Sniffing, Liz did as she was told.

"Good girl. Now—I know where they've stashed the spare bottles of fizz and I'm nicking one for you," Dave said, steering her towards the door. "No excuses," he told her, "I'll give you a lift home. Right now, what you need is a drink—and then a holiday."

Liz poked at a leaking eye with her knuckle and sniffed again. "I just want to go home," she said, "I'm not in the mood."

But Dave would not take no for an answer. "Elizabeth Marshall," he said, "you are getting pissed on Prosecco and that's an order."

2: The End of the Holidays

Another summer squandered.

Six weeks. Gone. Memories of late morning lie-ins, daytime television, and afternoons consumed by the vast, elastic internet confirmed it. Liz had neither cleared out the loft nor planned any lessons and the novel that was definitely inside her somewhere was still to be started.

"How the hell am I going to get through another year?" she wailed.

Jack stood up and gulped his coffee. "Just like you always do," he said. It was the same every September.

"But it's different this year," Liz insisted. "There's a new head. Shit—" she dragged in a breath. "What if he thinks I'm shit? What if he sees Pam Hooper's report?"

"He won't," Jack said. "Dave got it cancelled. Anyway, you've been teaching for years and they haven't sacked you yet, have they?"

This cheered her up, but she grimaced anyway. "It's only a matter of time."

Jack kissed the top of her head on his way out. "You'll be fine. Anyway, it's not *real* work today, is it?"

Liz's eyes narrowed in mock threat; he made this joke every time she had a staff training day.

"Daft bastard," she chuckled and launched her slipper after him as he opened the front door. It hit the wood with a soft thud as he closed it and fell to the floor.

"He's right, though," she thought. "Thank you, INSET day. Now, where are my jeans and flip-flops?"

Upstairs, Liz picked up yesterday's top from the floor and sniffed—it would do—and by the time she had pulled on yesterday's jeans too, her reflection looked gratifyingly unpremeditated. She was ready.

She opened her car door and sagged into the seat, trying not to notice the melancholy handful of holiday sand that had found its inevitable way to the footwell. Its grittiness taunted her as she felt for the clutch pedal with scantily shod feet and a gauze of early morning condensation veiled the windscreen, belying the belief that summer could not be over. Not yet.

Stoically, half-heartedly, she drove along roads that were untravelled, by her at least, since July. What did Keats know? Autumn was odious. She despised the season of mists; there was nothing mellow about its fruitfulness, and summer had absolutely not o'er-brimm'd any clammy cells she could think of.

Halfway to school, Liz spotted a small, navy-jumpered boy and his mother at a usually crowded bus stop. He must be a new year seven. She stopped and wound down the window. "Are you starting at King Richard's?"

The boy's eyes widened, alarmed, and he darted backwards, out of arm's reach.

His mother held his hand tightly. "That's right, why?"

"It's okay, I'm a teacher there." She rummaged for her staff badge and showed him. "You can go back to bed," she told them. "It's teacher training day. You're not in till tomorrow! Check the website."

The boy blinked and exhaled. "Thanks, Miss." He grinned unexpectedly, turned and they hurried away.

The atmosphere in the English block staffroom was heavy with coffee and dejection when Liz sloped in a few minutes later; they still had half an hour before the *welcome back* meeting so she grabbed a coffee and flopped into a chair.

"Good holiday, Liz? Glad to be back? How were your results?" enquired Dave, triply.

"Fine. No. Couldn't give a shit," she replied, only two-thirds truthfully (she had, in fact, disrupted the family holiday to find somewhere with a signal so she could check her class's results online, as soon as they had come out), but why would she let that get in the way of a good quip? "Morning, Bish," she added, "how was France?"

"Fucking French."

Uncertain whether this was a specific criticism of the Gallic people or simply an emphatic allusion to the bleeding obvious, Liz laughed anyway. "How's the new head?"

"Fucking... er... headish." Dave floundered, before shrugging sheepishly as if he realised his attempt to answer in the same vein had been poorly judged, but had soldiered on anyway.

"Good one," Liz tittered encouragingly. "You're on form."

Dave got into his stride: "Bedroom floordrobe this morning?" He nodded towards Liz's crumpled top.

"My ball gown's at the dry cleaner's. Anyway, the wine stain makes me look..." She deliberated.

Dave was amused. "What?"

"Edgy... louche," she finished.

"Dodgy lush, more like."

Just then, the tinny jangle of a bicycle bell sounded as a familiar woman free-wheeled across the wagtail-dotted playground. A moment later, the comfortably dishevelled, posset-stained Lucy Gray bounced in, unclipping her helmet, tousling her hair and rubbing at a dubious looking mark on the hem of her shirt, sniffing it and tutting.

"All right, losers?" Lucy beamed. "Coming to the pub for lunch, later?"

Liz's mood lifted as she remembered the traditional training day treat—two for one at The Snowdrop—she envisioned steak and chips. "I'm having a glass of red with mine. They haven't got me yet!"

But 'they' had. Liz shuddered as anxiety seized her; the new head would want to know his staff. There was every chance he would want to see her teach, especially if that report had found its way to him after all. Her ineptitude would be discovered.

Even after fifteen years, Imposter Syndrome was impossible to elude and despite reasonable (if not overwhelming) evidence of her competence (if not expertise) she still doubted herself, still dreaded exposure as a fraud, or worse: inadequate, the nadir of Ofsted ratings.

More members of the department arrived and the usual discussion of exams and whether all the hoped-for A level classes would run followed. Gareth Lincoln sauntered over and handed Liz a list of names. "Hey, Liz," he said. "Good news: ten year twelves have signed up for Film Studies."

That sweetened the pill of the end of the holidays considerably; Liz loved teaching A Level Film.

"Morning, morning, morning," Peggy Fletcher bustled in, weighed down with essential provisions, her voice chiming over the conversation. "I've got milk, tea, coffee and emergency chocolate!" She produced a huge tub of the kind of chocolates usually reserved for Christmas and placed it in the centre of the table.

"What emergency are you expecting, Peg?" Gareth nonchalantly shrugged his jacket and removed the lid. Absent-mindedly whistling the theme tune of *A Bout de Souffle*, he probed the tub with an elegant finger, selected a nutty one and sat down. He crossed his legs, adjusted his glasses and leaned back, scrutinizing Peggy while he unwrapped it pensively and put it to his mouth. Looking like

Godard with a Gauloise, he tapped his tastefully shod foot in mid-air.

Peggy rolled her eyes: "Running out of chocolate, obviously."

"I think you've got that covered," Gareth chuckled.

Before long, it was time to straggle across the playground for the meeting and, entering the hall, with its shabby stage, framed by frayed and faded velvet curtains, Liz cheered inwardly; rows of blue plastic chairs all faced the front. No group work, no anxiety-inducing small talk with people from other departments whom she didn't know well, no having to think, no pretending she knew what the hell was going on. They bagged a row of chairs that was just far enough from the back not to evoke disapproval and rooted around for pens. Liz's main concern was whether it was better to appear alert and neutral, so as not to draw attention to herself, or subversive and cynical, which was cooler, but might mark her out as a dissident. The former simply required her to sit about three inches taller than the latter and tilt her head an inch to one side. She opted for something vaguely between the two.

Liz perched her planner on her thigh and scrawled the new head's name. She was busy, doodling a spider, descending from the *N* of *Dillon*, and wondering whether there would still be free cakes and coffee at morning break when Dave slid in beside her. "Have I missed anything?"

"Nothing much," Liz replied. "The curtains are still held together with staples and there's still a felt tip cock on the wall."

"Wouldn't be the same without it," Dave said. "How long's it been there now?"

Before Liz could guess, a man stepped into the room, glanced about him and sprang up the steps to the stage. In contrast to Mr Woodfield, whose impeccably tailored grey suit—even on the first day—represented authority, this leader seemed determined to communicate casual ease to his newly acquired subordinates. A whisper spread throughout the hall. Colleague nudged colleague. Spines creaked and uncurled.

The new head was wearing jeans.

3: New Head

Optimism crept in on emaciated legs. Perhaps it would be all right after all. However, as Liz studied Gordon Dillon's obviously carefully selected outfit and recalled her own sartorial decision of that morning, optimism's frail limbs buckled and gave way. The too-stiff denim; the linen shirt with its ultra-casual but perfectly pressed grandad collar and the tweed waistcoat—universal sign of the consciously insouciant (and only ever partnered by the jacket and trousers of the suit from which it had been separated, until now, Liz suspected)—did not look as if they had been salvaged from his bedroom floor.

"It's still a suit," she thought, through gritted brain, and vowed to be on her guard.

Each garment seemed to shrink away from every other, as if they had all met for the first time today, not become acquainted in Cornish beer gardens or on Breton beaches. Those clothes had soaked up neither cider nor Cinsault. The faded areas of those jeans had been synthetically produced in a factory and the nylon umbilicus that joined shirt to shop label still pulsed its last in his bedroom bin, she was certain.

The room hushed. Gilded motes of dust waltzed and slowed in the sun-stripes from the high windows. Breaths became shallow as graves.

Gordon Dillon gazed round at the expectant staff from his elevated position on the stage. His eyes panned the large room, skittering from front door to fire exit. Visibly gratified that his entrance had been noticed and acted upon, he smiled and waited. But he did not speak. Caught between grin and grimace, his smile began to twitch. His temple fluttered. That muscle in his jaw flickered. The projector buzzed.

Suddenly, he swallowed and coughed before he rubbed his hands together in an oddly jubilant-looking gesture. He had, apparently, recovered and he commenced his assiduously practised (Liz was willing to bet) inaugural address: the speech that would both woo and warn his underlings.

"Good morning, everyone. I'm literally overjoyed to be here."

"What the fuck?" said the look that Liz and Dave exchanged.

Now that his false start was over, there seemed to be no stopping his messianic torrent of rhetoric.

"Welcome to the beginning of a new term at King Richard the Lionheart High School: *Dickie's*, I think they call it." He paused, observing the effects of his communication so far, then drew a decisive breath. "This post was a calling."

Gordon continued. "You're my flock and I'm your shepherd. I'm going to bring you to my folds."

Dave avoided an audible snigger by sinking his fingernails into his knees.

"Folds?" whispered Liz.

Dave's contempt surmounted his amusement. "Knob," he muttered.

Liz crossed out 'Dillon', scrawled 'Dildo' and nudged Dave, turning her planner towards him. Dave started to shake gently with silent mirth. Liz smiled, knowing Dave would see to it that the nickname caught on.

Unaware of all the rolling eyes in front of him, Gordon's own were misted with what looked like ambition and trained on the school emblem at the back of the hall: a golden lion, rampant on a blood-red shield. He reminded his flock that they had been lost, but he had found them and would guide them to greatness.

"You must have faith in me..." Gordon told them and paused dramatically. "...Believe in me," he continued.

"Halle-fucking-lujah," Dave whispered tmetically, "When do we get everlasting life?"

"And" Gordon's voice hardened and his eyes narrowed. "—do things my way."

Liz glanced around the hall and noted expressions ranging from half-concealed scorn to ill-concealed bewilderment. Suddenly, something more than dust seemed to charge the early autumn air with an unformed potency, as yet too elusive to galvanise the workforce.

Liz tuned back into the head's speech. He was holding forth again.

"I'm going to inject some passion into my teachers," he announced. "We all need our batteries recharging sometimes, and I'm going to make it my raisin d'été—"

A rasp of escaped laughter came from the languages department and was quickly suppressed, but its instigator did not seem to notice.

"—to excite you, to get you going, to give that buzz to each and every one of you."

Batteries. Buzz. This was textbook. Liz elbowed Dave and redirected his attention to the *Dildo!* she had just jotted, in case he was in any doubt about the pertinence of the sobriquet.

Liz's attention was brought back to Gordon as she became aware that he was now accompanied by a presentation on the big screen at the front of the hall. A procession of bullet-pointed percentages, perky Clip Arts and inspirational words and phrases appeared and Gordon informed them that, without his leadership, they would be unable to make the school outstanding—as if that bothered most of them. *Outstanding* was the inspection rating that was the Holy Grail of the profession and should be striven for at all costs, but it was exhausting; far better to aim for the happy zenith of *good*… enough—on a good day.

In front of Liz's vacant eyes, PowerPoint motivation bounced, flew, faded in and out, floated and zoomed in its manic, but fruitless efforts to hold her interest. It was not until the final slide that two details demanded her full attention. The first, a picture, wheeled its way onto the slide: a scarlet-vested, flaxen-haired, ray-gun-armed superhero. Perplexing. The second was a single word. It faded slowly in and then pulsated like some gross abomination: *Ofsted*. Petrifying.

The Office for Standards in Education meant inspections, lesson observations, special measures, even. Like the wind in the grass, a whisper rifled through them: *Ofsted*! The very word was a guillotine, a soft, metallic rush that ended with a sickening bump—and it was their heads on the block. Horror tightened in the pit of Liz's stomach as she tried to remind herself that it could be worse. Even if Dave had not got Pam Hooper's lesson write-up removed last year, Liz still stood a high chance of being in the firing line to be seen when Ofsted came in—and if she thought a normal lesson observation turned her brain to gravy and her legs to jelly, then it was a hundred times worse when it was Ofsted.

Then the screen turned black, but the obscenity had burned its after-image onto Liz's retinas and still throbbed there as they all made their way towards the main staffroom for mid-morning break.

"Please, please, let everything be all right," Liz willed.

And so it was—for now.

Celestial rays poured in through the high windows. The sublime aroma that greeted them was the answer to her recent prayer. Wantonly spread before them, piled on and spilling from trays were flapjacks, brownies, pastries and buns: a symphony in every scrumptious shade of brown.

Free cakes and coffee. Clever, very clever.

"He can't get round *me* that easily," Liz's words were muffled as she settled into a comfortable chair, sipped her coffee and rescued a flake of almond from the corner of her mouth with her tongue.

"Can't he?" said Lucy. "*Was ever woman in this humour wooed?*" she quoted.

"Smart-arse. I'm only having it to be polite." Liz was well aware Lucy was not fooled. "And just to prove how polite I am, I'm having a brownie as well."

"*Was ever woman in this humour won?*" smiled Lucy, scraping a dribble of jam from the front of her top and licking sugar off her finger. She patted her pocket and grinned. "Stashed a few goodies for the kids. Waste not, want not. Anyway, prick up your ears." She nodded towards where Gordon had taken up his position at the front. "He's off again!"

Conversations began to hush as the head, smiling hopefully, rattled his teaspoon against his coffee cup, planted his feet in a power stance, and rubbed his hands together expectantly. Gordon smiled round and, in the dying seconds of chatter, Liz noticed Dave whispering to some of the science department and gesticulating obscenely. They smothered guilty laughter and looked at 'Dildo'. Was Dave actually spreading the word? Liz caught his eye and thumbed approval.

The head began to speak. "Right, before I let you go off to your departments," Gordon said, "I thought I'd break the ice a bit more. I don't want you to think of me as your boss."

"Here we go," whispered Lucy.

"I'd like to think I'm more of a mementor."

"Not sure that's what he meant," muttered Liz.

"Don't be afraid to come and have a chat about anything you want," Gordon continued.

"We'll see," muttered Liz.

And his final guarantee: "My door is always open."

He had not finished demonstrating that he was a man of the people yet, however: "And I don't want you all kowtowing to me, either."

Time would tell.

"So, none of this *Mr Dillon*."

Liz was absolutely positive she heard the faintest *Dildo* whispered from over by the mathematicians. Excellent.

"I want you to call me *Gordon*." He paused conspiratorially and shielded his mouth with his hand in mock secrecy. "Not in front of the students, though. Don't want them calling me *Flash* like in my last school!"

The penny dropped. *Yes you do*, thought Liz. *That's exactly what you want!* She recalled the perplexing superhero from the presentation. *Well, over my dead body. Saviour of the universe, my arse.*

Gordon smirked and dismissed them, obviously congratulating himself on sowing the seeds of his preferred appellation. He had wasted his seed on the ground, however; Gareth arrived with news from the other side of the room. "Guess what they're calling Gordon! Greg from design tech just told me. He got it from the maths lot, who heard it from science."

Liz and Dave exchanged knowing glances.

"*Dildo*!" ejaculated Gareth.

4: The Snowdrop

"Was that your handiwork, Dave?" Gareth asked, as they went into Dave's classroom, where they held their weekly department meetings. "Well, the place is buzzing—with *dildo*es! *Dildo*es from art to zoology." He paused, distracted for a second. "I know we don't teach zoology, but it'll do. Anyway, they said you told them, Dave. Good man."

Dave gave credit where it was due. "Blame Machiavelli over there." He gestured towards Liz. "It was her idea. I just spread the word."

"Tell it to the judge," Gareth said.

"Good work, Bish. You've proved yourself a worthy ally," said Liz, sitting next to Dave.

"It was beautiful to watch," he said, "Like dropping a fag butt at a beauty spot in the middle of a drought."

He faltered, combing his brain for the words to express his awe. "It was like—fucking—whoosh! One minute a spark; next a tsunami," he said, mixed-metaphorically. Noting her expression, he backtracked: "Well, maybe not a tsunami. A fire, a fucking cataclysmic forest fire."

"And you know what's going to be even more beautiful, Dave?" Liz said.

"What?"

"When the kids get wind of it."

Behind his glasses, Dave's eyes shone with future wonder. "Fucking beautiful," he sighed before engaging professional mode and getting down to business: who was writing which scheme of work, what colour pens to mark in, class lists, seating plans, short-term plans, long-term plans, action plans, new initiatives, the latest pedagogy, how to ensure they were Ofsted-ready...

Liz felt the familiar, panicked tightening of her chest as the list of new systems to master, online training to complete and updated policies to remember grew longer and longer. She could feel herself getting further and further behind before she'd even started. She'd never be able to get all this done, so she resolved to resort to her usual failsafe method of hoping someone would remind her when she forgot something important or at least tell her when she got it wrong. Somewhat brightened, she daydreamed about lunch and the wine she would soon be drinking with it. Before long, the conversation caught her attention again.

"Anyway—and this'll please you, Liz—word has it, they've refurbished the bog. I haven't seen it yet, but apparently, it looks good."

This did please Liz. The only toilet in their block had been a source of resentment for as long as she could remember. With the flimsy inner-cubicle wall and door and even flimsier lock, it was shared by about twenty-five of them: the relatively civilised English department, the catering staff, the site team and the barbarians from design technology. Its proximity to students queueing for metalwork made it embarrassing to use between lessons and its general state of filth made it unappealing at break time too. This upgrade was long overdue and Liz could not wait to see it, so she high-tailed it down the corridor, bursting with anticipation. She paused before entering and gazed at the whiteness of the new door, imbibing the aroma of its fresh paint and conjuring images of a latter-day Grecian urn: all attic shape, silent form and fair attitude.

Here I come, thou still unravished bride of quietness! Liz grasped the shiny, stainless steel handle and opened the door.

Disappointment broke over her like a wave.

Inside, the cracked, yellowing toilet bowl crouched, yawning and dribbling, in the corner. Its foul, toothless mouth was crusted with scum as it watched over the grimy lavatorial accessories the way a vagrant guards his carrier bags. Beyond the new door, the room had not been decorated at all—not even a lick of paint—but there *was* one major change: the inner wall and door had been inexplicably removed, so that now there was no inner cubicle and only one degree of separation between a teacher at his or her most vulnerable and the casually savage teenage mob. Granted, there was a new seat, but there was still no mirror or toilet roll holder; the toilet still rocked alarmingly when sat upon, and brown liquid still oozed from its base in an obscene puddle.

Heaving a sigh of disillusionment, Liz realised also that there was still no extractor or ventilation either, despite desperate need, proven by obvious recent use (by a DT teacher, Liz deduced: their work on logs was legendary and their expertise with resistant materials was verified on the inside of the bowl). The odour was not improved by the liberal spraying of lavender-scented air freshener, the can of which now sat on top of the cistern like a parodic trophy. Mouth-breathing, Liz stared around at the filthy, stiffened rag, which still clung to the mildew-spotted pipes under the sink; the unmopped, corpse-grey scurf-drift, which skulked in the corner, behind the sanitary bin, and the desiccated, half-used bar of lard-white soap, marbled with dark brown veins, which was fused to the sink by its own scum. The final insult, Liz noticed: a hole the size of a fist had been punched through the artificial-limb-coloured wall to the brand new kitchen next door, to accommodate or remove some pipes, Liz supposed. It had not even been filled in.

People who worked in offices didn't have to put up with this. The other departments didn't have to put up with this. Even the bloody students didn't have to put up with this. Stirred by injustice and seething with purpose, she marched back towards Dave's room.

"You really haven't seen the toilet, have you, Dave?" Liz said.

Dave looked up. "No. Is it good?"

"No, it's shite."

Lucy sighed. "You can't polish a turd, I suppose."

"No," countered Liz, "but you can spray one with air freshener and hope no one notices it's still just a turd."

Dave looked properly annoyed now. "I was assured this morning that it had been refurbished."

"Who told you that?" asked Gareth.

"Gordon," Dave admitted. "We're going to have to be on our guard with this one. Anyway, that's it. It's lunch time. Last one to The Snowdrop gets the first round."

If Liz had had any misgivings about the head's nickname, they had just been flushed away. She shook her head sadly and allowed herself to be piloted towards the pub.

"Come on, Liz," said Dave gently, "Let's get you down the pub; you've had a nasty disappointment, haven't you? Nice glass of wine: that's what you need, you little alky."

"Sarky git! Come on then; you can drive."

By the time they got to the car park of The Snowdrop, it was already full. The handsome hand-painted pub sign swayed and creaked its cordial welcome in the late summer sunshine, the titular bloom, nodding palely against a background of purple hills. The porch door stood open and, above it, Farmer's Fare brandished its corporate ownership in brass. Ducking to avoid a hop-festooned beam, Dave led the way in. The lounge was clammy with humanity and the tired Axminster was beginning to exude an aroma of ageing canine and ancient beer.

The landlord was accustomed to the first Monday of September—when wave after raucous wave of Dickie's teachers crashed through the doors, baying for pub grub—and had called for reinforcements to cope with the onslaught: mostly Dickie's sixth formers and ex-students, who regarded them with tolerant amusement and addressed their clientele as *Sir* and *Miss*.

The bar was heaving with chatting teachers: artists and musicians expressed themselves, cooks and needlewomen mixed and made conversation, religious educators preached, philosophers debated and linguists were fluent. Here and there, civilians, who had forgotten what day it was, looked around, horrified, bolting their meals and retreating with their sticky-fingered progeny; it was not long before Dickie's had occupied almost the whole pub.

Around the quaintly uneven room, in accordance with corporate directives, was displayed all manner of discordant bric-a-brac. The Snowdrop had been rendered, not only quintessentially British, but also eccentrically unique, as were all four-hundred and thirty-eight Farmer's Fare pubs. Reclamation yards, charity shops and house-clearances for miles around had been ransacked and the resulting plunder regurgitated into the belly of The Snowdrop. Seventeenth century medicine bottles rubbed shoulders with milk maids' yokes; head-brasses flashed alongside incongruous miners' lamps, and a wooden handled, polished scythe hung pointlessly over a framed, age-wearied copperplate list of the fallen of both world wars.

"Christ, it's like a car boot sale in here," said Liz, as they elbowed through the assembly of educationalists towards the bar, "Watch out for low-flying pewter tankards."

"I'm more worried about that axe thing," said Dave and ordered the drinks.

"Get that down you." He passed Liz a glass of the blushful and gripped his pint, careful not to spill a drop, as they sought out the English table. Lucy patted the chair next to her; Liz plopped onto it, took a luxurious gulp and sighed audibly. Lucy crammed a forkful of vegetarian chimichanga into her mouth and grinned, losing a sprouting mung bean in the folds of her desert scarf.

"Man overboard! I'll find that one later." She laughed and slugged her *Badger's Bumfluff*, or whatever it was called. "All right, you two? You took your time."

"What the bloody hell are you drinking *today*?" asked Liz. "Looks like a sample."

Lucy laughed. "Yeah, one of those pregnancy ones with floaters."

"Don't get her onto bogs again," Dave warned. "I've only just settled her."

"Refurbishment? He's taking the bloody piss," Liz grumbled again.

Lucy jabbed an elbow into Liz's side. "Careful; he's coming!"

The volleys of conversation died a sudden death. In walked Gordon and paused for a second, haloed by the golden afternoon and—inappropriately—accompanied by his family. Mrs Dillon smiled round beatifically, indiscriminately; Gordon Junior, skulked in their wake, his face hidden by a curtain of dark hair and—the pièce de résistance—borne aloft upon his father's shoulders: Baby Dillon. What kind of trickery was this? From spin doctor to politician, through messiah and superhero, Gordon was employing every tactic in *The Headteacher's Handbook*, if such a thing existed.

Look how approachable and normal I am, he seemed to say, handed the baby to his wife and very normally approached the nearest male to him.

"Hiya, mate!" he exclaimed, eliciting a collective wince from the room. He clapped his left hand onto the man's bicep, as if to weigh him up, and grasped the reluctant right hand in his own sure one, pumping it and grimacing round the pub, eager to ascertain how many eyes were on the hearty greeting. Giggles were stifled as Gordon insisted, "Come and have a chat with me later. Tell me your vision for the year."

"Bloody teachers!" was the response. "You want locking up. I can't even have a quiet pint without you lot ruining it." The man swallowed the last of his ale and shuffled out, still muttering.

"And that's just the union rep!" sniggered Gordon, confident he had styled out his blunder. From a corner, a squeal of amusement erupted, unbidden, and was hushed. Somewhere else, the word, *dildo* caught in the air, snagging on Gordon's hearing like a silk scarf on a scab, puckering the smoothness of his gaze.

Recovering his equanimity almost instantly, Gordon continued to advance, still not sure who were his employees and who were not, but smiling and nodding anyway. At least Junior had the grace to look uncomfortable. Mrs Dillon, on the other hand, looked triumphant.

"The power behind the throne." Gareth incised to the heart of the matter.

"No, she's just a WAG," said Lucy.

"Look at her face," Gareth insisted. "Wife of a headmaster: the cat that got the cream."

"Oh my God, she's Lady Macbeth," said Liz. "Watch out, Baby Dildo; she'll pluck her nipple from your boneless gums and dash your brains out as soon as look at you!"

There was no underestimating the power babies have over otherwise sensible adults, though, and Peggy was first to cluck her way across the room to it. Lucy, still lactating herself, followed her over like a ferret up a trouser leg, cooing and gurgling.

"Oh well, might as well rack up a few Brownie points," said Gareth, heading after Lucy. "Tally-ho!"

"It's only a bloody baby," said Liz.

"Call yourself a girl?" said Dave. He shook his head sympathetically. "Those poor kids, though. Paraded around like that." Dave became contemplative—briefly. "Poor buggers. You know what Larkin said about your mum and dad, don't you?"

Liz raised her glass. "*They fuck you up.*"

5: Princess Belle

Half an hour later, as most of the teachers were finishing their meals, lingering over their drinks and trying to forget that they had to get back to the afternoon's meetings, Gordon approached the English department's table. "Now, I've got a surprise for English," he said. "Where are you, Belle?"

A voice chirruped, "Hiya! I'm Belle."

A tiny young woman stepped out from behind Gordon, her hands raised, her manicured, pink fingers shimmering and wiggling girlishly, level with her ears, in what seemed to pass for a wave. She giggled and there was a pause while everyone looked up from their plates at her and Gordon beamed. Was this another of Gordon's offspring, Liz wondered as other teachers began to pause their conversations and look over.

"Isn't she lovely?" Gordon must have read the room and decided that this audience would appreciate it if he channelled a pre-political-correctness game-show host, so he uttered the ill-judged imperatives, "Give us a twirl, gorgeous, and tell them about yourself."

The synchronised wince of every teacher in the pub seemed to go completely unnoticed by Gordon. In turn, Belle, apparently unfazed by the casual sexism, qualmlessly followed orders, slow-pirouetting, her shiny, blonde head tilting daintily, and then continued speaking. "So I'm really excited and I can't wait to work with you all?" she announced, the upward inflection of her voice making her statement sound like a question.

"This is our new English trainee," Gordon explained triumphantly.

Apparently, this was not his daughter, then—unless he was willing to commit nepotism as well as sexism on his first day.

"So I'm going to be working in the English department, on the Graduate Teacher Programme?" Belle continued.

"First I've heard about getting a GTP," whispered Dave, disgruntled.

She looked about twelve and was infuriatingly cheerful as well as sickeningly confident, by the sound of it. They would have to knock that out of her.

Dave addressed Belle now, smiling. "Hi—sorry—I didn't know anything about this or I'd have introduced myself earlier. What was your name again?"

She giggled. "Belle—Belle Jobson."

Dave shook her hand while Liz spluttered into her wine; she knew what Belle's staff code would be.

Just then, Serena Rochelle glided in and stood behind Liz's chair, glass of Pinot Grigio in her hand. Effortlessly soignée, she smoothed down her blouse and swept her golden hair behind her ear with an elegant finger. "She looks high maintenance," she murmured as Gordon steered Belle to the other end of the table. "Hope she's got a tutor group,"

Dave answered Serena with a puzzled look.

"BJ," she elucidated, before swallowing.

Dave snorted with delight and then greeted Serena properly. "What time do you call this, anyway?"

"Didn't you get the message?" she said. "My flight was delayed. I didn't get back till this morning. Have I missed anything?"

After a few minutes, pleasantly replete with red meat and wine, Liz and Serena dawdled back to King Richard's on foot, keen to drink in a few of the last dregs of summer sun. The lazy air was heavy with a trembling mantilla of gnats and liquid with the throaty warble of blackbirds and thrushes. They wandered towards their afternoon form tutor meetings, their feet reluctant and their shadows long.

They went through the staff room, to check their pigeon-holes on the way and heard a girlish sound that was somewhere between a squeal and a giggle and was followed by another: the skeuomorph of a camera shutter. A few feet away, the minute, tow-headed figure of Belle tapped her mobile phone's screen a few times, frowned prettily, and *squiggled* again, showing her photograph to the handful of attentive youngsters, presumably more trainees, who were with her.

"Christ on a bike. Now she's taking selfies," she muttered to Serena.

"What?" twinkled Serena, amused.

"That new GTP. She's just taken a selfie with the other students."

"Right. And...?"

"But she's only just got here."

"It's just what people do, Liz. People like to take pictures."

Bewildered, Liz shook her head. "But she's only just met them and she's organised a photo-shoot already. And we've got to work with her."

Serena raised an eyebrow. "It'll be fine; you'll probably hardly see her," she turned her attention to the tutor list she had just taken from her pigeon-hole, skimmed it and gasped.

"Oh my God! Hilarious! You're going to love this, Liz."

"What?" Liz asked hopefully. She needed a boost after the let-down of the toilet.

Serena handed her the printed list of form tutors, pointing to Liz's own name, about halfway down.

Liz followed Serena's finger. "Shit!"

There, next to *Elizabeth Marshall 7EM*, irrefutably added in blue biro: + *Belle Jobson, GTP*.

Both Liz and Serena were to be form tutors for the new year sevens and the upcoming briefing arising from the year sevens' primary school reports would forewarn and forearm them before they met their classes the next day. These often malodorous and misshapen whelps would need to be licked into shape. It was the same every year, when they read what their year six teachers had written about them: *delightful* girls turned out to be irritating tell-tales, *wayward* boys were entertaining, *introverts* turned out to be interesting and the *gifted* were often distinctly mediocre.

Inside the head of year seven's textiles classroom, the other tutors were gathering, pens and folders ready. Barbara Bosun, clad in a baby-pink twinset and preceded by her intimidating bosom, entered the room, lowered herself into a chair and welcomed them. She was an impressive spinster of a certain age, who traversed the school, like a ship in full sail: with gravity and dignity.

"Good afternoon, everyone," she said as she gave out the class lists. "We've got a huge number of extremely tricky little boys and girls, this year, so you're going to have to take no nonsense. Strict seating plans, silent registrations and definitely no smiling till Christmas." She laced her fingers and set them on the desk in front of her, both barrier to and defence against mutiny. Nobody dissented.

The door screeched open behind Liz and Serena, who were busily shoving lists of juvenile miscreants into folders, and someone hesitated.

"You're a day early, young lady." Barbara scrutinised the newcomer over the top of her gilt-framed glasses. "Sixth form registration isn't till tomorrow. Come back then, dear."

When the intruder did not move, Barbara removed her glasses and gave an impatient sigh. "Well, young lady, what is it?"

"Don't you remember me?" Belle tripped daintily into the room on exquisitely pedicured feet. "So I'm Belle Jobson, the new Graduate Teacher Trainee. I'm a year seven tutor?"

Barbara pursed her lips, heedless of her faux pas, hoisted her glasses from the front of her immense décolletage, where they hung from their chain, like a climber on a rock face, and planted them back on the terra firma of her nose. She looked at her list. "Actually, Miss Jobson, you will be assisting Liz Marshall with 7EM. Being a tutor is a highly responsible and specialised pastoral role..."

"Not the way I do it!" Liz muttered to Serena.

"...and, as such, it is not a privilege we can entrust, lightly." Barbara was stern; she had dealt with many trainees in her numerous years as head of year seven and found it so much easier not to differentiate between them and her sixth formers.

"Be guided by Liz," Barbara advised. "If you prove yourself competent, she will allow you more responsibility, as she sees fit." She turned to Liz now. "There's an extra boy coming into your form, Liz," she said. "I'll email you the information when I've got it. It's a last-minute thing, a very sad case, apparently. He and his mum had to be moved here by social services a couple of days ago. I don't know all the details yet."

"Okay," said Liz. "I'll look out for the email. We'll look after him; don't worry."

"That's what I thought," said Barbara. "He'll be all right with you."

Barbara focused on Belle again. "Well, have a seat then, Miss Jobson. We've got a lot to get through."

Belle's chin jutted, and she opened her mouth to protest, but, at a gorgon glance from Barbara, she closed it and, cowed, clambered onto a chair, next to Liz, where she sat, bottom lip protruding appealingly, and prepared to make notes.

After the meeting, Belle scuttled after Liz and Serena, who were on their way to their classrooms.

"Can you believe that tight-arse bitch?!" she exclaimed. "She can't speak to me like that. What a miserable old cow!"

Liz and Serena cast each other weary looks. They, too, had overseen plenty of trainees and had a well-honed sense of the pecking order; they had earned the right, through years of servitude, to say what they liked about Babs, but these youngsters needed to realise they were bottom of the food chain and show some humility.

"Barbara's a bit of a battle axe but she's a great head of year," warned Serena. "Don't get on the wrong side of her."

"Well, Gordon told me I'd get my *own* form," pouted Belle. "How am I going to pass my course if I can't practise on them?"

"Well, you're stuck with me and mine," said Liz, heroically lightly; these were kids, not lab rats. "Anyway," she added, keen to inject a note of humour, "at least the form won't have to be called 7BJ!"

Belle's look was granite. "Right, well, I'll need copies of all the class lists and data for the form so I can get started on the seating plan," she said. The stamp of her foot was not at the end of her dainty little leg, but in her voice.

"And how are you going to get those?" asked Liz, the bristle in *her* voice going unnoticed.

"Well, you've got them, haven't you?"

"Yes. *I* have."

Realisation's niggling fingers prodded Belle's consciousness. "Oh—could I have copies of them?"

"I'll let you have them later." Liz was gracious in her generosity. She looked at Serena, who observed the exchange with satisfaction. Their high-five was not in their hands but in their eyes. Liz had 'handled' an adult—albeit an almost embryonic one—and now there would be no stopping her. "Oh, and *I'll* be doing the seating plan. It has to be right," she added.

6: 7EM

Liz and Serena left Belle to absorb the idea and climbed the chilly back stairs to their classrooms. The window, halfway up, revealed a flat-roofed vista, still littered with discarded pens; faded, balding tennis balls, and a shoe. Beyond these, the Bremeldon Hills sprawled, like a languid dragon, among a tumbled patchwork of farmland and houses. Turning the corner for the next flight, Liz smiled as she saw the familiar graffiti: a pair of crudely drawn breasts, gazing down at her from above the double doors, keeping their vigil like Dr Eckleburg's eyes, although, like them, the breasts were dimmed by the passage of time; they had survived another summer holiday's rigorous deep-clean.

"The tits're still there, I see," Liz said.

Serena stopped and looked. "A bit old and grey, but there's still plenty of life in them," she said.

"Oh my God, that's so disgusting?" Belle caught up with them. "Someone should report it to the site team."

"Oh, they've been there years," said Liz. "I'd miss them if they went."

"They brighten the place up," Serena agreed.

"How can you say that? They're so sexist," insisted Belle.

"Don't worry; there're plenty of penises too. Did you see the one in the hall?" said Liz.

"No and I hope I don't." Belle was rummaging through her papers and did not notice the synchronised eye-rolls as Liz and Serena, once again forged ahead, towards their rooms.

"Rather you than me," whispered Serena. "She's going to be a handful."

Liz groaned. "Feel free to take her off my hands any time you like."

Serena opened the door to her classroom and went in. "No thanks. I've done my stint in charge of the student teachers. But don't forget," she cautioned, "Belle's not like the trainees we normally have; they've never done it before and they need TLC. Belle's done the theory and some practice already and she gets paid a decent salary to learn on the job so work her hard. Don't take any nonsense; she should know what she's doing, more or less."

Liz groaned and made for her room. *No wonder she's such a know-all*, she thought. *Still, how bad can it be? I'll only see her for a few minutes every morning and an hour once a week. She's sharing my form, not my life.*

She arrived at her door and smiled to see the sign she had made at the end of July: *7EM Mrs Marshall* it said. This was the best part of the first day back: when they got to go into their own tidy rooms; to enjoy the quiet solitude; to relish empty displays and blank pin boards, unpinned and full of promise. The desks were unadorned with chewing gum and graffiti; trays held nothing, and her desk was uncluttered with work. It would not be this good again for another year. Liz treasured this moment and lingered with fingers just touching the handle, anticipating the pleasant mustiness of the books, the tick of the clock, the warm stillness of the slightly stale air.

"*There* it is. My room." Belle jostled past Liz and bustled in, deposited her bag and planner onto Liz's desk and threw herself into Liz's chair.

"Needs brightening up," Belle announced, preparing to log onto the computer.

She was like a pug: tiny and headstrong, determined to mark her territory. Liz was going to have to train her; she wasn't going to let her bury her bone here. Liz's voice was a rolled up newspaper and she spoke slowly and clearly so there was no misunderstanding. It had taken her five long years to get her own room. This room.

"Belle. I'm afraid you don't have a room. This is my room." She gestured to her name on the door. "You'll be sharing with me—helping me and learning how to be a form tutor."

"Well, that's not fair," Belle spluttered. "I was told..." She trailed off. "I thought..." She started again: "But..." she tried, feebly. She was pouting again. She looked sulkily at her bag and planner, like a puppy next to a puddle.

Liz spoke more kindly now her point was made. There was no point in rubbing her nose in it. "Don't worry. Why don't you take those down to the staffroom and find Dave? He'll show you where you can set up camp and which computer you can use."

Belle skulked out of the room, tail between her legs, leaving Liz to reclaim her chair. Buoyed by victory, she logged on.

She looked at her class list and started annotating the twenty four names, according to the detailed information on each one that came with them from their primary schools: ticks and crosses, single and double, went next to each one, according to what previous teachers had written about them.

Kate, a good, level-headed name, Liz thought. She was right: *sensible*: two ticks.

Edward, again, the unbidden preconception she knew she should suppress told her that this was a name that spoke of sensible parents: *reliable*: two ticks.

Maisie, another nice, sensible name, Liz thought, pleased with her own perspicacity. She read the old teacher's remarks, which ended with: *tends to be rebellious*: one cross. Every year, her prejudgment of names was demonstrated to be inaccurate at least as often as not, but she enjoyed the game, nevertheless.

Jordan... was this a boy or a girl? Perhaps the photo would help. It didn't; she would have to get used to this. Liz added the two crosses indicated by the two most prominent words from the previous teacher's notes—*rude* and *boisterous*—and carried on.

Emin... she checked the list again... a boy; Emin Smith. She checked his primary school information—*defiant* and *disruptive* were both underlined—and added two crosses next to his name.

In her seating plan, double-tick students were paired up with double crosses, who were kept as far apart as possible, while still being near the front and her desk, where they would irritate the hell out of her. Liz felt a bit sorry for the double ticks; their reward for being the best behaved was to be saddled with the worst, in the hope that virtue would dilute depravity. Liz hoped, also, that diffusion might work both ways and a bit of mischief might seep into the goody-two-ticks. That could make life interesting. She wondered how many ticks or crosses Belle had been given by her first high school teacher and whether strategic seating had had any effect upon her—or her desk-mate.

To ensure the seating plan conformed to school policy Liz needed to find, not only names, but various other information, too, so it would be visible to anyone who might 'visit' a lesson. Liz undertook the time-consuming task of finding, copying and pasting the students' key stage two results, special needs and socio-economic data and target GCSE grades—each gleaned from a different file on the school system—and, with practised clicks, she inserted student names from the list, onto the grid, ready to print. A footstep at the door made her look up and there was Belle. With enormous effort of will, Liz tried to be friendly.

"I always try to guess what the kids are like from their names," she ventured, gesturing towards the class list.

"So, you can't tell anything about them just by their names. They told us at uni you shouldn't judge them?"

She'd learn. Belle's face became complacent. "What if people could guess what I was like just from my name?"

"I can't imagine it," Liz said. Belle took this as confirmation of her triumph and softened.

"Exactly! Actually, I was named *Belle* because of *Beauty and the Beast*."

"And which one were you?" joked Liz.

Belle looked a little mystified, but she pushed on. "Belle. You know, the princess," she paused. "It came out when my mum was pregnant with me?"

"You look good for your age. You must be at least two hundred years old," Liz said, smiling. Her attempt at humour was answered by a petulant *tut* and an exasperated shake of the head before Belle's expression calcified.

"No, the *proper* one," she said, "the Disney film. I was named after Princess Belle?"

"Yeah, I know. I was only joking 'cause it was written in..." Liz trailed off, deflated.

She sighed. Belle was probably used to being humoured, agreed with. She had probably been mollified and cosseted as soon as she had been old enough to turn tear-brimming eyes or trembling bottom lip towards her parents and teachers. This could be an interesting year.

Belle drew herself up to her full height and eyed the still seated Liz levelly. "Anyway, have you finished those seating plans yet?" she demanded, chin out and hands on hips. "I need a copy so I can learn their names."

"Nearly there," replied Liz, her teeth gritted. Sticking to her puppy training strategy, she gave Belle no extra attention now, but kept her eyes on her screen, as she finished her plan. Belle, taking Liz's preoccupation with the computer as a sign she was having trouble, thought she saw her advantage. Irrepressible, she bounced forward, grabbing the mouse.

"I'll show you how to do these," she said. "You just click here and double-click this. Then you can drop them wherever you want them—like this."

"I know," said Liz, jaw still clenched. There was no getting through to her. She pointedly took the mouse from Belle's hand and clicked *undo* three times. "I'd just finished. All I need to do is print it and you can have your copy."

Pachydermal and undeterred, Belle offered more technical instructions: "Just click that thing that looks like a printer. You'll know if it's printing because the icon will have a little picture of paper coming out," she said as she trotted out of the room.

Serena was just coming in. "Helpful," she chuckled.

"Unbelievable," Liz answered.

7: Gannet

It was the end of the first day. Downstairs, in the English staffroom, the sink was piled with a clutter of cutlery, plates, cups and glasses, as well as a sodden dump of spent teabags. It was almost as if the previous six weeks had never happened. Liz, Dave and the others basked in inertia, reluctant to let go of this precious, student-free day and go home just yet; going home would mean accepting that the following day would, indeed, follow, seemingly, even sooner.

Liz gazed at the crows and gulls, lined up on top of the school buildings surrounding the playground, and imagined them disgruntled by the lack of food. September's return of life to the buildings usually heralded rich pickings for them so they squawked their irritation and, still hungry, waited for tomorrow. The door on the other side of the playground opened and, from the main staffroom, Janet, the deputy head, tottered towards the English block. Liz watched her dreamily and daydreamed a prim-suited Tippi Hedren, beehive undone, cigarette forgotten, flailing against a cloud of murderous crows, which flapped blackly, like her eyelashes and were buffeted on the air like cinders.

She shook herself out of her reverie and warned the others cheerfully: "Lock up your biscuits. Here comes Gannet. I was wondering where she'd got to all day."

"Licking Dildo's arse, I expect," said Dave, professionally.

"I'll have trouble getting rid of *that* image," Lucy laughed.

"Can a dildo even have an arse?" Serena mused, trying to picture such a thing.

Lucy tried a few graphic, exploratory mimes, shrugging when she couldn't quite make it work.

Gareth laughed. "What would be the point in sucking up to Dildo?" he asked. "Gannet's retiring at the end of the year; why would she care what he thinks?"

"She's just a natural sucker-upperer," Peggy said. "If there's a boss to suck up to, Janet'll suck up."

"True," Lucy said and changed the subject. "Hey, Liz, what was that you were saying about the loo earlier?"

Liz's indignation resurfaced. "Haven't you seen it yet? It stretches the definition of refurbishment; that's all I'm saying."

Lucy stood up. "Intriguing. I think I'll pay a visit now."

"You treat yourself," chipped in Dave, who had just tuned in. "If you're as outraged as Liz, maybe you two can get a pressure group going."

"Great idea," Lucy beamed. "I love a protest."

Dave laughed. "You fucking hippy."

"Yeah, we could have a sit-in," Liz suggested, "or start a movement." A seed began to germinate in her mind. "Maybe we should take selfies in there and put them on Facebook," she said.

"Great idea! Belle'd like that," said Serena. "You should start a blog, Liz."

"That's what I was thinking," said Liz. "But are blogs still a thing?"

"Oh yeah! I was reading a hilarious one the other day. This blogger pretends to be a badger and just talks about what he sees around him." Lucy said.

"Why a badger?" asked Liz.

Lucy shrugged. "I dunno. Maybe it's just seeing things from a different perspective or something. Anyway, badgers are just funny, aren't they?"

"A blog's a great idea. Could be something Belle could definitely help you with," Serena suggested, raising an eyebrow.

"Fuck off!" said Liz good-naturedly. But her imagination was already beginning to conjure a vision of the internet-based musings of an anthropomorphised toilet and its countless, devoted online followers. She filed it for future use and focused on Janet again. "Anyway, sod all that. Janet's on her way over."

Liz nodded towards Janet, still in the playground. Janet had been waylaid but now made her determined way towards them, as if following a trail of biscuit crumbs. She leaned against the doorframe and inspected her coral pink fingernails, flicked her grey-rooted, holiday-blonde hair and tried to affect a casual demeanour. The hem of her frilled black and white cotton sundress brushed her leg mid-thigh, exposing the slightly baggy chamois of her knees. Her lower legs tapered towards her callused feet, which were crammed into a pair of staggeringly high wedge-heeled sandals, the final touch in giving her the appearance of a slightly unsteady ostrich.

"Anyway, hello, everyone!" Janet said. "Sorry. I've just been so busy, I haven't been able to get over to you sooner."

"Not while there were still cakes in the staffroom," Liz whispered to Dave.

Hawkish, now, Janet hovered for a second, as if deciding exactly where to swoop, and then lunged towards the still fairly laden table, snatching a chocolaty French biscuit in her talons and popping it in whole as she descended into a chair.

"Mmm—well done, English—best biscuits in school, as usual." She lined up another as she chewed. "Anyway, how's it all going? Ready for another year?" She trailed off, distracted, as her beady eyes scanned her quarry. Unconcerned about an answer, she sighted Peggy's family-sized tub of chocolates and reached mechanically, still chewing. There was no pleasure in her eating. Her talons plucked open the chocolates and swallowed them whole, grasping for the next as soon as the first had entered her mouth. This motion was repeated, joylessly, over and over again, until she became dimly aware that silence had descended and all eyes were trained on her. Peggy's were filled with indignation.

"Anyway, must dash," said Janet, fleetingly abashed. "Just came over to say *hello*. Got another meeting with Gordon now. See you tomorrow."

Peggy was not impressed. "The nerve of that woman," she said, but the door opened again and Janet reappeared.

"Oh—nearly forgot. Peggy—you're a year seven tutor too. Someone's dropped out and I told Babs you'd be best and you wouldn't mind. Here's your class list. Got to go. Bye!"

"What was that you were saying about nerve, Peggy?" Serena waited for Peggy's feathers to ruffle but she simply tutted and sighed, shaking her head.

"Babs said I'd have a rest from it this year. I was looking forward to a bit of peace and quiet. Now it's just going to be tears, runny noses and lost PE kits all over again." She scanned the class list with eager eyes, chucking and fussing at the twenty-five names and settling in her seat like a brooding hen. The rest of them understood and smiled indulgently: whatever she said, Peggy had taken on a glow; she was in her element.

The matriarchal purpose that coursed through her was clear to the rest of them and Lucy, in particular, recognised that primal pull. "Aww, Peg; you'll be great with them," she encouraged as Peggy began to think aloud, planning how she was going to train her charges.

"It'll be just like when I'm looking after our little Sophie. She's potty training at the moment," Peggy clucked, "and Nana has to show her how to do big-girl things. It's the same with year sevens," Peggy continued, confident of her opinion. "I don't care whether they're two or twelve."

Liz was amused. This looked as if it might turn into one of Peggy's gems.

"What sort of big-girl things?" Dave pressed and nudged Liz.

"Don't be crude, Dave," Peggy snapped. She was an innocent, unsullied by the modern world and continued recounting her tale, wriggling in her seat like a hen on the nest, and puffing out her chest with the pleasure of telling it. Dave opened his mouth to comment again, but was silenced by the blocking glance Peggy threw in his direction before continuing pointedly.

"Well, they've got our Sophie out of nappies and she'll use the potty, good as gold, but they still can't get her to use the proper loo. Anyway, last week, she was so proud of herself, she lifted her dress up over her head and said to me, *Look, Nana, I got proper pants on. I's a big girl*, so when she needed to go, I told her she shouldn't wear proper big-girl pants unless she went on the big-girl toilet like Nana does—and I showed her Nana's big-girl pants."

"What, the ones you were wearing?" asked Dave, "You'll be on a register!"

Peggy tutted and rolled her eyes. "Don't be stupid, Dave. They were some new ones from Marks's—and I'd got some for Sophie while I was there too. Anyway—" her expression turned into one of pride, "—so, *then* I said that if she did a wee-wee in Nana's big-girl loo she could have some new, pretty, big-girl pants from Marks's like Nana's.

That did the trick. *Okay, Nana, she says,* scampers up the stairs—" Peggy mimicked the two-year-old's bustling purposefulness. "—and uses the proper loo like a big girl."

A soft plop, made by Lucy's forgotten, dunked biscuit as it fell into her tea, punctuated the end of Peggy's point.

Smiling round at them, Peggy returned to her initial theme. "See, she only needed a bit of an incentive and someone to show her how. Year sevens aren't any different."

"Except you won't be taking them to the loo, will you, Peggy?" Dave pressed.

"Of course not, Dave; it's just an example," Peggy shook her head and sighed.

"Thank fuck for that," he sniggered.

Satisfied that she had made her point, Peggy shook her head and then tucked her chin into her chest and spread her hands on the table, preening delicately.

Liz shuddered and fought off the image of a crowd of year seven girls, holding their dresses up over their heads, waiting for Peggy to take them to the toilet.

"Jesus Christ," she whispered, turning towards Gareth.

"It's like Yew Tree never happened, isn't it?" Gareth smiled, ruefully, smoothed his trousers and crossed his legs.

"Don't tell her about that, for fuck's sake!" said Dave, "She'll be devastated. She's still hoping Jim'll fix it for her to meet Gary Glitter."

"What's that?" Peggy was stirred from her reverie.

"Nothing, Peggy, love; just saying what a brilliant form tutor you are," said Dave.

Peggy beamed with satisfaction.

"Now then, now then!" Gareth could not resist.

"How's about that, then?" added Liz, standing and picking up her bag. "See you tomorrow."

Half an hour later, when she stepped back through her own front door, Liz grinned as she caught the aroma of what would soon be dinner. "I *love the smell of barbecue lighters in the evening*," she announced, as she stepped onto the patio.

"*Smells like victory*... You won, then?" Jack put a glass of wine in her hand and gestured towards the bench, which he had positioned to catch the last rays of the afternoon sun.

"Just about. The real fun starts tomorrow, though." Liz ignored the faintest hint of chill as she settled onto the peeling, painted wood. She sipped her wine and gazed at the trees: birch, cherry and maple, their leaves like emeralds, garnets and amethysts, glowing on finger-like branches as they prepared for autumn. The children of tomorrow were far from her mind as she listened to the slow mumble of bees and the wood-fluted piping of the warblers. Jack tended the barbecue with expert tongs and, before long, their boys joined them and they savoured their final summer meal like lifers, pushing the spectre of the electric chair from their minds.

Evening gave way to night and, reluctant to go to bed early, the Marshalls stayed up and watched TV. When she did turn in, however, despite having drunk half a bottle of Shiraz, Liz still tossed and turned. Whereas she usually dozed off before the after-image of the lightbulb had faded from the insides of her eyelids, the night before seeing students again was different. The horrors that haunted her the night before teaching again never left her, even after fifteen years in the job. It happened every summer, Christmas and Easter—sometimes even half terms. Jack was used to it. He sleepily patted her cold-sweated arm and returned to his slumber. When she had finally managed to sleep, however, Liz was visited by dreams from the darkest recesses of her fevered brain. Insecurities deeply buried wormed their way through the labyrinthine furrows and convolutions and emerged as nightmares, seeking to annihilate the fragile self-assurance it had taken those fifteen years to muster.

In her dream, Liz arrived at work, late, unprepared and only half dressed. Instead of the compliant class of year sevens she was expecting to teach, the horde in front of her was made up of the whole of year ten, all crammed into one science lab, switching on gas taps, releasing locusts and pouring chemicals from glass flasks. The noise level rose as, scenting her fear, they began to jeer and bang out the rhythm of *We Will Rock You* on the wooden benches. Liz had to get control and the only way to do that was immediately to think of the most exciting lesson there had ever been, but her brain had turned to cotton wool: everything she had ever known or been taught, every ready-to-go, stand-by, decide-with-your-hand-on-the-door-knob lesson she had ever used in the past—and there had been plenty—left her mind and she froze. Desperate, she opened her mouth to talk, but all that came out were her crumbling teeth.

At the height of the chaos, the door opened and four bald men in pinstriped suits marched in, funereally, each one pausing to push a clipboard into her face, upon which a column headed *inadequate* was filled with crosses. As each inspector passed her, he turned his ashen face towards her and demanded in gravelly tones, "Despair and die!"

8: Invasion

Eight o'clock, Tuesday morning and the pavement outside King Richard's was already teeming with too-early parents and their children. Viewing them from a distance as she approached the main entrance, Liz was reminded of the multitudes of shambling corpses from the zombie show she had watched with the boys, the previous night. They seemed to wander vaguely, knotting themselves into sluggish groups and purposelessly dispersing again, limp-armed and vacant-eyed. Liz shivered and wove her way through, determined not to make eye-contact; she wasn't on duty until quarter to nine. If they realised she was not of their kind, the whole mob could be on her before she reached the English block. She imagined a herd of the undead, lumbering towards her, pawing at her, forcing her to the tarmac, where they would feast upon her twitching body before lifting their ruined faces and blackened mouths to the morning sun...

    Enjoying this vision, Liz indulged herself again as she entered the building. She pictured herself, restored to life now, but in fresh peril. This time, panting and dishevelled, she shouldered the double doors—just in time—against a forest of undead arms, which reached for her but missed, waving uselessly like coral on a reef. This imaginary Liz closed the doors with an almighty, grunting shove that scythed them. They squelched sickeningly, fell, and then lolled in their own treacly gore.

    Liz shook herself from this daydream—she needed to be alert now—and closed the doors behind her, in reality, severing nothing. She went into the empty English staff room. First in. That wouldn't last. She glanced out, across the playground and her view of the milling families was not obscured by a crush of reanimated cadavers, writhing in slow-motion and leaving their blood-blackened sputum on the glass. No, there was a time for that and that time was tomorrow, when, it seemed, most of year eight congregated right outside the English staffroom windows and watched them drink their coffee and eat their packed lunches, raising the question of whether they were visitors or exhibits in the King Richard's zoo, and causing a frantic yanking down of blinds every lunch time.

    Liz made a coffee and took it up to her classroom, where she could luxuriate in the last half hour before her year sevens—and Belle—made it their room too. For now, she was treasuring every exquisite second of procrastination. In thirty short minutes, she would have to transform herself from laissez-faire to martinet and venture down to claim her new students, not as Liz, but as Mrs Marshall. The computer whirred as it grudgingly roused itself. The corner of a grammar poster flapped in a gasp of air from the open window. The clock ticked, its hands, like Time's arrow, incrementally decreasing the time ahead.

    Quarter past eight and something seemed to be happening at the gates. Liz looked out. There were Gordon, Gannet and Barbara: the year seven Leadership Team. Convivial, deferential and formidable, they were like a cross between camp commandants and the Three Stooges. Gordon stood, capped and gowned in full headmaster regalia, feet planted sturdily apart, hands uplifted in welcome, under the arch that affirmed the name, KING RICHARD THE LIONHEART, in wrought iron letters, and spanned the entrance to the school. In fact, to Liz, it said, *TRAEHNOIL EHT DRAHCIR GNIK*, but today, as so many families assembled in the shadow of the square tower of the boiler room chimney, the black, metal proclamation that forged itself in her mind was *ARBEIT MACHT FREI*. Darkly appropriate for a school.

A constant stream of newcomers continued to drift in under the arch and gather in the playground, awaiting instructions in front of the low, red brick buildings of the older part of the school. Gordon swooped among the families, gown bellying and fluttering, mortarboard tassel bobbing. Liz imagined him, informing them that soon, the children would be wrenched from their families and placed with their tutor groups, to accept, unquestioningly, whatever King Richard's had in store for them.

She sighed and picked up her clipboard, grudgingly primed to follow orders. The hour was near. The bell would soon knell the end of freedom. She trudged back down to the English staff room, stomach churning, to find Serena, looking equally green and Peggy, radiant.

"Hi, you two. Where's everyone else?" she said; the room had not got much busier since eight o'clock.

"They're not in till later." Serena had obviously read her emails. "They're not year seven tutors so they'll wander in at the last minute, lucky sods."

"Christ, Serena, you look as rough as I feel. Bad night?"

"Just the usual nightmares," she confirmed. "There'd been a nuclear bomb and I had to protect all the year sevens from the fall-out, but they kept getting out. Every time I got one back in and locked the door, another couple jumped out the window and when I got them in, some more climbed through the skylights." Serena shivered at the memory of her nocturnal delusions. "More and more fall-out was getting in and all the kids were getting radiation sickness. Their hair was falling out, blood was coming out of their eyes and noses and their skin was going grey, but they wouldn't stay in. They just kept laughing at me and escaping."

"Christ! That was worse than mine—apart from when the Ofsted inspectors rated me *inadequate*."

Serena blanched at the reminder of impending inspection and a shadow dulled even Peggy's glow momentarily.

"Why the hell do we put ourselves through this?"

Serena jerked a thumb in Peggy's direction. "Well, I know why she does. Hey, Peggy?"

Peggy's face had gone into soft focus as she gazed out of the window. "Aww, look at all the little ones. I wonder which ones are mine."

"Notice, Princess bloody Belle's not here yet," Liz grumbled. "Probably taking a selfie to put on Facebook. Still, at least she's not here, trying to take over my form."

Liz's mind flitted elsewhere. "Hey, have you seen Dildo?" she nodded towards the playground where the head was grinning, rubbing his hands together and springing from group to group, predatorily.

"Isn't full academic regalia a bit overboard for year sevens?" Serena wondered aloud.

Liz readily supplied the answer: "How else could he show off about his two-two in sociology?"

Viewed from the vantage point of their staffroom, Gordon's flapping black gown and maniacally nodding cap, gave him more the appearance of the lollipop-foisting Child Catcher than the universe-saving Flash Gordon he aspired to be. But something more important gripped Liz now. She had noticed something. Something egregious in the extreme.

"Sneaky little shit!" she exclaimed. "She's not supposed to be out there till I go out. Why didn't she come over here and find me first?"

Peggy and Serena followed Liz's outraged glare to the playground, where Belle had appeared at Gordon's side with her clipboard and was working her nymphean sorcery, flaxen head nodding, lashes batting wildly. The tinkle of her laughter caught on the breeze and was carried in through the window. It was still only twenty-five to nine. Babs had not yet signalled for the year eleven prefects, who had come in a day early in order to help with the year sevens, to take up their posts along the brick wall and hold their tutor group signs aloft so each group would know where to line up. Seemingly determined that the new students—and their parents—would be imprinted upon her, rather than Liz, Belle marched to the wall, brandished her own *7EM* sign and looked around at the children, impatiently.

Liz was reassured. "Hey up; she's free-styling!" she said. "That'll go down well with Babs."

Indeed, Barbara, noticing a deviation from the usual running order, sailed across the playground, parting a sea of parents and children which closed again in her wake. What passed between Barbara and Belle could not, of course, be heard from where Liz and the others were, but its effect was unequivocal: having surrendered her sign to Barbara, who stowed it with her papers and turned her back on her, Belle skulked in the shadow of the tower, muttering, no doubt plotting revenge. Barbara glanced back at Belle and changed course again, bearing down on her, talking more animatedly and gesturing brusquely towards where the three of them were watching. Belle, subjugated once more, scuttled in the direction of their staffroom, towards them.

"Here we go," said Liz, bracing herself for another round.

"Be firm," warned Serena, "or she'll be a nightmare all year."

Belle burst in. "Did you see that? She's got it in for me, that woman."

Six eyebrows crept an inch nearer the ceiling. Barbara was old-fashioned, but she was not a bully.

"I was only acting on my initiative," Belle persisted. "How was I supposed to know she'd already organised it?"

"Well, she *is* head of year seven; it's her job," Liz pointed out.

"A job she's been doing for longer than you've been alive," added Serena.

Belle was not ready to let go of the bone just yet, though. "Well, she didn't have to speak to me like that. My course tutor said I should write it down in a notebook, whenever anyone's unprofessional, in case I need to make a formal complaint."

"Are you anticipating a lot of unprofessional behaviour, then?" said Liz, prickling with inquisitive amusement.

Belle squared her shoulders portentously. "Well, I've been bullied before."

"Have you?" Liz fought to keep the irony from her voice.

"Oh, yes; there was the owner of the café where I had my Saturday job, the manager of the student union bar when I was a student, one of the tutors on my degree course. I had to complain about all of them. The trouble is," she intoned, "you give someone a bit of responsibility..."

"Like helping with a tutor group," interrupted Serena helpfully.

Belle's look was dagger-like. "...and they feel the need to throw their weight around."

"Or confiscate your sign." Serena seemed to be enjoying herself now.

"It's not funny. I always get picked on."

"You'll be fine," Liz said briskly, but she couldn't resist, "Better log it in your notebook though. But be quick; the bell's going to go in a minute." Liz picked up her clipboard and she, Serena and Peggy moved towards the door, ready to stride onto the playground as soon as the first ringing sounded.

"Come on, Belle; you too," said Liz. "Don't worry about Babs; everyone makes mistakes, but you don't want to annoy her again," she added, a touch more softly. "Just follow me; it's all good."

The bell rang and the four of them put on their lanyards, checked their class lists and straightened their jackets, knowing the first-proper-day smartness would not last long. Belle followed them sullenly as they strode onto the playground, shoulder to shoulder, through the double doors, Liz humming *Little Green Bag* as they marched towards their posts.

"Why do you always sing that?" asked Peggy.

"*Why do I have to be Mr Brown? Sounds too much like Mr Shit,*" didn't really answer Peggy's question and she frowned at Liz, baffled.

"It's a film, Peggy, but you wouldn't like it," said Serena. They reached their destination and further explanation was curtailed as, at a nod from Miss Bosun, eight pairs of prefects raised their tutor group signs to chest height, like judges at a dancing competition. Barbara ascended the steps at the edge of the playground, hoisted her glasses to her face and, secure at the helm, eyed her charges. Parents nudged each other as many of them were transported a generation back to when they themselves had undergone this very ritual, overseen by this very Miss Bosun, not appearing too different from the one who now stood above them.

"Year seven," she commanded, "say *goodbye* to your parents and join your tutor groups."

The two hundred or so year sevens formed themselves into eight neat lines and their parents melted away. The year sevens stood quietly, awaiting orders and, at a word from Barbara, the tutors introduced themselves and the prefects and took the registers, arranging students into alphabetical order. Liz had assigned Belle to uniform duty and watched as she marched along the row of children, like a miniature drill sergeant, reaching up, now and then, to straighten a tie or standing on tip-toe to remove a gaudy hair ornament. At the end of the line, Belle paused and, after a few seconds, marched back towards Liz, her face fiercely determined, leading a tiny, tieless, blazerless boy.

"This young man is Alfie Willis," Belle began, officiously. "I told him to put his tie and blazer on and he said he wouldn't. What should I do with him? He's not on my list—*and* he's not wearing the right shoes, either," she added, with satisfaction, adding in a lower voice, "I think we should make an example of him."

Liz smiled at Alfie and put her hand gently on his shoulder. "Hello again, Alfie."

It was the little boy from the bus stop.

"I'm glad you're in my form," Liz said, noticing his neatly mended trousers, oversized, dazzlingly white, hand-me-down shirt and plain black plimsolls. "Don't worry; there'll be plenty of time to sort your uniform out."

"Sorry, Miss. I was going to go to another school but we had to move house in the holidays." Alfie's eyes were wide as he willingly put her in the picture. "I did my best with the uniform, but I haven't got a tie and Mum hasn't started her job yet, so I can't get proper shoes till she gets paid." Alfie patted down the vertical tuft of hair on his crown, an unconscious habit that seemed to be, at once, necessary and futile because the tuft sprang straight back up again, as if determined to add an extra couple of inches to its owner's height.

Liz had chosen her allegiance as soon as she had noticed that Alfie was one of only a very few of 7EM (comfortably-off and well-nourished as most of them seemed to be) who was shorter than Belle. "Well, Alfie," she said tactfully, "we can't have you feeling different from the others on your first day here. One of our prefects will take you to the lower school office and they'll kit you out with everything you need till your mum can get it."

A prefect stepped forward. "Hi, Alfie, I'm Tom. Come on, mate," he said and, putting a brotherly hand on Alfie's shoulder, steered him in the direction of the office, the small boy smiling up at the bigger one and chatting animatedly as they went.

"Is that it?" demanded Belle. "He has the cheek to turn up without a proper uniform and he gets away with it. I bet his mum never even bothers to get him his own stuff."

"Have a look at him, Belle," Liz said. "He looks as if he's on the bread line and there's obviously something else going on too. Remember what Barbara said yesterday?"

Belle tutted sulkily again and her eyes rolled, unbidden as she realised Barbara had been watching the incident and was now approaching.

"Well done, Liz. I see you've met Alfie, then. I emailed you with the details a few minutes ago, but I shouldn't think you've had chance to read it yet," she said. "I've only just had the paperwork through this morning. I'll photocopy the relevant stuff for you. Nasty case. He'll need plenty of TLC."

"Poor kid," Liz said.

"Yes," said Barbara. "Very sad. I'll find you later with the paperwork. I know he'll be all right with you, though."

Belle had licked her wounds and now listened, attentiveness replacing the petulance on her face.

"I'll do my best for him," Liz replied. *And they say there aren't boys like him any more*, she added to herself.

Flattered by Barbara's faith in her, Liz led her tutees, like ducklings: in single file, towards the hall. They paused in the foyer, where she instructed them to leave their potentially hazardous and distracting bags. Unquestioning, the children added them to the already mountainous pile left by the rest of year seven before entering the hall.

9: Alfie

Gordon swept into the hall to address the newcomers. He had taken care to leave the main doors open so that as he entered, his head master's gown was lifted by the breeze and it fluttered behind him as he made his impressive entrance.

"Welcome to King Richard the Lionheart High School," Gordon said. "Hands up who likes comics."

There was a ripple and about two hundred eleven-year-olds looked at each other, seeming unsure whether it was a trick question. Perhaps they were supposed to be above such puerile publications by now. Many looked, next, at their form tutors, who smiled encouragingly, hoping it was the right thing to do. Liz and Serena exchanged speculating glances and followed suit. Tentatively, about two thirds of the year sevens' hands crept up and a flicker of relief ruffled Gordon's expression.

"Well, so do I," he confided to the whole room. "In fact..." He paused and looked left and right, affecting anxiety at imagined discovery. "...I only became a head master so I could wear this cape." He grasped the edges of the gown and flapped it, to the amusement of the now secure year sevens.

"It makes me feel like a superhero from a comic," he said, conspiratorially. "My favourite one is Flash Gordon. Put your hand up if you can guess why I'm like him."

The assembled children were not as au fait with nineteen-thirties' comic book heroes (let alone their fifties or eighties TV or cinema equivalents) as Gordon had hoped. However, some were eager to please and a couple of hands inched up.

"Do you shoot baddies?" asked a boy near the front.

Gordon smiled and shook his head. "Good try. Anyone else like to guess?"

"Can you fly?" asked another.

"No, but it'd be useful," he laughed and motioned a sensible looking girl to answer.

"Tights?"

That wrong-footed him. He blinked and then, regaining his composure, pressed a button on a laptop at the front of the stage. The same comic book picture of Flash Gordon as he had used in the previous day's meeting appeared on the projector screen and Queen was blasted at them from speakers around the room: *Flash, ah-ah, saviour of the universe.*

"Well, year seven, you were close, but the reason is that Flash Gordon saved the universe and I want to do the same for this school. I hope that by the time you leave King Richard's, you'll all be superheroes too."

The hallful of eleven-year-olds gazed up at him, round-eyed as owlets, innocently sure of his ability to confer superpowers, and having faith that in seven years' time they would leave King Richard's, superior beings, capable of things inconceivable by other eighteen-year-olds. Their unquestioning acceptance was soon to transform, however, when Gordon delivered the next part of his assembly.

"*In loco parenthesis*," he said ostentatiously. "Who knows what that means?"

Liz and Serena avoided each other's eyes, biting their cheeks. No answer was forthcoming from the assembled young.

"It's nothing to do with trains; it's Latin," he prompted.

More blank looks.

"It means while you're at my school, I'm your dad."

The two hundred blank faces began to metamorphose; some became puzzled, others distressed and a few were incensed. When their faux father went on to elaborate, the year sevens' minds were still struggling to process the idea that their parents no longer held sway and failed to take the information in. They did not absorb Gordon's avowals that he wanted the best for them and that *in place of parent* meant that he would supervise their wellbeing and by the time the assembly was over, they were bursting with concern and consternation.

Alfie walked next to Liz as she led her group out.

"You got everything you needed then," she said. "You're a proper Dickie's kid now," and winked at him. Alfie beamed back, immaculate and equal in his new school tie and only slightly too big blazer. He patted the golden lion on its red, shield-shaped badge and whispered, "Well smart."

Back in the form room, Liz had some questions to field.

"What about if I've already got a dad, Miss?"

"Miss! Will he have to check with my mum?"

"He won't come to my house, will he?"

"He won't hug me, will he?"

Finally—from Alfie: "He won't whack me when I'm bad, will he, Miss?" Liz winced inwardly, experience telling her to take him seriously and respond gently, "Of course he won't."

Belle obviously felt her expert knowledge was invaluable, here, and interrupted: "Don't be silly, Alfie. Adults aren't allowed to hit children."

Liz hastily manoeuvred the answer back to safer terrain. "He just means he'll look after you when you're here."

"Will he, Miss?"

"He wants you to be safe and happy and to do your best. Now, off you go and find your seat."

Liz turned her attention back to the other students as they found their names on the seating plan and sat themselves down. One was missing—along with Ellie, the other prefect. A look at the plan confirmed which lamb had strayed from the flock.

"Do you know where Emin Smith went after assembly?" Liz asked Belle, but Belle was unable to help.

"Shit!" Liz whispered. "He was a two-cross kid. He'd better not have got into trouble on his first day!"

She didn't have to wait long to find out, however, because a pinch-faced, rat-like boy, eyes dark-circled from late-night gaming, swaggered in, led by Ellie. Liz indicated his seat, next to sensible, two-tick Kate and waited for Ellie to explain.

"He stayed behind to ask Mr Dillon a question, Mrs Marshall." She looked uneasy.

Swinging back on his chair, Emin hooked an elbow over the back of it and looked around at his classmates, smirking and nodding; he knew what Ellie was about to divulge. Liz glanced at him, taking care to veil the dislike that might become clear in her face. She was interested to see whether this *defiant, disruptive* boy would, as sometimes happened, prove to be entertaining or whether, as she suspected from his current demeanour, he would simply be obnoxious. He turned to his left and the light caught the intricately shaved pattern that curved around one side of his buzz-cut. That would have to go.

Ellie turned her back to him and whispered now. "He went up to Mr Dillon and said, 'If you're my dad, can I have my pocket money?'" Liz was careful not to let Emin see her involuntary smile and quelled it immediately. She had to hand it to him: that was sharp. However, it could prove dangerous to encourage such confidence on the first day, so Liz responded quietly, "What did Mr Dillon say?"

"He just took it as a joke, which it was... I think."

"Okay... did he see all this business on the side of his head?" Liz gestured, circularly, in the region of her right ear.

"No, I don't think so; he didn't say anything. I think Miss Bosun did though," Ellie replied.

Liz sighed. Emin could prove to be troublesome if she did not handle him carefully. She approached his desk at the front of the room and, firmly pushing the back of his chair so that all four legs were on the floor, bent down beside his desk, laying claim to his space, and showed him the uniform page in her copy of the student planner. She pointed at the rules about boys' hair: *Shaved and extreme hairstyles and colours are not permitted. Any student breaking this rule will be required to change their hairstyle before the next school day.*

"I'm afraid you'll need to get your hair sorted out as soon as possible. You can't have it like that at school."

"No way. My dad forked out loads to get this done yesterday."

"Well, I'm afraid it'll need to be fixed. All parents knew the rules when they applied to the school."

Before Emin could object, Barbara Bosun entered the room, on the same mission.

"Morning, Mrs Marshall. I've just come to check whether your year sevens are all up to scratch and behaving themselves."

She peered at them over her glasses and all but one sat up, alert, keen to make a good impression and not to be singled out. Liz straightened up and moved back towards her desk. Emin took his chance and casually tilted his chair back, looking at his head of year with insolently narrowed eyes.

"Sit on your chair properly and wipe that smirk off your face, Mr Smith. I've phoned home and I'll see you in my office before school in the morning with an acceptable haircut," Barbara said, sharply.

Emin coloured, but whether it was due to annoyance or embarrassment, it was impossible to tell.

Barbara's glance whipped across the rest of the students. "Jordan," she snapped, "remove that nail polish immediately. Mrs Marshall will give you the wherewithal."

That was that mystery solved, then. Jordan was likely a girl and as such, she could stay by Edward: Teddy-two-ticks.

Jordan strode towards Liz and bellowed good-humouredly, "Mum told me to take it off last night but I talked her round; I always do. Just my luck Miss Bosun saw. She taught my mum too."

The rest of the class tittered and Liz handed her the nail polish remover and a tissue.

"I remember," chuckled Barbara and stepped over to Liz's desk, lowering her voice. "Here's a copy of Alfie Willis's notes," she said. "Read them as soon as you get a chance. He's going to need gentle handling." She handed Liz an A4 envelope, marked *Confidential*. Glancing in, Liz saw Greater Manchester social services' headed paper and began, involuntarily, to predict its contents.

"By the way, if Mr Smith puts a foot out of line, send him straight to me," said Barbara. "What kind of a name is *Emin*, anyway?" She grimaced. "I'm not even sure how to pronounce it."

Belle, again, shared the bounty of her knowledge and this time it was more welcome. "It's after Eminem?" she said.

"Oh yes, according to the register, his middle name is *M*," said Liz. "Just the letter."

"What *is* the world coming to?" asked Barbara, not expecting enlightenment.

Belle's explanation did not surprise: "So, Eminem's a rapper?" she told Barbara, her smile at once complacent and obsequious.

"Thank you, dear. And this... er... Eminem, is he an American gentleman?"

Belle confirmed that he was.

Barbara sighed a sigh full of resignation and regret. "Why these young people can't have British role models, I don't know. This is Bremeldon, not the Bronx." She suddenly brightened and her eyes flashed a rare twinkle. "I'll call him *Emlyn*. That'll annoy him. I'll pretend I thought it was a misprint."

Barbara was almost never mischievous. Maybe she was mellowing.

The necessary administration followed and, when every child had been furnished with a planner, map and timetable, Liz sent them off, with their prefect guides, to their lessons. She sent Belle off to the staffroom to plan the form captain election lesson, which would take place at the end of the week: she should be ready to take on a whole lesson by then. Liz shuddered. Speeches, campaigns, ballot papers, popularity contests: that would be right up Belle's street.

Once alone, Liz picked up the A4 envelope that would disclose what had brought Alfie here with such haste. She pulled out the social worker's report, dated only a few days previously, and skimmed its contents, mindful that it would soon be time for break and she would need to cast an eye over the fruits of Belle's labours before then, too.

The report stated that Alfie and his mother had been living in a women's refuge near Manchester and, as her eyes slid over the dense print, Liz took in the reason as the salient details pushed themselves forwards.

... May 12th...Sarah Willis, mother... sustained attack, perpetrated by Sean Willis... miscarriage.

Liz searched for Alfie's name, trepidatious about what she might discover, and, finding it, read the sentence more closely. *Alfie witnessed the attack and was unharmed, although he tried, unsuccessfully, to protect his mother and called the emergency services as soon after the attack as he could.*

"How long does the election lesson need to be?"

Liz looked up. "What?"

Belle had trotted back in and waited for an answer. "The tutor group. The Form Captain elections. I need to know how much to plan."

"Oh, right—an hour," said Liz, distracted. "Maybe get them to start by thinking about the qualities a good captain should have. They could decide on a list they all agree on."

Satisfied, Belle bustled off to prepare her questions and activities. Liz turned her attention back to the report in front of her, skimming again, now. The phrases, familiar to her from television drama and the news, not real life, revealed themselves relentlessly.

...further injuries sustained by Sarah Willis... black eye... fractured ribs... injuries to the abdomen consistent with kicking... week in hospital.

Liz bit her lip as she imagined the small figure of Alfie, powerless against his father, and continued to skim the page.

Alfie was examined by doctors ... sustained some bruising.... older bruises noted... no hospital records of previous injuries.

"I could give the students group roles like idea-generators, scribes and reporters." Belle was back again, clearly desperate to share her theoretical knowledge of methods of group work.

Liz tore her eyes away from the clinical, photocopied white page; forced herself to consider Belle's question; administered the looked-for verbal pat on the head, and watched her trip away again, apprehensive about what else the report would reveal.

...Mr Willis arrested... Mrs Willis filed for divorce...temporary injunction... decided not to press charges...

The next phrase that forced itself into Liz's consciousness seemed to be what Liz was dreading reading: *...breached the conditions of the injunction...*

She slowed down, wanting to read the next part of the social worker's report more carefully, knowing it would disclose the reason for Alfie and his mother's sudden move and hoping that reason had been precautionary.

During August of this year, Mr Willis was seen near Sanctuary House a number of times and the police had to be called. He also made numerous telephone calls, asking to speak to Mrs Willis and Alfie. On 29th August, Mr Willis gained entry to Mrs Willis and Alfie's room and attempted to—

"It's okay if I try a few different groupings, isn't it?" Belle bounced in again, like a puppy with a spit-covered ball. Irritation got the better of Liz and she was sharper than she intended. "Do whatever you think. Give me two minutes—I just need to concentrate, okay?"

Belle scuttled off, startled.

—persuade her to leave with him. When this failed, Mr Willis made threats to both Mrs Willis and Alfie, although no physical violence actually occurred since staff on duty managed to calm him down and convince him to leave.

The breath Liz did not realise she had been holding escaped her as a relieved sigh and, cautiously reassured, she ran her eye down to the bottom of the page.

... St Anne's Women's Aid refuge, Bremeldon, Worcestershire...adults with a duty of care...vigilant... significant threat...gain access to Alfie.

Liz blinked. *Poor little sod*, she thought. *School uniform's the last thing he should have to worry about.*

Belle put her head round the door, ready to unveil her plan for the elections. "Can I come in now?" she asked.

Liz nodded, saying, "You ought to read these: Alfie Willis's case notes. It's all confidential, though. You can't mention it to him, unless he brings it up, okay?"

As Belle read, her face darkened. When she had finished, she looked at Liz, moist-eyed, and said, "God, that's terrible. You'll have to be really sensitive with him."

10: Alps

Chris Moran, unofficial poet in residence and official head of sixth form, smiled and strolled elegantly towards Liz and Serena as they went into the staffroom at break. He was about to give his annual 'welcome' assembly to the new sixth-formers, in which he would impress and bewilder them with a stream of erudition that would be over most of their heads. He was already limbering up and spoke with a familiar, measured cadence. "Hello, you two. You'll like this one." Chris smiled in anticipation and looked at them over his glasses, his ink black eyes darting around the room, gauging the attention of the rest of his colleagues as he prepared to flex his verbal muscles: "What do you call a sixth former with an identity crisis?"

Liz and Serena looked at each other, aware that he had entrusted them with his ingenuity and loath to let him down, either by guessing well and stealing his thunder or not having a clue and seeming too simple-minded to be worthy of his wit.

Liz floundered. "Er...normal?" she tried.

Chris took a seat and crossed his legs. He chuckled in acknowledgement of her answer, satisfied that he had prevailed. Polishing his glasses, he affected unconcern before enlightening them with an inscrutable combination of what seemed to be nonchalance and delight: "Addled essence!"

This elicited a mixed response from the room: after an initial silence, Liz snorted the required admiration, followed by Serena's complimentary response: "That's brilliant, Chris. Did you make it up?" to which Chris responded with a bashful affirmative. Lucy soon burst his bubble, though: "Bloody hell, Chris! That was awful, even by your standards."

Various groans and splutters followed as the wordplay was worked out, the rear being brought up by Peggy.

"I don't understand. What do you mean *adolescents*? That's just what they are, isn't it?" she said.

Chris was not listening, but basked in the appreciation of his joke. Dave leaned towards Peggy, kindly. "It's a pun—I'll explain later."

"Anyway," said Chris and cleared his throat, "No indolence for the iniquitous—"

"Tell you later," whispered Dave, as Peggy leaned towards him.

"—I'd better go and get my...er... PowerPoint ready for the assembly." Sheepish, Chris uttered the offending jargon almost under his breath as he hastened towards the door."

"*Et tu, Brute?*" Liz was not going to let him off the hook that easily. "I thought you hated computer presentations. Remember what you renamed them at the end of last term?"

"PowerPointless," Chris confirmed, "and I still find them entirely fatuous. Unfortunately, Gordon doesn't." He grimaced as if in actual pain. "He's prohibited me from giving one of my customary sixth form salutations and instructed me not to tell them anything irrelevant. He's insisted I simply deliver some inane slide show he's produced—all data and logos, if I may borrow from the ancients on both sides of the Ionian Sea for a moment—but I've augmented his fatuous address with something a little more highbrow; after all—" Chris smiled again, cheered. "—relevance is in the eye of the beholder."

Integrity reclaimed, Chris headed for the hall.

"Could be interesting, Bish," said Liz, finishing her coffee.

"Fucking priceless," said Dave. "Apparently, Dildo's making him tell the kids all about the A Level Performance System stats."

"Sounds bloody riveting."

"It's a load of old bollocks," Dave clarified. "Unfortunately, it's a load of old bollocks that we're going to have to get our heads round."

"Sounds like a load of extra work to me." Liz was irritated and terrified in equal measure.

"Anyway, Chris will explain all. Come on; let's bag seats at the front so we can put him off!"

Heartened, Liz drained her cup, shouldered her bag and followed Dave, Serena and the others towards the hall.

When they got there, however, their plan was thwarted. Gordon greeted them at the door, like an usher at a wedding, and gestured upwards to where a row of chairs squatted ominously on the stage. Horrified at the unnecessary formality and exposure, they climbed the short flight of steps onto the stage as if it were the North face of the Eiger.

"What does he think this is? Greyfriars?" Liz muttered and shot a questioning look at Chris as she took her place a couple of seats away from him, behind the lectern, but received only a shrug in return and turned her attention to the students coming in.

Excited chatter filtered up to the stage and here and there, the glowing screens of phones could be seen to light faces no longer afraid of their confiscation. In the three months since they had finished their GCSEs and left, last term's year elevens had undergone dramatic metamorphoses. Shoulders had broadened and décolletages bloomed: skinny boys had become masculine Vs and androgynous girls were now hourglasses. They had transformed from clones to individuals, now they were not forced to conform to strict uniform rules. Many had exercised this prerogative to the fullest. Boys' hair ventured way past collars most had now eschewed; beards, moustaches and sideburns had sprouted, burgeoned and been topiarised; girls' crowning glories blazed from all areas of the spectrum; a few of last year's 'boys' and 'girls' no longer identified as such, and, irrespective of gender, piercings and even some tattoos proliferated on hitherto uncorrupted flesh.

Liz looked down at the front row, where half a dozen or so girls, dressed in colourful summer vests, displayed acres of pale flesh. She nudged Dave. "Usual row of tits, I see. It's like a cowshed at milking time."

Dave turned his head in the direction of her gaze and, flinching, raised a hand to shield his eyes from the view. "Fuck me! I don't know where to look. I could lose my DBS just by being here."

Gordon, solemn in his black gown, introduced himself to the year twelves, thankfully without any references to comic superheroes or fathers, and quickly handed over to Chris, who would give the presentation Gordon had prepared for him. The heavy, velvet curtains were drawn back and the screen behind Chris lit up. He stood up and stepped gracefully towards the lectern. Coughing gently, he tapped the touchpad on his laptop and a picture of Turner's *Hannibal Crossing the Alps* came into view: Chris's addition to the Power Point.

Gordon's jaw and shoulders tensed and the line between his eyebrows deepened.

On the screen, the huge, turbulent sky dwarfed both men and elephants. The black, arching cloud gaped like an immense, otherworldly mouth, uvula hanging, yawning over the mountains, ready to devour. The students gazed, wondering what wisdom Mr Moran would impart—his assemblies being the stuff of legend—and whether they would understand a word of it.

"Good morning," started Chris. "For those of you as yet unacquainted with me, I am Christopher Moran, head of sixth form—your *caput sextus*, if you will. For the duration of your curricular enlightenment, I shall be scrutinising your conduct and coxswaining your scholastic advancement. I shall be omnipresent and beneficent."

Liz smiled at the sea of impressed, insensible faces.

"To which end," he continued, gravely, "I will first offer a small fragment of the wisdom of the great Romantic poet, Shelley, from his magnum opus, *Mont Blanc*: words that some of you might recognise..."

"Unlikely," Liz whispered to Serena.

"...and seem apposite on this occasion."

Seated to the right of the empty chair left by Chris, the head shifted and looked uncomfortable. Dave prodded Liz and whispered, "Look at Dildo."

"Proper Chris assembly," said Liz. "Knocks spots off Gordon's."

Serena sighed. "Yeah, schools need teachers like Chris."

Chris cleared his throat again and smiled. "Right...er...well..." he tapped his laptop and six lines of poetry in an elegant, cursive font gradually faded in, superimposed over the painting. Liz watched Gordon's philistine displeasure with satisfaction. Chris inclined his head forwards, a movement that told Liz and the others he was looking, not at the laptop or his notes, but professorially, over his glasses, at the students, his habitual pre-speech gesture.

He began to recite:
"*The everlasting universe of things*
Flows through the mind, and rolls its rapid waves,

*Now dark—now glittering—now reflecting gloom—
Now lending splendour, where from secret springs
The source of human thought its tribute brings.*"

Chris paused to gauge the effect of the words upon his students and continued imperiously. "You must each divine your own sources of thought."

Liz was not convinced they would, but Chris had boundless faith in the young.

He finished: "*Mont Blanc yet gleams on high:—the power is there.*"

He paused impressively before continuing. "Mont Blanc, as I'm sure you are well aware, is the highest mountain in the Alps and it is Alps of which I am—ahem—*required* to inform you this morning."

His cough was mannered and communicated much. However, Gordon's facial muscles relaxed as Chris's speech finally meandered towards the approved path.

"A. L. P. S." Chris indicated the Turner behind him with a nod before tapping for the next slide. Liz watched the acronym appear on the screen, complete with accompanying logo, a stylised combination of mountain range and line graph, the final peak of which, the Matterhorn, formed the 'A'.

"Advanced Level Performance System. A national database that—er—analyses your results..." Chris read the slide notes falteringly, as if he had never seen them before, adding, "...and, I'm—er—reliably assured," he glanced towards Gordon, "helps us to improve your—er—performance," and tapped for the next: *How your data is analysed.* That got his attention and he launched himself off piste again. "Actually, some of you might not be aware, but the word *data* is a plural."

"Here we go," said Liz. "Classic Chris."

"I fucking love it," smirked Dave.

Chris paused, his wisdom lost on the sixth formers. "The plural of *datum*: *that which we are given*, as those of you conversant with Latin will, no doubt, be aware."

The students were still blank. No one at King Richard's was conversant with Latin.

"So, if you'll bear with me, I'll just amend this asinine communiqué." He deleted *is* and typed in *are*, muttering that he could not see how any company could expect to gain the confidence of its users when it did not even demonstrate a grasp of basic grammar.

"That's better." He looked satisfied as he displayed the corrected slide. "How your data *are* analysed," he read.

Gordon's face was stone.

Chris presented the next slide. It was full of letters and figures too small to read, but a huge, almost phallic, cartoon thermometer showed that, as far as Liz could fathom, blue numbers were bad and red ones were good. Its glowing red tip illustrated that principle admirably. Liz bit the insides of her cheeks and tried hard to stay composed. Most of the students were less assiduous in their efforts, however, and titters rippled through the hall, rising to audible laughter when the thermometer, animated now, bounced along the bottom of the screen to illustrate the measurability of A level learning. Liz glanced to her right; Gordon was not laughing.

The presentation ended with a corporate slide showing several conservatively dressed A level students in the shadow of the company's Alpine insignia, holding their no doubt excellent and thoroughly analysed results aloft and smiling smugly at the priapic thermometer.

"To summarise, then." Chris attempted to tease some meaning out for the students. "Your A level studies will require unremitting endeavour on your part and, at times, it might seem like an arduous ascent, but persevere, acquire the utmost from it and, most profoundly, conquer the summit of your own Mont Blanc. Achieve your pinnacle."

Ardently, uncomprehendingly, in that moment, two hundred sixteen year-olds knew that they would.

Gordon sprang to his feet and hurried towards the lectern. "Thank you, Mr Moran."

Chris took his seat next to Liz and leaned towards her, not bothering to hide the disdain that showed in his face. His lip curled as he spoke: "It's like shovelling shit. Forget teaching and learning; just hand me a bucket and spade."

As if feeling the need to validate his own presence, Gordon, once more, addressed the bewildered students, underlining Chris's point: "Yes, young people. Data *is* important," he stressed, insensible of Chris's exaggerated wince. "Just remember the Alps and the way your results are measured."

Chris took this as his cue. "By the bucketful."

11: Normal Days

Liz was not ready for this. A normal day. A full timetable. She had not slept well again. This day seemed to get harder every year. The first standard day of term ushered in the irrepressible mob that had not been together in such numbers for six long weeks and whether she liked it or not, Liz would be part of their dynamic. They would be more concerned with the re-establishment of relationships and pecking orders; preoccupation with their peers' opinions, and the exchange of gossip, than anything she had to teach them, so she would need to be at her most competent. She felt her face start to burn with dread; she could not *require improvement* today.

Liz drove onto the patch of gravel next to the school, just behind Dave. Tucking her car in alongside his and getting out, she tutted and rolled her eyes, jerking her head towards Janet's two-seater, which had been abandoned diagonally in the middle of the car park, where it occupied enough space for at least two.

"Fucking typical," said Dave, by way of salutation.

"You'll miss it next year," she said. "Anyway, Bish," she continued, "what time do you call this?"

Dave had always arrived at the crack of dawn to stay one step ahead of the students, but this was only half an hour before the bell went. He hesitated, looked embarrassed. "I just suddenly thought, 'Why am I doing this?' so I had another half hour's kip."

"I did wonder," said Liz, rooting around in the bottom of her bag for her lanyard.

"Yeah, I—er—thought, *Fuck 'em; they're only kids*," he explained, over-egging the pudding.

Realisation struck. "I know that look," Liz exclaimed. "You had a better offer! Another half hour's kip, my arse! Have you even been home?"

Dave stifled a smile, looked away and reddened, clearly rifling in his brain for a way to divert Liz's attention. "What are you looking for?"

"Don't try and change the subject," she said, putting her lanyard over her head. "Come on; I want details."

"Okay," he laughed, "but you can't tell anyone else." His face became grave and he paused before adding, "Seriously."

"Of course I won't."

Dave noticed her with concern now. "Are you all right? You don't look too good. You're not actually ill, are you?"

"Thanks, you look pretty shit yourself." Liz replied. "I'm okay—just forgot to take my beta-blocker—that and the usual pre-school dread!"

"Thank God for that. I thought I was going to have to send you home," Dave said, but Liz brushed aside his unmerited alarm. "Don't worry—I'm indestructible," she laughed.

Dave's obvious relief liberated his humour. "Pickled by wine, more like," he said, nudging her. "You'll last fucking centuries! After the world's been destroyed by a nuclear holocaust and there's nothing left but cockroaches, there you'll be: scorched, shrivelled and clutching a glass of red in your bony little claw."

"Too bloody right," she smiled. "Anyway, I'm more interested in your love life."

"Come on, then; let's have a quick *breakfast meeting*." He indicated the irony with two crooked fingers of each hand. "We'll have a coffee, you can take some tablets or whatever and I'll tell you about my summer holidays—if you're *sure* you're all right."

In the few minutes it took for Dave to tell Liz about his first and only, outrageously successful foray into online dating and his subsequent headlong plunge off the cliff of singularity into the briny depths of coupledom, her equilibrium had returned and she was as capable as she ever would be of facing a pack of wild teenagers. First, though, she must take the morning register for her already tamed form.

By the time quarter to nine had tolled, Liz had wrenched Belle from the staffroom computer, brought her to heel and got her into the classroom for registration. Liz put her head out of the door to where Tom and Ellie had performed their prefectly duties perfectly and lined the year sevens up, ready to go in. Thank goodness: 7EM were not showing her up, but were as mouse-like and acquiescent as Serena and Peggy's forms. That wouldn't last. Liz invited them in and they all took their seats, and answered their names when they were called. Only one student was absent.

"Do you want me to let Miss Bosun know Emin Smith isn't here?" Belle asked. Impressed that Belle had tried to be helpful, but gratified that she had superior knowledge, Liz spoke kindly. "No, it's fine; remember, Babs told him to report to her with his hair cut, this morning," Liz reminded her. "She'll probably let us know in a minute. Check your emails later."

Tom and Ellie, charged with escorting the form for the rest of the day, stood at the back of the room, behind the diminutive students, and stifled knowing giggles when Liz impressed upon the year sevens how important it was to be quiet, listen and behave sensibly. Liz raised her eyebrows in the prefects' direction. "Tom and Ellie are two of our most sensible year elevens," she asserted, forcing the laughter from her voice, "and you should follow their example. In five years, this could be you."

Twenty-seven small heads looked towards the back of the room where the two prefects had smothered amused grins and replaced them with sagacious nods.

Ellie led the column of tutees off to their first lesson of the day. "How long are you going to keep that up, Miss?" whispered Tom as he brought up the rear of the line.

"Not long enough if you two keep making me laugh when I'm trying to be strict!" she replied. "Just 'cause I could never do it with your class!"

"I bet you've cracked by the end of the week."

"Probably," said Liz. "Now bugger off and catch up with them. See you later."

Liz turned towards her computer screen where a new email had arrived from Barbara, copied to Belle. She clicked and read its contents:

Dear Liz,

Emin Smith has neglected to follow my ruling regarding his hair and has, therefore, been sent home.

I have scheduled a reintegration meeting with him and his parents at 4pm.

In order to present a united front, it would be helpful if you could be there too, along with your trainee, if you and she are available.

Regards,

Barbara.

This would be interesting: Barbara in iron-clad battleship mode was impregnable. The Smiths didn't stand a chance. Liz almost felt sorry for them. For now, though, she needed to turn her attention to the gaggle of fourteen year olds catching up on the summer's gossip outside the room. She had not taught many of these students before, so she would need to manage their first impression of her judiciously.

She stepped out of the classroom and stood, arms folded, waiting for the students to hush naturally at the appearance of their new teacher. At the front of the line, one girl had her back to Liz, deep in conversation with her friends. As the rest of the students noticed Liz, they quietened and stood straight, expectantly. The girl at the front was consumed by her anecdote and her tiny audience's rapt attention. Her head bobbed with the joy of it, threatening to destabilise its unruly pile of bottle-blonde hair. Unbeknown to her, her audience had grown; now, the rest of the class listened with amusement too, while Liz exuded stern disapproval.

Now that the rest of the class was quiet, the climax of the girl's tale became audible to all of them.

"I just totally have a phobia of gone-off milk. Basically, Sam chased me round the library with a carton of it. He was, like, so-o-o mean, so I was like, 'That's so disrespectful'."

Nudged, at last, by one of her friends, she stopped and eyed first, her classmates and then her teacher. "Oh! Sorry, Miss." She waited, not knowing what would happen next.

Liz pressed her advantage and drew a menacing breath. "What is your name, young lady?"

The girl continued to look uncomfortable. "Um, Lauren Tyler, Miss."

Liz mustered her most viraginous expression and glared at Lauren stonily. "Well, Lauren, I think we'd all be interested to know—" she paused, registering the effect. She knew how much students loved falling victim to teachers' sarcasm. Lauren grew visibly defensive and squared her jaw.

"What?"

Liz relaxed her stance and laughed. "Is that when it all went *sour*?" She winked at Lauren who, fleetingly confused, soon gathered herself and smiled. "Yeah, I dumped him! You're better off without them, ain't you, Miss?"

Liz laughed and gestured towards the classroom door, but Lauren had caught a glimpse of the new teaching assistant, going into the year nine class next door. "Whoa!" She stopped dead. "I could make an exception for that! Hi, Sir!"

Next lesson was her year eleven top set, unchanged since last year. She could relax; she had known almost all of them since they had been in year seven. Many of them had been in her form for their first three years at King Richard's and they had already shown her they were the bosses. All she had to do was rely on their IQs and ambition and the run-up to their GCSEs would be plain sailing. Once the initial catching up had been done, Liz reminded them of their targets: vertiginous grades resulting from previous data (and woe betide Liz if any of them failed to achieve them) and set a typical exam-style piece of writing: *Describe the scene in a primary school playground at the end of the day.* Exciting stuff. She'd enjoy marking that.

Marking. Liz panicked. "No more than five paragraphs," she announced. "It's quality, not quantity I'm after."

The students tittered and looked at each other. "You've just realised you've got to mark this, haven't you, Miss?" Joe piped up from the back.

"Worried Dild—er—Mr Dillon's going to be checking up on you, Miss?" teased his tablemate, Dan, rubbing his arm after a sharp nudge from Joe.

"You know me too well, you lot," Liz confessed with a smile. "Anyway, Dan, what were you just about to call Mr Dillon? As if I didn't know," she added, "and, more to the point, where did you hear it?" She was eager to ascertain whether the name had been cultivated from her original sowing or self-seeded of its own accord.

"Pretty much the whole of year eleven started calling him that after assembly, Miss," interjected Becky from the other side of the room. "You see, there was this PowerPoint and it said his name and there was this animation of this superhero—"

More students started to chip in, delighted at the memory.

"And he was holding this laser gun thing—"

"Ray gun!"

"Yeah, and he sort of wiggled it up and down and it looked like a—"

"Okay, okay, you don't need to spell it out; I've got the picture." Liz gestured for quiet, laughingly, hands outstretched, palms downwards.

"You won't tell him, will you?" Becky was worried; she wanted to hang on to her prefect's badge for the whole year, not be stripped of it in the first week.

"You'd have laughed if you'd seen it, Miss," added Dan, "Ask Mr Bishop; he was there. I swear, he had to pretend to blow his nose 'cause he was bright red and made this weird noise into his hanky."

Liz would get the details from Dave at break. She answered, "Well, we did have a very similar presentation on Monday." She smiled as she recalled the heavily underlined *Dildo* from her notes as well as Dave's reaction, and with great effort of will, she forced herself not to regale them with the details of Gordon's speech and their own renaming of him.

"Ah, Miss!" roared Joe in glee. "You thought exactly the same thing, didn't you?"

Liz pleaded the fifth: "I'm not saying a word."

"Come on, Miss, we know you!" The class was elated.

"Don't worry, though—we won't tell him," Becky reassured her. "You're such a kid, Miss. You'll get the sack one of these days!"

12: Settling In

Three o'clock. Now, Liz really did feel as if the summer holidays had never happened. Already, she could not imagine getting up late and shuffling around in her pyjamas all day, unhaunted by the spectres of Ofsted inspections, lesson observations and reproachful bags full of exercise books. She had about an hour before the meeting with Barbara and the Smiths: just about time to make a coffee and a start on the year eleven marking. In the English staffroom, the others were recuperating briefly, before the work began again.

"You still okay, Liz?" Dave asked. "Going home to put your feet up?"

Liz grimaced. "I wish!" she said, stirring her coffee. "I've got a meeting with Babs and some parents later."

"Fucking hell. You in trouble already? What have you done now?"

She laughed and raised her hand, ready to let him feel the back of it. "Cheeky git! What makes you think it was me?"

Dave adopted a cowering pose. "Not the face!"

"You'll keep." She rinsed her spoon and picked up her mug. "Anyway, better get some work done. See you later."

Back in her room, Liz sank into her chair, faced with the pile of thirty newly-inscribed exercise books. Looking around, she sighed, noting the carnage wrought by the day. No longer parallel, the tables were finger-smeared, ink-blotted and grimy. Scraps of paper, a sweet wrapper, sundered fragments of eraser and the smithereens of broken pens strewed the as yet unvacuumed floor, like oblations. One awkwardly splayed, broken-spined dictionary sprawled, face down on the carpet, like a tyre-flattened magpie on the road. Its glossy cover was bent and thrust upwards implausibly, flashing blue-green like a damaged wing each time the breeze disturbed its feathery pages. Liz picked it up and replaced it on the latterly pencil-straight stack, shaking her head sadly as she stroked the cover back into place and considered the pithy observation penned on the page-ends, legible only when the dictionary was closed: *UR GAY*.

Settling back into her seat, Liz took a sip of her coffee and began to read the descriptions of playgrounds conceived by year eleven. Children and their parents were brought to life on the lined pages with varying degrees of success. Here and there, hackneyed eyes were cried out and vapid smiles stretched from ear to clichéd ear. One banal child was left alone, his predictable mother rushing in, late, to gather him in her platitudinous embrace and dry his passé tears. On the other hand, some students had approached the task with flair: extended metaphors involving ants and bees, battery hens and butterflies had been constructed with the dexterity of artisans. Some sentences grew and blossomed, becoming increasingly convoluted as clauses and phrases, long and short, separated by an embarrassment of punctuation (top grades could not be awarded to writing with unsophisticated punctuation; the students had obviously taken this idea on board and were determined to impress), jostled for supremacy and guided the reader along the meandering path of description to their ends: places entirely unconnected, however, with their beginnings, in some cases. By contrast, other sentences were kept short. That created drama. Impressive.

With a few minutes until she had to meet the Smiths, Liz opened Becky's book, casting a discerning eye over the loops and curls, strokes and dots that made up the artfully illustrated scene, a bird's-eye view that swooped elegantly from the general to the particular. Despite her mastery of grammar and vocabulary, Becky seemed to have had a mental block over the spelling of one word, however. The last paragraph began: *With a concluding crescendo*—nice alliteration—*of lunch boxes, book bags and PE kits*—list of three: good—*the last occupants of the soon-to-be-deserted*—compound adjective: tick—*playground squeezed through the creaking iron gates in a cacophony*—excellent—*of ~~caos~~*—Oh.

Liz chuckled and turned the page. She admired Becky's resilience (if not her common-sense; her desk was, after all, next to the dictionary shelf): the top line was filled with experiments in chaos: ~~kaos~~, ~~caosse~~, ~~chaos~~, ~~cahos~~ and ~~khaos~~, but she had given up and resorted to her original attempt. Liz circled the correct spelling in green (Gordon considered red too discouraging) and closed the book. She needed to get to her meeting, so the rest would have to wait. She made her way to the staffroom to collect Belle, but her bag and jacket were not there.

"Anyone seen Belle?" Liz asked the room.

"She left about half an hour ago," Peggy spoke through a mouthful of emergency chocolate. "She must have been tired after her first full day, poor love."

"Yeah. A full day of watching other people teach. Exhausting," Lucy chipped in, picking something whitish off her skirt and laughing.

Serena joined in. "She was just logging out of Tinder when I came down in my free to make a cup of tea." She eyed Liz eloquently from under an elegant sweep of hair. "She didn't even look embarrassed."

"Oh well, I'm sure I can manage without her." Liz side-stepped the problem; it would keep. "See you later."

Liz took the back route down to Reception, intending to keep a low profile until Barbara got there and took charge. In the foyer, occupying most of the ten, sociably grouped soft chairs in the visitors' waiting area, was the Smith family. The two other men who also waited there, sat uncomfortably close to each other but safely distant from them. Liz loitered in the corridor, at the far entrance to the foyer, where she could see the Smiths, and pretended to study the notice board, reluctant to tackle them on her own. Emin's posture betrayed somewhat less swagger now that he was newly shorn. A dough-faced woman with lank hair scraped into a spindly ponytail, which displayed slivers of pasty scalp, slumped beside him and Liz recognised, with a shudder of recollection, the motherly exhaustion she exuded. A child of about three or four climbed on the coffee table in front of them, scattering prospectuses and course leaflets in all directions. Mrs Smith's feeble entreaty of, "No, Ty," was ignored half a dozen times until the skinny, twitching, rodent-like man sitting opposite her swore loudly and turned to reveal the same shaved hair design as his elder son had lately sported.

"Tyrese!" he growled, "Fucking pack it in. You're doing my fucking head in," at which point, the child wandered towards the water cooler and set about dispassionately dropping disposable plastic cups onto the floor, one by one, with his right hand and dispensing ice-cold liquid onto the parquet with his left. Sensing further disapproval from his parents, Tyrese grinned jubilantly and turned, masticating a well-worn dummy and calculating their tolerance thresholds, while seeming to contemplate what manner of irritation he could wreak next.

"You're too fucking soft on him," his father informed his mother. "Oi! Ty, come here, you little brat." He fished a grubby baby's bottle out of his wife's bag, poured some cola into it, from the can he was holding, and handed it to the child. "Here you are: this'll shut you up." He leaned back in his chair; checked that the roll-up behind his ear was still in place, looked around smugly, and placed his scrawny, tattooed arm across the back of his wife's chair as if to stake his claim.

From her position on the other side of Reception, Liz watched them, willing Barbara to hurry up and appear; she was starting to feel ridiculous. Mrs Smith, feeling the proprietorial arm, shifted self-consciously and tugged at the back of her top, in a prim effort to cover the greyish flesh that was visible over the top of her jogging bottoms. Comfortable now, Emin's father leant towards her, seemingly in a show of affection. Mrs Smith, momentarily girlish, turned towards him, ready to receive his whispered endearment, but the harsh rasp that escaped him, unambiguously audible—even to Liz, was not from his lips at all, although the satisfied sigh that followed it was.

"Better out than in," he announced.

The other fathers, seeming chary of risking any altercation with Mr Smith, shifted uneasily and meticulously avoided eye contact—either with each other or him. Liz considered this studied obliviousness a wise move, but it was too much for Mrs Smith, whose sense of decorum overcame her weariness. "Wayne!" she exclaimed, glancing from side to side, mortified.

Emin did not share his mother's shame, however, and grinned. "Nice one, Dad."

Mr Smith's eyes narrowed and he looked around, nodding and smiling slyly, a gesture Liz had seen his son perform two days before. "Fucking sound," he replied.

"Kindly moderate your language, Mr Smith." Barbara hove into view. "You are in a school."

Perhaps it was the surprise, but Mr Smith sat up, scratched the back of his head self-consciously, displacing his greasy, peaked baseball cap slightly, and coughed. Liz stepped forward with what she hoped was the look of someone who had only just arrived and Barbara gestured towards her with an open palm. "You will not have met Mrs Marshall," she stated, consulting some papers and raising her eyebrows reprovingly in the Smiths' direction, "absent, as you were, from the new intake information evening, in July."

Liz smiled and shook hands with the couple, noting Mrs Smith's blush and her pale eyes, which only met Liz's fleetingly before skittering sideways.

"Right," Barbara continued, "let's keep this brief; I'm extremely busy, as you can—" she paused, "—perhaps, imagine." She marched to her office with the assurance of one used to being obeyed and, when satisfied she had been, bade them sit.

"Now," she said, "I take it you've read the details of the home-school agreement as I asked you to."

Mr and Mrs Smith nodded meekly and signed just below Barbara's imperious finger.

"And I see that Emlyn's hair—"

Mr Smith opened his mouth and his hackles seemed to rise, but Barbara's words swept his objections aside.

"—is more compliant with our requirements, although it should be cut to a centimetre or more—as long as it doesn't grow beyond collar length—in future."

Mr Smith regained some of his nerve at these infringements of his son's rights. "So, it has to be longer than a number three?" he asked sulkily.

Barbara settled back in her chair and laced her fingers on her lap. She fixed him with a wearisome look, a look so full of sorrow and pity that Liz was both embarrassed and impressed. "Yes." She sighed, a small, sad shake of the head acknowledging Mr Smith's own hairstyle, "anything shorter than that makes boys look like hooligans."

Wayne Smith's expression oscillated between outrage and anxiety.

Barbara continued: "We don't want anyone in a King Richard's uniform to give that impression. We have a reputation to maintain." Her gaze, now stony, bore down on the Smiths and she continued, "I seem to remember having a similar meeting with you about Mariah a few years ago. What year is she in now?"

"Er, year eleven," said Mr Smith.

"Ah, yes," said Barbara, "Pink streaks, if I remember correctly. Now, I must get on." She stood up, a signal they recognised, so did the same. However, as Barbara moved towards the door to show them out, Mrs Smith ventured, "Miss Bosun?"

Barbara stopped and looked back at her. "Yes?"

"Can you make sure school's got his name down right? It's Emin, not Emlyn."

Mrs Smith seemed to stand a little taller and when Liz smiled, she met her eye for longer now.

"Oh, I'm so sorry," Barbara replied. "I thought it could only be a mistake. I'll just make a note of that and pass it on."

Liz winced at the dig and looked away. Barbara seemed so carried away with the mischief she had dreamt up on first meeting Emin that she failed to recognise its cruelty, but Mrs Smith had not noticed and smiled as she shuffled out of the room.

13: Electioneering

Friday already. The end of the week meant a whole hour of form time—an hour in the company of her year sevens. That was a tolerable enough prospect, but it also meant an hour with Belle. Liz was not sure she had the patience. However, the argenteous edge of this cumulus suddenly revealed itself as she remembered granting Belle the authority she had so coveted: *she* was taking charge of form elections. Oh, happy day. Liz deposited her bag on the staffroom table, retrieved her mug from the sink and rinsed it. There would be time for a coffee before registration now—and perhaps a biscuit if she could find one.

Having located the tin at the back of Peggy's emergency cupboard, where it had been stowed safely away from Janet's scavenging talons, Liz settled into her chair to enjoy a few minutes' contentment before the bell.

"Miserable old cow. She can't speak to me like that!" Belle stomped in, puffed up with indignation.

"What's happened?" Liz fought the instinctive eye-roll.

"That bitch, Bosun," Belle elucidated. "Apparently, there was a meeting with Emin Smith and his parents on Wednesday."

"I know. I was there," said Liz.

The creak of the door announced the appearance of Dave and Gareth. They hushed at the sight of Belle, hands on hips and pink with fury. Dave's face betrayed apprehension—presumably at the prospect of having to reassure or reprimand and he narrowed his eyes, trying to gauge which conversation might be demanded.

Belle shot an angry glance at them and then turned her attention back to Liz. She swept away a flaxen strand from where it had become tethered to the corner of her mouth by an angry little stretch of spittle. "Well, why wasn't I there? I'm his tutor. I just went to Bosun to see why I wasn't told and she acted like *I'd* made a mistake." Belle mimicked Barbara poorly with a childish whine: "*No need to apologise; the trainee doesn't have to attend all meetings*—as if *she* was forgiving *me*!"

"You should record it in your special notebook," Gareth chipped in, accompanied by a snort of mirth from Dave, visibly relieved now someone else was dealing with the situation.

"Don't worry, I will," Belle said, "and I'll report it to my tutor when I'm in uni."

"Before you do, though, when did you last check your emails?" Liz did not have the heart to actively encourage Belle to make a fool of herself.

"I don't know. Why?"

"Well *Miss* Bosun did copy you into the email about that meeting on Wednesday morning and invited you along after school. If you remember, I did say she'd probably email and that you should check." Liz hoped her voice was steady; being firm with another adult was way out of her comfort zone.

"Oh." Belle reddened. Evidently, Liz's voice had not betrayed her.

More confident now, Liz continued. "If you'd been at registration *yesterday* morning, I could have saved you the embarrassment of storming into Barbara's office, all guns blazing."

Impressed, Dave nodded and nudged Gareth. "She's learning," he muttered.

"Well, she should have given us more notice." Belle was off again. "I couldn't have gone anyway, if it was after school; I had a date."

"Why are you worrying about it, then?" Liz was starting to feel at ease.

Belle would not drop the bone. "It's the principle. I'm the tutor."

"*I'm* the tutor and *you* should have checked your emails," Liz said sharply. "Anyway, never mind that." She was loath to get into another skirmish with Belle, especially with Dave in attendance. He was, after all, Belle's line manager and no matter how infuriating Liz found her, she did not want to throw her under the bus in her first week. Besides, she had scented gossip. "You had a date at three o'clock in the afternoon?"

Fortunately, Belle was easily distracted. Her eyes widened and she smiled now, sat down and leaned forward sororially. "No, my date was later, but I had to get my gels and my spray done. Oh, and my wax."

"No. Didn't get a word of that."

Belle laughed, all resentment gone. "You're so funny! It's my nails, my tan and my lady parts."

Just in time to catch the unsavoury end of Belle's sentence, Serena and Lucy arrived and were instantly rapt; an edifying narrative was clearly about to unfold.

Though cringing at Belle's euphemism, Liz tried to be nice. "Aw, how long have you been going out with him? Was it a special occasion?"

"Oh, he's not my boyfriend. I just met him the other day on Tinder." Belle's openness was startling, but impressive. "I had to make a good first impression; he'd booked a hotel and everything."

"Where were all the girls like her when I was growing up?" Gareth muttered.

Liz chided him good-naturedly. "Being subjected to a load of double standards, probably." She turned back to Belle, encouraging her with an eager nod and she continued her explanation of the previous day's tardiness, undaunted. "Anyway, that's why I didn't come to registration yesterday morning." Belle shrugged and flicked her hair prettily.

"Right...and?" Liz awaited further clarification.

"Well, I didn't have my car 'cause we got a taxi back to the hotel after dinner, so I had to get the train back to my flat in the morning and change into something more suitable for school, so I couldn't come to registration."

Liz looked at Belle's short, cotton dress with its delicate straps and low neckline and wondered how much less suitable for working with school children last night's outfit could have been. She might have to get Peggy to have a quiet word about it later, but for now she was more interested in hearing about the apparently burgeoning whirlwind romance and pressed for more detail. "I see. It was pretty special, then—so, when are you seeing him again?" Liz asked.

Belle giggled. "Oh, I don't think I will. I've got a date with someone else tonight." She shifted gear. "Anyway, I'll be up a bit later. I just need to plan some stuff for this afternoon and do some photocopying."

Liz steeled herself. "You've got five minutes till the bell goes."

Belle pouted, but Liz persisted. "You're in charge of form elections, remember. I'll see you up there in five minutes. Don't forget all that stuff you planned the other day—and don't forget what we talked about either."

"What was that?"

"Check with me before you announce the winner," Liz reminded her. "We have to make sure somebody decent gets in or it'll be a nightmare all year."

Serena joined Liz as she made her way upstairs. "You're getting the hang of this," she smiled, "Give it another week and she'll be putty in your hands."

Liz doubted it, but she had to hand it to Belle: she could plan a form election, even if it was somewhat transatlantic in flavour. She watched as Belle grouped the students, explained the duties of form and sports captains and asked them to consider the qualities of a good leader. A few eager eleven-year-olds grasped the proffered black marker and wrote a variety of character traits on the board: *fairness, good listner, confidance, fitness, sensableness, braveness, pursuasive, onisty, good at sport* and nominations followed shortly after. Liz was not surprised by four of the six names that were put forward. The best and worst behaved always made an appearance: sensible and fair, Kate and Ted were recommended and agreed with by some of their peers; persuasive and confident, Jordan and Emin were likewise proposed and backed up. Liz was not worried; Belle had been primed to rig the votes; eleven-year-olds could not really be allowed complete power to choose their leaders.

	The students had noticed good things in other class members too, having had a week to get to know each other. Gratified, Liz read Alfie's name along with Maisie's. Branded *outspoken, stubborn and inclined to be rather silly* by her last teacher, Maisie had gained the confidence of many of her classmates, despite knowing none of them previously and Liz was curious to find out why.

	Belle got the attention of the class with unanticipated authority and revealed to the students which of them would be running for the four positions: two form captains and two sports captains. She allocated a campaign team to each nominee and gave each group a sheet of A3, a board marker and twenty minutes to prepare for the hustings. The classroom soon filled with lively conversation and the sheets of paper gradually filled with ideas. Snippets of conversation emerged here and there. From Kate's party, a sigh, followed by, "Yes, but you have to make the speech fun."

"No, you can't just promise to make lunchtime longer," came, unsurprisingly from Emin's team.

Ted's voice was next, "I'd ask everyone their opinions about everything we decide. I could use questionnaires," a statement that elicited approving sounds, followed by a smaller voice, asking, "How do you spell questionnaire?" and another, shushing the speaker, afraid their genius would be copied.

True to form, Jordan could be heard answering a question of her team, "Well if they don't want to, I'll just make them," followed by anxious glances and nervous laughter as *just make them* was duly transcribed on the sheet. In the corner of the room, Alfie's team was deep in discussion, all faces turned towards him and nodding and smiling as he looked round at them and whispered earnestly. The team supporting Maisie took a more arcane approach to the task. Giving the impression of a Roman testudo, they spoke in low voices and leaned inwards, momentarily, raising their arms and spreading their blazers, to form an impregnable barrier.

With a mixture of nostalgia and admiration Liz spotted a clandestine black and white badge pinned to the underside of Maisie's lapel. Its capital *A*, breaking out of the confines of the circle that surrounded it, told Liz that things could be about to become interesting.

The twenty minutes came to an end and it was time for the election speeches. First to declare his intentions, Emin swaggered up to the front of the class, where he looked at them with his now familiar narrowed eyes and complacent smirk. He placed a crumpled piece of paper, covered in uneven, blotchy writing, on the corner of Liz's desk, where he could see it as he addressed the electorate, and started lurching back and forth, one hand hovering, worryingly, at the front of his school trousers and the other throwing poorly formed gang shapes.

"Yo!" he started. "Emin's in da house—" His lyric degenerated into uncontrollable giggles before he continued, "you better vote for me." It seemed to be some sort of ill-conceived rap. He continued emceeing a few half-hearted statements filled with forced rhymes and lacking scansion.

"Homework sucks totally." More unrestrainable laughter from the performer intruded. Undaunted by his loss of vocal control, however, Emin continued. "E to the M to the I to the N. Emin's fresh on the mic so you've gotta give him ten out of ten."

Liz couldn't see many signs of freshness—or a mic, for that matter, and as for the rest...

"School uniform's shizzle and the tie's lame."

The weaknesses in the rhythm and rhyme were becoming ever more apparent, especially when he resorted to, "I'll pimp it up if you vote for Em. That's my name."

The bar spitting limped to its conclusion now and after some woeful beat-boxing, Emin finished with his final promise to the class. "Em will ban Maths and English and make all lessons PE." and his closing imperative: "Vote for Em; he's the blazin' MC."

Actually, Liz mused, the last line was its saving grace; she almost looked forward to presenting him with Shakespeare and the iambic pentameter. However, she still rejoiced silently; he must have ruined his chances completely. His fellow students were more easily impressed than Liz, though, and clapped enthusiastically, quashing her untimely relief.

Belle, presiding, thanked him and, immersed in the role he had adopted, Emin leered and scrutinised her shamelessly from legs to chest as he clutched at the front of his trousers again and attempted to throw another bogus hand signal. Naïvely, she did not appear to realise and invited the next nominee to the front of the classroom. Kate spoke with the wisdom and aplomb of one used to having greatness thrust upon her. Next, Ted made his grinning way forward, eager to share his manifesto. Jordan made up for what she lacked in articulation with a force of will so strong as to be comical. Her style of persuasion was of the sledgehammer variety and Liz could not imagine her cohorts daring to defy her.

By complete contrast, Alfie made his appeal next.

"I won't actually promise anything," he began, "'cause we probably won't be allowed stuff like banning homework and having longer holidays." The other students chuckled and groaned before Alfie assured them, "But I'll try and make sure us year sevens get listened to."

The many appreciative nods that came from the rest of the form were contagious and Liz noticed, with a smile, that even Belle had warmed to Alfie, after their initial unfavourable encounter, and was nodding along with the others. Laughter erupted when Alfie added, "And if they won't listen, I'll just—I'll just bloody shout till they do!" He gasped, shocked at his slip. "Sorry, Miss."

Belle stepped in here, motioned him back to his seat to the audible mirth and applause of his classmates, and invited Maisie to the stage. Her address was full of references to *the man*, flowers in firearms, lone protestors taking on tanks and sit-ins against oppressors. Most of the year sevens did not quite comprehend what she said, but the faint edge of danger that crackled behind her words charged the atmosphere with life, even if she would be a David against the Goliath of authority, Liz thought. Belle shifted uncomfortably. This bore no resemblance to the bunting, pompoms and rosettes she had had in mind, but Liz appreciated dissidence and crossed her fingers for a successful pairing of rebel and cause.

A secret ballot followed, made dramatic by the exaggerated secrecy with which Belle insisted it be conducted. Belle counted the votes while Liz, fatally distracted, rummaged for the four leaders' badges in her tutor's pack, but they were not there. Liz remembered shoving them in her desk drawer and leaned over to try to open it. It was locked. She managed to find the key, unlock the drawer and rifle through its contents, eventually finding the envelope that contained the essential emblems of office. However, her distraction was to prove ruinous. By the time Liz had turned her attention back to the class, Belle had announced, "Okay, the votes have been counted and the students with the most votes are..."

She paused theatrically. Liz attempted to get her attention with a discreet, yet frantic wave, but Belle was relishing her moment and did not notice. Perhaps it would be all right.

The clock ticked. A raven croinked from the roof of the block opposite. The tiniest whirr emanated from the computer as it processed some new bit of information.

"Form captains... Maisie and Alfie —" her voice was drowned by a cheer so that she had to shout, "and for sports captains, we have..." She paused again and waited for the voices to recede.

"...Jordan." Liz could see how that would work. Jordan glowed with pleasure and pride; so long unappreciated, she exemplified the tenacity of Robert the Bruce's spider. Belle continued. "and... by a majority of one..."

Another dramatic pause. Ted and Emin looked at each other, Emin, swinging on his chair, Ted, biting on his lip.

"Emin."

An affirmative hiss, accompanied by a clenched fist and curled bicep, came from Emin. Ted congratulated him without hesitation, but Liz was far less generous—in her thoughts, at least. Sports captains were ambassadors; Emin would be called upon to represent 7EM on the field. This could be a disaster. She approached Belle as the class was packing up and growled, "You were supposed to rig the voting!"

"Oh!" Belle replied. "I forgot. Anyway, it wouldn't be very democratic."

"Sod that!" Liz said. "I'm with Churchill."

"What do you mean?"

"The best argument against democracy is a five-minute conversation with the average voter."

14: Learning From the Master

"Who the hell launches a new course the week before half term?" Liz grumbled as she and Lucy wandered over to the main staffroom, where tables equipped with paper and pens had been arranged for Gordon's modestly named professional development initiative: *Learn from the Master*.

"It must be from that heads' conference the other week," said Lucy. "Apparently, they're all going mad for this new teaching method that's doing the rounds."

Liz groaned and looked around for the rest of the department.

Dave waved from the back of the room and they headed towards him, glad he had bagged a table outside of their leader's likely range.

"Well done, Bish," Liz muttered and slid into the seat beside him. Lucy took the one opposite and they were joined by a blinking, hunch-shouldered man in his late thirties, who shuffled to their table apologetically and introduced himself.

"I—I'm Colin McGee. Er—maths." His tiny, colourless eyes avoided theirs and he twitched his nose in an effort to push his thick, round, rimless glasses up. In doing this, he bared tiny, almost pointed teeth and gave a gentle snort, perhaps an expression of embarrassment or amusement; it was impossible to tell.

"I remember," Lucy lied, "How's it going?"

He emitted another minute snort, paused and answered, "Hrhmm."

He was going to be hard work.

"Looking forward to Dildo's training?" Liz asked. Dave looked at her sharply and Colin blinked again, and looked at Liz, frowning. He placed his unfeasibly large, pale hands on the table, as if receiving enlightenment from beyond. Seeming to remember something important, he raised his index finger, displaying long, yellowish fingernails, and stood. "Hmm, excuse me," he said and shuffled away.

"Fucking hell!" chuckled Dave. "What did he say his name was?"

"Mr Magoo, I think it was!" Liz laughed.

Just then, Gordon came in and stood by the door, smiling as the last few staff came in. Inexplicably, he had changed out of his suit and donned his favoured jeans-waistcoat combination and, even more bizarrely, a long, apricot coloured scarf was draped around his neck. Lucy grinned and nudged Liz, who looked over to where Gordon was rubbing his hands together affably.

"What's with the scarf?" Liz asked, bemused. "Has he been listening to Carly Simon?"

"He looks like a fucking theatre director," said Dave.

Gordon started to bounce, slightly, on the balls of his feet: limbering up. The tasselled ends of the scarf jiggled. He rubbed his hands again and gestured expansively as colleagues found their seats.

As soon as everyone seemed to be settled, Gordon stepped to the front of the room.

"Looks as if it's show time," said Liz. *"Fasten your seat belts; it's going to be a— "*

Dave cut her off with a warning look as Colin shuffled back to their table with his folder and sat down.

"Afternoon, guys," Gordon started, "and thank you for coming."

Lucy leaned towards Colin. "Well, it's not like we had a choice," she chuckled.

His answer was humourless: "Well it is, nnh, directed time."

Liz raised an eyebrow as Colin ran a curved claw down his file.

"Yes, er, the staff handbook says, er...phfhh." Colin's point fizzled out; his lack of resolution failed to keep Lucy's attention and she turned towards Gordon, leaving Colin to blink lashless eyes at the back of her head.

"Guys." Gordon clapped his hands together and rubbed them briskly with a smile that, from a distance, looked oddly like glee. "We must be Ofsted ready."

A susurration disturbed the room and Gordon addressed them again, palpably impatient to share his expertise. "I am an outstanding practitioneer," he crowed, unaware of the bristle that swept through the staff like a Mexican wave. "And by the end of this course, all of you will be too."

The staff exchanged disgruntled looks; most of them had been judged 'outstanding' before and had the paperwork to prove it, which suggested that he had not even looked at anyone's files.

Gordon persisted, certain of his virtuosity. "According to the latest paedogogy, the key to progress is independent thinking," he expounded, "and I'm going to tell you exactly how to do this in my 'Learn from the Master' sessions. I'm going to model outstanding teaching so that you can do it too."

Liz looked towards Chris, on the table nearest Gordon. She was keen to gauge his reaction. Chris could never toe the party line and this time was no exception. His eyes clouded and his hand went to his forehead in a gesture more mournful than mocking.

Gordon continued. "My inspiration has been this guy." He held up a theoretical book on teaching. "Rhys Owens. Emirates Professor of Education."

Chris's frown intensified and jaw tensed. His sorrow turned visibly to indignation at the malapropism.

Liz leaned sideways. "Bish," she whispered, "look at Chris... *Emirates!*" She shook her head.

"Priceless," Dave chuckled, "Have you seen Gannet?"

Opposite Chris, Janet was nodding vigorously and beaming up at Gordon like a star struck groupie.

He sighed. "Yes, the teaching methods I'm going to pass on to you are truly outstanding."

Gordon resumed his homily, holding forth about surveys and statistics and displaying graphs and tables that corroborated the veracity of his words. He stressed the importance of getting students active as soon as they sat down to allow them ownership of their learning, rather than standing, talking at them. Liz glanced surreptitiously at her watch. Twenty minutes had gone by. There were marker pens and paper on their tables, but no indication of what was to be done with them—or when.

Liz leaned towards Dave again. "Is this the outstanding bit?"

Her attention drifted until she became aware of Gordon, again extolling the virtues of his favourite book, *Inspiring Independence*, from which all his ideas about autonomy of thought were gleaned. He wrote the name of the method it expounded, *The Pedia Lesson Structure*, on the flip chart and announced, "Using Rhys Owen's Padua Structure theory for lesson planning is the best way to be outstanding. Write that down."

Liz was confused by the difference between what Gordon wrote and what he said and asked the others, "*Pedia* as in *Wiki* or *Padua* as in the Italian city?"

"Neither!" Dave had Googled Rhys Owen. "It says here it should be Paideia: P. A. I. D. E. I. A, a teaching method that encourages independent thinking and learning. I think it's Greek."

Colin frowned. "Actually, er, ngh," he protested, ignored by Liz and Dave.

"Christ, you couldn't make it up," chuckled Liz. "He's managed to write it one way and say it another—and neither of them's right! The book's right in front of him, for Christ's sake! What with that and 'emeritus'. Wait till we see Chris!"

"Inspirational stuff, that's for sure," said Dave. "Definitely outstanding!"

They looked towards the front table. Gannet was still scribbling eagerly, but Chris had picked up Gordon's copy of *Inspiring Independence* and was reading the contents page. He shook his head slowly and his shoulders ascended and descended, betraying a heavy sigh, less of surprise than disappointment.

Liz redirected her attention to Gordon's interminable sermon.

"So, in essence," he said, "teacher talk should be kept to a minimum."

"No arguments there." The comment was a stage whisper from somewhere in the vicinity of the maths teachers' table. It obviously touched a nerve because Gordon's expression became steely. "What I'm doing here isn't just teacher talk," he asserted.

"Isn't it?" the dissent was a touch louder now and definitely from maths.

Gordon snapped flick-knife eyes to the maths table and when he spoke, it was a throat-opening slash, designed to silence his unknown underminer. "It's *totally* different, thank you."

His apricot scarf trembled ominously.

Suddenly, pens, paper and planners became fascinating as people strove to remain unnoticed.

Gordon took this as a revolution quashed and resumed. "No," he said, mustering some of his former joviality, "what I was doing was what Rhys Owen calls the didactyl phase': importing expert knowledge to the listener. It's all in his book."

Satisfied that it was now safe to recommence normal behaviour, Dave jabbed Liz with his pen and whispered, "Have you got that down?"

"Should that be 'didactic'?" Liz smirked and stuck her tongue out of the corner of her mouth in mock concentration. In a careful, rounded hand, she wrote in her planner: *Teacher talk bad. Didactyl phase good.*

The head was back on course. "I'd recommend that you all follow the leading thinkers in education, like Rhys Owen, on Twitter. You can get ideas any time and anywhere."

Gannet whipped out her phone and started frantically jabbing it and looking baffled. Chris shook his head sadly.

Liz was less amused. "I'm not polluting my phone with work shit," she groused. "I've got a bloody life."

"Go, girl," Lucy laughed. Colin snuffed his disapproval and wrinkled his glasses further up the bridge of his nose.

Didactic phase over, Gordon announced the task that would begin their transformation from inadequate amateurs to outstanding professionals: writing imaginary lesson objectives. Glad to have something to do—finally—the English teachers got started, discussing the precise use of language that would be at once accessible, challenging and measurable. Colin seemed reluctant to join in.

After a minute or so, Liz became aware that no one else seemed to be doing anything. She looked around the room and nudged Dave who kicked Lucy under the chair. An uneasy quiet had settled on the room. Some of the others were looking at Liz's table with amusement, some with anxiety. Gordon was counting backwards from five. "Bloody hell!" she said, "I didn't realise we had so little time. Better hurry up." She wrote their contribution down, not accounting for the silence that had fallen.

Suddenly, Gordon's voice rose. "Am I going to have to embarrass people by naming and shaming?"

The rest of the room seemed to shift uncomfortably, but Liz, Lucy and Dave were oblivious to whatever it was that the others were so anxious about.

Gordon raised his voice still further and added to his previous sentence pointedly: "...English department!"

Colin moved his chair slightly further away from Lucy and the others: "Ngh."

Liz, Dave and Lucy looked up. No one else had begun the task. Gordon, it dawned on them, must have been waiting for them to stop talking and listen to him. Counting backwards was his method of getting them quiet. It had probably been tweeted by one of his professional crushes and it was conceivable that it bore more fruit with students than it did with adults. Gordon watched them, arms folded, while they modified their behaviour. Metaphorical wrists figuratively slapped, they sniggered like naughty children.

At last, Gordon allowed them to embark. Liz's group had already finished so they chatted until the time was up, although Colin would not be drawn in and carried on considering the learning objective until the countdown that signalled Gordon's expectation of silence began again. True to form, the mostly English table did not notice straight away and Gordon had reached minus two before they realised and ended their conversation.

It did not go down well. Gordon picked up a heavy duty hole-punch from the shelf beside him and, face like thunder, wove through the other tables, towards them, advancing on Lucy, nearer to him than the others. Lucy smiled apprehensively, wondering what weird thing he was about to ask them to do next. Then, in a move so ill-judged as to be farcical, as if he were a villain in a melodrama, Gordon flicked one end of his scarf over his opposite shoulder, raised the hole-punch above his head with both hands and mimed bringing it down upon hers.

The room held its breath. Lucy, unamused, for once, shook her head at him, curled her lip and turned away in a rare display of disgust, and Gordon, wind withdrawn from his sails, lowered the offensive weapon and stepped away, laughing nervously.

"Was that the outstanding bit?" Liz asked Dave.

"Yep. Write it down," he replied.

"That's what happens when people are off-task," Gordon said as he walked back to his spot at the front.

"Er, Gordon," volunteered Colin, blinking his anaemic eyes and moving his chair well away from the English table, but Gordon did not seem to notice. "Er, *I* was on task," he whined, obsequiously.

"Sanctimonious twat," murmured Dave to Liz.

"Judas," Liz muttered back under her breath.

Chris watched them over his glasses and, catching Liz's eye, raised a brow and lugubriously shook his head. Heartened, Liz made a note in her planner and tilted it towards Dave: *Dildo- putting the aching into teaching.*

Smothering forbidden laughter, Dave added: *dick.*

Now he had made his point, Gordon continued, instructing them on the importance of creating a safe classroom environment in which students could flourish, before, in another dizzying change of tack, he launched into a tale of his family.

"I've got to tell you about my youngest son," he began. "His dog-earedness is amazing; he keeps trying until he succeeds and that's what I want for all the students here at King Richard's. My wife and I made the decision to put our baby son on the floor and leave him there to work out how to crawl when he was five months old. After a few hours of us watching him crying and flailing around, he finally taught himself! Now that's persistence. We *gave* him that. The average kid doesn't do that till they're about seven or eight months."

Gordon looked around, proud of his parenting. Liz and Lucy looked at one another, appalled, although in no doubt that the poor baby in question would, later in life, be a 'winner' of sorts, albeit a *dog-eared* one.

His next anecdote involved the older son: eleven years old, shy and friendless. Gordon's solution was to buy the most state-of-the-art games console on the market and invite the other boys in his class round. Liz imagined the self-conscious boy she had seen on the first day of term, sitting awkwardly in the corner of his own bedroom, while his paternally picked guests availed themselves of his video games and excluded him, bringing his isolation into his home as well. She wondered what life-lesson he might have learned from that.

Liz caught Dave's eye. "Why is he telling us all this?"

Dave supplied his wisdom: "Fuck knows."

Lucy, also unimpressed, grumbled under her breath. Colin sniffed and nodded. Around the room, the teachers were becoming restive. What was the point of this, especially when they had so much work to do? Chris's face was, again, a picture of grim disbelief.

Gordon, for once, sensed the prevailing mood and stated, "Some people don't like it when I talk about my life. They think it's a waste of time." He paused, daring anyone to challenge him. Nobody did.

"To them, I say," he paused. Then his voice rose aggressively, "TOUGH!"

Sibilance sliced through the staffroom as the assembled staff sharply drew breath.

"As Rhys Owen says, to build the safe environment that is the cornerstone of learning, I need to build a relationship with my students and I do that through sharing myself with them. That's how they learn to trust me."

The teachers exchanged dubious glances.

"That's what I was doing with you. Now I've shared part of my life with you, I've gained your trust; you feel safe enough to learn from me."

Lucy swivelled back towards him, folded her arms and raised her chin. Noticing movement, Gordon turned towards their table, forcing a smile, which froze as his eyes met hers fleetingly, before skittering off towards the exit. He swallowed and coughed before recovering himself.

"Anyway, that's nearly it for tonight. Look out for my email in the next couple of days. It'll also contain details about the new Learning Walk system I'm introducing."

Liz's anxiety rose again. *Learning Walk* was just a friendlier-sounding name for lesson observations. An image of Pam Hooper's judgement of her lesson at the end of last year flashed into her mind and she wondered again whether Dave had actually managed to get it removed from her file.

Gordon looked around at their reactions before adding, "Nothing to worry about, but if anyone wants to talk to me about this after the meeting, I'll be in my office for an hour or so, going through your files."

He paused again, a lengthier pause this time. "As I said, nothing to worry about."

His smile was smug now. Immediately, everyone started worrying. Gordon scanned the room, looking for something—or someone: "Colin!" He had found his man. "I'm sure you all remember Colin McGee, my right hand man."

Colin seemed to perk up, having been noticed at last.

Liz nudged Dave. "Uh-oh."

"Or, at least he will be once I've completed his training," Gordon added.

Colin squinted and sniffed, baring his miniscule teeth. "Yes, er, thank you, Gordon."

"Colin will be the head practitioneer of professional development and internal training. He'll be the one stood here," —Chris and Liz winced in unison— "leading these sessions next term, won't you?" Gordon smiled almost fondly at his protégé.

Colin made one of his small noises: "Snhth," and made his way to Gordon's side.

"You'll have your own suite of rooms, where you'll be able to host workshops with external participators as well as our staff too, won't you?" Gordon was like a new stepfather, trying to ingratiate himself with a ready-made son.

"Hnngh."

"Colin'll be helping me keep an eye on teaching and learning, to get us Ofsted-ready, so don't be surprised if he pops into your lessons."

"Ffnh."

"And don't worry; it's nothing to do with the redundancies I mentioned earlier this week," he threw in casually. Then he left the room.

Colin blinked down at his spatulate hands and wrinkled his nose.

"I knew it," Liz hissed. "Dildo's mole."

Dave sighed, "We're fucked."

15: Bog Blog

It was the last Friday before October half term. Liz wound through the lanes, on her way to work. Swallows twittered in the skies and settled on the telephone wires. Oak trees stooped blackly at the edges of the fields, their branches heavy with crows, until the sound of Liz's engine sent them, complaining murderously, into the air. The damp hedgerows were flanked by brown cow parsley: a ravaged chorus line, all drooping headdresses and jutting hips, holding their final flourish with crooked arms. Morning glory—no longer glorious, but wilted and past its prime—sagged behind them like shrugged-off feather boas. Half term could not come soon enough.

Once at work, Liz managed to pass the morning without incident and soon it was afternoon. The threatened email had arrived from the head entitled *Learn from the Master: are you ready for Ofsted?* Having a rare few minutes free, she skimmed its contents, scanning for the explanation of the learning walks Gordon had tried to slip in under the radar the previous day. She took in the key information:

With reference to the learning walks I eluded to in yesterdays training session, myself and/or any member of the senior management team will pop into lessons and ensure that appropriate learning and progress is taking place. We will also offer support to any co-workers that have any areas for development in a non judgemental way.

Liz fought her simultaneous instincts to correct the email and to panic at the prospect of more terrifying lesson observations: they would have to wait until later because today, Liz had more important work to do. She had enlisted the help of Lucy, who was younger than Liz, to help and advise her in a technological endeavour and went down to the staffroom to see how she was getting on.

"There you go," said Lucy, tapping one last key flamboyantly and leaning back like a slightly crumpled concert pianist—one with a silvery nose-trail on the hem of her jacket: at toddler height. "All done. You're registered. Bog Blog's ready to roll." She looked at Liz and grinned. "Loo roll!"

"That's terrible!" Liz laughed and then: "Actually, that's *it*!"

"That's what?"

"Lulu Rolls," Liz clarified, "my Bog Blog alias. It's all coming together."

Liz peered over Lucy's shoulder at the pale blue screen and its tantalising stripes and boxes. She had been gathering blog fodder since the beginning of term and had plenty of material. There was photographic evidence of the many and various unpleasantnesses that had occurred within the lavatory's trembling, fleshly painted walls; a complaint relayed by Peggy, regarding the unfitness for purpose of the bolts fixing the plastic seat to the porcelain rim (not to mention the dampness and bruising resulting from falling off), and an anecdote about a recent lock malfunction and subsequent short-lived imprisonment of a supply teacher who arrived at her lesson, hoarse and traumatised, fifteen minutes late.

Liz would have to wait until half term to upload the anthropomorphised musings of what might be the internet's first ceramic raconteur, though; there was still one lesson before half past three and the beginning of the holiday.

Lucy deposited a handful of home-wasabied peanuts into her mouth and stood up. "Well, I think I'll just pay Lulu a little visit," she said and bounded down the corridor while Liz started gathering her resources ready for her lesson. After a few seconds, Liz's phone chirped. It was a message from Lucy. Opening it, Liz was assailed by a close-up photograph of such obscene horror that she gagged. The message accompanying it read, *Look what somebody dumped in Lulu!*

Lucy bounced back in, a minute later, laughing. "You got my message, then?"

Liz was appalled. "You didn't just do that, did you?"

"God, no!" Lucy shrieked, "It was there when I got there. A present from DT, I should think. You'd think I'd be used to shit, the number of nappies I change, but this was in another league." Still giggling, she continued, gesturing in the manner of an angler. "It was this big; I had trouble getting it all in the photo."

"I thought you were a long time," laughed Liz.

"And when I tried to flush it, it was like Robert De Niro at the end of Cape Fear," Lucy elaborated. "Yeah, I thought it was going to start speaking in tongues before I managed to get rid of it!" she continued.

Liz made a pantomime of retching and Lucy continued: "Bobbing back up, gurgling and bubbling..." she paused. "I can't believe you thought I'd do a massive, great shit at work, though!"

Liz scrutinised the photograph. "You're right," she conceded, "it looks too meaty to be one of yours," she said and headed for her classroom.

Just over an hour later, Liz lugged bags full of holiday marking and preparation down the debris-strewn stairs, past the fading mammary scrawl and into the staffroom. It was like the Marie Celeste. Partly consumed cakes, packets of biscuits and half empty cups lay, forgotten and used teabags littered the table, their string and cardboard labels like toe-tags on corpses. It was as if the occupants had dashed out for just a moment and would be back to finish their snacks any second, but Liz knew her colleagues better than this; they'd be halfway home by now, gleefully forgetful of the provisions they had so lately prized. Sighing indulgently, Liz rounded up the food and placed it in the various tins and containers left over from the beginning of term, now empty of the foreign sweets and biscuits they had latterly held.

Just then, Serena drifted in and put her bag on the table. "You still here?" A response being superfluous, she ploughed on. "What a day!"

"Bad lesson?" Liz asked.

"No, the lesson was fine. It's that Belle. She's supposed to be teaching my year nines and all she could do was flirt with Rob."

Liz was horrified. "Rob? Rob in your year nine? I know he's big for his age, but—"

"No, no." Serena cut her off, "although, I wouldn't put it past her," she added darkly. "No, Rob, the new teaching assistant. You know: the new one. Looks like that one off that TV show."

"Bloody typical," Liz encouraged.

"There I was, sitting at the back, trying to get a bit of marking done, when I had to step in because she was too busy trying to flash her tits at Rob to teach." Serena said.

"Slut shaming: that's not like you," Liz said.

"Sorry," Serena continued, "it's just, I wouldn't mind if she was even trying to teach; I'd be happy to step in, but I'm only supposed to be there because she's not *actually* qualified yet. She's supposed to plan and deliver the lesson with me there just in case. Peggy's her mentor, isn't she? I'll have to have a word with her. It's not the first time either."

"Yeah, just think yourself lucky she's not taking your sixth form," Liz said, forgetting her earlier right-thinking comment. "She wouldn't know who to try and shag next. Mind you, I bet Rob was loving it, wasn't he?"

"Oh, he was lapping it up so neither of them was doing their job," Serena said. "Anyway, speaking of sixth form..." She perched on the edge of the table and looked around. "Now, bear in mind this is only gossip, but my group said they've seen her in a club in town a few times."

"I'm not sure I want to know," Liz said. "Go on."

"Well, there's not much to tell really, just a bit of dirty dancing and 'hooking up with randoms', as they so delicately put it." She paused and looked pensive. "Still, she'd better be careful; it'll be one of them next."

"Yeah, a word with Peggy might be an idea," said Liz. "Belle probably wouldn't recognise the sixth formers when she's out."

Lucy nodded. "Well, they certainly recognised her."

"Anyway, you going home?" Liz asked.

Serena confirmed that she was and hoisted her handbag onto her shoulder, groaning as she heaved up the other one, full, as it was, of books.

"Wait for me, then; I'll just nip to the loo. Then I'll walk to the car park with you." Liz said.

Serena dropped the heavier bag with a thump. "Hurry up then; there's a bottle of ice cold Pinot waiting for me at home!"

Liz strolled down the corridor, grinning as she remembered the blog she intended to start, wondering how much mileage she would actually get out of Lulu Rolls. When she got there, it was occupied and, from the muffled sounds coming from within, she deduced that one of the DT lot must be wrestling with a monster—again. Revolted, she turned to leave, but the door opened and Belle emerged— backwards. She wiped her mouth with the back of her hand, brushed some dust from her knees and adjusted her skirt. She hadn't seen Liz and made straight for the staffroom without looking round. Liz shrugged and stepped towards the door of the toilet, but as she did, the lock clicked again. Someone else was in there.

Unwilling to leave without discovering the identity of Belle's clandestine paramour, Liz loitered, like a gold prospector, anticipating the richness of this seam. Two nuggets in one day. This yield was beyond the dreams of avarice and Liz could not wait to get started on Bog Blog. The metallic rasp of a fly, rapidly zipped, followed by a rush of water and rustle of paper towels told Liz she was about to lay eyes on her quarry. A final clatter of the lock sounded and the door swung open, revealing Rob, the TA, smiling—and ruddy with exertion.

"All yours," he said and sauntered down the corridor, clearly not realising how long Liz had been outside.

"I thought you'd fallen in," scolded Serena when Liz got back to the staffroom.

"No, I just had to wait," Liz replied and added more stridently, "There was someone in there."

From the other side of the room came a crash as Belle dropped the cup she was rinsing into the sink.

"Bye, Belle, have a good half term," called Liz as she and Serena stepped out of the room. "Have a rest; you'll need it."

Belle did not turn round. "Yeah—er, bye," she responded feebly.

"Oh, and get some antiseptic on those knees," Liz called through the closing door.

"What was all that about?" Serena asked when they were out of earshot, on their way to the car park.

"Guess who was in the loo when I got there."

"Belle. Obviously. She came into the staffroom a couple of minutes before you."

"Got it in one." Liz's voice crackled with the sheer deliciousness of the gossip she was about to divulge. She paused and looked at Serena so she had her full attention. "Belle got it in one as well." Serena stopped walking and Liz continued. "Actually, I think maybe she was giving more than getting..." she trailed off and gazed into the middle distance in mock contemplation. "She was certainly earning her staff code."

"What are you talking about?" Serena wasn't usually this slow on the uptake. "Come on; spit it out!"

"I think that's what Rob said." Liz started walking again, laughing, and Serena followed, realisation dawning. "Oh! Belle Jobson... BJ...What, you mean she was in there with Rob?" She reached her car and unlocked it with a cheep. "In *that* toilet? Dirty bitch!"

"Oi! What about *him*?" Liz said.

"Dirty bastard," Serena added and got into her car.

Back at home, Jack read Liz's mind. "Do you want a drink before dinner?"

"Does the pope shit in the woods?" Liz smiled as he placed a dark red tulip of wine into her waiting hand and stirred something fragrant on the stove.

"Get that down you," he commanded and sipped his own.

Ever obedient, Liz did as she was told and sank into a chair by the window, drinking in the homely welcome as well as the October sunset. In the sky above the garden, the sun was sinking, gathering the smoky violet chiffon of the clouds with apricot fingers as if to cover the sky's nakedness.

"Liz?"

She was suddenly aware that Jack was speaking. "You've gone into one of your reveries again," he said.

"Sorry, love," she said, "what was that?"

"Gorgeous sunset, isn't it?" he repeated.

"Yeah, not bad," Liz said and sighed contentedly, gulping her wine.

The sun dropped low, becoming a crimson disc, shrouded by a now indigo veil of cloud. A distant chirruping arose and the sky was briefly visited by a murmuration of starlings, a billow of unity, curling and swelling and folding before sinking to its rest. Liz and Jack cradled their glasses and watched the sun slowly diminish and disappear.

16: Stolen Afternoon

Hands clamped round her coffee mug, a week and a half later, Liz watched, fascinated and amused, as Dave made his usual mug of tea, moving from fridge to kettle and back again on unusually light feet and humming tunelessly as he did so. Even the prospect of Open Evening that Thursday did not seem to impinge on his mood.

"Good half term, was it, Bish?" she asked.

Dave glanced around; no one else was in yet. "Fucking bliss," he said.

"Oh yeah?" she encouraged. "What did you do?"

"I just told you."

It was too early for riddles and Liz's face bore witness to her confusion.

Ever helpful, Dave elucidated. "Or, to put it another way: fucking. Bliss."

He sighed and his eyes glazed slightly as he revelled in memories obviously too unwholesome to share.

"Still going well, then, is it?" Liz deduced. "Did you go away anywhere?"

"No, we just slept late in the mornings and stayed in most afternoons." He grinned. "In one room, pretty much."

This euphoric Dave was something new; Liz pounced on the opportunity to winkle more details out of him. "Love made one little room an everywhere, did it?" she pressed.

"Didn't it just?" He flushed, consumed, again, by recent memory. Dave stirred his tea contemplatively. "And since we're quoting Donne, I've got five prepositions for you." He set his mug and spoon down on the draining board carefully. Liz raised her eyebrows in mirthful anticipation.

"*Before, behind, between, above, below.*"

If the graphic mummery that accompanied these words was anything to go by, Dave's recent activities were definitely more carnal than Cartland.

"Okay, I've got the picture!" Liz groaned. "Drink your tea and stop being a twat!"

Dave obeyed and looked at Liz properly for the first time that morning. "Big night last night?" he asked, pointing circularly to Liz's mouth.

"Oh God, have I still got a wine smile? I thought I'd managed to scrub it off!" She licked a finger and rubbed at the corners of her mouth.

"Not quite. I guess some of us just manage to hide our vices better than others," Dave sipped his tea and sat down. "You didn't fall asleep with a glass of wine in your hand again, did you?"

"Not quite." Liz filled in the details of the previous night, when, in desperate denial of the last day of the holiday, she had taken her glass of wine to bed with her, in the hope of staving off insomnia. "It did the trick; I fell asleep before I'd finished it."

"What a waste," said Dave, but Liz had not finished. "Don't worry; when I woke up at half past two, it was still there."

"You didn't drink it!"

"God, yes." Liz said proudly. "There was half a glass left so I thought, 'Waste not, want not,' knocked it back, turned the light off and went to sleep."

"You're such a fucking lush," Dave laughed.

"Yeah, I had a mouth like the Joker and black teeth when I woke up," Liz chortled. "Can you believe, only an hour ago, I looked like a meth addict?"

"Yes," replied Dave, nodding sagely, "yes, I can."

Ten minutes later, they shuffled over the playground towards the main staffroom for the usual Monday morning briefing. Students were already trickling in under the wrought iron guillotine of *TRAEHNOIL EHT DRAHCIR GNIK*, which arched above them, as if impatient to dissever unwary heads from shoulders. Beyond the gates, mothers cackled and gossiped like tricoteuses, before jumping back into their cars and getting on with the rest of their days.

In the staffroom, the post half term chatter died down as Gordon came in, took his place at the front and waited for the last sounds to dissipate. Satisfied they had done so, he clasped his hands in his familiar, pseudo-jovial gesture and opened his mouth to speak, whereupon, from the back of the room, a whining roar, like the engines of a jet firing up for take-off, obliterated his words for all but those most eager staff closest to him.

"What's he done to annoy her this time?" Serena wondered in a whisper. Liz and Dave turned towards the source of the noise: the photocopier where Jean, a severe woman in her late forties, hair dyed maroon as a substitute for personality and still smarting from her recent divorce, stood, face like thunder, grimly jabbing buttons. Gordon continued, unaware, but as the job finished, there was a lull in the grumble of the machine and the phrase, *Open Evening displays* surfaced before the pre-flight engine revving resumed. When the sound faded again, Gordon's last sentence could be heard: "So, your displays and flyers need to be sent to Jean in Reprographics by the end of tomorrow if you're going to have them by Thursday."

Jean's expression was murderous as she squinted at the photocopier's controls, but Gordon continued, undaunted. "That'll keep you busy, won't it, Jean?"

Her reply, if there was one, was drowned out by the stabbing of a button, followed by the crunch of spiral binding battering its way, deafeningly, into newly printed pages.

Liz leaned towards Serena. "Does that answer his question?"

Gordon leaned forward and whispered something to Janet who looked over, stood up and started to totter towards them.

"Hey up," said Liz, "what's Gannet coming over here for? We haven't brought any biscuits."

However, Janet did not have the English department in her sights; she passed them, stopped beside Jean and spoke quietly to her. Jean met Janet's eyes coldly, dropped the pile of papers she was holding onto the table, snatched the photocopier's plug from its socket and, accompanied by the moan of the huge machine powering down in the middle of its job, she left the room, disappointingly thwarted of door-slamming drama by self-closing fire hinges.

Dave had been stifling his amusement since Jean first started the photocopier up and his long-imprisoned laugh escaped, now, as a hoarse rasp of hilarity.

"Unbe-fucking-lievable!" he choked, his exclamation disguised by the ripple of reaction in the room.

However, Dave's high spirits were soon curtailed when Gordon began speaking again. Whether the head was giddy with the anticipated success of Open Evening or, perhaps, had spent his week's holiday graduating with flying colours from a residential course in winning friends and influencing people was hard to tell, but when he made his next proclamation, he was visibly jubilant. Not for the first time since September, outrage swelled in the assembled staff as he informed them that the usual half day, which allowed time for Open Evening preparations, had been scrapped and that students would be in school all afternoon as well, meaning that after teaching all day, they would need to spend three hours getting their rooms and activities ready and then be back on duty, ready to sell the school from half past six to half past nine.

"When do I see my kids? When do we get to eat?" wondered Lucy—and she was not alone. Gordon swept aside their clamour with a benevolent smile: "Don't worry; you'll have plenty of time to go home first," he said, which glib reply elicited further objection. Dave raised a hand and asked. "But if people go home, how can they prepare properly?"

"It will be up to them to manage their time as they see fit," Gordon said, still grinning, "Don't forget, in a time of recession, with the threat of redundancy always looming, jobs depend on the success of the business and in our case, Open Evening is our shop window."

Dave, cowed, made a tactical retreat. "Did he just slip in the word *redundancy?*" he whispered to Liz through clenched teeth. "How can he look so fucking cheerful about it?"

Liz just shook her head sorrowfully and muttered back, "*One may smile and smile and be a villain.*"

Gordon's response occupied hazardous terrain, in terms of employment law, though, and had Glyn Evans, the union representative, reaching for his notebook before asking whether this decision complied with union guidelines on the entitlement to enjoy a reasonable work-life balance, as outlined in Section Two of the School Teachers' Pay and Conditions Document.

"Will you, for instance," pressed Glyn, "compensate us for the time we spend by cancelling Directed Time in other areas? It is, after all, an extra six hours on our working day, since we have no real choice but to stay and get our rooms, activities and displays ready between the end of school and the beginning of Open Evening."

Gordon's smile froze; his stare was ice. "There is no requirement to stay between half past three and half past six, so—no—I won't." His words flashed like the glint of a cutthroat razor, produced without warning in a back-alley fist fight.

A battle-scarred old unionist, Glyn was undeterred. "With respect," he lied, "I believe there *is* such a requirement and the union agrees."

"Open Evening has been on the calendar since the beginning of term," Gordon said, withdrawing the cold steel of his smile swiftly, like a blade from flesh. His next words dealt what he anticipated was the fatal laceration: "You should have come in at half term to get your rooms ready."

A collective intake of furious breath scythed through the staffroom and fear flickered behind Gordon's eyes.

"For the record, Gordon," Glyn sounded calm—and dangerous. The hush intensified and Glyn continued, "are you saying that working in our designated—and, by the way, unpaid—holiday counts as directed time, then?"

Gordon laughed, demonstrating the whole thing had been a joke, and assured everyone that they were professionals who could be relied upon to rise to the challenge and give their best for their school—and their jobs. He stopped, comfortable now, and his look was distinctly triumphant. Glyn continued to make notes.

Glyn looked up from his notebook and held Gordon's eye with the fearless stare of the timeworn. "Just one more thing, Gordon."

Gordon was on his guard again. "Yes, Glyn?"

"Are we to understand that redundancies might be in the offing?"

A shutter seemed to snap closed in Gordon's eyes and his smile became glassy, inelastic. "At this stage, redundancies are hypothetical," he replied coldly and, leaving the comment hanging in the air, he turned and stalked out of the room.

Belle was sitting at a computer in the English staffroom when they got back. "Did I miss anything?" she chirped.

"You could say that," Liz said, "We could all be made redundant and Gordon's cancelled prep time for Open Evening."

"Open Evening?" Belle looked alarmed. "When's that?"

Liz told her and Belle wrinkled her nose and grunted. "But I might have a date." She flicked her hair back sulkily. "I'll speak to Peggy; she'll let me go early."

Hearing her name, Peggy wanted to know what was going on and dismissed any ideas Belle had that she was a push-over, dealing with her deftly, as she did her younger pupils: "I reminded you about it at our last meeting, so you're going to be there, date or no date, young lady. It's a requirement of your training so you'll just have to rearrange your social life."

If there was any awkwardness, the registration bell smothered it and Peggy swept Belle up the stairs with matronly briskness. "Come on, let's get these year sevens registered." She looked over her shoulder at Liz and winked. "Have a sit-down for a few minutes, Liz; Belle can do registration today. There are some nice chocolate biscuits on the table."

There were indeed some nice chocolate biscuits. Lucy testified crummily to their merit as she popped the second half of hers into her mouth and licked her thumb. "Mmm, gorgeous," she said. "Good old Peggy!" Lucy suddenly sat up. "Hey, well done with Bog Blog. I was pissing myself, reading it last night. I sent the link to Gareth and Serena, by the way."

Liz was delighted. She had painstakingly uploaded all her pictures at half term, accompanying each one with a what she hoped was a witty—and untraceable—commentary or anecdote in the voice of Lulu Rolls: her disappointment at the make-over that never happened; the repeated degradation suffered at the bowels of the DT staff, and the enforced witnessing of an act of carnal depravity too indecent to mention by name, which had to be described tangentially to ensure anonymity, and therefore rendered at once more salacious and more detailed.

Gareth sauntered towards them, unpocketing his phone and flicking open its cover as if it were a silver cigarette case; what he drew from it produced almost the same satisfaction. He cleared his throat and read. "*Bog Blog: the porcelain perspective according to Lulu Rolls. I think it was a philosopher who first said, 'Some come here to sit and think...' but you know the rest.*"

Gareth noticed Liz's embarrassment. "You may well squirm, Elizabeth," he said, mock-severe, scrolled down the page a bit and continued. "*In this blog, I will lift the lid on what goes on in a typical workplace—from the bottom up. This is the power on the throne, the seat of knowledge and it's all cisterns go. This is all the shit that goes down—except sometimes it doesn't.*" Gareth glanced at Lucy and raised his wry right eyebrow. "Puntastic, Liz. Be careful what you say, though; you'll soon get flushed out."

Lucy groaned.

"God knows when I'm going to have time to keep on top of it, anyway," said Liz. "Certainly not on Thursday."

Lucy shook her head in sympathy. "We'll be lucky if we have time to *use* the bog on Thursday, let alone blog about it," she said as the bell went for lessons and she hurried out of the room.

17: Open Evening

Thursday afternoon came. Liz and Serena moved tables and set up laptops to transform Dave's classroom into a sham news room and further enhanced the illusion by stapling photocopies of journalistic phrases around the room until it bristled with slogans like, *STOP PRESS!*, *HOLD THE FRONT PAGE!* and *ABOVE THE FOLD*. Finally, Liz enlarged a copy of the Open Evening newspaper's title, *THE LIONHEART*, in true tabloid style—red sans serif, all caps, extra bold—and pinned it to Dave's door where it shouted wonkily to any passing parent.

Next, they shoved Dave's exercise books, already grubbily thumbed and scruffy, into cupboards, along with all the ancient, dog-eared class readers and piled the most immaculate novels on the desks to demonstrate how up-to-date King Richard's was. They could not allow parents who had not yet made up their minds where to send their offspring to see musty, spineless copies of books that they, themselves, had probably read when they were there. They might even find their own names in the front of To Kill a Mockingbird or *Fuck you* scrawled, in a classmate's hand, inside The Catcher in the Rye. Liz picked up a broken-backed copy of Of Mice and Men, which was sprawled on the floor at the back of the room, and gently closed its cover. As she did so, a scrawl, at once insolent and exuberant, caught her eye, a spoiler of both book and story: *George shoots Lennie.*

"Looks great," said Dave, coming in just as the last novel had been arranged. "I've just been for fish and chips for everyone; it's in the staffroom when you're ready, but go and have a look in Peggy's room before you come and eat."

"Wow! Just what we needed. Thanks, Bish," said Liz. A chip run. Dave did have his uses, but as she and Serena moved towards the other classroom open to parents that evening, Peggy's poetry room, he stopped them. "Actually, hang on; you need some background first."

This sounded interesting. "Go on," Liz prompted.

"Okay, one of Peggy's activities involves massive cardboard fingers."

"Right... Why?" said Liz.

Dave elucidated. "It's a poetry thing. Kids get given cardboard fingers with similes or metaphors written on them and there are cardboard palms with things written on as well and if they match the right fingers to the right palms they end up making whole hands."

"Okay..." said Liz, but Dave was not convinced she had understood so he tried again.

"There's a palm with, like *eyes* or something on it and kids have to find a finger with, say, *as blue as the sea* or *deep pools of mystery* or some shit like that on it and stick it on the palm. Each palm has five simile-metaphor fingers that go on it to make a whole hand."

"Oh, that's a good idea," said Serena. "I might use that in lessons."

Liz was more cynical: "So why do you want us to go and look at it?"

"You'll see," he said.

Intrigued, Liz and Serena ducked into the room next door. "Hi, Peggy, Dave's just sent us to look at your amazing poetry fingers thing," said Serena. Peggy had just begun to lay out her cards, each one a simple, eight-inch representation of a finger, on a table at the front of the room, where they would attract the attention of the visiting masses.

Liz's eyebrows shot heavenwards. "Glory be!" She looked again. "Why's there a line at the top?" she asked.

"Oh, I'm no good at drawing," Peggy said, "so instead of a fingernail, I just drew a line across." She paused and looked at one, head on one side. "They're stylised," she said.

Serena gasped. "They'll certainly bring the mums in, Peggy!"

"Thanks. Dads too, I hope."

"Maybe not the dads so much," said Liz, picking up a finger and studying it musingly, "although, maybe—we do live in modern times." She paused and held the finger up. "Can I ask you something, though, Peggy?"

Peggy looked up from her finger arranging. "Go ahead."

Liz continued: "Did they have to be so..."

"What?" said Peggy.

"So ...pink?" finished Liz.

Peggy was still bewildered when Lucy strode in. "Bloody hell, Peggy," she laughed, "you can't give cardboard cocks to ten-year-olds!"

Dave appeared behind Lucy. "Come on Peggy, love; have your chips and we'll help you make some new fingers," he said kindly, "I've nicked some more card from Jean's cupboard. Yellow."

"Fingers aren't yellow," grumbled Peggy.

"Neither are cocks, though, Peggy, and that's what's important," said Dave, gently steering her out of the room and towards the staffroom, where he had put both the chips and the yellow card.

Peggy sat down, muttering about filthy minds and wondering what the world was coming to. "Anyway, where's Belle disappeared to? She was here a minute ago. I'll get her making them; we've got twenty minutes before it starts."

"I expect Belle might like to keep the pink ones; I'm sure she could find a use for them," offered Liz, helpfully, through a mouthful of chips. "She could have BJ bookmarks when she has her own form."

"She could decorate her room with them," Serena said.

Dave completed the image mentally before verbalising it: "Cock bunting."

Shaking her head, Peggy clicked a resigned tongue just as Belle trotted in, oblivious.

They wolfed what was left of their fish and chips in somewhat hysterical silence and hurried to their posts, smelling of grease and vinegar.

Back in Dave's classroom, Liz manned the news desk. She had bribed Alfie, Ted (sports captain, Emin, being predictably unavailable), Maisie and Jordan to take part in this, their first official form engagement, with promises of cakes, pop and house points: a heady cocktail for a year seven. When they arrived, Liz furnished them all with notepads, pens and trilbies with cards announcing *PRESS* in their hat bands and sent them off, in pairs, to make notes and interview parents and teachers, after which, they would return to the *press office* and write up their stories, creating an edition of The Lionheart that they believed would be printed and circulated and Liz and Serena knew never would.

The first small flock of parents wandered in, shepherded by Tom and Ellie, 7EM's year eleven prefects, who announced that Mrs Marshall and Mrs Rochelle would tell them about the English department and the tutoring system for year sevens. Liz hung back; Serena was so much better at this, but Tom was not about to let her escape that easily. "This family is especially interested in the way the buses are organised, Mrs Marshall," he said, eyes glinting. "I said you could give them some information, since you did bus duty last year."

"Thanks, Tom." Liz said brightly, struggling not to sound sarcastic. "I'll get you back," she growled at him as she turned towards the family of two. The mother, panting, laboured towards her on grimy, aluminium crutches, her mouth pinched in a thin, pink line. She appraised Liz with obvious distaste. Liz smiled expectantly. "How can I help you, Mrs...?"

"Coghill," she bellowed. "I have to bring Carol to school and pick her up on the bus every day 'cause she can't be trusted." She nodded her head towards a smiling girl of ten, who was eating a bag of pork scratchings. Both mother and daughter were holding the large, cardboard fingers from Peggy's room, but these were pink, not yellow. Liz smothered a smile; evidently, someone in the next room had not hidden them well enough. She would have to check later. Maisie, who had smelled a scoop, followed the Coghills back into the room, listened and scribbled in her notebook.

Mrs Coghill continued. "I had to complain last week, though. The teachers won't stop kiddies getting on and off the buses while I'm waiting there. I *am* disabled, you know."

Carol explained: "Mummy nearly got knocked over when they all ran onto the bus."

"Don't talk with your mouth full of scratchings, Caz." Mrs Coghill turned to Tom. "She loves them. I tell her to have an apple or summat but what can I do?"

"Mummy stands in front of the bus doors till I come out, but I'm always last, aren't I, Mummy?" Carol had a mischievous spark in her eye and grease on her chin.

"Yes, and they bump into me, but the teachers don't care; they say I should let her go on the bus on her own like the other year sixes. They tell me not to come 'cause, apparently, I get in the way," whined Mrs Coghill.

"Oh dear." Liz nodded sympathetically, avoiding Tom's eyes.

"That was 'cause of the walking frame you used to have as well, wasn't it, Mummy?" Carol added helpfully. "And 'cause you wanted them to lift you onto the bus."

Maisie's pen flew back and forth across her notepad and her trilby bobbed and tilted as she took it all down.

Her mother shushed her, but Carol carried on, her head turned by the audience. "And 'cause of that time you brought Harry."

Liz imagined another, smaller child, adding to the chaos of the situation.

Mrs Coghill turned to Tom, absent-mindedly turning the cardboard finger over and over in her hand. "He had the operation no man wants to have, but he got an infection."

Tom nodded, sagely, empathising for all he was worth.

"Poor Harry was slipping all over the place and crying and bumping into things. I could hardly hold onto him and his little winkle was hurting him." Tom eyed the now slightly battered, pink organ clenched in Mrs Coghill's hand and winced.

Liz was horrified: "And nobody helped you?"

There was a faint rustle as Maisie turned her page and a scratch as she jotted. This was Lionheart gold.

"It was hard to manage, what with the frame and Harry's cage, but they still wouldn't help," Mrs Coghill added.

Cage?

Carol spoke evenly to her increasingly agitated mother: "But you can't just bring a rat to school, Mummy."

Mrs Coghill rounded on her with the air of someone who was explaining this for the millionth time. "Well, you kept picking him up and prodding and poking at him with your pork fingers. He got an infection on his boy's part and I had to get him to the vet somehow."

Teacher, prefects and form captain-come-newshound shared a second of stunned silence as realisation bloomed. They looked at each other and then at Mrs Coghill, who, forgetting her original mission, span on her crutches and hobbled off. Carol looked at her greasily wilting cardboard simile finger and read, "*As smart as a whip*," then shrugged and pocketed it. "Thanks. See you next year," she finished and skipped after her mother.

Liz was stunned. "What the f—sorry—what the hell was that?"

Maisie giggled and scribbled.

"Pork fingers? Boy's part?! I feel sick," said Tom. "And what was *that* she was holding?"

18: The C Word

The next day, Liz thanked a maker in whose existence she did not believe that it was Friday as she staggered into the staffroom, groggy and cantankerous. Dave and Peggy were already there.

"Morning," Liz managed. "Christ, you two are early. Have you even been home?"

"Just long enough to go to bed and then come straight back here," Peggy grumbled.

Dave was preoccupied by his tablet. He tapped and swiped, frowning at the screen, finally tutting.

"Fuck!" he vociferated indelicately. "Talk about a sting in the tail!" he continued. "Have you seen Dildo's latest email?"

The answer was written all over Liz and Peggy's vacant faces so Dave continued, quoting, "*Thanks for all your hard work at Open Evening*, blah, blah, fucking blah."

So far, so predictable. Then Dave read the end of the email. "*Finally, may I remind all staff to arrange their proffesional development lesson observations with their head of departments. They have to be completed by Christmas so that we are ready for Ofsted, whenever they dein to inspect us.*"

The mandatory lesson observations became the main focus of Monday's department meeting. Dave produced the two-page Ofsted list of criteria by which he would be judging them and started organising their observations. Desperate to get it over with, Liz made it as easy as possible for herself and arranged for Dave to come into her year seven class, the following Tuesday morning, when they were most tame, and reminded herself that this was only Dave; this was not an Ofsted inspector. Not yet.

Still, dread blossomed in Liz's stomach like a tumour and her blood raced, roaring in her ear drums. A glance round the room revealed the strained, grey faces of her colleagues, each trapped under a similar sword of Damocles. She stared out of the window, as if searching for an escape route, but all she saw were the last few students wandering home after their clubs, greyed out and ghostly in the fading light. One figure, however, oddly unmoving and bagless, seemed to be watching the English staffroom. Liz nudged Serena tensely. "Who's that man?" she asked, but before Serena had focused on him, he had dissolved into shadow.

"Did he have a suit and clipboard?" Serena said, shuddering, theatrically. "You're hallucinating inspectors now."

Dave decided to lift the mood of the room. "Cheer up, you lot," he said cheerfully. "Think yourselves lucky; I'm doing you and I'll be gentle."

A few managed reassured chuckles and Dave continued. "I'm getting done by Dildo and he won't be." He clarified the metaphor, allowing for Peggy's unworldliness: "In other words, I'm buggered."

Gareth mimed a drum flourish before adding wryly, "He's here all week."

Tuesday came and Liz congratulated herself on her foresight: the year seven English class in question was her own form. They were already in her room for registration, so they would avoid the hysteria-inducing rigmarole of lining up, coming in and sitting down; when Dave came in, they were engrossed in their reading books and hardly noticed him. That was the box ticked for having a calm and efficient start to the lesson, anyway. Although the palpitant quiver of her heartbeat still registered, Liz forced herself to breathe, gave out the books with only slightly trembling hands and switched on the electronic whiteboard to reveal the PowerPoint lesson on sentences she had prepared.

"Right, year seven," she started, hoping they would not be too taken aback by the unaccustomed effort she had put into the lesson's preparation, "put your reading books away and let's impress Mr Bishop with what we know about sentences. How many different types can you think of?"

Remembering Gordon's faith in the current 'no-hands-up' principle, she lopped the forest of arms that had shot up with a swipe of her hand and chose Alfie to answer, thus demonstrating her special consideration of disadvantaged students. Alfie responded with 'simple'. Next, Ted remembered 'complex', which Liz had hoped he would. Jordan was visibly relieved to be asked early and offered 'compound'. Finally, Liz selected Kate, who could always be relied upon to give correct answers to difficult questions and, dependably, she suggested 'compound-complex'. So far, so good; Liz had remembered to alternate boys and girls in her questioning, gaining another tick and was just about to start the next activity when Emin's hand rocketed into the air. "You missed one, Miss!" he called, without waiting to be invited. "Suspended," he added triumphantly.

Dave smiled from the back of the classroom, but Liz, fully focused on her lesson, did not follow. "I don't think that's a type of sentence, Emin."

"It is," he asserted, "It's a good one as well, 'cause my dad got one in a text from my uncle, the other day, and he was well happy."

"Okay," said Liz, "I'm still not with you though. What did the text say?"

"Well, I don't know what it actually *said*, but when Dad read it, he said, "Cool. Suspended sentence."

Dave could not resist. "Don't forget 'custodial', Miss," he chuckled.

Kate, ever diligent, asked, "Should we write those down, Mrs Marshall?" but Liz assured them that they would tackle the more advanced sentences later in the year, praised Emin for his excellent contribution and ushered them towards the next activity.

Liz put the class into mixed ability groups of four, earning another tick from Dave, delved into a bag and brought out an object, meant to inspire creative writing, for each group: a long, black glove; a compass; a peacock's feather; a trilby (familiar from Open Evening); a spent World War One brass bullet, and a glass paperweight. The students passed the objects between them eagerly, watching and listening as Liz demonstrated how to write a group paragraph with six different sentence types, each determined by the throw of a die. After this, came a solo paragraph and, finally, the inspectors' favourite: peer appraisal, before the bell went and it was all over. Dave hurried off to his lesson, giving the thumbs up as he left; drained, Liz sank into her chair.

By lunch break, Liz was back to her usual self. Dave came in and sat down next to Peggy. He opened his lunch box, eyes glinting, and winked at Liz. "Well, I've got my observation booked in with Dildo, Peg," he said. "Year eight. I've got a spectacular lesson planned."

His eyes said 'just play along' and the rest of the department was happy to be transported in the slipstream of one of his wind-ups.

Peggy listened, at first with wondering admiration, then with increasing dismay, as Dave described his ersatz lesson in all its inglorious detail. He was studying Anne Frank's diary with his year eight class; that much was true, but the truth was merely a gateway to the growing heap of fabrication that followed as he skilfully layered fib upon falsehood while the rest of the department enabled the hell out of his trickery. He outlined the way he would line the students up outside the classroom; turn off the lights in the corridor; stand, unsmiling, in the doorway, and shout their surnames in alphabetical order, allowing students in one at a time and dictating where each would sit. Next, Dave explained that he had enlisted the help of Gareth, who had a free lesson at that time, to goose-step in from the corridor and scrutinise each child, sending the blue-eyed to the back of the classroom and the others to the front.

Peggy gasped. The rest of the department nodded and expressed their fraudulent approval. Gareth would then give each of the children at the front of the room a yellow sticker to stick on the lapels of their blazers. These students would have to leave their books and pencil cases in a pile and Gareth would march them back out of the room, along the dark corridor and across the playground, towards the gym. Peggy looked indignant, while Liz, trembling with mirth and fighting to keep the hilarity from her voice, asked, "What's your learning objective, Dave?"

He had obviously been waiting to be asked this. "Well, it has to fit in with Dildo's training on higher level thinking skills, so I thought I'd better get all his key words in so that box gets ticked in my observation."

"Good thinking," said Liz. "So, what is it?"

Dave's eyebrow twitched and his colour deepened as he forced a snigger back. "To develop empathy for characters, using previous knowledge and comprehension of *The Diary of Anne Frank* in order to..." Dave faltered as he groped for the rest of his sham learning objective. Liz could almost hear the cogs whirring in his fertile brain. After a couple of seconds, he was back on course. "... to apply the principles to an analysis of our own experiences and synthesise our findings to enable us to evaluate our reactions in the context of our learning," he finished terminologically.

Peggy blanched.

"Bit complicated, isn't it?" Liz commented. "It'll take them the whole hour just to write it in their books."

Dave nodded. "Yeah, but remember the training." He signalled wildly with his eyes. "It's the latest research, isn't it? You've got to get all the key words in to take the students from the low thinking skills to the high ones."

"Oh yeah, I remember," Liz reinforced, "So, how are you going to show that they've actually learned something?"

Dave had an answer for this, too. "Well, I did this lesson at my last school and the students were noticeably affected by it—so that was the *visible learning* box ticked. Half a dozen were actually in tears, so it was really measurable too."

Ever accommodating, Gareth cut in. "And there were the letters from concerned parents too, weren't there, Dave?"

"Fuck, yeah! They're all in my professional development folder: proof of secure learning of the issues raised by the book as a means of stretching empathy skills."

This was too much for Peggy. Far from warning Dave about the inappropriacy of his lesson, as they had expected, she slammed her sandwich box down on the table and, despite her natural aversion to profanity, said, "Oh, that's bloody marvellous!"

Dave looked at her questioningly.

"My lesson's going to look bloody rubbish compared with yours," she continued, "Now I'll have to start planning all over again."

Liz caved first and disabused Peggy of this conviction. "He's winding you up, Peg," she said. "And don't forget you've got me too," she said and reminded Peggy that she was on the support rota for that lesson and would be an extra pair of hands in the classroom.

The day of Peggy's observation came and she was as convinced as she had ever been of the efficacy of her teaching. Dave followed her up to her room after break, positioned himself in a corner and waited for the students to arrive. Like most of the department, Peggy had chosen to be observed teaching her year sevens, the youngest students being generally the most biddable. Liz hovered, lending pens here and bestowing tissues there, so that the students settled without the usual fuss. When the students saw scary Mr Bishop with his clipboard, they gasped and sat wide-eyed and still, making sure they were on their best behaviour. One or two, for whom primary school habits died hard, even put their fingers on their lips. Unfortunately, impeccable conduct was not conducive to demonstrating—visibly to an assessor—a relentless lust for knowledge and the students were abnormally unresponsive, forcing Peggy to work hard to encourage them to contribute. When asked for the constituent parts that made up the example sentence she had written on the board, she had to coax the answers, 'verb', 'noun', 'adjective' and even 'adverb' out of her class and wrote them up. Finally, she drew a circle around the word 'but' and invited a student to tell her what sort of word it was. When this student failed to answer, she tried another, and another, before opening the question to anyone to answer. "Come on." She fought to keep the panic from her voice. "We did this last lesson."

Still no response.

"It's the 'C' word," she prompted. Risky. Liz held her breath and glanced at Dave. He was rigid with soundless hilarity and growing pinker by the second.

Twenty-six eleven and twelve year-olds did not have the common sense to look at the previous pages in their books.

"Okay, year seven." Peggy was getting impatient now. "Mr Bishop wants to be amazed. Surely, someone knows the 'C' word."

When the same twenty-six heads turned towards Dave to see just how much he wanted to be amazed, he was crimson and shaking, now, with suppressed laughter. Like lightning on the uptake, the students seemed to realise he must have thought of a rude word. A few of the youngsters eyed each other, wondering which of them would be brave enough to speak.

Peggy asked again, "Anyone? Come on. Shout out the 'C' word."

There was a long silence. Peggy sighed, exasperated and snapped the top off her board marker, irritated, but as she raised her hand to write the answer on the board, a small voice bravely suggested, "Crap?"

Liz handed Dave a tissue to stifle the guffaw that she knew was about to escaped him.

"Bless you, Mr Bishop," she said.

19: All Fingers and Mums

Ordeal over, at least until the next one, Liz hummed as she emptied her pigeon hole the next morning. The school newsletter was out, the main story being the report on Open Evening and she felt a pang of guilt that, after raising her student helpers' hopes, the fruits of their labours would never ripen on its pages. Previous years' offerings had taught Liz that year sevens made the most useful volunteers, but not the most erudite journalists, so she never submitted their feeble testimonies to the newsletter. However, not one volunteer had ever remembered they had written a report or asked why it had not appeared in print, so remorse did not trouble her for long. Hoping to hide the evidence of her false pretences from the duped volunteers in her form, she tried to hide the offending pages underneath the weekly lists of lost property and late library books, but as she did so, she noticed something worrying. Printed—below the fold, admittedly, but there, in black and white—next to the undeniably brilliant headline, *All Fingers and Mums*, was the name, Maisie Harrison, 7EM's form captain and would-be political activist, and underneath that was a photograph of a handful of parents and children, including the Coghills, in Peggy's poetry room. The picture, she noticed gladly, was credited to Alfie Willis; Liz was more interested in the contents of the article, however. She recalled Maisie's rebel-rousing speech and anarchy badge from the form elections and shuddered. Maisie must have handed another copy in to Jean, but what subversion would grace its columns and, of paramount importance, who would have proof-read it?

    Liz had already 'filed' Jordan's effort, *natsie mr lowe*, which had nearly found its way into the newsletter during Jean's afternoon off at the end of the previous week. It had not only libelled DT teacher, Greg, and his colleagues' Open

Evening activities, but had also ridiculed their dress sense, personal hygiene and liberality with detentions. Worse than this, however, was that it had been written with as much proficiency as would have been demonstrated by a chimpanzee with a computer. Not the best advertisement for a King Richard's education, *as any fule kno*, she thought.

Jordan's report had opened, *this is my artical on open evning and what I thouhgt to the dt activity's*, and continued, unchecked: *their was alot of parent's and kids and they whatched natsy mr lowe showing stuff in his werk room, he showed them how to make box's and that but it was boreing and some kids where tarking but he didnt give them detension like he dose to us, enyway they didnt stay long they when't to see English witch was rearly exiting.*

Fortunately, the vigilant prefect, who had been requisitioned to print the newsletter in Jean's absence, had returned Jordan's handiwork to Liz and, she now realised, must have replaced it with Maisie's.

"Thank goodness Maisie ran this one by you first, Liz," Jean said, on her way back from the photocopier. "Very nice piece of writing. She's got a real flair for journalism, that one. Little Alfie's not a bad photographer either."

Disinclined to admit to a lack of control of her form, Liz thanked Jean and hurried to her room to read Maisie's magnum opus before registration. Jean's appraisal had been right; Maisie was a natural. The article began with a florid account of Mr Dillon's speech to the parents, complete with impressively eclectic descriptions of the *brooding shadow* cast over his *saturnine features* by the mortarboard on his *domed forehead*. Maisie had evidently trawled her parents' book shelves before writing. She also described, without any detectable suggestion of irony, the shock of the prospective parents when the *blond superhero*, familiar to King Richard's staff and students from September, appeared on the projector screen, unexpectedly accompanied by the *strident tune that proclaimed his status as a redeemer of the cosmos*. Liz pictured Maisie, bent over her keyboard, back hunched like a pianist's, making full use of shift and F seven, and chuckled in the knowledge that Gordon would undoubtedly accept this as complimentary and carried on reading. She raised an eyebrow at Maisie's account of the DT department's demonstrations of *outside-the-box packaging*, the *rapt attention of the gathered throngs*, the *avuncular assistance* given by Mr Lowe, and wondered whether Maisie and Jordan had been at the same Open Evening.

The next section detailed the activities in the English department: *the cut and thrust of an authentic newspaper office*, the desks *festooned with literary tomes*, the *doting parents and their eager offspring*. Liz chuckled as she read about Peggy's yellow simile fingers and barely recognised herself in the *enthusiastic educator* who gave *stimulating consultations*. Maisie described a small girl, *filled with fascination* and her *incapacitated* mother who *limped away, grasping a mysterious pink member* and Liz wondered how ingenuous Maisie's choice of synonym had really been.

As soon as the bell rang to signal the end of morning registration, Liz dismissed her form, but asked her two captains to stay behind.

"Well? What have you got to say for yourselves?" She picked up the newsletter and looked at Alfie and Maisie severely while her sixth form Film students started drifting in and taking their places, mildly curious about what mere year seven students could have done to provoke such a harsh reaction from her.

"Do you remember I asked you to give your reports to me so I could check them before they went to the newsletter?" Liz asked.

Alfie reddened and looked at his well-worn, but freshly polished shoes. Maisie gulped and spoke for both of them. "Sorry, Miss, but I did check it really carefully." She rushed on, sensing an abatement of disapproval. "I just thought you'd be too busy and I didn't want to bother you because you've always got so much marking and you looked tired after being on your feet from eight in the morning till nine at night and—"

"All right, all right," Liz interrupted, "I've got the picture."

Lana and Frankie, slowed down by brimming cups of coffee, arrived, followed by Jimmy, who loped in, gape-kneed, on skinny-jean-clad, gangling legs.

Maisie smiled gratefully, glad of the distraction, and Liz continued. "Luckily, it was brilliant!"

"Thanks, Miss."

"Is this the newsletter?" asked Jimmy. "My mate printed it. Apparently it's well funny. Makes Dildo look a right dick."

"Jimmy!" Liz hissed.

A giggle erupted from Alfie, no longer shamefaced. "She wrote it. I just took the picture," he said.

"No way!" Jimmy replied. "That's mega." He crooked his sinewy arm, curled his fingers and bumped, first Alfie's small fist and then Maisie's larger one. "Respect."

"Did you read it?" Maisie asked.

"Not yet," Jimmy replied, "but I'll have a look now. Sick title!"

Maisie displayed no discomposure, but Liz noticed her lowered eyes furtively following Jimmy's lanky form as he dropped into a chair, plonked his high-topped feet onto the table, shoved his wayward mop of hair out of his eyes and began to read the article.

Liz ushered the two year sevens out. "Off you go, then. First lesson's about to start."

"Later, dudes," said Jimmy as they went.

"Let me know what you think." Maisie smiled and straightened her blazer as she left, making sure she flipped up the lapel. As she had obviously intended, Jimmy noticed her badge and raised his fist. "Anarchy!"

"Pretty cool for a year seven," said Ethan.

"Paedo," said Jimmy. It was the standard accusation, delivered as a matter of protocol, rather than outrage, and was ignored by Ethan who had been taking it all in quietly, happy to let Jimmy take the reins. Now he held his hand out for the newsletter. "Let's have a look."

Jake smiled a knowing smile and raised his head from his folder. "She seemed pretty keen for you to read it, Jimmy," he commented.

Lana smiled. "'Course she was, bless her," she said. "She's got a crush on you."

"They're right," said Liz. "Be careful; I don't want to be nursing broken year seven hearts."

Jimmy snorted. "Chill, Miss; *I'm* not a paedo."

"Who's not a paedo?" Bradley came in and took his seat just as the bell rang. "If you mean Jimmy, he is, though."

Jimmy wasn't having that. "Yeah, with your mum."

"That doesn't work." Kai, sitting alone and aloof, rarely spoke, but clearly could not ignore an opportunity to get the better of Jimmy.

"Owned," commented Brad.

Jimmy took the criticism with characteristic grace: "Your little sister, then," he laughed, undermining his previous objection, and passed the newsletter to Ethan who nodded, impressed and said, "I couldn't have written any better than this."

"I'll have to get her to help me with my coursework," said Jimmy.

"Jimmy," Liz sighed, "what have I just said?"

"Relax, Miss! I'm only winding you up," he said. Then, unable to resist, he continued: "I bet she would, though; chick's only human."

"Oh my God, can't a girl look at a boy without you lot saying she's got the hots for him? Women don't just exist in relation to men," Frankie cut in. "She's done the most amazing piece of journalism and all you can talk about is her fancying Jimmy."

Ethan took advantage of the brief silence that followed. "Yeah, for about a microsecond," he laughed.

"True, dat," Jake added, diffusing the argument. He was looking at Alfie's photo. "That little kid's pretty good with the camera too," he said. "I like the way he's got that weird, funny pair in the foreground with their cardboard finger thingies and then all the other people milling about, but then he's got the background in focus too, so you can see that creepy bloke, on his own in the playground."

Liz had not looked closely at the picture, but now she was interested: "Where?" she asked. Jake pointed to the tiny figure of a man, just visible through the window at the back of Peggy's room. He was difficult to make out in the darkness, but he seemed to be looking straight at the camera.

"I'm sure I've seen him here before," she said. "He must be someone's dad." She shrugged. "Right, you lot, let's get started. We're moving away from eighties' Neo-Noir now and we're looking for the ways French New Wave reflected the ideas and attitudes of France in the late fifties."

"It's not going to be disturbing, is it, Miss?" Ethan shuddered.

Jimmy snorted. "He's only just got over *Blue Velvet*!"

"You know when we watched that scene when Frank first comes in and— " He paused, not having the words. "It was just before lunch and afterwards I was going to the canteen and I had to go the long way round just so I wouldn't see anyone 'cause I couldn't talk to anyone after that. I needed a few minutes on my own to get my head together."

Ethan looked around at the others and chuckled at himself, but Lana patted his arm, saying, "Aww, Ethan, that's so sweet," and even Frankie nodded her approval.

The quiet moment of sympathy was fractured, inevitably, by Jimmy. "What a pussy!" he guffawed, gripping Ethan in a brief, but good-natured headlock before releasing him, digging his pen out of his jeans pocket and slamming it on the table. "Come on, then, Miss. Let's watch *Breathless*."

Liz switched on the electronic whiteboard. "Good idea."

The students sighed and opened their folders while Liz set up the film, drew the blinds and switched off the lights. Frankie tutted as the film's first image appeared: a close-up of a newspaper with a drawing of a young woman, standing in her underwear, smooth, bare legs, slightly apart, smiling coquettishly back over her shoulder at the viewer. The first words of the film, however, drew more laughter from the class—and hearty agreement from Frankie—with its protagonist's assertion that *After all, I'm an arsehole*.

"No arguments there," she said as the cool sounds of a jazz trumpet meandered around the thrum of double base and the newspaper was lowered to reveal the owner of the voice, the disreputable Michel, removing a lolling cigarette from his mouth to rub his thumb across his fleshy lips, Bogart style. The expected discussion of the pre-sexual revolutionary objectification of women ensued before, towards the end of the lesson, Liz got to the introduction of gamine American, Patricia, and Godard's presentation of the new feminine ideal in an intelligent, independent woman, unimpeded by bourgeois sexual repression.

"The thinking man's fantasy, really," she joked.

Frankie's pen scribbled profusely and she rolled her eyes. "Typical man."

Mindful of losing the backing of the male component of the class, Liz thought it was a good time to mention the example of Nouvelle Vague they would be studying alongside *A Bout de Souffle*.

"Tomorrow, we'll have a look at Trouffaut's presentation of a female character: the mother in *Les Quatres Cents Coups*, which is a film about a misunderstood teenager's struggles with those responsible for him," she explained.

"What does the title mean?" asked Ethan, eliciting another well-informed smile from Jake. One of his other subjects was French.

This was definitely going the way Liz wanted. "*The Four Hundred Blows*," she answered.

Jimmy's response was immediate: "The thinking man's fantasy, really."

20: Theatre Trip

The term wore on, growing chillier, damper and more dismal by the day, but before Liz could slack off and start the novelty Christmas lessons, there was one last impediment to her natural propensity for sloth: the year eleven theatre trip. She could not afford to take her eye off the ball just yet. They had been studying *An Inspector Calls* since September and were looking forward to seeing the famous Daldry version with its ingenious staging. A hundred students needed to be rounded up and registered. Uniforms needed to be checked, undesirable groups divided and contraband confiscated—and the coaches were due any minute.

Dave shoved Liz her class list. "There you go. Get stuck into that lot. Where are Gareth and the others?"

Liz nodded to where Gareth stood, remonstrating with a ferrety-looking boy.

"I haven't got any more, Sir, honest."

"Well, you'll have to sit at the front, by me," Gareth growled. "You can be in charge of the sick bucket, since you were so keen to ensure it was filled."

"Oh, sir," the boy whined, "It was only a stink bomb."

Serena glided towards them, was handed her clipboard and floated among the students, whispering their names and ticking her list.

Next, Lucy bounded up and grabbed her list. "Right, you lot. Heel!" she shouted. Laughing, her class shambled towards her, jostling and bickering until she put a finger and thumb to her lips, let out a long whistle and pretended to cuff a six foot, bearded sixteen-year-old around the back of the head. He roared with laughter and put his arm round her shoulders.

"Can I sit with you, Miss?" he boomed and lifted her off her feet.

"Put Miss down, Giles," Dave sighed. "You don't know where she's been."

"I do, sir. She's my next-door neighbour."

Back on solid ground, Lucy whacked Giles over the head with her clipboard. "Sod off, you silly bugger!" she yelled.

Giles ducked before she did it again. "Did you see that, sir? That's abuse, that is."

"I'll give you abuse in a minute!" Lucy brandished her clipboard again.

"Promises, promises," said Giles.

Gales of laughter erupted from Lucy's class. "And you lot can shut up," she pretended to snarl. She loved it.

Dave shook his head and wandered off towards his class, chuckling.

Belle padded towards them, snug in pink puffer jacket and snow boots. She was horrified. "You can't let them behave like that; they'll be representing the school. What will the public think?"

Liz nudged Lucy and whispered, "Who invited her?"

This must have been part of Belle's training; the 'taking part in a school trip' box needed to be ticked and so here she was. Her dainty, pink face was pinched with disapproval and, tutting, she took out her special note book and looked over at Giles, scribbling.

At last, when the last few names had been cross-checked with late parental permission slips, the coaches arrived. Once again, the students cheered. There was one name unticked, from Liz's list, though: Kayleigh Bates. She had probably forgotten—or decided to stay in bed; with no one at home to get her up, she did not always make it to school. Liz let Dave know and he agreed to wait a few minutes.

"Why don't you go and check the school registers," he suggested. "Maybe she's not in today. Have you checked with Fray Bentos?"

Kayleigh's best friend, Freya Bentley, was almost as scatter-brained as she was and lived with her parents, several siblings and some nephews and nieces, it was said, squeezed, anachronistically, into a tiny, rented cottage where rabbits and pheasants were hung, dripping, in the kitchen, ready to be made into stews and pies and clothes were dried inside, absorbing the whole gamy aroma. Her nickname, therefore, was a no-brainer.

"Freya's phoned her and left a message," Liz replied and hurried towards Reception. On her way back towards the bus bay, Liz noticed the students leaning close to Dave, who was talking animatedly and gesticulating.

"No luck?" he asked. "Give her a shout to make sure."

"I'm not sure it'll do much good," said Liz. "She's obviously not here."

"Just one try," he urged. Liz wondered why the students had suddenly gone so quiet, but she shrugged, cupped her hand around her mouth and called. "Kay-leigh!"

The ninety-nine gathered students responded, out of tune, but as one Marillionesque voice: "*Is it too late to say I'm sorry?*"

Liz groaned and punched Dave in the arm.

"Sir! Sir!" shouted Giles, "That's abuse!"

There was a hiss and a clank and the coaches' doors opened, allowing the students to charge on.

Just as they were settling the last few into the coach she and Dave were on, Liz heard pounding feet and a cry of, "Wait for me!" An unkempt figure panted up the coach steps, waving a permission slip. "Sorry, Miss, I overslept." She dropped into the seat next to Freya.

"All right, Frabe?"

Liz was, exasperated. "Kayleigh!"

"*Could we get it together again?*" This time, the chorus came just from Dave. The students burst into another cheer as the coach pulled out and they were on their way.

The theatre was only an hour away, but after twenty minutes of winding through the countryside, retch-related prophecies reached their ears and could not be ignored. Dave tapped the driver on the shoulder and he grudgingly pulled over into a layby. The culprit was a girl in Liz's class, so she clambered past Dave, and helped her off the coach, hoping the fresh air would alleviate the symptoms. However, Eloise turned a worrying shade of green and lurched towards the hedge, bending over the jetsam of crisp packets and cigarette ends and heaving. Her stomach churned ominously.

"Hold me hair, Miss."

Liz did as she was asked. "It's a while since I've done this," she commented.

By way of a reply, Eloise disgorged a stomachful of atrocity, wiped her mouth with the back of her hand and smiled, normal colour returning to her cheeks. "Have you got a mint?" she said.

As they climbed back onto the coach, Liz noticed Dave was now at the back. What was he up to now? As Eloise sat down, he called to Liz, "What's her name?"

Liz called back, "Eloise."

"*Do-do-do-do-do-do-do-dooo*," chorused the students, gleefully, hastily choir-mastered by Dave in the few minutes she'd been on vomit detail.

They arrived at the theatre half an hour early. The coach doors shushed open and the students scrambled out, a buzzing, navy-blue swarm on the paved neo-classical plaza outside the main doors. The grey December day did nothing to strengthen the impression of Italianate sophistication and the numerous coffee shops, delicatessens and wine bars bordering the plaza seemed to shrink from the cold, their outside tables all but empty. Giant concrete-come-marble planters holding olive and citrus trees shivered in the winter air, as if yearning for some Mediterranean sun.

The students started to fret like toddlers.

"Can I go and get a drink, Sir?"

"Is there a toilet, Sir?"

"Can I ring my mum, Miss?"

Weighing up the Canute-like endeavour of keeping them there for half an hour against being considered a legend by allowing them twenty minutes' off-leash time, Dave bestowed a brief freedom.

"Stay around this square and be back here at ten to," he said.

Like cockroaches when the light goes on, the students skittered out of the plaza in the direction of cafés, clothes shops and side streets: anywhere the teachers were not.

"Remember, you're representing King Richard's," he called, but school was the last thing on their minds.

Liz and the others sat down on benches to enjoy a few minutes' peace. Scanning the perimeter of the plaza, Liz noticed two delicate ribbons of blue-grey smoke, rising from behind one of the denser olive trees like the graceful lines bordering an Art Nouveau illustration. Lucy spotted them at the same time.

"Kayleigh and Freya: guaranteed!" I thought they'd at least get out of sight before they lit up!" she laughed.

"Blind eye?" Dave whispered to them perspicaciously.

Belle leapt to her tiny, furry feet. "So, we'll have to report it and they shouldn't be allowed the privilege of seeing the play?"

"Thanks, Belle," said Liz, "but I think we were mistaken, weren't we, Dave?"

"About what?" he replied. "I've literally no idea what you mean."

Belle was in pug-with-a-bone mode again. "I can definitely see smoke? We need to get over there and catch them in the act?"

"I definitely *can't* see any puffs of satisfying cigarette smoke being blown out—and those are definitely not smoke rings over there," Lucy told her, laughing.

"Come on," Belle yelped, "they'll have finished them by the time you've stopped messing around and we won't be able to punish them."

Dave turned to Belle sternly. "Sometimes, you need to pick your battles," he said. "If we report them, they'll be excluded."

"Well, they deserve it," Belle insisted.

Liz joined in. "Those two girls might pass their exams if we can keep them in school. If they get kicked out, they've got no chance. Their parents know they smoke; they buy them their ciggies, so what's to be gained by reporting them?"

"It's the principle."

In the minutes it had taken to have this discussion, the two miscreants had obviously finished their cigarettes and were heading back towards their teachers. Seeing that there were no other students there, they looked at each other, worried and quickened their pace.

"Are we late?"

Liz gave Belle a warning look and, huffing, she sat down.

"No, you're first back," said Liz.

"We didn't want to look round," Kayleigh replied; "we were just desperate for a sm—"

"Toilet," Freya cut in, jabbing Kayleigh with her elbow. "Desperate for the toilet," she finished.

Dave raised his eyebrows. "Well, it *is* a nightmare when you're desperate for a sm—toilet," he agreed. The girls nudged each other and giggled. "Mrs Marshall, I think the girls might like one of your mints."

This was too much for Belle. She snorted, got up again and padded over towards Gareth and Serena, on another bench, where she took out her notebook and began to write furiously.

Once inside the theatre, they dispersed themselves amongst the students, splitting any rowdy combinations. Almost every year eleven for miles around was here. Blocks of colour tessellated throughout the auditorium: navy against grey, burgundy next to black. There was even a row or two of bottle green. An unwitting handful of bewildered members of the public sat, singly or in pairs amidst the sea of raucous teenagers, looking around, dismayed.

Within the teenage sector of the audience, there was no such dismay. Familiarity with their own school's matching-uniformed potential life-partners had bred contempt and now they investigated opportunities for new colour combinations. A complex semaphore of hand signals, eyebrow twitches and phone jiggles flickered through the stalls as negotiations were entered into and possibilities pursued.

Suddenly, the lights went out and the room gasped and whispered. A small, sad-looking boy, wearing grey flannel shorts and a fraying knitted tank top, wandered in front of the plush velvet curtain and lifted it, peering underneath. The students looked around in confusion. Was this part of the play? The curtains rose, golden tassels quivering, to reveal a man in a trilby and trench coat, leaning against a telephone box. Head wreathed in the smoke from his cigarette, he gazed up at a crooked oversized dolls' house, teetering on rickety iron stilts that raised it above the rubble of a blitz-weary street. People in worn, drab clothing stood in the background, watching glumly as the sparkle of champagne and laughter tinkled down from the house, bright and brittle. The students relaxed, reassured by the familiar scene, as the front of the dolls' house opened to reveal the Birling family, just as Priestley described, in the dining room of their *fairly large suburban house*, with its *heavy and substantial furniture*.

The audience was noisy, but appreciative, treating the performance as pantomime, so when the inspector's final speech reached its crescendo of *fire and blood and anguish*, the students were vocal in their surprise at the theatrical thunderclap and flash of lightning. The characters were 'thrown' forward in the blast and the dolls' house toppled and fell into the rubble of the blitzed street beneath it. The dining table lay on its side, its top facing the audience, and smoke rose dramatically from behind. Flames licked the table's underside and became visible to the audience, who marvelled at this innovative interpretation, as their teachers had told them they would. The smoke rolled downstage and reached the actors, who—far from lying, motionless—sniffed, raised their heads and looked at one another, nervous, as the sound of the thunder died away.

A man in black shirt and trousers entered stage left with a fire extinguisher and sprayed the fire with foam. Staff, students, and civilians alike looked at each other, puzzled. They were still not certain whether this was part of the show—another layer of time-loop trickery, intended to bring the message to a contemporary audience. After a minute, the curtain came down and the lights came up. The audience applauded politely. The man in black emerged through the red velvet, still gripping the extinguisher, and addressed them: "If you could stay in your seats, we'll get the play started again as soon as possible," he said. "We've just had a minor issue with the pyrotechnics."

The penny finally dropped and there was an explosion of cheering, whistling and foot-stamping. The stage manager blushed and took a bow to even more raucous applause, before the lights went down again and the curtain rose for the dénouement, the twist and a standing ovation from the audience.

"Another classic Dickie's trip!" Liz said as she and the others herded the chattering swarm back towards the coaches.

"Vintage!" Dave agreed.

Kayleigh and Freya caught up with them, smelling of pie and ash, as usual.

"Hey, Sir, Miss, did *you* know that fire was real?" asked Freya.

"What did you think when you saw all the smoke?" Kayleigh said.

Liz winked. "We thought it was you two, gone to the toilet again."

21: Christmas is Coming

The last day of the autumn term finally arrived and, as Liz drove to school, the frost-silvered hills floated, ghostly, into view, affirming the festive time of year. Trees stood root-deep in mist, which stirred and settled gently, like discarded tissue paper on Christmas morning. As Liz approached the school's main door, a robin carolled from the crimson-berried rowan tree next to the entrance.

Gordon's little helpers had woven some Yuletide magic the previous evening and the entrance hall was heaving with Christmas spirit. A huge, almost real-looking Christmas tree groaned under the weight of tinsel, baubles and lights, and piles of imitation presents nestled under its branches. Cello and bassoon called and answered as Prokoviev's *Troika* was piped into the foyer. At the sound of the sleigh bells, feebly, fleetingly, Liz felt the elusive childhood tingle of Christmas. However, like the shadow of a dream that disappears when focused on, it was gone, forever resistant to re-creation in the adult consciousness.

Despite the school's appearance of relaxed festive cheer, Liz was not convinced that, under Gordon's regime, that this, the most untroubled day of the year, would retain its traditional congenial disposition. Much would depend upon which version of himself Gordon would decide to communicate: humbug or hallelujah. Reading her emails delivered the answer soon enough, though; a message to all teaching staff forbade the traditional last-day viewing of Christmas films and warned that Gordon would not be expecting to see them being screened in any lesson he might just happen to walk into. Bloody Scrooge. She wouldn't even be able to show *A Christmas Carol* to her year elevens, even though they were studying it for GCSE. So much for honouring Christmas in his heart.

"Miserable sod," Liz muttered just as a Christmas jumper clad Peggy arrived, tin of home-made mince pies under one arm and bag of DVDs over the other. As she put her bag down on the table, she triggered a tinny rendition of *Jingle Bells*, which emanated from a small speaker in a plum pudding on her chest.

"No one can be miserable at Christmas," she said and the lights on her Christmas bell earrings twinkled in agreement. "Well, no one can be miserable when they're watching *A Muppet Christmas Carol*, anyway," she continued, producing the DVD in question with the triumph of a television game-show's glamorous assistant: "Ta-dah!"

Liz disabused her of this conviction: "Dildo can," she said.

Peggy rolled her eyes and sighed with a shrug of forbearance, but Liz continued. "We won't get a chance to find out, anyway. The Grinch has stolen Christmas."

"I've got that one in here too," Peggy put in, rummaging.

Liz tried again. "Peggy, he's banned Christmas films."

Peggy's expression turned murderous. She folded her arms indignantly and set *Jingle Bells* off again. However, now it had a discordant, almost sinister sound.

"Battery's going in that, Peg," said Dave as he walked in. "Last year's is it? Sounds fucking terrible!" He looked from her face to the bag of DVDs and the penny dropped. "You've heard about Scrooge, then?"

"Another one I can't show!" Peggy wailed.

Dave put his arm round her and triggered off another dissonant, mournful chorus. "You'll be fine," he said. "I've got a shed load of Christmas shit you can give the kids: word-searches, poems, anagrams, The Twelve Language Features of Christmas..."

"Anyway, it's only the morning," Liz told her. "It's the Christmas concert this afternoon, don't forget. That's one good thing he's done for the school, anyway."

Peggy had always loved the Christmas prize-giving and now that Gordon had combined it with a traditional Christmas concert, she looked forward to it even more and forgave him his curmudgeonliness. She revelled in the successes of students she might only have passed in the corridor almost as much as those she had taken through from year seven to the day they left. She smiled and headed towards her classroom, clutching the pile of engaging Christmas learning activities that Dave had given her.

Liz followed her upstairs and, when she got to her room, she was greeted by the usual year-seven-ish kerfuffle over cards and presents. She was almost sorry Belle was at university, instead of here, today. Almost. The girls had given every one of their class-mates cards and most of the boys, perennially lacking in social skills, had not—much to the girls' chagrin. They would know better next year. As she sat down, Liz was bombarded with one of the great perks of being a year seven tutor: gifts from parents still concerned with what was de rigueur at primary school. If only more of them would realise it was perfectly acceptable for eleven-year-olds to come to school with bottles of wine in their bags—as long as they were gift-wrapped and labelled *To Mrs Marshall*—more than acceptable.

The bell sounded and Liz wished them a merry Christmas, sent them to their lessons and settled in for a morning of film deprivation related disappointment, cheesy Christmas music and chocolate fuelled hysteria. She wondered vaguely whether either of the bottle-shaped Christmas presents among the haul from her form was a screw-top.

Once the year nines were set up in groups, making fun-but-educationally worthwhile board games based on *Z For Zachariah*, and the glitter, glue and gel-pens were flowing, Liz settled to prepare her own game. She wrote individual Christmas-related words, gleaned semi-at-random from the activities on her desk, onto small pieces of paper, folded them up and placed them in the green fabric pouch from a *Scrabble* game, the better to rummage in silence with. She stashed the pouch in her pocket for the traditional limerick writing game she and Dave would have later, while Doug (the head of governors), the local vicar and the guest speaker, gave their interminable speeches. They had devised the game to combat the brain-ossifying tedium of the first hour of Prize-Giving a few years ago and had played it ever since. Dave would lose; he always did, having not the slightest grasp of poetic metre, not even that of a limerick. For Liz, the challenge came, not from the task of writing a limerick containing three words randomly picked from the bag, but from that of reducing Dave to a shuddering hulk of hysterics. One year, he had struggled for ten minutes with his three words—*list*, *goose* and *plum*—and the resultant offering was too pitiable even to be amusing. Liz, however, had come up with a limerick whose conceit was both unexpected and filthy. Dave had been done for. How had it gone again? Liz could not remember the whole thing, only that one of the words she had picked had been *pluck*: a gift.

The morning went by with something that, despite her cynicism, looked very like good humour. Liz tidied her room, gathered up her cards and presents and, festively laden, made her way down to the English staffroom for the pre-prize-giving lunch. Dave had just taken delivery of the traditional Christmas pizza and was laying the table with holly-wreathed paper napkins, champagne flutes borrowed from the caterers and a rectangular present, roughly eight inches by five, for each of them. He rubbed his hands together. "You up for the limerick challenge this year, Liz?" he asked.

"Certainly am," she said. "I've done the words. Have you got Serena on the Last Clap again?"

"Abso-fucking-lutely!"

As if by Christmas magic, Serena appeared with two bottles of Prosecco. "Look what I've got to wash our Christmas lunch down with," she smiled, twisting the first one until it popped gently and sighed. "There should be just enough for a glass each."

"Ooh, and proper glasses too." Lucy said. She was just behind Serena and sat down, grinning.

"Oi, Bish! Are these for us?" Lucy said, pointing at one of the slightly sloppily wrapped gifts. "You didn't need to do that, you soft git."

Dave nodded and coloured. "Well, it *is* fucking Christmas."

Peggy joined them, flashing and jingling, and picked one up, studying it and turning it over in her hands. "Probably books."

"Really? How do you know?" Liz ironised.

Gareth had come in from bus duty, "Look at the shape," he said, quoting his sit-comical namesake. He sloughed his trench coat "You crazy kids ready for some fun?" he chuckled, and patted his rakishly scuffed briefcase.

"Right, Gaz," said Dave, abbreviatorily, ignoring Gareth's flinch at the diminutive, "what have you got for us this year?"

Over the past few years, Gareth had run a Christmas book on the incidence of the multifarious quirks of the staff and governors who sat on the stage during the prize-giving.

"I can give you odds on how many times Doug touches his todger, the vicar picks his nose—"

"The good old pick and flick," interjected Dave.

"Oh no," Gareth corrected him, "he rolls and eats it; he's not an animal."

"Any more?" Liz urged.

Gareth smiled and continued. "How many times the head boy says 'like' in his speech, how many people trip over, going to get their prizes."

"Nice," said Dave. "Anything on Dildo?"

Gareth drew out a notebook. "Loads," he confirmed. "Grammatical mistakes, malapropisms, offending parents, getting people's names wrong, offending governors, mentioning superheroes, offending staff. It's quite a list."

"I've got another one for you," said Liz. "Have you seen what Gannet's wearing today?"

Gareth leaned back in his seat, pushed his glasses up the bridge of his nose and hooked his elbow over the back of his chair, smirking. "No, why?"

Liz had seen Janet going into her office on her way in. She had been dressed for the season, but hardly the weather.

"Well, she's got on a lovely, Christmassy, Fair Isle jumper, a festive hat and scarf and knee-length snow boots," said Liz.

"Sounds fine," said Gareth, "so what's there to bet on?"

"That's it," said Liz.

"What, no trousers?" asked Dave, Chaddishly.

Liz shook her head.

"Skirt?" Gareth pressed.

"Nope," said Liz. "I mean, she does look good, but it *is* short, considering she'll be on the stage and we'll all be looking up at her." Liz glanced out of the window. "You'll see for yourself in a minute, though; she's on her way over."

They all followed the direction of Liz's gaze to where Janet had paused at the doorway on the other side of the playground, to call something back over her shoulder, and their eyes widened.

Gareth licked the end of his pencil. "Right, Liz, start giving me colours and I'll work out some odds."

"Christ in a manger!" gulped Lucy. "I mean, I know we're sort of in mufti, but still, when she's higher up than us..."

"Actually, I think I can see her mufti," chuckled Dave.

Peggy frowned. "Dave!"

"Sorry, Peg," said Dave. "Now everyone, stop twatting about and let's get started on this." He unboxed the pizzas with a flourish. "Merry fucking Christmas. Dig in."

Serena had just finished pouring Prosecco into each of the glasses, and echoed Dave's imperative: "Yes, grab a glass, everyone. You can do a toast, Dave."

Before anyone had the chance to obey, Janet breezed in with the icy wind. "Merry Christmas, English," she said. "Do you like my Christmas jumper-dress?" She didn't wait for an answer, however; her ravenous eyes darted to the table and evaded contact with those of her colleagues. "I thought you'd have a good spread. Cheers." She dropped into the chair, snatching a slice of pizza on the way, and drained the nearest glass in one gulp. Oblivious to the shocked stares of her colleagues, she fell upon one of the bottles like a vulture and attempted to refill her glass, but it was empty, so she reached across the table for the other one—with the same result. Undeterred, she seized another full glass and gulped before devouring her slice of pizza and lunging for another. Initial shock gave way to self-preservation and Liz and the others all grabbed their glasses and handfuls of pizza before she cleared the entire table.

"Mmm." Janet's voice was muffled by tomato and mozzarella. "Well, got to go," she said, jumping up and making for the door. "See you at the prize-giving."

"What just happened?" Peggy seemed genuinely baffled.

Serena just laughed: "Cheeky sod! Lucky I poured one for Belle by mistake."

Lucy screamed with laughter. "Christmas jumper-dress? Whoever sold her that as a dress must have seen her coming."

"Well," Liz answered, "it *is* short!" she laughed.

"Yeah, you could nearly see her cracker!" added Lucy.

"You know what's really Christmassy with a Christmas jumper, though," Dave chipped in. This was bound to be good.

"What?" they asked.

"A nice fur muff," he replied.

Gareth grimaced. "As long as she doesn't let the vicar put his hands in it!"

Liz adopted what she thought was a fair approximation of the maid in Tom Jones and curtsied: "*La! Mr Jones,*" she lisped in a West Country brogue, "*you will stretch my lady's muff and spoil it!*"

"Okay, Dave," Gareth laughed, "I'll give you ten to one on Gannet's pants. What colour?"

"She'll definitely have gone for red today." Dave fumbled in his pocket. "Where's my wallet? Gannet's Christmas pants are worth a quid of anyone's money!"

"So I've heard." Liz fished in her purse. "Do you do accumulators?" she asked.

"No," Gareth replied, "but I think the vicar does."

22: Christmas Concert

Lunch dispatched, they strolled, chattering, into the garlanded hall, where the school choir was already dispensing festive ambience with its sotto voce performance of *O Little Town of Bethlehem*. Again, the tingle of Christmas alighted, briefly, on Liz's shoulder, but when she tried to capture and keep it, like a robin eluding a cage, it was gone.

Liz and Dave headed for the back row of seats, followed by the rest of the department. Photocopied programmes had already been distributed, one to each chair, so they picked theirs up and sat down. A quick check at the back confirmed that the last two pages were blank—perfect for their limerick composition—and Liz made ready her pencil. The senior leadership team, governors and local vicar ascended the stairs to the stage, their way gestured superfluously by a grinning Gordon, resplendent in his academic regalia.

Gordon coughed. His gown flapped and his mortarboard bobbed as he welcomed the guests, pausing for the obligatory applause after he had introduced the first speaker, Doug, the chair of governors. He stepped to the side and, in the few seconds before Doug had laboured to his feet with a scrape of his chair and approached the front of the stage, Janet, who was sitting directly behind the lectern, revealed the answer to the sweepstake in all its festive glory. Red.

Liz elbowed Dave. "You've won a quid," she said as Doug's shambling frame blocked the view again. Serena, seated on the other side of Liz, nudged her gently and gestured, with her head, towards Gareth.

His pencil was poised over the Book. At the first nervous, unconscious flutter of Doug's hand towards his fly, Gareth made the first confident, deliberate stroke of his pencil on his page: the plank that began the picket gate of the tally. And they were off.

Doug's speech was as long-winded as ever, so Liz and Dave settled themselves in for some serious wordplay. Dave's fingers crept furtively towards the green pouch, then plunged in and rummaged. He drew out three pieces of paper and unfolded them quietly: *candle*, *snow* and *turkey*. He pulled a face and set to work straight away, bitten lip and beetle brow evidencing the near impossibility of the task. While Liz composed with composure, Dave chewed his pen, scribbled, tutted, drew a line through, started afresh and scribbled again, this time with visible inspiration, until he was ready and they swapped.

Ignoring Dave's expectant face, Liz began to read his limerick: *One day it was dark + murky*.

The first line did not promise very much and delivered... well, even less. Perhaps the second line would be better: *I went in search of a massive turkey*. Nope.

Still, the anapaestic dimeter of lines three and four could still save it.

But in snow

I didn't know. Hmm, nearly. She carried on, not holding her breath for evidence of poetic genius in the final line.

So I lit a candle—it was quirky and I felt perky.

Liz had the greatest respect for Dave's intellect, but the less said about the end, the better. She looked at Dave, who was pink with mirth again. At least he recognised his shortcomings.

Doug's speech drew to a close and he shuffled back to his seat to more clapping. Gareth scribbled in the Book and mouthed, *Seventeen*, at them. The applause petered out, with just a few isolated claps prolonging the time until

Gordon would start speaking again. When they had died down completely, he started to speak.

"Well, it's that time of y—"

A single clap, like a pistol shot, reverberated round the hall, cutting off his words. Liz froze and waited. The head was not speechless for long, however; he continued, undaunted. When it was safe, she looked at Serena. Serena's expression bore no suggestion of the subversive act she had just committed and she smiled coolly and gazed, in apparent innocence and admiration, up at Gordon.

"—year again," Gordon continued, forehead puckering slightly, "and I thought I'd share the school's new mission statement with all of you." His face took on a smug expression and he clicked the remote control he was holding, causing the screen behind him to light up. He read aloud the words that loomed above their heads: "To actively encourage students to never give up so they are able to truly succeed."

Liz giggled and craned her head to see Chris's reaction to Gordon's syntactical tmesis. "He missed *to always split the infinitive*," she whispered. On the stage next to Janet, Chris wearily removed his glasses and, before replacing them, rubbed his denuded eyes with a melancholy hand. Next to him, the vicar's little finger strayed, seemingly of its own accord, to his impressive proboscis. Liz glanced at Gareth, who was busy with his pen. She nudged Dave.

"Vicar's in up to the elbow again," she commented.

Gareth was watching, pen hovering, now, above the Book. The vicar looked guardedly from side to side before popping his finger into his mouth, withdrawing it and giving it a quick wipe on his jacket.

"Yes!" hissed Gareth, ticking it off in his book.

Dave nodded, smiling. "You treat yourself, Rev."

Gordon's speech gathered pace, and Liz and Dave engrossed themselves in the next round of the limerick challenge and filtered him out. Liz was just grappling with *poinsettia*, *egg-nog* and *wassail* when she noticed a sudden change in the atmosphere of the room. The air in the hall seemed to have become hard and brittle and Glyn Evans, in the row in front, had become markedly more alert. Gordon's voice ricocheted off the walls as he finished what he was saying: "...and all I've wanted to do since I first worked with her is have her on my team again, so I look forward to making that dream come true in the near future."

Liz realised they had just missed something momentous. "On his team again?" She elbowed Dave and refocused her attention on the head, following the direction of Gordon's stare as he stretched out his hands, palms upwards, Christ-like, and gestured towards a spot on the front row of seating. His eyes misted and he gulped down the lump in his throat, managing to say, "Join me in a round of applause for my wife, my inspiration, the Dale Arden to my Flash Gordon. Yvonne Dillon, everyone."

The audience could do little but obey and, noticeably consternated, roused itself in somewhat less enthusiastic manual appreciation than they had for Doug.

"I thought he was threatening redundancies," said Serena. "He can't give her a job."

If ever there was a time for Serena to administer the Last Clap, it was now and, with searing audacity, she delivered that final, insolent clap a good seven or eight seconds after its most recent predecessor, to the puzzlement of the head.

Tension broken, Dave whispered, "What the fuck was all that about?"

Liz reminded him of the first day back and her appraisal of Yvonne Dillon then. "I told you in September:

Lady Macbeth." She took advantage of the muted hubbub to continue: "Remember, he mentioned redundancies at half term? Now he's trying to sneak the missus in."

Dave nodded his head towards Glyn. "That'll go down well with the union."

The prize-giving was next on the agenda and they endured half an agonising hour of students climbing the steps, shaking hands and descending again, punctuated by increasingly apathetic clapping and only enlivened by one minor stumble. Gareth would have to decide whether to pay out on that one.

The final part of the assembly made way for tradition and spirits began to lift. At least this was a change Gordon had made for the better. The choir led the singing and Christmas was restored again. Liz's figurative robin perched momentarily on her shoulder once more as, collectively, their voices belted out *O Come, All Ye Faithful*. Her vocal chords tightened and a sentimental tear blossomed in her eye as Gareth and Serena, unforeseen tenor and soprano, harmonised freely. In the final chorus, Gareth's tenor swelled and rose as his *O come* coaxed Serena's soprano, at first breathy and tentative. Soon, her vocals gained confidence and mounted to a joyful crescendo of *O come let us ado-o-o-ore hi-im*, which elicited admiring looks from those around them. Perhaps even more impressive was the emerging predominance of Glyn's dramatic basso profondo, intoning *Christ the Lord* in the final line, suppressing all other voices and extending the final note of the carol with its comfortable, earthy throb.

"Postcoital cigarette, anyone?" whispered Dave as they sat down. "Didn't think I'd feel *this* satisfied by God."

"That's the downside of being an atheist," said Liz. "I do miss the singing."

In the hush that followed, Lana, who studied drama and English as well as film, and was renowned for her clear speaking voice and impeccable pronunciation, climbed to the stage, moving with the beguiling combination of grace and awkwardness as a foal. Regarding the audience demurely from under thick lashes, the slight cast in her eye only increasing her appeal, she tucked her hair behind her ear, took a breath and began. Everyone in the hall was further palliated by the familiarity of the story and savoured its Biblical inaccuracies, craving stables and inn keepers, camels and kings, and when Lana informed them, in mellifluous tones, that, Mary had ridden on a monkey, nobody in the audience seemed to notice the mistake. Lana faltered, however, causing the listeners to double-take.

"What did she just say?" whispered Dave, chuckling.

Lana went back to the beginning of the sentence and tried again: "And so it was that Mary, heavy with child, rode upon a monkey to Bethlehem."

"Think I prefer this version." Liz was giggling now. "Poor Lana."

Lana's mistake had superseded the intended word and muscle memory seemed unwilling to relinquish it. Lana tried again, ignoring the few titters that came from the choir. A desperate tremor crept into her usually steady voice: "A m—, a monk—," she said forlornly, glaring at the sniggering choir before capitulating and rushing to the next part of the story.

Dave and Serena, either side of Liz, were shaking with silently uncontrollable laughter, and a glance at the stage told her that Chris was in the same predicament, although, thankfully, he was better able to disguise it and smiled kindly, urging her to continue, when Lana glanced behind her for his reassurance. Gareth thumbed through his Book, tallying and adding up.

At last, it was the final carol and after a euphoric delivery of *Ding Dong Merrily on High*, complete with harmonies, the concert was over. Chris filed off the stage, after the dignitaries and with the rest of the leadership team and must have run the length of the corridor that went along the side of the hall because he appeared behind them, having slipped in through the back door.

"Is Lana all right?" Liz asked him.

"Yes," Chris replied, "she's fine now; it'll be one to tell her grandchildren. Even better, it's all been recorded!" He stopped and glanced around him, lowering his voice. "I couldn't believe it: Mary rode a monkey! I had to stick my pen in my leg to stop myself laughing. I mean, I actually had to injure myself, physically!"

"Good work, Chris," said Gareth, "Now, let's repair to The Snowdrop for a few ales. I've made a packet today."

Liz drove home under a radiant, pregnant moon, which lolled, wanton, on its bed of crumpled clouds, the very antithesis of the virgin of the nativity. When she arrived, Jack had collected the tree from the local farm shop and they imbibed its resinous perfume as, pleasantly exhausted, they watched over their tumblers of iced Irish cream, as the boys decorated it. Then they lit tea lights, which glimmered, gem-like, in the various festively beaded and coloured jars for which Liz had scoured the local junk shops a few years before, and settled down for a few days of cosiness, predictability and traditionalism.

"This is my favourite bit," Liz said, passing round the drinks as they sank into the sofas, around the television. "Everyone's home and no one's got to drive anywhere so we can shut the world out and get our Christmas started."

"Well said." Jack pressed the 'play' button on the remote control.

A familiar picture book page appeared with its monochrome snow-scene illustration of log cabins, trees and waving children in their horse-drawn cart. A church bell tolled, fading into the jingle of sleigh bells and an orchestral version of *Buffalo Gals* played as the pages turned slowly, one by one. Bedford Falls was revealed with its Christmas lights strung between the shops and snow falling like feathers from angels' wings. The drug store, the bar, the church and the old Granville house were as familiar to the Marshalls as their own home and by the time the camera had tracked up above the roof, through the falling snow, and the shot had dissolved into one of the firmament, at least two pairs of Marshall eyes had moistened, not to dry up until well after the final *Auld Lang Syne*.

23: New Year

All too soon, the holidays were over and real life resumed, the only difference being that every fresh conversation was preceded by the mandatory salutation of 'Happy New Year', which had rapidly lost its novelty after the half-dozenth time Liz had heard it.

"It's the fifth of January now, for God's sake," she grumbled over her pre-registration coffee.

Students were gathering on the tarmac outside, their foreheads and necks strangely exposed by short new haircuts as they exchanged Christmas holiday anecdotes and compared their recent acquisitions: games and gadgets, phones and fragrance, clothes and cash.

Serena had also paid a visit to the salon. Her blonde hair shone even blonder than before, and was swept back smoothly and tucked behind her ears.

"Wow! Great hairdo, Serena," Liz commented. "Sorry—*happy New Year*—great hairdo, Serena. Growing out the fringe?"

"Thanks," Serena replied. "I mean *happy New Year*, thanks. This is fun; it's like *Simple Simon Says*."

Gareth looked up from his pile of photocopying and raised an eyebrow. "Yeah, nice—very Grace Kelly."

"Wouldn't have killed you to have had a new do for the new year, Gareth," Liz joked.

"I thought I might go for the beatnik look this season." Gareth tossed a make-believe tress over his shoulder and smoothed his imaginary Fu Manchu moustache.

Lucy bounded in, grinning. "All right, losers? Good Christmases?" She shrugged her coat off and threw it into the corner. Tutting, she licked a finger and rubbed at a stain on her top. "Shit, I thought I'd got that port out of this. Does it show?"

Liz shook her head. "Nah, it's fine. You'll never get me spilling my Christmas drink, though," she said significantly.

Lucy settled into a chair and beamed. "Sounds like there's a story there," she said. "Go on; I can tell you're dying to tell!"

It was true. Liz had been desperate to get the conversation round to her finest hour and the others listened as she regaled them with the account of her Christmas morning.

Some people unwrapped parcels in their pyjamas; some invited rosy-cheeked offspring into king-sized beds to delve into stockings full of nuts and clementines; some even went to church. Liz, however, had taken her glass of pre-lunch sherry to enjoy in the bath and, as she soaked with the foot of her delicately stemmed glass resting on her stomach, smelling the turkey's increasingly mouth-watering aroma and humming along to the swing of Frank Sinatra's *Jolly Christmas* that drifted up from the kitchen below, she had let her eyes close and enjoyed a few seconds' undiluted relaxation.

Having set the scene for her colleagues, Liz described the way she had opened her eyes, enjoyed another sip, resettled the glass among the perfumed bubbles, which had disappeared more quickly than expected, and used her toe to turn on the tap and add more hot water. She paused to assess the effect of her narrative on her audience. As she had intended, they were amused and unsuspecting.

"Anyway, I thought I'd better not leave Jack to do all the cooking on his own," Liz continued. "So, I put my glass of sherry down on the side, by my watch, and guess what!"

"Oh no," Serena gasped. "You spilt it on the watch! Was it your Christmas present?"

"That wouldn't have been much of a story!" Liz said, laughing. "No, I saw the time. I'd been asleep nearly an hour, holding my sherry. I thought the water had gone cold quickly!"

As Liz had hoped, her colleagues reacted with exaggerated gasps and flabbergasted laughs.

"But, do you know what the best thing was?" Liz waas proud of this.

"What?" said Lucy.

"I hadn't spilt a drop!"

Dave had wandered in and heard the end of her story. "Legendary lushery. You're basically just a high-functioning alcoholic, aren't you?"

Liz laughed. "Define *high-functioning*."

Dave sat down by Liz and she said quietly, "How was your Christmas, then, Bish? Romance still going well?"

Dave sighed and his eyes softened. He rested his chin on his hand. "It was Perfect. Cottage in the countryside, frosty walks, roaring fires, the lot."

Reluctant to draw attention to his liaison, Dave changed both the subject and his expression and spoke more loudly now. "Anyway, Liz, Belle's just coming over. She's just been telling me about this blog she's been reading over the holidays. Bog Blog ring any bells?" he said.

"Uh-oh," said Liz. "Some of it's about her!"

"This could be interesting," said Lucy.

Belle pattered into the staffroom with a steaming coffee in a cardboard cup and her own new hair style, which, perched on top of her head, gave her the appearance of a miniature cottage loaf. She took a dainty sip. "Happy New Year?" she announced to the room. "Like the bun?"

Indifferent to Belle's coiffure and keen to instigate some fun, Lucy acknowledged the question, but immediately took the bull by the horns. "Happy New Year. Love it. Dave says you've been telling him about a new blog."

Liz tried to look innocent.

"Ooh, yes," Belle replied. "Someone at uni. told me about it. Bog Blog. Hang on; I'll find it for you?" She tapped her phone a few times and chuckled. Liz was puzzled. Why was she so chirpy about it?

"I've read it." Lucy said. "It's a blog, but written as if it's a bog. The way it's described, it could almost be our loo, couldn't it?"

Liz's eyes widened as she tried to make them bore into Lucy's, but Lucy, enjoying the fun, just winked.

"Don't be silly!" snorted Belle. "As if it'd be this one." She chuckled and shook her head.

Liz did not relax just yet, though; she could do without being added to Belle's list of disgruntlements and being reported to her university tutor. However, she was thankful that Belle, so often sensitive to imagined injustices committed against her, was equally often impervious regarding actual ones. This combination of high self-belief and low self-awareness also enabled her to expunge her more blameworthy actions from her memory completely. It was this quality that saved Liz from exposure as the lavatorial scandalmonger.

"Listen to this entry," Belle said cheerfully and read. "'*Exits and Entrances: Engaged or Vacant?' by Lulu Rolls*. That's the blogger's fake name?"

"Good name, isn't it, Liz?" Lucy said pointedly.

Liz stayed quiet. Instead, she waited for Belle to carry on reading, which she did, revelling in her position at the centre of their positive attention for once.

"*Ladies and gentlemen, you've spent your penny; now please take your seat. All the world's a stage, or at least a stall. And all the men and women have their exits and their entrances, to paraphrase a fellow commentator on the human condition—*that's Shakespeare?" Belle interjected before continuing: "*In my tiny theatre, where there is only one seat—and it's flush rather than plush—an exit usually occurs before an entrance is made—*"

"Ooh, Lulu does love a pun, doesn't she, Liz?" Serena teased, knowingly. A frown from Belle saved Liz from having to respond.

"Listen; it's getting to the good bit," Belle said. "*However, today was different. Today, I hosted my first romance, or was it simply erotica: a peep show, 'sans eyes' to watch it? Today, the lover didn't vacate the stage before his mistress made her entrance (or did he make his?) and soon they were engaged, 'quick and sudden' with 'strange oaths' and 'sighing like furnaces'.*"

Belle paused again to explain. "So, it's all to do with 'All the World's a Stage'. Do you remember, Liz? I did a lesson with this speech. The year sevens had to make up their own poems about the seven stages of life, except not with toilets."

Liz nodded, laughing. It was where she had got the idea for her take on Belle's extra-curricular shenanigans. "Keep going," she urged, confident, now, that Belle had not made the connection.

Belle returned to the account, unaware that her afternoon triste, a couple of months previously, had been its subject. When she approached the end, she giggled. "It's quite rude," she explained before resuming. "*The final act was awash with 'mouth', 'cannon', 'pouch' and 'youthful hose' until... 'mere oblivion'.*

Liz became audacious: "Is that the end?" she said, knowing full well it wasn't.

Belle scrolled down and finished: "*As you like it? I think* they *did. But this show wasn't about bums on seats and something tells me they won't be lifting the lid on this one. Until next you pay a visit, bog people.*"

With faultless timing, the bell sounded for registration. Liz drained her coffee cup and heaved a sigh. "*Once more into the breach.* Come on, Belle, Let's go and register the form. Can you believe that sort of thing really happens?"

Belle reddened, remembering Liz's comments just before half term, now. "I'll be there in a minute," she said. "I just need to nip to the loo?"

When she got to the top of the stairs, Liz bumped into a student from Gareth's last year thirteen form she had not seen for a while. "Hi, Ben," she said, "what are you doing back here? I thought you finished ages ago."

Ben grinned. "I did, but I needed to come back and retake French and German to get onto the uni course I wanted," he explained. "I've been on an exchange placement since the September before last."

Some more of Gareth's sixth form tutor group joined them, waiting to go into registration with Ben and, while they were talking, Belle appeared, trotting up the stairs to catch up with Liz. The others nudged each other and whispered, looking at Ben. Noticing Belle with an expression of surprise, Ben stopped and smiled. Noticing Ben, Belle froze and gasped.

"Hi, Belle," he said, "I didn't know you came to this school. Good New Year's, wasn't it?" He blushed before continuing. "You never gave me your number, though."

Liz cut in. "Ben, this is Miss Jobson. She's a trainee teacher."

Behind them, Ben's companions unsuccessfully tried to stifle their laughter.

"Hi," Belle managed and rushed past them, to the form room.

"The *bell* was definitely banging away on top of Big Ben on New Year's Eve this year, wasn't it, Ben?" his friends teased as he joined them, stunned but even prouder of recent achievements than he had been hitherto.

Liz went into her classroom and Belle busied herself with taking the register, signing students' planners and avoiding Liz's eye.

Alfie arrived with Maisie, as usual. "Morning Miss," they said in unison, "did you have a good Christmas?"

"Morning, captains," she replied. "Lovely, thanks. Did you get anything nice?"

Alfie beamed. "Mum got me the whole set of *Harry Potter*s," he said, excitedly. "I've read them before, but now I've got my own, I can read them again." He delved into his PE bag and brought out a pair of football boots. "And she got me these," he said.

Emin had just come in. "Umbros?" he sneered, "I got Adidas Aces. They're well expensive. And I got an X Box 360." His derision went unrecognised, though; Alfie just answered, "Wow! Nice boots. Lucky you," before the boys went and sat down.

Maisie lingered by Liz's desk and lowered her voice, commenting, "At least Alfie's mum paid for his presents. I reckon Emin's mum and dad'll still be paying for his *next* Christmas."

Liz looked over at Belle, who was studiously avoiding her eye. She knew she would have to have another conversation with Peggy later, although, this time, Liz sympathised. Ben and Belle were both adults and Belle's only transgression was in not having the common sense to find out where the sixth formers did their socialising and avoid casting her net there—and she would definitely have to throw this one back.

After her form had left for their lessons, Liz broached the subject with Belle. "We'll have to let Peggy know," she said.

Belle's reaction was a fusion of mortification, terror and defiance. "Why do we have to tell her? I haven't done anything wrong," she whimpered. "How was I to know he was a student here?"

Liz commiserated. "You're right, but we also need to think about protecting you," she said. "At best, this could be embarrassing and, at worst it could ruin your career before it's even started."

Subdued, Belle scuttled out of the room and down to the staffroom to prepare her lessons and lick her wounds. Something told Liz Belle was not going to log this one in her special notebook. Talk about shitting on your own doorstep.

24: Leaders' Wives

Later, at the first whole-staff meeting of the new year, Gordon bent over his laptop, prodding and prepping, while the projector whirred into life and a slide appeared, bearing an animation of ping-pong balls flying towards a row of cups. It was juxtaposed with a stock illustration—in a completely different style—which depicted cartoon colleagues, high-fiving each other and grinning. At the top of the slide, a speech bubble with the words, *New Year, New Friends*, sprang from the face of Gordon's signature ray-gun waving superhero picture.

Liz curled her lip. "We're never going to call you *Flash*," she muttered, shaking her head.

From somewhere over the other side of the hall, where the mathematicians and scientists sat, her cynicism was corroborated by a loud uttering of the phallic nickname, thinly disguised as a cough. Dave snirtled audibly and Gordon jerked his head up—half a second too late—and glared in their direction.

On discovering nothing amiss, however, Gordon gilded his face with a smile and stood up, rubbing his hands together in what he clearly imagined looked like an avuncular gesture. He explained that they were going to play an ice-breaking game which he had learnt over the Christmas holidays. It involved pairing up and one of the pair guiding his or her blindfolded partner to blow a ping-pong ball into a polystyrene cup. It was supposed to motivate them or strengthen their relationships—or something.

"Where did he go for Christmas? Bangkok?" Dave asked as a ping-pong ball hit him just below his blindfolded left eye.

The hall was soon filled with gentle clicks and taps, as balls hit and missed their targets, and miniature drum-rolls as they half-rolled, half-bounced along table-tops. Meanwhile, there was, indeed, a mood of relaxed bonding between colleagues who had found their competitive sides, despite their initial scepticism and continuing confusion as to the point of the exercise.

That point was made no clearer when everyone settled back into their seats and Gordon switched to the next slide on his projector. Smiling photographs of the leadership team appeared (Chris Moran having been typographically rechristened *Chris Morgan*) alongside the heads of year (including one who had left the previous July) and even last year's head of special needs (would Liz *ever* be allowed to forget Pam Hooper and her bloody report?). Gordon's own picture was at the top. Its caption read *Gordon F. Dillon*.

"Wonder what the *F*'s for," said Dave.

Lucy immediately offered *Fred*; Gareth came in with *Fabian*, and Serena, insightful as ever, proposed *Flash*.

Liz waited for their chuckles to subside. "Fucking?"

The others looked blank, so Liz put her suggestion into context for them: "Oh shit, here comes Gordon Fucking Dillon. What a tit."

When the voices had died down, Gordon began to talk about his New Year's resolutions and his desire for a school that was worthy of its students and their aspirations. He also referred to a survey that had been sent to the students and their parents at the end of last term, unbeknown to most members of staff, who looked around at each other, frowning and confused.

"It is vital to know what our kids think about the direction in which their school is heading in," he said.

The whole row of English teachers winced and, even though only able to see Chris's back (seated, as he was, on the front row), they all felt him bristle. Gordon did not notice, though, and carried on: "As education-givers, we have an ethnical obligation to our clients," he intoned.

"Not to the staff, though," whispered Dave. "Where was our survey?"

Liz shuddered. "Clients?"

"They are our perspective-takers, so we must listen to their views," Gordon continued, "so we can help simulate social mobility and opportunity."

Glyn had obviously made it his business to be aware of all the behind-the-scenes machinations and had obtained a copy of the survey results, presumably through the union. He raised a hand. Gordon turned a stony stare towards him, seated just in front of Serena, which he struggled to conceal with an air of cordial approachability. "Yes, Glyn?"

"You asked them whether they would prefer—and I quote—*the current old-fashioned pastoral care system, run by heads of year, which does not meet the needs of today's student or a modern, success-focused system, proven to effectively facsimilate student achievement*."

Gordon looked smug. "That's right."

"Facsimilate?" mouthed Liz.

"And even though the question was designed to lead them to give the answer you wanted, a good forty-five per cent still preferred the 'old-fashioned' system," Glyn said. "Is that right?"

The smug smile started to slide. "Well, yes, there's always a core of disinfected students, obviously."

A collective rasp of hastily smothered laughter followed and Gordon, flustered, seemed unaware of the specificity of his mistakes, while vaguely aware that he had undermined himself in some way. Chris shook his head, pained yet resigned.

Next, Gordon introduced his new idea, the 'Climate of Cultivation', which he fleshed out by recasting the school as a garden, talking about crop rotation, nursery beds and pruning. In this scenario, he was the head gardener, both nurturing and ruthless in equal but necessary measure. To ensure his garden continued to flourish and produce crops, he might need to rely less upon traditional, organic methods and initiate a fresh approach to gardening, one which would cost less, but yield more and would work alongside some established practices, but replace others all together.

Liz smirked, distracted from the magnitude of the message by the idiocy of its metaphorical communication. "What's he on about? He's talking gibberish," she whispered.

Serena was not laughing. "Redundancies," she mouthed.

"What?" Liz's shock was more than just a whisper and once again, Gordon's glance shot in their direction, just missing its mark once more.

Serena waited for him to return to his spiel before muttering, "Glyn just told me, the heads of year and some of the teaching assistants are for the chop and we're not going to have any new teachers or student teachers next year."

The extension of metaphors continued apace and Gordon began to talk about the pain involved in removing a dying branch from a tree, rather than propping it up, so that the rest of the tree would not be infected. His moral responsibility was to the tree, apparently. He paused to display some helpful comparison tables and illustrations.

As Gordon explained the images on the screen, Liz looked around, hoping to gauge the reactions of her colleagues. Barbara, head of year seven and linchpin of the current pastoral care system, had obviously unpicked the metaphor well enough. Like a dying branch, she bowed her head and a tear dripped from the end of her nose onto her formidable bosom. The other heads of year had a variety of reactions, ranging from incomprehension to fury, despite their *ethnical obligation* or their *moral responsibility*, and seemed not to be listening as the head went on to assure them that, as prunings and dead wood, they would be made use of if they wanted to be. Every part of the garden was valued.

"Are we the trees or the branches?" Liz whispered, genuinely worried.

"Fuck knows," answered Dave, covered by the rising hum of voices.

Serena explained in a whisper that was disguised by the general hubbub: "The heads of year are the dead branches. He's planting a new sapling next to the tree now, listen. They don't need as much water—i.e. money."

He outlined the way he had found a tiny seedling growing in a shady corner of another, neglected, garden. He had lovingly potted it up and grown it on, ready to replant it here at King Richard's, where it would give generously *to* the whole ecosystem while not taking much *from* it.

"That sapling is married to myself," announced Gordon, dendrophilically, his grammar eliciting another departmental intake of breath.

Gordon took the rapid swell of muttered conversation to be a measure of their excited anticipation and he was smiling and rubbing his hands together again, now.

Liz leaned towards Dave again. "He'll never get the blood off them!" she said, less quietly than she had intended.

Gordon's eyes flicked, unnoticed, to Liz. She was not anticipating the conversation to wane even more suddenly than it had waxed and the abrupt return to silence coincided with her slightly-too-loud follow-up: "Cue Lady Macbeth."

The gasp that rushed through the hall was the perfect sound effect for the whip-pan swivel of Gordon's head as it twisted towards Liz and she was impaled on the cold, steel blade of exposure.

Gordon kept his eyes on Liz's for a few excruciating seconds while he addressed his next suggestion to the whole room: "Anyone unhappy with decisions I make about personnel is welcome to discuss them, in my office, after this meeting."

Mortified—petrified, Liz dropped her gaze in a tactical admission of defeat. Years of cheerfully and cynically passing under the radar and never raising her head above the parapet had been sliced away in one fell swoop.

Dave squeezed her arm, sympathetic. "Fucking Hell, Liz, that's your card marked."

Gordon returned to his introduction, bruised, but undefeated. "Yvonne Dillon is spreadeagling a new King Richard's system and here she is to explain her pioneering role."

He turned the lectern towards the door and raised his hands as if to invoke applause. However, no other hands rose to join in and the room was soundless, save for the uncomfortable creaking of a hundred people shifting in their seats.

As Yvonne stepped towards the lectern, the silence within the room seemed only to intensify. The telephone in reception rang. A motorist outside changed gear. The projector hummed. She had obviously achieved her ambition and stood in front of them. However, far from being triumphant, she seemed smaller than Liz remembered; her face was red and, when she spoke, her voice shook.

"I want to—to thank you for welcoming me into King Richard's," she barely managed to utter. All around the hall, the staff looked down, to the side, at their planners: anywhere but at Yvonne—or Gordon.

Liz almost felt sorry for her until she reminded herself that, just like in *Macbeth*, Yvonne might look like an innocent flower, but she could still be the serpent under it. Yvonne mustered her strength as she spoke: "Yes, this is the opportunity I've been hoping to be granted," she said, "and I hope we can work together to enable this school to fulfil its ethical obligations to the children."

The emphasis she placed on the second part of her sentence was accompanied by a straightening of the back and a raising of the chin that gave her the appearance of a cobra, about to strike. Her initial hope now seemed like a threat. The serpent had ventured out, cautiously at first, and then had crushed the innocent flower under its ground-crawling, reptilian belly: "Of course, if that is not possible, then—to continue Gordon's metaphor—we can always consider replanting surplus plants in other gardens. We must have pride in our garden. Our Eden."

Many of them were frozen now, their faces expressionless under the potential scrutiny of twice as many Dillons, as they waited for the Fall.

Yvonne continued. "My role will be pastoral and will focus on the wellness of the children, both physical and mental, and to this end, I will liaise with social services and the educational welfare officer as well as improving attendance and safeguarding procedures."

Liz risked a furtive glance at Barbara, whose shoulders softly quivered. These were all jobs that Barbara and the other heads of year had been performing admirably up until now, but, to Gordon, presumably, the financial benefit of downgrading five heads of year and allotting the pastoral aspects of their jobs to his wife must have been too attractive to overlook.

At the end of her speech, Yvonne assured them that, "King Richard's deserves this. King Richard's deserves me." Maybe it did.

25: Ropy

That night, Liz's sleep was populated by a succession of black-cloaked shadows, which slashed their demented way through her nightmares, discharging torrents of incomprehensible jargon from gaping mouths while their heads span like Linda Blair's in *The Exorcist* and their eyes lanced through her skull like lasers, extracting her every thought before plotting their diabolical revenge.

She woke, clammy and shaking with the phrases, *education-giver* and *perspective-taker* still reverberating around her skull. It was well before dawn, and anxiety stove off sleep for the two hours before her alarm went off: two hours during which she rehearsed what she might say to Gordon if he brought up her Lady Macbeth gaffe of the previous day:

"Dave asked me to find a suitable excerpt for the year ten Shakespeare assessment."

Plausible...ish.

"Peggy asked me about the Iconic Women project."

Less likely.

"Serena asked me about my costume for World Book Day."

But nothing seemed credible. She would just have to avoid Gordon for the rest of her life.

When she got into school, Liz went the long way round to the English staffroom, thus managing to avoid walking past Gordon's office, which was near the entrance of the main school building. She briefed Dave on the *Macbeth* assessment story she had plumped for as an excuse and they sat down with coffees.

"Don't worry," Dave reassured her; "just keep your head down for a bit. It'll soon blow over."

Liz smiled wanly. "Thanks, Bish," she said and sighed before hoisting herself to her feet, giddily.

Dave looked at her with more concern now. "Seriously, are you okay?" he asked, "'Cause you look fucking terrible."

"Yeah, I'm fine," Liz replied. "I just feel a bit light-headed; I didn't get much sleep last night."

"Well, don't do any exciting lessons today," he said.

Liz chuckled. "Way ahead of you."

"I'm serious," Dave pressed, "and if you start to feel worse, go home."

Liz dragged herself up the stairs to her classroom, wondering whether minor hypertension was grounds for early retirement.

Her form arrived on the bell and they were still in such a state of mild hysteria, even a few days after the Christmas holidays that her unease was soon subsumed into their juvenile concerns. Belle had more adult concerns in that she had heard about Gordon's decision to streamline the staff.

"I suppose that means there's no chance of being kept on here, doesn't it?" she said.

Chary of kicking a pug when she was down, Liz did not, therefore, enlighten her as to Dave's low opinion of her. Instead she just said, "It does look that way. We're all at risk, though, and you're in a good position to find something else because you're cheap and you can go for anything that comes up after the May deadline."

"What's that?" Belle asked.

"Well," Liz replied, "when you're in work, you have to hand in your notice, preferably by Easter—May at the latest—if you want to start a new job in September, otherwise you have to wait till the following term. That's why you're in a good position; you can go for anything that comes up after that—and there are usually loads."

Belle seemed heartened by this and, with characteristic resilience, readjusted her plans. "Well, I suppose it opens up lots more possibilities for me."

Liz and Belle registered the year sevens and sent them on their chattering way so she could get ready for her first lesson: year eleven. They were going to be going over the mock exam papers that Liz had spent a large proportion of the Christmas holidays marking and every student had corrections to make, improvements to add and individually tailored tasks designed to address their particular areas for improvement and, with Dave's instruction in mind, she decided that it was about time they did this independently.

A smiling face appeared round the door. "All right, Miss? Remember me?"

"Laylah! How are you?" Liz hadn't recognised her from last year's nightmare year nine, at first; she seemed so calm and civilised.

"I'm doing good," she replied. "I'm doing Functional Skills instead of GCSEs, so I'm mostly in the Learning Support Room."

"Well, you look like you're enjoying it," said Liz.

"Yeah, we've got a new teacher now Miss Hooper's left. She's really nice, so I'm good now."

Liz shuddered at the mention of Pam Hooper and her lesson report. Laylah wasn't the only one glad to see the back of her.

Laylah carried on. "Guess what; I can still spell *Macbeth*, though. See ya," and off she went.

Macbeth. Liz shuddered, remembering her faux pas and wondering when Gordon's retribution would be meted out.

The students arrived, some still groggy and yawning, and took their seats.

"Have you marked our exams, Miss?" Becky asked as she came in.

"Morning to you too," said Liz, "and yes, I have, actually."

"That was quick," said Dan, "for you!"

Liz laughed. "It was the highlight of my Christmas, doing those." She picked up the scruffy sheaf of papers and started to weave in and out of the desks, stepping over bags here and round PE kits there, giving the scrawl-covered pages back to their owners.

"What's this, Miss?" called Tom from the back, holding up a page with something dark brown and sticky-looking clinging to it.

Liz went over and scrutinised it.

"Careful, Miss," Tom warned, "it looks pretty dodgy!"

Liz prodded it, evoking a collective groan of disgust from the class. She sniffed it and provoked a louder wail. "Mince pie," she said, turning the wail to laughter. "Well, I had to keep my strength up."

"What about this then?" Joe held up one of his pages, grinning. It bore a tell-tale purple ring, the same size as the foot of a wine glass.

Liz smirked. "Thirsty work, marking."

"What's it worth for me not to show Dildo?" Joe teased.

Liz winced at the memory of yesterday's indiscretion in the meeting. The flinch was, nevertheless, noticed by Joe. "I wouldn't really show him, Miss. Anyway, our marks are better when you've had a drink!"

The class settled into a leisurely lesson of chatting while they read (or tried to read) Liz's barely decipherable comments, actioned their corrections and reluctantly completed additional tasks as directed. Liz circulated, chivvying and explaining. It was a routine they all knew well and the atmosphere in the room was more cheerful than challenging, the progress more incremental than incredible.

Sitting with Dan, absorbed in translating, for him, a particularly illegible green ink scribble, Liz suddenly felt a horripilant prickle at the back of her neck as the hairs on it stood up—even *before* the students fell quiet—at which, Dan nudged her and hissed, "Dildo and Magoo."

She jerked her head towards the door; the head and his acolyte, Colin McGee, were standing in the doorway. Gordon's reprisal was clearly being dispensed with remarkable alacrity.

What the fuck do they want? Liz thought. "Hello. Come in," she said.

"Hnnh," Colin managed to utter and he shuffled in, blinking and wrinkling his nose to push his bottle-end glasses up its bridge, towards his pale, lashless eyes. He had probably been dying to spy on her ever since the 'Learning From the Master' training and made his way towards the back of the room where he began leafing through other students' exercise books. Gordon, on the other hand, plastered his face with a stony smile and rubbed his hands together slowly, deliberately. "Morning, Mrs Marshall. Learning walk," he said icily.

Liz tried to cover her look of dismay. She had forgotten about those. They sounded so beneficial, pleasant even. A member of the senior management team popping in—gentle exercise for both the mind and the body—so, why did she feel like an Eastern Bloc dissident cornered by the Stasi? She knew that a learning walk was supposed to mean that they could simply ensure that learning was occurring within the classroom, but, given the timing, this seemed more like intelligence-gathering, dirt-digging, ammunition-stockpiling.

Gordon glanced at the board. Thank God she had bothered to write a learning objective on it: *to understand how to improve by reflecting on exam performance.* She looked over to where Colin was talking, in a whisper, to a group of students, and tried to gauge his opinion. He was holding Tom's mince-pie blighted exam paper, shaking his head and writing. As long as he did not pick Joe's up, she would be fine. As usual, Joe read her mind and surreptitiously slipped the paper under his exercise book—not surreptitiously enough, though. Colin leaned over, whispered something to Joe and eased the paper out from under Joe's exercise book. He put it back down, sighed and wrote something in his notebook.

Liz turned her attention back to Gordon, who was leafing through her seating plans.

"Can I see your development plan for this class?" he said.

Liz swallowed. She had not updated it yet, this being only the second day of the new term—just one day after the student data had been revised and renewed. "Um, I haven't had a chance to do a new one yet," she admitted, reddening. "Sorry."

Gordon's smile disappeared and he glanced at Colin, who scribbled something else in his notebook. Then, he looked into her eyes without speaking: a classic technique for allowing people to fill the silent space with words, to condemn themselves from their own mouths. Liz tried to make light of it, adding brightly, "That's not very good, is it?"

"No," he said and turned away.

Liz continued her attempts to stay afloat and dredged up a reference to Gordon's 'Learning from the Master' training. "I've been putting your training into practice," she said. "Er, building a safe environment and a relationship with the students. It's been working really well."

Distracted by the flattery, Gordon looked more interested. "Go on," he pressed.

"Yes, I was really impressed by what you said about trusting the teacher being the—um—cornerstone of learning."

Some of the students had overheard and backed Liz up, smiling, nodding and looking as trusting and learned as they could.

Gordon looked around at them. "Well, good. It's something to build on, anyway."

He beckoned Colin with a jerk of his head. "Do you have any questions for Mrs Marshall, Mr McGee?"

Colin sniffed and blinked. "Fngh. Why have their books not been marked since the beginning of December?"

Liz's colour deepened as she panicked momentarily before remembering herself and reinstalling her backbone. "I marked their mock exams over Christmas," she said steadily; "that's what they've been reviewing today."

"Mmvnh. School policy dictates—"

Liz, less steady now, interrupted him. "School policy dictates each book should be marked every half term and I've done that."

Colin scoffed, cast his eyes down and started to rifle through a folder. Liz continued, "There are twenty-eight students in this class. Each of them sat two papers. An English paper takes at least half an hour to mark."

Gordon watched the exchange impassively. Colin blinked and humphed. Liz continued; she was so far above the radar, now, that she might as well stick up for herself. "It's different for English. With adding up the marks and converting them to grades, that's nearly four days' work. How long did your maths exams take to mark?"

Colin hnnhed, gulped and then stayed quiet. Even he couldn't argue with that. He turned to Gordon and raised acquiescent eyebrows.

"Thank you, Mrs Marshall, we won't take up any more of your time," said Gordon and they left.

The class held its breath for a few seconds to allow the interlopers time to be out of earshot and then erupted all at once with long suppressed giggles and shrieks.

"Go, Miss!" said Ellie.

"Are they checking up on you, Miss?" asked Dan.

"Sorry about wine-stain-gate," added Joe.

Liz sighed with relief. It could have been much worse and she could not help feeling she might just about have dodged a bullet.

After school, Dave came up to her room and sat down opposite her desk. "Dildo and Magoo came to see me after their *learning walk*." He accompanied his acerbic tone with equally acerbic crooked fingers.

"Right," said Liz. "Is that a good sign or a bad sign? What did they say?"

Dave paused, swallowed and sighed. "You're not going to like it."

Hollow nausea punched Liz in the stomach.

"Gordon said it was—" he paused again "—ropy."

"Ropy?" said Liz, plummeting into her seat. "What the fuck does that mean?"

"Fuck knows," said Dave. "He wouldn't say specifically, but he said Magoo's got to come into your year eleven class to *support* you in your *areas for development*." The ironically crooked fingers, again, underlined Dave's attitude. "I asked him whether it was anything to do with what you said at the meeting yesterday and I told him about the Macbeth assessment," he added.

"Did he believe you?" Liz asked hopefully.

Dave looked dubious. "Well, he accepted it, but I'm not sure he was convinced."

Liz put her head in her hands. "This bloody job," she groaned. "Why do we put ourselves through it?"

Dave shook his head sadly. Liz's self-belief was fragile, especially after the last day of last year. "You did get Woodfield to get rid of Pam's report last summer, didn't you?"

"Oh yes, don't worry. Fair play to him; he was as outraged as I was," Dave said. "Gordon never saw it."

"Oh well, that's something," Liz said. "He doesn't need any more ammunition against me."

She was far from being totally reassured, though. Being thought of as someone who, after fifteen years, needed a colleague to show her how to teach was almost too much to bear and when she asked Dave, "So, when are they going to do it?" her lip trembled and her voice cracked.

"Monday." Dave dragged his chair nearer to Liz and put his arm round her shoulders. "It's not you; it's that fucker, Gordon," he said. "He's just flexing his muscles—showing you who's boss."

Liz sniffed. "Thanks, Dave," she said, "Why did I open my big mouth yesterday? Bet I'm top of his redundancy list now."

26: Magoo

The rest of the week went by at a pitiless pace and Liz had a feeling of disconnection, watching each lesson—each day—recede the way a train passenger watches the passing landscape: as a blurred streak of scenery through a steamed-up window. She tried to tell herself that Colin McGee's lesson observation had genuinely been organised, as Gordon had told Dave, in a spirit of collegial support, not ordered, as she suspected, in a show of autocratic castigation. However, what could not be cured had to be endured and, having so publicly alluded to the Dillons' vaulting ambition, Liz realised she would just have to accept her punishment and hope that Gordon had not quite understood the exact nature of her unintended heckle. If that was the case, this observation might be the snuffer of the brief candle of her ignominy.

Might be.

Sunday dwindled, Monday came around and all too soon, the metaphorical train had slowed, delivering her to her doom. It was nearly the end of break and Liz sighed, hauling herself to her unwilling feet. Her observation was next and her blood seemed to be rushing more forcibly through the labyrinth of her circulatory system. She just needed to grab her work sheets from the photocopier and get to the classroom before Colin arrived. When she got to it, the photocopier was beeping malevolently, lights flashing on its control panel.

Panic thudding in her chest, Liz jabbed at its buttons and the beeping stopped, but still nothing emerged from its depths. A mechanical creak emanated from the bowels of the beast and its black mouth stretched in a silent scream. Its stomach groaned and rumbled and it vomited forth a litter of crumpled white pages.

None of them was hers. She would have to run upstairs and resend the document to a different printer, but time was running out; the class and Colin would be there in a couple of minutes.

Liz's gut plummeted as the bell went for the end of break: the knell that summoned her to Heaven or to Hell. She wrenched the office door open and dashed towards the stairs, but her way was barred by a knot of students, jostling and shrieking and thrusting pieces of paper towards her: forms to sign, permission slips to read, homework to collect. Their numbers multiplied and the stairs grew more and more out of reach as the students crowded round her, shoving and calling in slow motion, guileless and deadly as a herd of cows.

Five minutes late. Liz knew her class would have arrived before her and dreaded to imagine what havoc they might be wreaking. She struggled through the lumpen horde, making it to the bottom of the stairs just in time to see Colin's running feet disappear from the top, round to the second flight. Thumping-hearted and painfully aware of the pandemoniac thuds and screeches coming from her room, Liz swung round the metal newel post and launched herself up the stairs two at a time. She still had a chance of arriving at the same time as her feared assessor, even if she could not get there before him.

The stairs, however, had other ideas; as she looked up to check her progress, they lengthened and proliferated to become countless flights leading to innumerable floors and her room was at the top, wherever that was. She struggled on, breathless, clinging to the handrail and clawing at the walls, always a flight behind the now jack-booted feet of Colin McGee, until she could carry on no more and sank onto a step, defeated, deflated, done for.

From far away, the beeping of the photocopier mocked her failure, growing louder and louder. Liz became aware of softness around her: blankets and a pillow. That beeping must be a monitor. She must be in hospital. The stress must have been too much for her hypertensive body. She would probably get the rest of the year off; strokes were a serious matter. Or had it been a heart attack? She wondered sleepily whether they had got the air ambulance for her, but even as she was wondering, she began to recognise her own bed and the sound of her alarm. Disappointed at her good health, she turned off, not her life-support, but her alarm.

God, she'd have to go through all that again in a couple of hours.

As it happened, there were no such disasters and when the lesson started, Liz was prepared, PowerPoint displayed, worksheets and books ready on the desks before Colin arrived, which he did, just before the students.

"Ngh," he said as he shuffled in, blinking through his bottle-end glasses. "Where shall I sit?"

Liz handed him the required sheaf of papers—lesson plan, work sheets, seating plan, student data sheets, individual education plans and class improvement plans—and indicated a spare chair at the back of the room. He sat down and began leafing through the papers, squinting up towards Liz as she straightened papers on her desk and tried to stay calm.

The bell rang—for real this time—and Liz's year elevens trickled in, chattering noisily and greeting her as they took their places. One or two looked startled and nudged each other as they noticed 'Magoo' sitting at the back. Becky, nearest to him, grimaced at Liz and opened her book, soon cheering up. "Yay, a house point! Thanks, Miss."

Colin sniffed loudly and scribbled something on his clipboard.

Joe was last to arrive. "Sorry I'm a bit late, Miss," he said. "I've just had my Spanish oral."

Liz looked up from her plan. "Have you?" she replied. "How did it go?"

"Okay, I think," Joe said, taking his seat and opening his book. "I made a couple of mistakes, though."

"I'm sure you'll be fine," said Liz. "Let me know when you get the result."

Taking the register, Liz was aware of Colin's pen, scraping disapprovingly against the page clipped to his board, and the light flashing as it caught the lenses of his glasses every time he moved his head. She fought to regulate her breathing and her hand trembled as she reached for the electronic whiteboard's remote control and pressed the button.

The learning objective came into view: *to evaluate how the features of conversation are represented in a transcript*. The students duly wrote it down, sensitively concealing their surprise at the unexpected formality of their lesson, sensitive also to the continual scrutiny of Colin as his puckered little eyes darted from one to the other of them, searching, it seemed, for evidence of Liz's inadequacy. The first task was to match up the key terms they would be using with their definitions: an accepted way to recap the previous lesson's learning and prepare for this one's.

Colin stooped to his feet and shuffled around, snuffing and grunting at the students and rifling through freshly marked books before the next part of the lesson, in which Liz wanted the students to analyse a transcript.

"Before we start," she said, "What are the two most important things to remember about a transcript?"

Unusually orderly and well-behaved, a few students' hands went up: a change from the usual casually called-out contributions. Keen to get a correct answer, Liz scythed the forest of arms with a sweep of her own and selected Ellie.

"It's written down *after* the conversation has already happened."

"Well done, Ellie," smiled Liz. "Tom, you had your hand up before. Do you know the other thing?"

Tom, ever reliable, replied, "There's no punctuation, apart from dots in brackets for pauses, so you have to try and work out things like their tone and where sentences end and stuff like that."

At the back of the room, Colin had sat back down and his long, yellow fingernails scrabbled against the paper as he scribbled and scraped his notes and quietly 'hnnf'-ed.

"Yes, that's right, Tom," Liz said and displayed the slide that confirmed this information. "Now, you have ten minutes to work together to annotate this extract from a transcript," she instructed. "Label it with the key terms you matched earlier and later we'll explore what it tell us about the speakers." She paused, sure she had forgotten something. Colin's lenses flashed again in the harsh morning light. He wrinkled his nose and a small smile twitched around his thin lips as he wrote—something unflattering, Liz presumed. However, his premature celebration had lowered his guard and given Liz the reminder she needed: "Any questions before you start?" she remembered to ask, careful to keep the relief from her voice.

Colin 'ffn'-ed, hastily erased the note he had just written and squinted at the worksheet, replacing the earlier expression of triumph with one of bafflement that only deepened as the students completed the task and Liz circulated amongst them, silently congratulating herself on her adequacy, as Colin gave up and left his chair in order to scrutinise the displays.

He stared portentously at an empty board. Shit. Liz had lent Dave the posters she had made (that outlined each GCSE assessment criterion) for his observation with the head. They gave colour coded examples of how students could take writing from one grade up to the next and had been picked out as an example of outstanding practice when Dave had had his formal observation a couple of weeks previously. That would have been an extra tick in her favour, but she could not change that now. At least she knew the lesson was sound. It had a proven track record, being based on the one recommended by the exam board. Liz had improved it by creating more eye-catching worksheets and a PowerPoint as well as building in direct relevance to this particular class. Not only that, but Liz had already passed the lesson on to a teacher friend in another school, who had taught it for an observation lesson and received a rating of *outstanding*, so she did not worry unduly when Colin slunk back to his seat, squinted and 'nng'-ed before scratching down his little notes.

The students did her proud and adorned their transcripts with colour-coded annotations which, later, they converted into sample essay paragraphs, each fulfilling the demands of the criteria they were to be assessed by. When the lesson came to an end and Colin shuffled away to write up his report, Liz breathed a sigh of relief; it had gone as well as she could have hoped and all she had to think about now was the minor inconvenience of the feedback after school.

Liz approached Colin's office on her way out of school at the end of the day. She took the flaccid utterance that responded to her knock as an invitation to enter, went in almost gladly and sat in the chair indicated by Colin's yellowing claw.

"Nnnh, how do *you* think that went?" Colin said without looking up. The clichéd opening gambit, misguidedly believed to demonstrate tact and sensitivity on the part of the assessor, jerked the rug of Liz's complacency from under her feet. The question only ever ushered in criticism.

Liz regained her balance just well enough to avoid humiliation by pretending she was not too pleased with the way the lesson had gone: "Erm, well, not bad," she faltered, "but I think they were a bit subdued. Maybe having someone watching put them off a bit," she added, "and it was challenging work."

Colin clenched his glasses with his eyes again. "Yes," he agreed, "The tasks were sufficiently challenging, but they weren't working as hard as they might have been," he asserted, "so I can't rate the lesson *good*."

Liz was uncomprehending. "But they all achieved the objectives I set and you agreed that they were challenging, so they must have been working hard enough."

"Yes."

"So, you'll change your rating, then?"

"No."

Colin now attacked from a new angle: "I wondered why you didn't—ghh—use the methods stipulated in Gordon's 'Learning From the Master' sessions."

Liz was floored; she'd forgotten all about those. "I—I tried to use some of them."

"Have you even read—fnh—Rhys Owen's book on independent learning?" Colin pressed. "Where was the consultation phase of the lesson?"

"I planned the lesson around what the board suggested," Liz said, "and they're the ones who set and mark the exams. There wouldn't have been time for a consultation phase." She trawled through her memory of the training session. "Anyway, doesn't the idea of a consultation phase contradict Gordon's idea that teacher-talk should be kept to a minimum? I got them active straight away and enabled them to learn independently. Those were methods Gordon wanted us to use too."

Colin was obviously not in the mood to deviate from the path that had, presumably, been decreed by Gordon. He ignored her responses and continued: "It's—erm—just that you seemed—ngh—less than receptive to the methods in the training session, if I remember correctly."

Liz sighed and wondered how long Gordon's reprisal would go on. If only she had kept her mouth shut at that meeting and not tried to be clever. Colin's fingernail scraped down the form in front of him until he came to the next item. The displays. As Liz had predicted, he found fault with the empty display board. Liz took that one on the chin; it was unfortunate, but she could not change the fact that Colin had not seen the display and, therefore, could not tick a box to say he had.

The next criticism was baffling. Colin asked her about the piece of writing she had given the students to analyse.

"Where did you get this extract? I didn't understand it."

Liz was not sure what he was getting at. "Well, it's the transcript provided by the exam board to prepare them for the assessment," she said.

"It was so strange," Colin pressed. "Hnngh...you could have given them something easier to analyse."

"Well, it had to be a transcript and the board recommends that one."

"Yes, but—mmh—an extract from a novel would have been better," Colin continued.

"But that's not a transcript. It has to be real speech." Liz stuck to her guns.

"Well, some *dialogue* from a novel, then."

"Fictional dialogue isn't a transcript; it's totally different."

Colin had not grasped it, but this was of no comfort to Liz. Her earlier sense of reprieve had disappeared and been replaced by mounting horror at what this actually meant for her. She tried, tactfully, to explain why an excerpt of dialogue would not have done the job. "Remember when I recapped the two main points to remember about transcripts for the students?" she asked him. "It's actually real; it's transcribed—written down *after* the event and it's not punctuated like speech in a novel."

Colin continued to stare at his form, seemingly unable to understand what she was saying or alter his original verdict. She tried another tactic. "Did you ask the students? They all understood."

He did not respond.

"So you're not going to change whatever you've written about that either, then?" Glancing at his sheet, Liz caught sight of the neat circle pencilled around the *requires improvement* box.

Colin just 'hff'-ed gently, shook his head and prepared to hammer the next nail into her coffin. He hunched over the piece of paper on his lap again and brought up another matter: the 'inappropriate' conversation at the beginning of the lesson. Liz could not fathom what he meant, but she did not have to wonder for long. His objection was to Liz asking Joe how he had got on in his Spanish oral exam.

"What was I supposed to do? Ignore him?" Liz was incensed.

Colin suggested that in her place, he would have told Joe that it was inappropriate to discuss this in the lesson and told Joe to come and talk about it at break. This was too much for Liz. "And that's why your students have such a good relationship with you," she said, aware that the sarcasm would probably not find its mark. "I thought Gordon was all for the relationship with the students being the cornerstone of the effective classroom environment," she added. "That's what he said in the training."

"Gordon's—mmnh—not writing up this report," he mumbled, "I am—and I stand by my original assessment that the lesson needed improving, particularly in light of your report at the end of last year."

Sucker-punched, Liz was shocked into silence. The fight had been ripped out of her, along with her breath. How the hell had Colin found out about that? Had Mr Woodfield not shredded the sensitive documents in his office before he left? And if Colin knew, Gordon must know too.

So this was how Gordon was going to slim the English department down: besmirch her impressive reputation as a just-about-good-enough classroom practitioner and get rid of her—and all on Colin and Pam's specious recommendations. Liz dragged in a breath, got to her feet and left the office, leaving Colin squinting and saying something about mentoring and support. When she texted Dave to tell him, his knee-jerk response was simple: "Twat," followed by the more considered, "Jumped up little Caesar. Don't worry—I'll sort it out."

27: Snow Day

January wore on, but the novelty of the new school year had worn off long since and the impending exam season was too far away to generate any sense of urgency. February half term—that longed-for half-way point of the academic year—was weeks away. The bleak, midwinter view out of Liz's window had been dismal all term; gulls hunched, shivering, on the walls surrounding the playground and freezing groups of students, wrapped in prohibited colourful scarves and bobble hats huddled, like sheep in their woolly folds. The chill was bitter in the extreme and the weeks ahead, grey and monotonous.

One morning, late in the month, Liz awoke to eerie quiet. She sensed it before she knew it; instinct more than information, compelled her to find signs to confirm what she suspected. A car went past, improbably slowly, making almost no sound. The far-off call of an early worker was peculiarly without reverberation. The light was both soft and vivid—and very, very white.

"Please," she thought, "Oh please."

She put out a hand behind her and touched the curtain, hesitant to open it; while the curtains remained drawn, she still had hope, but if she opened them and there was none, she felt she would never see snow again.

She yanked the curtain back, like a child ripping off a plaster. The street outside was white; flakes the size of babies' fists tumbled, in slow motion, from the yellowish, otherworldly sky and the world shivered in its daybreak dusk.

Snow. Inches of it.

Jack was already up. "I've checked the website; school's closed," he said when she had bounded downstairs. "Full English to celebrate? There's proper coffee on too."

"This," Liz stated simply, "is the best day of my life."

Breakfast eaten, the four Marshalls dug out their wellingtons and sledge and headed for the local golf course, where the best slopes could be found. The snow was still falling heavily; the dozens of figures that converged on the sledge-friendly undulations of the links from every direction loomed, wraith-like, from the nebulous pallor as if from the hereafter. Appearances were definitely illusory, though; there was nothing ethereal about these individuals. They hadn't materialised from the other side; they were simply everyone from a radius of about a mile who had, like them, been given this gift, this bonus holiday by the auspicious precipitation. Shrieks of euphoria resounded as sledges were mounted, snowballs lobbed and angels imprinted on the ground until, at last, the chill outdid the thrill and the Marshalls trudged home, passing ten-foot snow-boulders and smiling, carrot-nosed snowmen as they went.

The next day, the snow still covered the streets, although it no longer fell, unless the wet plop of a branchful dropping onto the ground below counted. Whereas yesterday's snow had been dry and playable, its drifts sharp-edged and its flakes fulsome and feathery, today's was flaccid and sheened with moisture. Yesterday's yielded underfoot with a satisfying squeak that was felt, not heard; today's squelched and dissolved with the warmth from the foot that trod it. However, King Richard's website still proclaimed closure and displayed a photograph, taken by Andy, the site manager, of the familiar iron gates, chained and padlocked, and a jaunty snowman, in a King Richard's scarf and tie, with a cardboard sign on a string around his snowy neck, saying 'SCHOOL CLOSED' in black marker pen.

Liz settled in for a cosy day, glad of the time to catch up with some marking, and curled up on the sofa, green pen in hand. She had marked about half a dozen books when her phone beeped. She could hardly believe the text message, which had come from the school office: King Richard's was opening after morning break and all staff and students who could get there were expected to do so. Liz cursed and considered pretending she had not seen either the text or the website—now amended to reflect the current situation. The new picture showed open gates and the same snowman, although the upturned row of pebbles that had formed his smile had been realigned to form the downward curve that echoed the attitude of everyone who looked at it. The sign had been crudely edited and the *CLOSED* had been crossed out and replaced with *OPEN*. Liz assumed that Andy, not Gordon, had been responsible for this exhibition of solidarity, this small act of defiance.

Still swearing and muttering, Liz kept her huge, unprofessional woollen jumper on in protest, but swapped her denim jeans for corduroy ones, combed her hair and slapped some make-up on. She grumpily shoved her feet into snow boots, buttoned herself into her warmest, full length coat, pulled a hat down over her ears and drove cautiously the few miles to school, noticing the snow becoming less melting and the weather more biting, the nearer she got to the Bremeldon hills, which were still fully clothed in white. Had Gordon *seen* the weather in Bremeldon? The staff car park had not been cleared and she slithered into it, sliding dangerously close to another car as she parked. Gordon was all right though; that was the main thing. His four-by-four was parked in his reserved space, which had been shovelled clear, presumably at his request. No wonder he looked so bloody cheerful, standing at the entrance to the playground in a long, dark coat and Cossack-style furry hat like the enemy at the gates, welcoming students, rubbing his hands together and stamping. Liz slunk past, loath to be seen and greeted; she was still smarting from

Colin's retributory lesson observation and was too resentful to feign even civility, let alone joviality, if Gordon spoke to her.

When she got to the door, she stopped to read the A4 sheet of paper taped to it. *SNOW RULES*, it read, but this wasn't a statement of the excellence of snow; it was a list, for the students, of what they should and should not do in conditions such as these. Liz glanced along the corridor and saw the same sign attached to each of the doors by which students would enter or leave any of the school buildings. They were instructed to stick to the paths that had been cleared in the snow by the site team, so as to keep their feet warm and dry; to move around the school carefully, and to wear their coats during lunch break. Most importantly, however, they were not to utilise the snow inappropriately.

The bottom half of the notice bore the instruction, in bold: *Do not misuse snow. The following will result in severe consequences* and the subheading, *Misuse of Snow*, under which was an exhaustive list of such misuses. It started with *Putting snow down the back of someone's neck* and also included *Rubbing snow into someone's eyes (especially when stones have been put into it)*, *Forcing someone to eat snow* and *Filling someone's hood with snow*. Liz's eyes ran down the list. It was full of wrongdoings, but might just as well have been introduced with: *Are you stuck for inspiration when it comes to bullying a fellow student using snow? Follow these simple instructions and you'll be making someone's life a misery in no time!* The final offence listed had the potential to be catastrophic, however: *Putting animal fecies into a snowball and throwing it at someone.* 'Someone' had obviously inspired all these misuses, and that someone's identity was, perhaps, something that should stay between Gordon and his psychiatrist. Liz made her way over to the English block and prepared herself for *Snowmageddon*.

She had no need to worry, though; any students likely to attempt such heinous acts had stayed at home, having had the sense to pretend they had not seen the website. In fact, because of this and the impassable roads further up the hills, only about a quarter of the school's population had made their grumbling way in, they too wearing non-regulation scarves and snow boots or wellingtons instead of school shoes, and the atmosphere was jolly, despite the obvious waste of everyone's time, it being impossible to teach proper lessons with three quarters of the students missing.

At the end of the day, Liz was disinclined to stay much beyond the three-thirty bell. The sky was already darkening and the slushy roads would become more treacherous, the colder, darker and later it got. Liz put her enormous coat and hat back on and stumped back along the cleared pathways, through the rapidly re-freezing snow towards the car park.

Gordon, still behatted and with the lapels of his overcoat turned up to protect his neck, was at the gates again, making a show of ensuring students were safely delivered to parents' cars and the smaller ones helped over the mounds of shovelled snow onto the waiting buses, where, if they slipped and broke their necks, they were no longer his responsibility. Liz could not avoid him a second time and, as he hopped onto the bottom step of the bus to speak to the driver and then turned to jump back down, she braced herself to receive and return the requisite—if uncomfortable—pleasantry. From Gordon's demeanour, Liz could only assume he had endorsed Colin's assessment of her lesson and felt he had made his point.

Gordon fixed a grin to his face as she shuffled towards him. "'Night, Liz," he called from the step of the bus.

"'Night," Liz responded and mustered a smile.

Evidently more at ease with simulating geniality than Liz was, Gordon opted to play the magnanimous leader. "And thanks for coming in," he said—as if she had had a choice—and, warming to his role, continued: "I love the snow." He touched his hat and nodded towards Liz's ankle-length coat. "We look like something out of Dr Zhivago, don't we?"

Liz laughed feebly and decided she had better join in with his ersatz bonhomie. "Yeah, be careful getting off that bus, Omar," she joked as she passed him, noting with satisfaction the lack of recognition in his answering chuckle. Buoyed by the tiny victory, Liz rode the wave of her daring; waiting until she was sure she was out of earshot, she added, in muttered tones, "Come the revolution..."

28: Stuff Mums Should Cover

At last, the winter began to limp towards a close. The snowdrops had eased their shy, white heads through the black earth and glanced timidly about before giving the all-clear and beckoning the rest to follow. The white had made room for yellow: constellations of wood anemones, primroses like tiny lemon slices and sunny winter aconites with their stiff, green ruffs had emerged like debutantes, at first bashful, but each brighter and braver than its predecessor. Birds flapped and twittered hectically in the race to attract mates, find nesting spots and continue their species. Finally, March arrived, heralding Spring with its strident trumpets of golden daffodils.

March also brought World Book Day and it was the tradition for the English teachers, and sixth formers— still nostalgic about their primary school days—to dress up as characters from books for the day. For a week before, the talk among the female population of the English staffroom was all of characters and costumes; Dave and Gareth, equally consistent with their gender, did not show quite as much enthusiasm when Liz enquired about their outfits.

"You'll have to wait and see," said Dave, establishing that he had not given it a moment's thought.

"And don't just go to a costume hire shop the night before; that's cheating," said Liz. "Don't forget, last year, all they had left was a nylon Superman—in medium."

Dave was quick to defend himself. "Well he *is* a character."

"Out of a comic," said Liz, "and your costume was so tight we could see what you had for breakfast."

"Yeah, a—er—" he faltered, "—jumbo sausage and two plum tomatoes," he finished, inspired, "and you loved it."

Liz laughed. "Remember, those massive red shorts from the lost property cupboard we had to make you wear over the top? Those budgie smugglers that came with the costume would've got you onto the sex-offenders' list."

"Those shorts were fucking rank," he replied. "Anyway, dressing up's a girl thing. You lot can get excited about anything as long as clothes are involved."

Liz remembered past World Book Days and the disproportionate amount of satisfaction she had obtained from the internet-trawling, charity-shop-rummaging and clothes-altering that went into making a costume compared with the mundanity of the day itself, it being pretty much the same as any other day, except for the fancy dress. A couple of years ago, when the A Level Literature students were studying *The Great Gatsby*, she had meticulously researched nineteen twenties' fashion and had made herself an authentic looking Daisy Buchanan outfit. However, she had faltered on the way to work, reflecting on her age—what had made her think she could pass for a glamorous, twenty-something socialite?—and by the time she had arrived, she was demi-centenarian, Clarissa Dalloway, instead; the costume served equally well for both and it was far better to have people say she was more Daisy than Dalloway than the other way round.

Then there was last year; she had been in the middle of berating a student for some misdemeanour or other and had suddenly remembered she was dressed as Hermione Granger and her stuffed Crookshanks was slipping off her shoulder and undermining her authority. However, her wand was actually a pretty serviceable pointing device so it was swings and roundabouts. Indeed, the Hogwart's cloak had given her leave-taking of the student in question a drama she had not anticipated, too. Perhaps there was something in

Gordon's love of the academic robe... She forced her mind back to the matter in hand: Dave's costume.

"What about the year before?" she continued.

Dave remembered: "Police man," he said. "What's wrong with that?"

"What character were you?" Liz challenged, laughing again.

Dave tried, unsuccessfully, to look shamefaced. "Didn't have one," he smirked.

"We had to tell the kids you were PC Plod from *Noddy*, didn't we?" Liz said.

"You looked like a stripper in that costume," said Gareth, looking up from his *Sight and Sound* magazine. "I'm sure those trousers had Velcro down the sides. And as for the handcuffs and mirror shades..." he broke off, chuckling.

"And I notice you're keeping quiet about your costume, Gareth," said Liz. "Whose turn is it for you this year? Are you going for the undone bow tie and martini glass combo or the fedora and trench coat?"

Gareth had two costumes for World Book Day, both of which consisted of his best black suit, varied with accessories so that, whether he was James Bond or Philip Marlowe, he still managed to look like Gareth.

"I bloody hate dressing up," he said simply.

Just then, Janet came in, closely followed by Lucy and Serena. Her eyes darted to the table, but it was bare. She raised her voice slightly. "Anyway, as I was saying..." she paused, enabling everyone present to be reminded of the dizzying heights she had attained at King Richard's. Satisfied all ears were on her, she continued. "As deputy head, my line manager's Gordon, so he'll be doing my lesson observation this year. Anyone got any ideas for an outstanding lesson I can steal. I haven't got a clue what to do."

"What about one of those ideas *you* trained *us* in at the beginning of the year?" said Dave. "You know, when you gave that presentation."

Janet looked blank so Dave prompted: "After you got that pay rise for leading on Teaching and Learning."

Janet giggled weakly. "Oh yeah, I forgot about that," she said. "But, seriously, has anyone got anything I can do that actually *works*?"

Pausing to acknowledge the Mexican wave of raised eyebrows and muffled splutters of astonishment, Dave asked Janet, who was oblivious to the reactions, "When's your observation?"

"Next Thursday," she replied, "but it's World Book Day. Should I dress up or not?"

Serena answered before the others had had time to think. "You should definitely wear a costume. It'll get you a tick in the SMSC box and you can't get *outstanding* without that."

Liz displayed her ignorance—or was it apathy? "What's SMSC?" she asked and looked to Janet for an answer.

Janet cast about with her eyes. "Oh, what is it again? It's something to do with awareness of religion and people and British values," she said, obviously expecting a verbal lifeline, but it was too entertaining to watch her flounder on one of the things that were central to her remit. Realising she would have to try to keep herself afloat, she mused to herself in a low mutter, seeming to have forgotten the rapt audience of English teachers, "S, S, S—'society'? No, that wasn't it. What about the 'C'?"

Suggestions were soon offered from around the staffroom, but whether these were meant to confuse or help, was unclear.

"You said it had something to do with religion, Dave reminded. "Christian?"

"Muslim?" Gareth added, upon which bandwagon Lucy jumped: "Sikh?"

"No, it wasn't just religions," Janet urged, clearly having decided, shamelessly, to pretend she was testing them rather than admit ineptitude or ignorance, demonstrating, therefore, the very trait that had ensured her continual promotion.

"Was the 'C' for 'community'?" asked Lucy. "Or 'civilisation'?"

"You're all supposed to know this." Janet was becoming impatient now, believing her own propaganda. "I would have sent an email round in September."

Liz had already shown her lack of awareness on the subject, so she did not mind evidencing it further. "I can't remember, Janet. Can you just tell me?" She smiled and waited, knowing not to hold her breath.

Janet, still operating with the conviction that no one had fathomed her lack of knowledge, deflected the question. "Serena. You always know what's going on. You tell her."

Of course Serena knew; she had brought it up, but it was much more amusing to prolong the hoax a modicum. "Sacred, Municipal, Society and Community," she said, decisively.

"That's right," Janet affirmed, equally decisively, her relief at maintaining her façade of proficiency preventing her from giving Serena's salvatory answer her full attention. "Well done, Serena. At least someone reads their emails."

Serena glanced up with a playful glimmer. "Oh no. Wait; that's wrong," she said. "I've remembered now; it's Social, Moral, Spiritual and Cultural awareness."

Janet looked startled. "What?" She floundered again and then giggled. "Well, they're always changing these acronyms; it's hard to keep up, isn't it?"

Dave took pity on her and broke the tension. "I just call it 'Stuff Mums Should Cover. But, seriously, he might ask you what it stands for; he asked me about an acronym once."

"Oh, I'm sure it'll be fine," she said breezily; "I still don't know who to dress up as, though."

Lucy had an idea. "Talking of stuff mums should cover, how about Carrie White? I was going to do it, but it'll frighten my kids when I pick them up; they're only little."

That interested Janet. "Who's Carrie White then? What would I have to wear?"

"From *Carrie*," she said. "It's just a seventies' high school prom dress with a sash and tiara, 'cause you'd be the prom queen."

"Ooh, I like the sound of that," said Janet. She put her head on one side and fluttered her eyelashes self-consciously, smoothing her skirt and straightening the sleeve of her jacket. "Do you think I'd look a bit ridiculous, dressed up as a teenager, though?"

"No, you'd be fine," Lucy reassured her, "and your hair's the right colour; you'd just have to do a centre parting and straighten it."

Janet continued to preen, passing her hand over her hair, "Oh, is Carrie White blonde too?"

"Yeah, *she* is, but you'll have the blood in it, so no one will notice," Serena put in.

"Blood?" Janet seemed to lose confidence in the idea.

"We can just use red paint. It'll be fine; we'll help you." Again, Serena pacified her.

Liz couldn't resist adding to the intricacy of the costume by including every reference to the book she could think of, knowing Serena's penchant, even fiercer than her own, for assembling fancy dress costumes. "Remember Carrie's mum and the shower scene? You're going to need a massive crucifix, a bucket and some tampons. What about a fake dead pig too?"

"And a *plug it up* sign," added Serena.

Lucy squealed with enthusiasm. "Oh my God! Remember in the film?" she asked and artlessly started clapping the chant from the film, promptly joined by Serena: "Plug it up, plug it up, plug it up!"

Liz winced, unsure whether Janet, in her eagerness to portray this victim, had actually become one. Janet had no such fears, however; she smiled with a mixture of exhilaration and bewilderment, delighted to be the centre of attention.

Serena noticed her perplexity and overrode it. "Don't worry, Janet; leave it to me. It'll be amazing." She started scribbling down notes and doodling, swept away with the imagined upcoming preparations. Janet would have no say in it now; in Serena's hands, she would be spectacular. Horrifyingly inappropriate, but spectacular.

29: World Book Day

Thursday came around and Liz watched as, true to their word, Serena, already dressed as Miss Havisham, and Lucy, who still had her coat on, helped Janet into her costume before the day began. They had already found a pink satin nightdress, very like the prom dress in the film of *Carrie*, in a charity shop and daubed it with simulated pigs' blood. They helped Janet into the gory garment and adjusted it over her shoulders.

Janet looked concerned. "That neckline's a bit low, isn't it?" she said.

Liz laughed. "You have to show your dirty pillows for Carrie," she said.

"Dirty pillows?" said Janet.

"It's what Carrie's mum calls boobs," Lucy said. "Don't worry; they'll be mostly covered with the prom queen sash."

Serena approached Janet with the squeezy bottle of fake blood and squirted dollops of gore across the front of Janet's dress and in her hair. Lucy placed a tiara into the mess on her head, adjusting the angle and standing back, satisfied with the result.

"Nearly done." Serena unwrapped a few tampons and sanitary towels and began to pin them to the back of Janet's dress as a final dash of realism.

Liz was uneasy. "Isn't that going a bit far? You don't want to make her look too ridiculous," she said, "and it's a year seven class, isn't it?"

Janet dismissed her concerns, unfathomably heedless of the inappropriateness of bogus sanitary items in a year seven lesson, observed by the head. "It'll be fine; Serena and Lucy know what they're doing."

"What time's Gordon doing your observation?" Liz asked.

"First lesson," she said, "So, if you've finished, I'd better go in early and get set up. Thanks, ladies."

"Oh my God, she looked brilliant," said Lucy when she had gone. "I wish I could have worn it, but it would have terrified my two. Anyway," she added, "What do you think? I borrowed it off one of my sixth formers."

Lucy took off her coat, revealing rakish attire: cream jodhpurs and a hacking jacket, accessorised with riding boots, crop and hat. Her shirt was partly untucked, her hair deliberately dishevelled and bits of straw stuck to various parts of her clothing. "Guess who I am."

In answer to their questioning looks, Lucy smacked a thigh with her crop and said, "Some woman out of *Riders*. Who are you, Liz?" she continued, looking at Liz's frilled dress and black boots.

However, Belle had come in and with an impatient swish of acres of buttercup silk, she made it impossible for them to ignore her costume. When all eyes were on her, Belle graced them with a slow twirl. "So, guess who I am?" she demanded, as if she would have dressed herself as anyone other than her Disney namesake.

"Miss Jean Brodie?" ventured Liz.

Belle giggled and shook her head. "Don't know who that is," she said. "Try again."

Serena had a turn. "Scout Finch?"

Belle laughed scornfully. "She hates dresses; even I know that!"

"Lady Macbeth?" suggested Lucy.

Peggy approached with an expression of contempt at their idiocy, so Liz, sensing their fun was coming to an end, threw in a final suggestion: "Fanny Hill?"

"Come on, you lot, haven't you seen Beauty and the Beast?" said Peggy, gesturing towards Belle's voluminous yellow skirts. She and Belle chorused, "Belle!"

Liz, however, was far more interested in the *quality* of the costume. This was real silk with an authentic-looking crinoline, not to mention the layers upon layers of petticoat. Belle hadn't rented this from some high street hire shop. "That's a top quality dress, Belle," she said, where did you find it?"

Belle adjusted her décolletage proudly. "I just—" she paused, searching for the right word, "er—reconnected with a drama student I was at uni with? He's got a job with a theatre company now? Anyway, better go and get my stuff ready." She rustled out of the room and up the stairs, leaving a collection of stunned faces in her golden wake.

"Well, don't I feel stupid now?" said Liz. "I could have looked like that, but I paid for mine contactless."

Dave came in, giggling, his costume drawing raised eyebrows from all of them. "I've just seen Gannet. Fucking incredible." He plonked a pile of sanitary items, pins and a 'plug it up' sign, handwritten in fake blood, in front of Serena. "I couldn't let her go in with those jam rags all over her, though. I'm not sure the head would see the funny side, SMSC or no SMSC."

Lucy and Serena scooped up a handful of ladies' accoutrements each, disappointed, and went to deposit them in the sanitary bin. Dave's sense of propriety and his pride in running a halfway decent English department seemed to have overruled his desire to be involved in Janet's gulling. Liz smiled; perhaps he was starting to mellow. Musingly, she picked up one last cherry-daubed pad, missed by Serena and Lucy, and chuckled.

At that moment, Gordon himself arrived. Apparently unwilling to undermine the authoritative mystique befitting his position, yet seemingly desperate to join in the fun, he had replaced his headmasterly black robe with a scarlet satin cloak, emblazoned with Flash Gordon's lightning bolt logo.

"Morning, er, Marla?" he said, eying Liz's oversized *Hello I'm...* name badge, "Which room is Janet teaching in?"

"Morning. She's in yours, isn't she, Dave?" Liz replied. Dave confirmed this with a biscuit-muffled grunt that came from the depths of a fake beard. Remembering she was holding it, Liz fumbled with the grisly sanitary pad self-consciously, inadvertently drawing attention to it. Gordon stared at it for a second or two, scowled and then left the room in a flutter of scarlet.

Dave looked at the pad too. "Still an impressive costume without them."

Agreeing, she turned her attention to Dave; now Janet had gone, she noticed he had made an effort with his costume for the occasion. As Mr Twit, he wore a stained, fraying blue suit, many of whose buttons were missing and whose knees had worn into holes. He had spiked his hair and wore what appeared to be scuffed gardening boots. The pièce de résistance, however, was his beard, which was, faithful to Roald Dahl's creation, crammed with corn flakes, fake sardines, bits of spinach and fish fingers, although the latter were plastic and from a child's play set. The most impressive thing about this costume, though, was that, for the first time ever, it was unmistakably home-made.

"Brilliant costume, by the way, Dave." Liz said, "Did Peggy help you?"

Peggy was dressed in a pink floral dress and pink cardigan. She looked over the top of her pink-framed glasses and said, "No, Miss Honey's the only Roald Dahl character I could whip up."

Dave reddened slightly. "What makes you think I couldn't do it for myself?"

"I've no doubt you can," laughed Liz, "but what about the costume?"

"All right, Sherlock," Dave said, stepping back so that he was behind Peggy and signalling wildly with his eyes, "a *friend* helped me." He still seemed inexplicably determined to keep his relationship a secret.

Serena and Lucy came in at that moment and caught the end of the exchange.

"Yes, we were just talking about your costume, Dave," Serena said. "It must have been a very good friend to help you like that. There's a lot of work in it."

Lucy joined in: "Such a good friend would have to work with you for hours on that," she said. "Might even have to stop over."

"And you with only the one bedroom," added Serena, smiling, apparently ingenuously.

"Morning, Dave." Gareth walked over to the fridge and retrieved his gourmet-style deli-salad; he could not, apparently, wait until lunch, "that internet dating finally worked out for you, then?"

Dave was keen to deflect the attention away from his love-life and lashed out against the one person who knew the truth. "Why are you so interested in my costume? It's Liz's you need to pay attention to—especially if you've seen those two year thirteens from her film class," he continued enigmatically.

All eyes turned to Liz. She and her film studies students had agreed on a mini challenge: dressing up as characters from books that were also films. Liz herself had dressed up as Marla Singer from *Fight Club*. She had sourced a tired-looking, chiffon bridesmaid's dress from a charity shop, satisfied that, like Marla's, it would again be loved intensely for one day and then tossed. A shaggy, black, fake fur jacket, dug out from the back of her wardrobe and chunky ankle boots, completed the costume, together with backcombed hair, sunglasses, a fake cigarette and an oversized support-group badge that read 'Hello, I'm Marla'. If only she had Marla's pillowy French lips and her huge, anime eyes, she would be really happy, but she couldn't have everything.

"What are you talking about, Dave?" she asked.

He just smiled, went over to Gareth and whispered something in his ear. Gareth spluttered, emitting a fine spray of baba ganoush onto the table in front of him.

"What?!" Liz demanded, as prickly as her fictional counterpart.

Gareth was almost as enigmatic as Dave had been. "I said *Fight Club* could be risky," he said jubilantly.

Lunch time heralded the traditional English department photograph and they all gathered on the steps in front of the English block while Chris, expert with a camera, attached his wide-angle lens and adjusted his tripod, preparing to take the shot that would adorn the website and newsletter at the end of the month. He ensured that the most spectacular costumes were given centre stage, so Belle and Dave stood, resplendent at the front of the group, like some freakish bride and groom, with Janet as their maid of honour, and flanked by all the others, Gareth, gladly at the back. Students began to gravitate towards them, keen to see their teachers dressed so outrageously, and soon there was a glitter of phone screens and flashes as they were photographed by dozens of students and instantly uploaded.

As they walked back in, Liz asked Janet how her lesson observation had gone.

"Oh, all right, I think," Janet said, breezily, "It was hilarious, actually; Dave missed one of the tampons stuck to the back of my dress."

"Oh no!" said Liz. "What happened?"

Still laughing, Janet said, "Well, this little boy noticed it and asked what it was. Of course, I couldn't see 'cause it was at the back, so I asked Gordon and he just unpinned it, put it in the bin and told the boy to get on with his work, so that was okay."

"But was he annoyed with you?" Liz was worried. "Did affect your grade for the observation?"

"Oh, don't worry," Janet replied, "I told him I didn't know it was there 'cause you lot had done round the back."

Liz felt a leaden plummet in her stomach as she remembered Gordon's glare at the sanitary towel she had been holding earlier. Just her bloody luck to be caught red-handed, especially when the smoking gun in question wasn't even hers.

Film studies was after lunch so Liz didn't have long to wait until she found out what Dave and Gareth had found so hilarious earlier. Brad and Kai arrived first, dressed in the obligatory boys' fall-back costume of dark, but otherwise ordinary, clothes teamed with whitened faces, purple-bagged eyes and fake-blood crusted wounds. They sat down, self-consciously, muttering about the funny looks they had got from younger students on the way. Liz could not think of anything Dave and Gareth could laugh at about that.

"Don't tell me: *World War Zed*," Liz said.

The boys groaned, zombie-like. "*World War Zee*, Miss! It's American."

Liz feigned indignation. "It doesn't mean *I* have to be," she retorted. "This is Film Studies, not Movie Class."

The next to arrive, trying to avoid spilling their coffee on their outfits, were Lana and Frankie, mimicking red-robed Offred from *A Handmaid's Tale* and Lisbeth Salander from *The Girl With the Dragon Tattoo*, respectively, and following them was Jake, masked, straitjacketed and carrying a bottle of chianti. Jake looked at the girls as he sat down and chuckled, "Bit rapy."

"You can't say that!" Lana exclaimed, laughing. "We're wronged women, making a stand for all wronged women," she added, her tongue only partly in her cheek.

Frankie agreed, but there was no irony in her statement. "We're making a point by confronting you men with the legacy that patriarchal societal norms have imposed upon women," she said, "and if that's 'a bit rapy'..." She made inverted commas with her many-ringed fingers. "...you'll just have to deal with it."

Lana put a placatory hand on Frankie's arm. "He's only joking," she reassured her.

Jake just smiled quietly, shrugged and surrendered, palms up; Frankie was preaching to the converted.

Liz thought. The girls' characters' themes were not, perhaps entirely suitable to be examined too deeply by the younger students, but they could easily gloss over the details if asked, so it was not likely to be that that had caused Dave and Gareth's amusement. Anyway, Dave had said it was something to do with boys in the group.

"Hannibal Lecter, I presume," Liz said to Jake, regretting, now, that they had decided this book-and-film character challenge: most of them were from films certificated eighteen.

"Hi Miss, or should I say Marla," Jake replied, "Wait till you see Ethan and Jimmy," he added, a meaningful tone in his voice. So he knew as well.

Just then, they heard the worrying sound of a scuffle, followed by a loud voice—Jimmy's— outside the classroom: "What's the first rule of Fight Club?"

This question was answered by Ethan's voice: "You do not talk about Fight Club."

They rushed to the door to see what was going on. Ethan and Jimmy stood, facing each other, grinning and covered in theatrical bruises. This must have been what Dave and Gareth were talking about. She couldn't see the harm in it; it was only once a year and these skits would raise the profile of the film studies A level, so Liz leaned against the door frame to enjoy their performance.

"I want you to hit me as hard as you can," Jimmy said theatrically, in a generically inaccurate American accent, acknowledging the audience of students and costumed teachers, who had also come to the doors of classrooms. Rising to the occasion, he gurned, half sneer, half smile, leaned back from the waist, tilted his head and nodded unhurriedly, mock-arrogant, Tyler Durden style.

"Face or stomach?" Ethan asked, almost as ostentatiously, though, knowing his limitations, he did not attempt the accent.

"Surprise me," Jimmy replied and Ethan obliged, swinging his arm and clenched fist in slow motion into Jimmy's cheek, at which Jimmy embarked on a slow-motion clasp of his face, distorted cry of pain and backward leap, ending with him sprawling against some filing cabinets, still smiling. He bounded to his feet and the pair bowed to their spectators, who were ushered back into lessons by James Bond, Miss Havisham and Mr Twit, the cornflakes in his beard, rustling dramatically as he span round to return his students to their lesson. There was one character missing, however; 'some woman out of *Riders*' was nowhere to be seen. Presumably, Lucy was running late for her lesson, but her class was a paragon of virtue and, ushered in by Serena, they sat quietly with their reading books and were immediately forgotten about by the other teachers, who quickly became absorbed in their own lessons.

Ethan and Jimmy came into the classroom at last. Jimmy, with even more swagger than usual, wore a shiny, reddish leather safari jacket with wide, seventies' lapels, a Hawaiian shirt and mirrored aviator sunglasses. His face was daubed in simulated blood and a replica cigarette drooped from his mouth. Ethan was dressed conservatively in grey trousers (torn), a white shirt (blood-spattered) and tie (crooked). His face was made up with a luridly green, purple and yellow black eye and, like Jimmy, he had made good use of the counterfeit blood from the drama department, which trickled from his nose and mouth, dripping onto the *Hello, I'm Cornelius* badge that was pinned to his chest.

"Wow, you've really gone to town on those costumes!" Liz said. "It must have taken you ages to find that shirt and jacket, Jimmy."

Jimmy grinned again. "Nah, we already had them. We went to a fancy dress party as Tyler and the other one in half term," he said. "We'd have invited you if we'd known you had a Marla costume."

Realisation dawned on Liz at last. She blushed as she remembered the graphic sex scene between Marla and Tyler—or was it the other one?

"See what I mean, Miss?" Jake said, smiling.

Liz laughed nervously and deflected their attention to the two boys. "You went to a party together, dressed like that? Isn't that a bit couply?"

Jimmy pulled Ethan into an embrace. "How do you know we're not a couple, Miss?"

"Maybe they're subconsciously responding to the homosexual-slash-homoerotic subtext of the film-slash-book," Jake suggested helpfully.

Kai rolled his eyes. "Typical psychology student."

"It *is* pretty gay, though," commented Brad.

Jimmy did not mind in the slightest: "Massively gay," he said proudly and kissed Ethan loudly on the cheek. Ethan laughed, wiped his face with his hand and shoved Jimmy off him.

A cheer came from Lucy's classroom and Liz instinctively cocked her head to listen in case help was needed. No further sound followed it, however, so Liz concluded it had been good-humoured and continued.

"Right, before we start, I want a photo of you lot," Liz said and positioned them all in front of the film studies display board. Before she had time to take the picture, she heard her door open and a familiar 'Oi'. Lucy was in the doorway, jerking her head manically to beckon Liz towards her.

"You all right, Lucy?" Liz asked. "What's up?"

"Didn't you hear me banging?" she said, but before Liz could insert a witty response, appropriate to Lucy's assumed character, Lucy continued. "I've been locked in the loo," she explained.

Now the cheering made sense.

"I slammed the door and the bloody lock fell off! I was shouting and banging for twenty minutes before anyone heard me and called Andy. He came over with a screwdriver and let me out."

Liz's gasped and clapped her hand over her mouth, part horrified and part amused. "Didn't Greg hear you? That loo's right next to DT and they've got loads of screwdrivers there, surely."

"No, he was on a cover so the tools were locked away," she said. "Anyway, better get back to my class. Lucky they're angels!"

Liz turned to the amused sixth formers and shrugged. "Right, where were we?" she said before capturing them in all their dubious glory on her phone. "That's one for the album."

Jake spoke up next, a mischievous twinkle in his eye. "Now, let's have one of Miss with Ethan and Jimmy." He got out his phone and made them stand in front of the *Fight Club* poster. "That's it, Miss; you go in the middle," he said. "Perfect. Now, say 'Project Mayhem'." He looked at the picture, gratified with his handiwork. "Great photo. I can see it now: on the website, in the newsletter, even in the tabloids with the headline, *Teacher and students in bizarre film-based ménage à trois*. It could even make the 9 o'clock news."

30: Private's on Parade

One misty Friday morning, towards the end of the Spring term, Liz crossed the haze-shrouded playground, nodding to a few early students, who loomed, ghostly, from the fog as she neared them and faded back into it as she passed.

She arrived in her classroom and logged into the timetable on her computer. Her heart sank as a fluorescent yellow square leapt out at her, radiating malevolently. A cover lesson: year ten PSHE. The lesson PowerPoint had been emailed to her so she clicked it and laughed grimly as she realised that this half-term, the year tens were doing a carousel course on sex and relationships. The lesson Liz was doing today was improperly titled *Private's on Parade*, which augured well. There was nothing like a pun, not relevant since the eighties, to pique the interest of the average fifteen-year-old, especially when it included a grocer's (or was that *grocers*?) apostrophe. She would let the students correct the spelling, punctuation and grammar on the slides as they went along, as usual. At least then they might learn something useful.

The email instructed Liz to collect the lesson resources from the teacher who had delivered this lesson the previous week, so she checked the rota and wandered along to the design technology department, where Greg was waiting for her.

"Come for the cocks and cunts, have you?" he beamed and handed her a lidded plastic box.

"Well, I thought I'd do a bit of teaching first," she said. "Shouldn't mix business and pleasure."

"Funny," he commented and added ominously, "You won't be laughing for long."

Liz had heard about PSHE's infamous box of delights and, peering at the vague, lumpen shapes through the translucent lid, she decided this would not disappoint.

"Good luck," Greg wished her, "the sex lessons are shit, by the way," he added.

Liz sighed. The course had been put together some years previously by the current head of PSHE, Kelly Brown, a promotion-hungry opportunist with a third in sociology, killer heels and a thigh-gap. Armed with the essential tools of the doggedly ambitious: unshakable self-belief, non-existent self-awareness and, perhaps most important of all, extreme pachydermy, she had netted herself a substantial pay rise for these lessons.

Greg obviously held the same opinion as Liz did. "I don't get it," he said. "How did she get that job?"

"Tits," Liz dysphemised and carried her precious cargo back to her room, where she snapped open the fasteners and slowly lifted the lid. A dozen forms, each just the right size to nestle in the palm of a curious hand, quivered slightly, with the movement, like shiny party blancmanges just out of their moulds, some vanilla, some caramel and some chocolate. So, these were the legendary replica genitalia, faithfully reproduced in silicone rubber. The multi-racial penises and pudenda bumped together, winking and smiling merrily, a pornographic Benetton advert in the uncanny valley.

Liz delved into the capacious box to grab the master copy of the *Male and Femail Sex Organ's* worksheet. Badly photocopied in black and white, two indistinct and, frankly, disturbing photographs dominated: the titular organs, which had been reproduced so often that they were barely recognisable any more. Students were supposed to label them and harsh, black lines stuck out from them at all angles, indicating the specific parts to be named. At first glance, one grotesque picture resembled a pale Saint Sebastian, martyred with arrows and moribund, though still standing. The other was like an anguished bull, lying on its back, stuck full of spears by a toreador and in its death throes. At the bottom of the page, a number of anagrams waited to be worked out and written in. Liz headed to the photocopier to furnish herself with twenty-five of the off-putting worksheets, which would lose even more clarity and be rendered even more repellent by the time she had reproduced them. Perhaps that was the point.

While she waited for the photocopier to ejaculate the sheets, Liz picked up a pile of someone else's word-searches that had not yet been claimed and put it to one side. As she did, she glanced at it, always keen to pilfer a resource wherever possible. However, on reading the title, Liz recoiled, disgusted, and thrust it away from her.

Then door swung open and Peggy came in. "Morning, Liz," she said, looking at the copier. "Have you got a PSHE cover too? You haven't seen my female genital mutilation word-search, have you?" she asked with an unsettling lack of distress.

What would be next? Paedophile Top Trumps?

Just then, Serena drifted into the room. "Anyone got any condoms? I've got to teach contraception to year ten and the box is empty; last week's class must have stolen them all."

"Blown up like balloons, as usual," said Liz. "Bloody hell! Have we all got sex with year ten? Where are all their tutors?"

"Signed off with stress after last week, I should think," explained Serena. "No, they're on a course—how to teach sex ed."

"Meanwhile, we're teaching it without the training," said Liz. "Oh, the irony. Look out for a spike in teenage pregnancy some time soon."

"Quite," said Serena. "Anyway, I still need those condoms."

"I bet Kelly's got some," Peggy said ingenuously.

"What about Princess Belle or Rob-the-TA?" Liz said. "Or, you could always send an email round to all the staff. I bet you'd soon round up enough for a class."

"Doesn't bear thinking about!" Serena laughed. "I could send it to the sixth form tutors. They can get their forms to donate theirs!"

Liz's lesson itself was just before lunch and the students were obviously eager to be edified. They had already done some of the other lessons in the *Sex and Relationships—the In's and Out's* programme, they informed her, including the somewhat aggressively named, *Gays Have Rights Too, Got A Problem With That?!!!*, the sinister, *Its Not ok* and the old-school, *Cap's and Rubber's*, which Serena was teaching later. Many of the boys, being, as they were, in the grip of a fifteen-year-olds' hormone rush (not to mention excited by its being Friday as well as by the mere mention of sex) wrestled, mounted or dry-humped each other as they came in, instinctively craving physical contact and unlikely to get it from any of the girls. *Private's on Parade* evoked guffaws and crude mimes involving trouser fronts and water bottles, pelvis waggling and shouts of *Att-en-shun!*

Laughing presciently, Liz settled them down; the next hour could be hard work, judging by their level of excitement. She switched on the whiteboard, gave out their books and set them to copying down the title, reminding them to miss out the erroneous apostrophe.

The first task was designed to enable the students to be disencumbered of their immaturity about genitalia at the beginning of the lesson, ensuring that they would refer to *privates* using correct physiological terminology thenceforth. That was optimistic. Had Kelly actually *met* any teenagers when she designed this lesson?

Your teacher will give each group a sheet of flip chart paper and some marker pen's, the slide told them. Liz put paper and pens on each table and pressed the button for the next instruction to appear. *Write down all the slang words you know for penis and vulva,* an imperative that triggered an eruption of sound and movement that was almost volcanic and soon the pages were bristling with the expected wangs, clams and shlongs as well as some appellations Liz was sure had been invented: *dick-filled splatty-puss,* being particularly ingenious. Far from encouraging mature discussion of purely functional body parts, the exercise had furnished even the most overprotected students with an impressive glossary of crudity that it would surely be impossible to resist in the rest of the lesson and beyond.

Next, Liz gave out the poorly reproduced sex organs worksheets so that the students would be well prepared to deal equably with the silicone models (which lurked in the box behind the desk, like pigeons in a basket, quietly waiting to be released) later in the lesson.

"Urgh! What the hell is that, Miss?" Lauren, whom Liz knew from her year ten English class, said as she handed round the anagram sheets she had photocopied earlier. The other students expressed their repulsion in a mature and sensible way, as they had been primed to do.

"Oh my God, look at the state of that knob!" came from the back of the room, followed by, "Miss, there's something wrong with this fanny!"

Liz struggled to stay professional: "Correct terminology, please, guys." However, her sense of the absurd won and she could not resist smirkingly correcting their comments. "No—this *vulva* looks like it's been run over," and, "He should see a doctor about his—er—*urethral meatus*; what *you* called it is a teensy bit racist." She glanced at the teachers' answer sheet and did a double take. "Meatus?" she repeated, dubiously, checking the answer sheet again and shuddering at the phrase, whose ugliness was an exact match for the photograph upon which it would be written. Liz much preferred the lyricism of *HEAR A LUTE STRUM*, its anagramic counterpart.

The students soon settled to the task of decoding the other anagrams and writing the answers next to the appropriate arrows on the photographs and Liz enjoyed a few minutes' respite as competitive streaks took over and they each rushed to be the first to transform such puzzles as *FAST H*, *S M GAME*, *REFS OINK*, *LICE TESTS* and *IRIS CLOT*. Liz considered the neatness of *POSSUM BIN* and *I PRUNE ME* and her opinion of Kelly soared as she imagined her, painstakingly working out her anagrams, getting carried away, and being unable to resist the compulsion to include the vulgar yet apposite *CUM ROTS*, even though she must have known its message would be lost on most of them.

Finally, the lesson dictated that the students would now spend twenty minutes 'exploring' the silicone facsimiles, presumably so that they would become mundane and familiar and lose their power to fascinate, tempt or petrify. Liz lifted the innocent-looking box onto the desk, amused that only she knew its contents.

It was time to release the bits.

She unsnapped the lid and placed it back on the floor. A few students looked mildly intrigued. Liz pressed the button to reveal the next slide: *Knowing the Opposition!!* At the next press, Liz's pedantry went into overdrive as she dissected the multitudinous inaccuracies. The words, *Now your teacher will give you a model of a penis (if there a girl) or vulva (if there a boy), hold it!! feel it!! examine it!!!!!* appeared, denticulate with unnecessary exclamation, alongside a photograph of one of the replicas—or should she say repli*cants*?

The students exploded with hysteria and, as Liz gave them out, shrieks and whistles ricocheted around the room, making her thankful she had been forced to close the door at the beginning of the first noisy exercise. Surprisingly, the frenzy quickly died down as the students became absorbed by the intricacy and accuracy of the reproductions and she even overheard students using their new-found correct anatomical jargon to name the different parts, cross-referencing them with their worksheets, comparing their organs with their neighbours' and, inevitably, investigating how well they fitted together.

The lesson finished and Liz counted the 'privates' back in, retrieved the pudendum that had accidentally found its way into a boy's bag, dismissed the class and stepped into the playground to go back to her department.

The mist had not dissipated and, though the ghost of the hills—all but invisible—continued its draconic vigil, the playground was eerily quiet and veiled in grey. The scene was other-worldly and sub-oceanic and students were silhouetted and hazy, their movements seemed strangely slowed-down. Among the milling students, whitish, rounded, semi-transparent shapes moved slowly like jellyfish or sea toads, staying close to the ground, some gently drifting, others bouncing softly. So Serena had managed to find her replacements. Liz chuckled. *Cap's and Rubber's* always ended like this.

A dark-suited figure loomed, silent, shark-like, from the depths of the fog and revealed itself to be Gordon. One of the inflated items bobbed against Liz's foot and rebounded into his path, eliciting a disapproving glare. Liz opened her mouth to try and offer a jovial explanation, but this time, Gordon had glided past her without biting.

31: The Poet Laureate

Shortly before the Easter holidays, King Richard's hosted an evening that was intended to be a feather in the cap of the English department. Chris had persuaded his old friend, Carolyn Murphy, the poet laureate, to run a poetry workshop with aspiring writers from years eleven to thirteen and later, to lead the cultural culmination of the day with a reading of poetry at a cheese and wine evening in the drama studio. Parents, governors, and even the Bremeldon Echo had been invited and Chris was buoyant as he went through the arrangements with Liz, who had volunteered to help.

"This will unquestionably establish us as a centre of excellence for the teaching of the arts," Chris smiled, handing Liz a pile of freshly printed programmes to fold as they went to check the drama studio's metamorphosis into a refined entertainment venue.

"It won't do your sixth form numbers any harm, either," Liz replied. "How do you even know the poet laureate, anyway?"

Chris smiled enigmatically. "We're old friends. It's quite a lengthy narrative," he said. "I'll tell you one day."

She looked around the room, impressed; the scruffy little studio had been transformed into a cathedral of creativity by the art, design and drama departments. The finest students' pictures and sculptures adorned its walls, alongside posters advertising past theatrical productions and mannequins displaying garments designed and made by students. The stage had been furnished with chairs and music stands, ready for the chamber orchestra, which would accompany the poetry readings.

Chris checked his watch. "Carolyn should be arriving just about now. I'll go and meet her and see you in the hall for the workshop. If Gordon materialises to greet her before we arrive, tell him we won't be long."

The site team had put out tables and chairs in the hall to enable small groups to work together, and as Liz distributed paper and pens, the students began to arrive, brimming with inspiration and ideas, closely followed by Chris and Carolyn.

"Hi, we're so grateful you've given up your time to do this for us. The students are really excited. This'll be so good for them." Liz made a supreme effort not to gabble in the presence of such a stalwart of the British literary scene.

Carolyn turned slowly towards Liz and offered her hand, stateswomanlike. Her grey eyes seemed to have measured the philosophies of ages and looked through Liz's corporeal self into her very soul and beyond and she appeared to be channelling the very essence of the universe as she took a long inward breath, blinked deliberately and said, "Fuck, I'll do anything for a bit of cheese."

Meanwhile, the fifty-or-so carefully selected students had all arrived and Carolyn approached the front of the hall and started to take a few books from her bag, helped by Chris, while Liz seated the students at the tables. Gordon appeared just outside the doors and peered in, frowning and scratching his head. Chris gestured to him, inviting him in, but he slunk away, still frowning.

Chris came over to where Liz was and whispered angrily, "What's he playing at? He's supposed to be welcoming Carolyn," he hissed. "What will she think of us?"

Shortly afterwards, someone else arrived. Darren, the PE teaching assistant seemed an unlikely volunteer to help with creative writing, but Liz was not one to judge. He stood in the doorway, blocking the light almost completely. A plastic fork from the canteen dangled from his slack, spittle-sheened mouth and his tiny eyes blinked drily. His arms curled as he began to lumber towards Liz, vast biceps preventing his fists from meeting his sides, hugely muscled thighs thwarting a natural gait as he reached her.

"Hi, thanks for helping," said Liz. "She'll be starting in a minute, I think."

"Dance," he grunted.

Liz was puzzled. "No, poetry," she said.

"No," Darren insisted, "dance practice. It's booked."

Chris strode over. "Hello, Darren. Everything all right?"

"The hall. We booked it first." The plastic fork in his mouth wagged up and down, turning his words into exclamations in a way his vocal delivery could not.

Chris smiled, confident that this minor hiccough would be easily rectified. "Look, there's evidently been some error with the reservation, but if you rehearsed in the dance studio, just this once, it would give us considerable succour in our hour of need," he said. "There *are* only eight of you and this *is* the Poet Laureate."

The blonde-ponytailed figure of Keeley Clarke, one of the PE teachers, followed by half a dozen girls in leggings and hoodies, appeared, beetle-browed and indignant. She did not acknowledge any of the writers, but addressed Darren instead: "What's the problem?" she demanded.

"They won't go," he told her. "They've got this Loretta poet and they want us to go somewhere else."

Keeley got out her phone and showed Chris the booking confirmation.

"Sorry. We booked it first," she said. She did not look sorry.

"I know and I offer my deepest apologies," Chris conciliated, "but the hall is the only free space large enough for an activity of this magnitude and you do have the dance studio. This is the poet laureate."

"It's not free. It's booked for dance rehearsal." Keeley turned and started to push the tables back to the sides of the room.

Liz gestured for the students to pick up the paper and pens and follow her, feeling it best to avoid an undignified argument and make a tactical withdrawal. Chris outranked Keeley; he could wreak his revenge later. "Let's decamp to the drama studio," she said.

"We can't use it till this evening," Chris reminded her. "The GCSE performances are being assessed there this afternoon; we can't disrupt that."

"The dance studio?"

Chris shook his head again. "I can't risk damaging that new floor and I'm not asking Carolyn to take her shoes off."

"The library, then," Liz suggested.

"Bloody good idea," agreed Carolyn. "I did the official opening when it was first built. It'll be like going home." She gathered her bags and books and patted Chris's arm. "To the library!" she directed cheerfully.

The silence in the library crackled when Liz, as scout, pushed the door open. The eyes of Glenys Kane, the librarian, whip-panned towards her and the cold glitter of her half-moon glasses signalled her disapproval even before her forefinger had shot to her pursed lips.

"It's only me," whispered Liz. "Since it's not busy in here, I was hoping you'd be able to help us."

Glenys smiled just with her lips and waited. Squirming inwardly under her stare, Liz continued. "We're running a creative writing workshop with Carolyn Murphy and we were supposed to be using the hall."

Glenys nodded.

Liz continued: "Anyway, it was booked for a dance rehearsal so we had to leave. Could we do it in here?"

Glenys shook her head. "Sorry, Elizabeth, as you can see, I have children in here, doing homework."

Liz looked over at the two year sevens in the corner. "They'll be fine," she said. "They'll be finished soon and we won't disturb them; they can stay in that corner."

"Sorry." Glenys did not look any sorrier than Keeley had.

"But it's Carolyn Murphy."

"Sorry."

"You know: the Poet Laureate."

"I know."

"But she *opened* this library."

Glenys remained unmoved.

Liz's voice, incredulous, rose in pitch. "There's a plaque with her name on it above the door!"

"I can't make exceptions, Elizabeth." Glenys turned away and began tapping on her computer keyboard, indicating that the conversation was at an end and Liz had no choice but to walk away, shaking her head and muttering.

"Genghis won't let us use it," she told Chris. Fortunately, Carolyn seemed to be finding it more amusing than either Chris or Liz and was regaling the students with tales of previous turnings away to rival the holy family's fruitless quest for hotel accommodation two thousand years previously. "Such is the poets' lot," she told them: "a long and proud tradition of persecution."

Liz was suddenly struck by inspiration. "What about Magoo's new training suite?"

"Perfect!" said Chris. "He's not using it till the first week back, so it'll be free now."

They headed over to the rooms in which Colin had just been installed in his capacity as leader of professional development and internal training. The double doors had been painted glossy red and a Perspex sign bearing the training room's name had been put up above them, a Perspex sign that caused the wordsmiths to gasp.

Ignorant of the precise nuances of language, as Liz already knew to her cost, Colin had employed what he must have believed was ingenious word-play in his naming of the training suite. Gordon was obviously similarly obtuse, since he must have authorised it. Therefore, *The You-Genesis Suite* had become a permanent fixture.

"You-Genesis?" Liz read, dumbfounded. "Wasn't that outlawed at the Nuremberg Trials?" she said.

"I despair." Chris shook his head sadly. "My sincere apologies, Carolyn," he said. "What must you think of us? Sent from pillar to post, and ending up in *The Torture Chamber*."

Carolyn was still seeing the funny side. "Glorious!" she declared and went in. "Come on; it's fine. Perfect for our workshop."

So, for the second time that afternoon, Liz distributed paper and pens around tables and bade the students sit down, while Carolyn got her books out and started the first activity. The students were busily composing group sonnets when Liz heard the shuffle of feet and Colin appeared.

"Fngh," he began, "What's—er—going on?"

Liz explained what had happened and assured him that they would not move anything, take anything away or leave any mess, but he was still not happy. He adjusted his glasses with a scrawny finger and rasped. "You can't stay here; I've got forty bottles of water to put out before my training session after Easter."

Chris had joined them and was losing his equanimity. "Look, Colin, this is the Poet Laureate," he hissed. "Do you know how important that is?"

Colin made another disapproving sound in the back of his throat.

Chris pressed his point. "It's like the Science faculty inviting Stephen Hawking to speak."

"What's this about Stephen Hawkins?" Gordon had arrived to check on his protégé's progress with the water bottles. "Great signage, Col." He turned to Chris. "You'll appreciate the pun, being as you're a classic scholar."

With superhuman effort, Chris responded politely. "Indeed."

"It's 'You' for the people we're training and 'Genesis' is like genetics so it's science-y and all that, so..." Gordon trailed off, waiting for Chris's complimentary response.

"Yes, well, it's just that—" Chris hesitated, searching for the right words.

His pause was filled by Carolyn. "Sounds a bit like 'eugenics'," she supplied.

Colin sniffed, affronted.

"That's it! Like I said: science-y," Gordon said and turned to Carolyn, obsequiously offering his hand. "Ah, you must be the lady poetess." He shook her hand. "How nice to meet you, Loretta, I'm Gordon. Now, I'll leave you to get on with your ditties," he smarmed and left.

Carolyn erupted with raucous laughter and nudged Liz. "Chris tells me Dildo was your idea," she said. "Nice work."

The students, coming to the end of their shared sonnets, caught the tail end of the conversation and the word *dildo* rippled laughingly through their groups like wavelets at the turn of tide.

However the mood was immediately quashed as the door burst open and Gordon stepped back in, looking around sharply and cutting off the whispers. Young heads bent back to their work and Liz reddened and fell to giving out more paper. Gordon grunted and retreated, taking care to leave the door ajar. Bemused, Carolyn watched him leave, then began to move from group to group, offering guidance to the aspiring poets. The exercises in poetry that followed were as fruitful as they had hoped and the afternoon's workshop culminated in each student choosing the piece of which he or she was most proud, which they would read at the cheese and wine event later that evening.

Just before they were due to leave, Carolyn treated them to a first recital of the latest poem she had been commissioned to write, an elegiac piece to observe the centenary of the battle of the Somme, later in the year. Birdsong poured through the window along with the spring sunshine; the students lost themselves in her words, and the room took on an atmosphere of reverence. As Carolyn spoke, however, a familiar sniff was heard from behind a door at the back of the room and Colin scuffled in, squinting theatrically at his watch. Appearing not to notice, Carolyn continued, consumed by the enormity of what she was describing. She paused, words choking in her throat and tears brimming in her eyes, composing herself, ready for the final stanza.

"All done?" There was a hiss of steel. Colin hooked his retractable tape measure at one end of the wall behind Carolyn and was walking backwards with it, towards the other. "Ngh. Must get on," he said, blinking at the disbelieving gathering in front of him.

Carolyn regained her equilibrium and lost her sense of humour. As Colin bent to angle the steel strip right into the corner for the measurement, she strode towards the hook end and calmly unhooked it. The steel tape thrashed its way back into its housing, delivering him a punitive lash as it did so. Colin recoiled from the room, his hand clasped to the angry nick on his cheek. Carolyn returned to her post, her eyes remisting as she finished her recital.

After the workshop, Chris again expressed his regret to Carolyn for her treatment at the boorish hands of so many King Richard's staff. "This is what I have to put up with," he despaired: "A phalanx of Philistines!"

Carolyn rummaged in her bag and pulled out a bottle. "Don't worry about it," she said. "Let's repair to your office for a quick snifter of the old Poet Laureate's sherry."

Liz's ears pricked up. "Sherry?" she said.

"Yes," said Carolyn, "it's tradition. The people of Jerez give you a lifetime's supply when you're made Poet Laureate."

"That's it; I'm going to practise my poetry!" Liz licked the end of an imaginary pencil and started to compose. "A man from the island of Muck," she began. "Nope," she continued, "can't think of anything." She paused again, as if waiting for the muse to strike. "There was an old man called Frank... No," she said, "nothing. That sherry'll never be mine!"

Later, in the drama studio, where Liz had been roped in to serve drinks and nibbles, Chris's evening of culture was a huge success and parents watched proudly as their offspring took the stage alongside Carolyn. After the readings, the guests were invited to sample some of the local cheeses with some wine. A reporter from the Bremeldon Echo mingled discreetly, interviewing guests and participants and taking photographs and towards the end of the evening, Chris stepped up to the stage, and spoke. "Ladies and gentlemen, thank you all for coming to support us this evening. Before we all go, I have a final presentation to make, so if our esteemed guest would join me on the stage..."

Carolyn finished her drink and made her slightly tipsy way up the steps to Chris and followed his expectant gaze towards the back of the room, where two of the sixth formers from the workshop earlier were bearing a hefty gift aloft, on a tray, as if it were a middle-Eastern princess on a litter. Followed by a procession of student waiters and waitresses (until recently, the chamber orchestra) with trays of cheese samples and glasses of wine, the students made their way slowly towards the stage with the present, a plump, shiny Bremeldon pie: Carolyn's favourite.

Chris spoke solemnly. "In recognition of *Ode on a Meat Pie*," and for the benefit of the audience, he added, "the humorous poem Carolyn recently wrote in praise of our local delicacy."

A voice behind Liz broke the spell. "They've taken my—fnyh—mini whiteboards." Colin had skulked in, pink-faced and trembling.

"Haven't you been home yet?" Liz pictured him, counting his bottles and checking his inventory in the 'Torture Chamber' before she responded to his statement. "And we didn't take anything."

Colin was too incensed to listen and began to shuffle purposefully towards the stage where students, cheese and wine were now in position and Chris had been handed the gargantuan pie, ready to present it.

"Colin," Liz hissed, "can't this wait?"

She rushed after him. The applause instigated by the appearance of the pie was still dying down and masked the scuffle of feet as Liz reached Colin just as *he* reached the steps at the side of the stage. However, the clatter of metal on wood as he swerved away from Liz and knocked a music stand over was less easily masked and guests, performers and press alike hushed and turned as Colin, flailing, fell sideways, causing a domino fall of stands, waiters, wine and cheese, inevitably resulting in the toppling of the poet laureate, who sprawled on the floor, surrounded by finger-food.

There was a few seconds of utter silence, during which, the only sounds were the skeuomorph whirr and click of the Echo reporter's camera, before Chris's panic-stricken voice could be heard: "Oh my God! Carolyn! Are you hurt?"

"Sod me," she replied. "Is the pie all right?"

32: Parents' Evening

The spring term had been a long and difficult one, not made any less exhausting by the fact that year seven parents' evening was on the penultimate day before they broke up for Easter and, for some of the staff, it would be the last one at King Richard's. Gordon's pruning of dead wood had not been as dramatic as feared and most of the few teachers and administrative staff at risk had found other jobs, with the notable exception of Barbara. She would be demoted to the status of an ordinary teacher and her pastoral responsibilities assumed, along with other non-teaching administrative duties, by the far cheaper Yvonne, who did not teach.

Chatting about how hard-done-by they were, Liz and Serena forged a direct path through the haphazard groups of students, oblivious to their scattering and parting, never having to deviate from their straight line, until they reached the English block.

"Don't look now," Serena said, nudging Liz gently. "Here comes Princess Belle."

Liz looked. Belle was weaving and zig-zagging through the same students who had parted for them a few seconds earlier, her face puckered with irritation.

Peggy was already there. "Morning, you two," she said, "kettle's just boiled and there are chocolate biscuits over there. We're going to need them today."

Liz thought it best to warn Peggy. "Belle's on her way over, Peg. Does she know about tonight?"

"Well, I told her last week, so she should do," she said.

"Talk of the devil," Serena murmured, as Belle came in, pink-nosed and panting slightly. "Peggy..." she started.

Peggy turned towards her decisively. "Yes, Belle." There was no question in her voice.

Belle blinked and then opened her eyes wide, tilting her head to a more winsome angle. "It's about parents' evening. I wondered..." she wheedled.

"No, Belle." Peggy turned back to her planning.

Belle seemed surprised. "But you don't know what I'm going to say."

Peggy decided to give her a chance. "Are you going to ask not to do parents' evening?"

"So, Liz won't mind; she's got to be there anyway and they're her form, really, not mine," she pressed.

Liz raised her eyebrows and started to speak, but Peggy spoke for her. "It doesn't matter whether Liz minds or not; this is your job and you're paid to be here."

Belle knew better, by now, than to argue. She sniffed and followed Liz upstairs to her form room. At the top of the stairs, the door was held open for them by Ben, the sixth former behind Belle's embarrassment at the beginning of term. Liz thanked Ben and went through. Poor Belle—she had been genuinely shaken after New Year, but Peggy's stern, motherly guidance had limited the damage. Glancing back protectively, Liz offered Belle tacit support to help her deal with her embarrassment. However, Liz's glance caught the last microsecond of something: Belle's hand was returning to her side; her face, as she turned back from Ben, was pink, and a recent smile was fading from her lips and eyes. She met Liz's searching gaze with a defiant jut of her chin and trotted into the form room.

There was a buzz in registration; a few of the students were clustered round Maisie's World Book Day report, which was in the spring newsletter, with photographs of some of those who had dressed up. Liz looked over Kate's shoulder. Through the tangle of small hands, pointing and grabbing, she could just about make out some captioned photographs.

"Great pictures," Liz said.

Alfie looked pleased. "I took all of them, except the one of you."

"Have you seen it, Miss?" Maisie asked. "It's at the bottom." She swatted away a couple of hands to reveal the picture. It was the one of Liz with Ethan and Jimmy.

"How did you get hold of that?" Liz said, laughing.

"Oh, I follow Jimmy from sixth form on Instagram," she said breezily, her deepening colour belying her casual tone. "He shared Jake's photo so I copied it from there. They said it was okay to use it."

"I bet they did," Liz thought, groaning inwardly. So the photo had done the rounds of the sixth form and now it was in the newsletter.

Kate leaned in towards the picture and studied it. "It's not embarrassing, Miss; you look pretty," she said, reassuringly.

"Let's see," said Belle and prised it from the remaining few fingers that still had purchase.

"I just copied the caption Jake used on Insta," Maisie explained. "Except I made it a bit shorter. It was in French, so I used Google to translate it."

Belle read the caption: "Jimmy Fox, Mrs Marshall, and Ethan Radley: a household of three from *Fight Club*."

Liz gulped, remembering the joke Jake had made when he had taken it.

Maisie explained: "It said *ménage à trois*."

Belle yelped and giggled.

Maisie continued, "I think it makes sense because there are three of them and I think they must have lived in a house-share—I haven't read the book and the film's too old for me," she explained cheerfully.

267

"Yeah, that's right," Liz said. *Just as well she translated it*, she thought. Anyway, Jean in Reprographics had obviously deemed it suitable and her impropriety radar was set to 'low', so maybe it was fine.

After they had sent the form to their lessons, Belle said, "So, there was a Bog Blog about World Book Day?"

Surprised yet relieved that word had not reached Belle of the blog's true author, Liz professed that this was news to her. "Oh?"

"It's definitely about a school toilet 'cause it's only schools that dress up as books?"

"And book shops," said Liz.

Belle continued. "Well, my uni friend thinks it's his school 'cause his head dressed up as Batman?"

What is it with head teachers and superheroes? Liz wondered.

"But it's not going to be anyone we know, is it?" Belle tapped her phone a few times and began to read. "*Greetings, bog people, Lulu Rolls here, your Bog Queen—*" Belle frowned and shook her head in confusion, confirming Liz's fear that adding a layer of poetic allusion was probably a step too far, but once thought of, it had been hard to resist. Belle continued: "*—flushed with excitement about today's comings and goings*," she read. "*Today is World Book Day and all manner of literary characters have graced my porcelain—*So that's why we think it's a school?" Belle explained.

Glad she had had enough sense not to mention the actual character names, Liz hoped fleetingly that Gordon would be as incapable of identifying himself as Belle was, if he ever saw it, and urged her to continue.

"Okay—*I'm sure you canny bog people can guess the identities of these visitors to the hallowed stall where I am the artful voyeuse. First, a top secret agent who shook, but thankfully didn't stir, although his pistol was magnificent.*

Next, an old-fashioned jilted bride and an oft-ridden equestrian, placed bloody libations, like soiled bandages, bruised berries, in my collection box—Don't get that bit." Belle paused.

Liz remembered the discarded elements of Janet's *Carrie* costume. "Sounds like a Heaney reference," Liz supplied. "Whoever this blogger is, sh—" Liz corrected herself quickly. She still did not trust Belle not to let Gordon know the blogger was her if she thought she could profit by it. She continued: "—*he* certainly likes to throw it all in. Talk about more is more."

Belle did not notice, more concerned with the currency of what she clearly assumed was greater knowledge that Liz had. "But this is the bit my friend thinks is about his head—*Later, a superhero engaged my services and I waited, open-lidded, as he prepared to unleash his shooter. This superhero's weapon was a disappointment. A pale imitation. A child's water pistol. And it was set to sprinkle.*" Belle giggled again. "That must be his willy? Anyway—*his cape was majestic, though*—That's the Batman bit," she interjected before continuing: "*Fluttering behind him. If only it had stayed behind...but a little water cleared him of his deed*—Don't get that bit either, but do you see what I mean?" said Belle. "It could almost be my friend's school."

At the end of the day, Liz printed out the obligatory tracking sheets and progress charts needed for parents' evening and headed towards the inexplicably unrecognised convenience. When she came out, Ben was there in the corridor. He looked confused.

"Sorry—I thought..."

"This one's just for staff, Ben," Liz told him, "and it's not as nice as your brand new sixth form block loos!" she chuckled.

"Oh no, I was just waiting to see..." Ben's eyes widened and, looking beyond Liz, he gave his head the tiniest shake. Liz looked behind her to where his eyes were fixated. Belle had appeared silently from the technology department corridor. She froze mid-tiptoe at the sight of Liz and reddened.

However, a microsecond's thought furnished her with a believable excuse to turn tail: "Forgot my bag," she yelped as she hastily retraced her steps, more noisily this time.

Liz looked back at Ben; his face was the same colour as Belle's.

"Surely, she wouldn't," Liz thought, "again. Would she?"

However, by the time they were in the hall, ready to meet parents, Belle's incredible capacity for wilful forgetfulness had erased the episode and she chattered away as if nothing had happened.

Yvonne had been placed at the front of the hall, where she smiled and nodded, keen to dispense platitudes and allay concerns. Her acrylic name plate bore the words, *Mrs Yvonne Dillon, Director of Pastoral Care*, a role that should not officially have been active until September. Barbara also sat at the front, dignified and stately despite this being her last parents' evening as year head. Her sign indicated her not-yet-defunct position as *Head of Year 7* and a queue of about half a dozen parents waited to speak to her. Yvonne had no such queue.

Gordon strutted around, exchanging pleasantries with parents and giving his academic robe another airing. He picked up a copy of the newsletter and began to flick through it, stopping after only a few seconds, frowning and strolling over to Dave, perhaps to comment on Maisie's World Book Day piece. Liz's heart rate quickened. What if he worked out what the caption had been translated from? What if he'd seen the film (possible)—or read the book (less likely)? She had begun to think she had shaken off Gordon's wrath and could start to relax, but this could put her right back on his radar. She risked a glance towards him, but misjudged it and made eye contact. A brace of parents arrived to hear about the aptitudes and inadequacies of their offspring and Liz forced herself to focus her attention on them instead. When she looked up again, Gordon had gone.

During a brief gap in the traffic, Dave dived over to Liz and said, "Don't worry; Dildo hasn't got any more idea about it than Maisie did."

"Thank God for the culturally bereft," Liz replied.

Next, a small, bird-like woman approached the desk and extended a hand whose tremor was hardly noticeable. Liz and Belle shook it in turn.

"Sarah Willis," she said.

"Alfie's mum!" Liz said. "Lovely to meet you properly at last."

Mrs Willis spoke softly, "I know I'm supposed to ask about how well he's doing in all his subjects, but I'm not worried about that yet. I just want to say thank you to the school for helping him settle in so well. He's got loads of friends and he's really happy."

"Well, he's a lovely young man," Liz replied. "He's a great form captain and he's been getting involved with all sorts of activities: helping with Open Evening and taking photos for the newsletter."

"He's putting everything behind him at last," Mrs Willis continued, but recent memory clouded her eyes and she paused before swallowing painfully and taking a ragged breath. "He loves the new house and he's got his own room too. He's even stopped having nightmares."

Liz struggled with a lump in her throat as Mrs Willis told her about the change in Alfie and how secure he felt at last and she got the distinct impression that she spoke for herself as much as her son.

After Mrs Willis, Liz received an uninterrupted stream of parents, most of whom only wanted to prove they were decent parents by being there and to know that their offspring were happy and behaving well, and when the flow of parents slowed, Liz looked around to see how her colleagues were faring. Peggy, thorough and verbose as ever, still had a lengthy queue to get through; she would be the last to leave, as usual, but the others all seemed to be packing up. Liz had no more appointments and availed herself of the facilities before leaving. Lucy was in the ladies' too.

"You'll never guess what I've just done," Lucy said.

Liz grinned. "What?"

"Well, I was talking to this parent and I could smell this shitty smell the whole time, so I thought the dirty bugger'd farted," she said. "Anyway, I could still smell it after he'd gone and I kept looking round to see if I could work out what it was. I even checked the bottom of my shoes, but guess what it was."

Liz dreaded to think and luckily, Lucy put her out of her misery straight away.

"Well I'd changed the bub's nappy just before I came back to school," she explained, "and I had a bit of baby shit on my cuff!" Lucy dissolved into helpless laughter before demonstrating the way she had shown the parents their children's books, pointing out clever vocabulary and sage advice—all the time, unknowingly waving a foecally festooned sleeve under their noses. "Look," she said, doing the same to Liz, "have a sniff of that!"

"I think I'll pass."

Lucy laughed again. "Don't worry; I've just rinsed it in the sink." She picked up her bag. "Right, I'm off. Later, loser," she said and hurried out towards the car park, chortling.

When Liz got back, a man whom Liz recognised, presumably from the year sevens' first day, had arrived. He glanced at Liz's name plate before shaking Belle's hand, leering wolfishly and not letting go. Belle batted her lashes and flicked her hair; she was used to men introducing themselves to her this way. Liz smiled and held out her hand for him to shake. He grudgingly relinquished Belle and slowly turned towards Liz. As he did so, she caught the metallic scent of strong lager, interlaced with the musty sweetness of marijuana. Ignoring her proffered hand, he hooked his thumbs into the greasy waistband of his jeans and looked Liz up and down derisively before sitting in front of Belle and displaying a grimy crotch by leaning back and widening his thighs into a predatory grin.

Liz's flesh crept as she tried to place whose father he was. "I'm Mrs Marshall, year seven tutor," she said. "I don't think you're on my list. Whose dad are you?" There was always at least one child who forgot to book.

Slowly, deliberately, he turned to face her and rolled the match he was chewing to the other side of his mouth with his tongue. His eyes flicked from side to side furtively as he sniffed and wiped his nose with the back of his grimy hand.

"Alfie Willis's," he said.

Thankfully unnoticed by Sean Willis, Belle quickly stifled an involuntary gasp.

The words catapulted the Greater Manchester social worker's report that Liz had read in September back to the front of her mind: the women's refuge, Alfie's bruises, now disappeared, his mother's cracked ribs and lost baby. The statement also conjured two other images from the depths of Liz's memory like rabbits from a hat: the dark figure in the playground, glimpsed through Dave's window and the mysterious man staring, unnoticed by Alfie, into his camera lens from outside the classroom on Open Evening.

Alfie's father had been watching him for weeks and now, here he was, breaking the conditions of his restraining order. They would need to keep him there and call the police.

Liz controlled the gasp and shocked expression that might have warned him that they knew his history and thought quickly.

"I think you might be better talking to our head of year," she said calmly and gestured for him to follow her. He got to his feet with a disrespectful lack of alacrity, clicked his tongue twice in the side of his cheek and winked at Belle, who winced perceptibly now, before allowing himself to be led over to where Barbara's queue had finally disappeared.

"This is Alfie Willis's dad," Liz told her.

Barbara knew exactly what to do, as Liz had known she would. She politely asked him to take a seat and nodded to Liz, who went discreetly to inform Gordon and to call the police while Barbara kept him talking for as long as she could so they could intercept him before he left.

Liz came back and sat down and she and Barbara set about explaining all the school's routines and regulations: any neutral information, in fact, that would force Mr Willis to stay and listen, but would not be specific to Alfie, which might put him in danger.

Stifling a yawn, Mr Willis listened to Barbara's detailed information about the systems for setting, the rewards and sanctions procedures and the management of the transition from primary to secondary school. Mr Willis's leg jiggled impatiently as his expression became glazed.

Suddenly, his stare snapped back into focus and a cunning frown deepened on his forehead. His posture became taut, like a longbow at full draw. He clearly wanted something from them.

"Contact details," he said. "Can you check you've got my contact details?"

Glad of something else that would keep him there longer, Barbara found a piece of paper and a pen and passed them to him. "If you could write them down for us, I'll make sure we get them onto Alfie's record."

"Can't you just check now?" Sean asked, his tone betraying impatience.

Barbara remained patient. "We haven't got the records here, Mr Willis, but we'll add them to the database in the morning,"

He wrote and then paused, seeming unwilling to hand the paper back to Barbara just yet. Yvonne had noticed the exchange between Barbara and an obviously dissatisfied parent, but clearly did not comprehend the gravity of the situation. She pulled her chair alongside Barbara's and introduced herself to Sean, asking, "How may I help you today?"

Having found his nocking point, Sean took aim. "I was just trying to get them to put my contact details on Alfie's record."

"This is *Alfie Willis's* father, Mrs Dillon," Liz said, pointedly enough, she hoped, to indicate Yvonne should be cautious—she was supposed to be fully conversant with the details of all the 'at risk' students at the school—but not so emphatically as to raise Sean's suspicions and scare him off before the police arrived.

Obviously imagining herself professional, Yvonne rifled through her folders.

"Willis, Alfie," she muttered before pulling one out. "Here it is," she said, opening it.

"Thank you, Mrs Dillon, I'll see to it," said Barbara quickly and tried to take the folder out of Yvonne's hands, but Yvonne's grip was vice-like.

"It's fine," she said through gritted teeth.

Liz dived in, trying to divert Sean's attention.

"Alfie's an excellent form captain. He's—" but Yvonne cut across her.

"I see Alfie's moved house recently," Yvonne said, taking out the top page and smoothing it down, just out of reach of Barbara and Liz's reaching hands.

Sean leaned forward as he prepared to loose his arrow. "Yeah, to—er..." he said, stretching his neck towards the paper. "To—um..."

There was still no sign of the police. Liz desperately tried to signal to Yvonne; they couldn't let her disclose anything to him. Surely, she knew how serious this was.

Yvonne's finger scanned the page. "Ah, no, we don't have your details here."

She turned the page towards Sean.

Desperate, Liz snatched the piece of paper. She had to stop Yvonne, even if it meant Alfie's father realised and bolted.

"Sorry, it's confidential," she said.

But in one movement, Yvonne plucked the paper from Liz's hands and placed it in front of him. He had hit his target.

"Don't be silly, Mrs Marshall, this is his father," she hissed. "Mr Willlis, can you write your contact details in that box?"

But Sean stood up abruptly without writing anything else. He had what he wanted.

"17, Hillside Road. Thanks, ladies; you've been a great help," he said before striding out of the main doors.

Yvonne rounded on Liz and Barbara. "What was all that about?"

Barbara had more important things to do than answer her, however. She rushed towards Gordon.

"You'll need to call the police back straight away," she said urgently. "He's gone and he knows their address."

33: Off the Radar

Liz and Barbara were loath to leave until they knew Alfie and his mother were safe, so they helped the site staff to stack chairs and fold tables, ready for the following day. Yvonne had scuttled off to Gordon's office, muttering that she could not have been expected to know, while Gordon himself stood, tense of face, in Reception, alternately glancing at the door, the telephone and at Liz, but his expression was inscrutable and, despite her concern for Alfie, Liz could not help but remember, with a shiver of dread, Gordon's frown as he had leafed through the newsletter earlier and seen the potentially compromising World Book Day photograph.

At last, the telephone in Reception rang. Liz and Barbara froze and watched Gordon from their position in the hall as he spoke briefly and nodded before replacing the receiver and heading towards them, his features still strained and uneasy-looking.

"The police picked him up before he got there, thankfully," he told them. "They've cautioned him and they're issuing a protection order so he should be out of the picture now."

Liz was still worried. "What if he breaches it like he did when they had to move here?"

"The Willises still have the option to start again somewhere else, according to the police," Gordon said, "but they want to stay. They'll have to move house again, though."

Barbara looked at him unflinchingly, over the top of her glasses. "It was lucky that Liz and I were so familiar with his case and that we knew how to implement the correct procedure," she said. "It could have worked out much—" she paused and deliberately removed her glasses— "much worse."

Gordon shifted uncomfortably from foot to foot and coughed gently before speaking; the elephant in the room was already in his office and would, doubtless, be addressed before long and in private, but for now, Gordon managed, "Yes, thank you, both, for your swift actions," and, gathering momentum, he salvaged his headmasterly veneer and continued. "The wellness of our learners is my number one top priority." He snapped his smile back on, as if to underline his soundbite. "'Night, ladies," he said and performed a hundred-and-eighty degree turn before marching, with a corvid flap of his robe, towards his office and his waiting wife.

By the time Liz left work, it was nearly nine, but the twin triumphs of the thwarting of Sean Willis and the retrieval of Gordon's approval, however grudging, buoyed her. The sky glowed apricot and violet, the evening star glimmered and, as in the old ballad, the new moon held the old moon in her arms.

When she arrived home, she kicked off her shoes and flopped onto the sofa.

"Only one more day," Jack pointed out cheerfully as he placed a plated-up, heated-up, home-cooked meal onto her lap and a welcome glass of red into her hand.

"One more day," Liz repeated sleepily, an hour later, when she got into bed, comforted by the almost papery crinkle of the duvet and the down-soft sigh as its feathers settled around her, soothing her to sleep.

The next morning, Liz was logging onto her computer, ready for morning registration, when a duo of heads popped round the door. Alfie and Maisie, inseparable since forming their successful journalistic partnership as well as their twin form captaincies, asked whether they could come in, even though the bell had not yet gone for registration.

"Alfie!" said Liz. "I wasn't expecting you in today. Are you all right?"

Alfie smiled and gave Liz an envelope. "I'm fine," he said. "Mum asked me to give you this."

It was a card from Sarah Willis.

"I've given one to Miss Bosun too," Alfie said. "The policeman said it was you two who we've got to thank."

Liz laughed. "I'm not sure he meant it that literally. It's our *job* to look after you."

"Well, Mum said Mrs Dillon didn't, so I'm glad you two were there." Alfie's smile faded as the same memories that had troubled his mother the previous evening flourished in his mind like the wind passing through grass. "It could have been really bad."

"Well, tell your mum there was no need for thanks, but thanks anyway," Liz said.

Maisie had been atypically quiet, but now she joined in. "And guess what the best bit is." Without waiting for the demanded speculation, she plunged on. "Alfie's staying at my house."

"Yeah," Alfie confirmed, "Maisie and her mum and dad were at our house when the police got there 'cause they'd given my mum a lift."

"And we've got loads of room and they couldn't stay at theirs any more," Maisie added.

Liz looked down at the card she had just been given. *Dear Mrs Marshall*, it read, *Thank you for everything you did last night— Alfie and I are safe thanks to your quick thinking.*

She set the card discreetly on a shelf behind her desk just as the bell went and the other students arrived. Emin swaggered in last, wearing a pair of luminous orange trainers.

"Where are your school shoes, Emin?" Liz asked.

By way of response, Emin handed her a note, scrawled on lined paper, torn from an exercise book: *Emin is not waring his school shoes today hes gone and got dogshit on them.*

At the end of the day, Dave intercepted Liz on the way out. "Well, you can actually enjoy your Easter holidays now," he said. "I've just been talking to Dildo about you and you're flavour of the month after last night."

"I didn't really do anything, though," Liz replied.

Demonstrating an understanding of school politics that he rarely flaunted in the normal course of his work and which went some way towards explaining his successful stewardship of the department, Dave enlightened Liz. "Ah, but if you and Babs hadn't done what you did, Yvonne's cock-up would've had major consequences. Dildo would've had to suspend her for not following correct procedure, neglecting her duty of care and endangering a student."

"So, do you think he'll reinstate Babs as head of year seven out of gratitude, then?" Liz said.

"I don't think he'll go that far," Dave said; "she rubbed his nose in it too much. Lucky for you, you had the sense not to criticise his wife to his face."

"Christ, after Lady Macbeth-gate, I wouldn't dare!" Liz laughed. "Anyway, I was trying to keep a low profile about the *ménage à trois* thing in the newsletter!"

"I told you you didn't have to worry about that; he didn't take it seriously. He didn't even get it," Dave said before looking at her mischievously and adding, "As if you'd ever get up to anything with a sixth-former," he snorted. "You wouldn't get the fucking chance!"

"Cheeky bastard!" laughed Liz. "I'll have you know, I'm a renowned milf!"

Dave became serious again as he reassured her. "Seriously, though, you should be all right now. I even reminded him of everything that was wrong about Magoo's lesson observation," he said. "He pretended it was nothing to do with him and Magoo did it wrong, but he said he'll have another look at it with my objections in mind. But that's not all." Dave grinned now.

"What?"

"I mentioned Pam Hooper's report and that Woody had cancelled it before he retired because of the way she did it."

"And?"

"Gordon said he must have had a paper copy from Pam's files *somehow* and they'd make sure any files they look at from now on will be the official ones from the right folders."

"So does that mean he's discounting it? I'm off the hook?" Liz was beginning to smile now.

Dave nodded. "It does. For now, anyway,"

Relief consumed Liz. "Thank God for that. You're a miracle worker," she said.

"Luckily for you, I just know when to press an advantage," Dave replied.

34: Countdown

The summer term was, as ever, a term of two very different halves: the first was packed and panic-stricken as year eleven and thirteen students were made ready for their exams and the second was a slow winding down as students left, exam season started and timetables lightened. It was this lightening that occupied Liz's mind as she drove home on the sunny Friday afternoon before the Whitsun break, for once, not dreading, prematurely, the next half term. The late May lanes were effervescent with cow parsley and the air was sickly with nectar, clotted with willow-fluff, and bubbling with the fluid melodies of thrushes, robins and wrens.

The same lanes had somewhat less appeal ten days later, when Liz returned to King Richard's, batteries recharged and loins girded, for the final push. First on the agenda was a mammoth revision session in preparation for the English Language exam, later that week. The hall had been booked and the English teachers had to bring their classes down after registering them in their own classrooms. Liz greeted her year elevens in her room and handed out books, past papers and highlighters, reassuring them that everything would be fine and that this revision session would just remind them of all the things they knew already anyway. After the register had been taken, they had a few minutes to wait before they went to the hall so the students chatted while Liz gathered together everything she would need.

The tranquillity was abruptly rent asunder when a year eleven boy from another class thrust his head round the door frame. With all the arrogance and selfism of youth, he seemed to have forgotten the time he had spent in Liz's year nine class, two years previously, when he had repeatedly endeavoured to drive her to psychosis with his exploits, and, grinning maniacally, he yelled, "Hiya, Miss. Do you miss me?"

Ever sincere, Liz answered, "Every minute of every day, Jamie."

"Really?" he said, incomprehensive of the sarcasm, which she had made no attempt to conceal, and dived into the next classroom, where he would, indubitably, hail Serena in the same manner.

"Twat," Liz muttered under her breath as she picked up her pile of spare pens and papers.

A gasp made Liz spin round. Unheard by Liz, Becky had come to her desk to ask her a question. Liz's hand flew to her mouth. "Sorry," she said, "deeply unprofessional of me."

"Don't worry, we won't tell anyone," Ellie chipped in, her lip-reading skills clearly having been honed to perfection.

Becky giggled. "He is though, isn't he, Miss?" she agreed.

"We'll just write it down in the book," Dan teased. "Oi, Ellie, have you got the *Miss's Misdemeanours* book. Need to get this one on record."

"Oh yes," said Joe, miming opening a reporter's notebook and writing, "never know when it might come in useful."

Liz laughed. She was going to miss this lot. "Come on, gang," she said, standing up; "we're going to be late."

Peggy led the session, supported by the rest of the department, who would circulate among the students, helping them implement the skills they had been learning for the last two years. She was guiding the students through a past paper and had prepared a PowerPoint presentation to support the session. The students had read and annotated an extract from a short story and purposeful quiet settled on the hall while they were given exactly twelve minutes to analyse the way the writer of the excerpt had created a 'chilling tone' in the first paragraph. This gave the teachers a few minutes' break to check their phones, whisper or daydream before they were needed again.

Suddenly, Liz became aware of the sound of wheezing. She scanned the room with her eyes; the heat and stress had given students asthma and panic attacks a few times before, but she could not see who was in distress. She turned towards the back of the room. Dave was doubled over, gasping with broken, laboured breaths, his face purple and his eyes streaming.

"Shit!" she stage-whispered. "You all right, Bish?"

With what looked like considerable effort, he sucked in a rasping breath that sounded more like a death-rattle and raised a feeble hand. Pointing at the whiteboard, he regained control of his breathing and stood up straight.

He was not in imminent danger of asphyxiation; he was helpless with laughter and students were starting to notice.

"What?" Liz hissed, but he just pointed again, unable to articulate an explanation.

Liz glanced at the board where Peggy had entitled the PowerPoint slide, *Countdown to the Exam*.

"What about it?" Liz said and looked again.

Peggy had used her, at best, mediocre design skills to prepare the presentation, and had taken real pride in this one. The heading was in vibrant purple san serif capitals, emboldened for impact and clarity, and the font was so big that the nine letter word would not fit the space and Peggy had had to split it so that *down* was on the next line. The *to* and *the* were in much smaller, italicised black letters and were, at first, hardly noticeable so that, from a distance, it read COUNT DOWN EXAM. Except it didn't really. The thing that had obviously rendered Dave insensible, was that Peggy had replaced the *O* in *COUNT* with a Clip Art picture of an alarm clock, whose resolution was so low that it was far less distinct than the letters either side of it and seemed to recede into the background, whereas the *C* word of which she had so nearly fallen foul in her lesson observation earlier that year screamed out of the whiteboard all the more loudly. Dave would think she was doing it on purpose.

Liz read it out in a whisper, realisation dawning as she read: "Cunt...down...exam!" She laughed. "It's a pube inspection!"

At this, Dave was overcome by a fresh gale of laughter and all around the hall, students had come to the end of their practice question and were looking up and noticing him, as well as what he himself had observed. Year elevens nudged, whispered and pointed as audible amusement spread through the hall and most seemed more entertained by their teachers' merriment than by the slide itself. Peggy clucked and shushed them, looking at the slide in bewilderment before ushering them to the next part of the session: reviewing their answers, helped by one teacher to each table of students.

Aware that her writing time had come to an end, Kayleigh, there against all odds, sat up and surveyed her three paragraphs with satisfaction.

"Will you check mine, Miss? I've been practising how to do this all week."

"Have you shown Freya?" Liz asked, "We're doing peer assessment first."

Liz had heard that Freya had appointed herself, in loco parentis, as responsible for piloting Kayleigh through her revision and GCSEs, dragging her into school at the crack of dawn for her many revision sessions and exams.

Kayleigh pushed her paper over to Freya. "There you go, Frabe. Enjoy."

Liz read Kayleigh's first paragraph over Freya's shoulder: *I dont agree about there being a chilling tone because the boy is shouting 'give them back!' not chilling out. I know this because of the ~~explan~~ exclaimation mark. There is definately nothing chilled about that and I persionly think that insted of chiling, the tone is wierd and frightning.*

Liz was trying to formulate a tactful and encouraging response, but Freya, serious about her role as exam guru, screamed with laughter.

"Not that type of chilling, Kayleigh, you dozy cow," she advised.

For the last part of the session, Peggy focused on the writing part of the exam. She recapped the examiners' marking criteria and, somewhat paradoxically, advised a checklist of ways to demonstrate creativity, which, she hoped, would silence the hackneyed refrain—or was it just a pre-emptive excuse?—of the GCSE student: "You can't revise English."

This checklist *could* be memorised and included such creative writing course staples as using a surprising viewpoint, not revealed until the end; assuming a persona different from oneself, and, for the extremely confident, employing and sustaining an unorthodox idiolect. Students were also encouraged to experiment structurally and Peggy's Power Point summarised *in medias res*, flashback and cyclical structure as well as the structure within sentences. Peggy outlined some of the different ways sentences could be made, not only entertaining and varied, but also technically adept. Patiently, she explained the foregrounding effect of the leading adverb. She provided examples, which had been painstakingly reproduced on coloured paper, of the extra detail endowed by the embedded subordinate clause. The passive voice was also expounded by Peggy as an indicator of a student's ability to manipulate the reactions of the reader deliberately: proof to any examiner of creative prowess. The final piece of advice about sentences and structure would, again, enable the students to achieve credit for the conscious crafting of their writing by using one-word 'sentences', preferably presented as discrete paragraphs.

Simple.

Soon the students would be given some writing prompts from past papers and challenged to use the checklist and write their own creative pieces: a difficult enough feat in a hall full of their fellow exam candidates, but surely impossible, Liz thought, when it came to the real exam; youthful resilience and useful adrenaline would obviously have to be key factors in the success of students of English. However, before she let them try a couple of paragraphs of their own, Peggy reminded them of the need to use a range of punctuation marks and displayed a slide with some examples of sophisticated ones they might otherwise forget.

Peggy paused, looked at the teenagers gravely and said, "It's important that, when you get to the original writing section of the exam—" but she was cut off, mid-sentence.

From several parts of the hall, students called, asking what section of the exam paper that was, as if they had not attended a single lesson since year ten, nor been reminded of this every English lesson since before the mocks.

"Section B," said Peggy with unwavering patience.

Liz promised herself she would emulate Peggy's forbearance from now on, a promise that would, undoubtedly be broken before the day was out if past performance was any indicator of future behaviour.

"Which paper is it on?" Different voices, now, from different parts of the hall.

Lastly, Kayleigh's plaintive voice asked, "How many papers *are* there?"

Once these worries were dealt with, Peggy continued: "As I was saying, when you get to section B, it's important to plan your writing before you start."

Again, a few of the youths in front of her were reluctant to accept the wisdom of experience, not to mention the advice of the exam board; a flurry of assertions that planning was unnecessary ensued and when Jamie, arrogant as ever, called out, "Planning's a waste of time. *I* never do a plan," Peggy responded, placid as ever.

"You're right, Jamie," she appeared to concede. "Some of the most able students don't need to."

Jamie, pacified by Peggy's pretence, smirked and looked around, nodding smugly before Peggy continued in an unusually caustic manner. "How *did* you do on this section in the mocks?"

Jamie stopped smiling and slid a little further down in his seat.

A triumphant shout came from another table: "Owned!"

Peggy carried on, visibly gratified that her conquest of Jamie had been recognised and celebrated, however briefly by the other students. "Now, if you've written a list of what you need to remember at the top of your exam paper, you can tick off all the items, including, the best punctuation marks, when you check and edit your writing at the end."

There was a ripple as students wondered whether they dared to give voice to their opinion that editing was unnecessary. Jamie, with the skin of an elephant, and memory of a goldfish, asserted loudly that he never proof-read his writing—as if his teachers were in any doubt about that.

"So," said Peggy, "Start writing now and don't forget your colons, semicolons and parenthetic commas; they'll impress the examiner most."

The year elevens quickly chose from the list of writing tasks on the board and began their practice paragraphs. Some were meticulous in their application of all the items Peggy had specified; others fell to writing immediately and without stopping, forgetting the ten minutes that had preceded their efforts and almost certainly setting themselves up for crushing disappointment in the very near future.

Liz circled the table to which she had been assigned and looked over Kayleigh's shoulder at her paragraph. Her 'description', inspired by a photograph of a busy beach, was a story completely devoid of adjectives and written solely in one, long compound sentence: *'I was walking along the sand eating a candy floss when suddenly a man ran past and he had a handbag but it wasnt his because it was this womens and she couldnt catch him but she tryed to run and she was shouting for help but noone helped her and the man just ran off towards the arcade so she had to call the police but they didnt come quickly enouth and he got away.'*

"Okay, Kayleigh," said Liz, sitting down, "you've got a great story here: really exciting."

Kayleigh beamed with pride before Liz continued. "But you've got to get all the things in that the examiners want or they can't give you the marks."

By the end of the time the students had been given, Liz had coaxed Kayleigh to make her one sentence into six; put in some adjectives, adverbs and a subordinate clause or two; change a couple of her lacklustre verbs, and supplement her description with a simile. The redrafted version showed a marked improvement: *'I was stroling peacefuly along the golden sand eating sweet candy floss when sudenley a dodgey man sprinted past. Anxously he was griping a posh hand bag but it was'nt his. It belonged to a elegent women who could'nt catch him because she could not run in her stileto heels like dagers stabing into the soft sand. Even though she was shouting franticly, noone helped the poor woman and the evil man just ran off as fast as a cheeta towards the colorfull arcade. She called the police but they were as slow as a snail and the wicked man excaped.'*

"Now let's see if you can get in those punctuation marks Miss told you about," prompted Liz and lowered her voice to remind Kayleigh about semicolons. Kayleigh shrieked with laughter at Liz's suggestion and passed the information on to Freya. There were two students who might remember that advice, anyway.

From Liz's table, the recommendation quickly spread around the room so that, by the time Peggy had stopped them writing and initiated peer assessment, most of the students had been made aware of it and Peggy, realising something was inspiring the students, called for quiet so she could ascertain what it was.

"Miss Marshall just told me a really good tip, Miss," Kayleigh volunteered eagerly. "Go on, Miss Marshall."

The hall was silent. Most of the students knew roughly what she had told Kayleigh and now they wanted to hear it from her mouth. Liz rolled her eyes. She might as well tell them; at least they would all remember it. "I was just telling Kayleigh that it's a good idea to know what to do with a semi—" she said and paused, amused by the titters of appreciation, not least from Dave. "—colon," she continued, utterly straight-faced.

Peggy nodded, smiling, oblivious to the double entendre, and reiterated the advice for the benefit of the year elevens. "Precisely, Mrs Marshall," she shouted over their clamour. "Remember, always get a semicolon in if you possibly can," she said, regarding the students with an expression that betrayed a mixture of pleasure and puzzlement. Her revision sessions did not usually go as well as this.

Dave hiccoughed noisily and Peggy continued: "You'll never be sorry you did. The results can be surprisingly rewarding, can't they, Mrs Marshall?"

Liz glanced at the crimson-faced, weeping Dave before delivering her reply: "Always worth squeezing in a semi."

35: Exams

The wind-down to the end of the school year began with years eleven and thirteen having officially left with nothing before the end of term but exams and the leavers' balls. The first English Language exam was on the Thursday after Peggy's revision session and as soon as it was allowed, Dave looked at the paper so he could report back to her, which he did at morning break.

He waited until most of the department was sitting with coffee and biscuits and Peggy was rooting in the back of the cupboard for emergency chocolate—coffee break being the emergency—then made his 'just play along' face to Liz and the others. "Weird choice of non-fiction extracts this year," he threw in.

The rest of them made encouraging comments, knowing better than to try and predict Dave's latest hoax, but Peggy seemed not to have noticed. Dave spoke more loudly. "Must have stumped a lot of our kids."

Still nothing from Peggy, half inside the cupboard now. At last, her tenacity paid off and she emerged, brandishing something promising, judging by its purple wrapper.

Liz came to Dave's aid. "What was that you were saying about the exam, Bish?"

Dave tried again. "*I*'d have thought it was a bit inappropriate to have extracts about Operation Yew Tree on the exam paper, but I suppose they know what they're doing," he announced.

Peggy had been about to take a bite of her chocolate, but she stopped and her eyebrows shot up. "You're joking," she said, little suspecting the accuracy of her comment.

"It's true," stated Dave, mendaciously. "There's a bit of Wikipedia—"

"Wikipaedo," interrupted Liz.

"Too far, Liz," Dave replied, winking.

Peggy's horror mounted. "Go on. What else was there?"

"I bet it was a Daily Mail article—" Gareth said. "The board's bloody obsessed with the Mail Online," he observed. "There's always something on the exam from there."

"I thought teachers were all supposed to be socialists," said Lucy. "What are they even doing on the Daily Mail website anyway?"

"Go on, Dave; what was the other extract?" Peggy said, impatiently.

A mischievous glimmer crept into Dave's eye. "Extract from Savile's diaries."

"Well, that's just bloody typical." Uncharacteristically, Peggy had raised her voice. "I haven't done anything on Yew Tree with my class. They won't know how to tackle that."

Dave, fully on the brink of collapse now, replied, "That's not the worst bit."

Peggy postponed the chocolate again. "Oh my God! What?"

"Section B was: *Write a letter to Jim'll Fix It*."

This was too much for Peggy and she slammed the bar down on the table. "Well, that's scuppered my results, anyway! Are you going to complain?"

The howls of laughter that exploded from the rest of the department informed Peggy of her gullibility and she beamed.

"You silly bugger!" she chided and had another attempt at the chocolate.

As soon as the external exams were over, the year ten mocks began, resulting in the staff having a blissful week with very few lessons to prepare or teach, although the hiatus in workload would end soon enough, when it was time to mark their papers. Unlike the externals, which were supervised by professional invigilators, the mock exams were supervised by teachers and the already demob-happy English staff stove off exam-hall boredom by playing all the customary exam-hall games.

"Right, you lot," said Dave one lunch time before they had to go over to the hall for the afternoon exam, "usual rules. Five sheets of paper each and the first to get rid of all theirs wins."

Belle, having already voiced her opinion about why they shouldn't have to invigilate in the first place—an opinion that fell on deaf ears—looked up from her phone, confused.

Liz furnished her with an explanation. "When kids need an extra piece of paper, they put their hands up," she said. "The object of the game is to be the one who gives them that paper, so you have to race to get to them before anyone else."

Belle sniffed. "Isn't that a bit disruptive for the children?"

"Fuck 'em," Dave said, provocatively; "they're only kids."

Belle rose to the bait, opened her mouth to protest and then closed it again, perhaps remembering that Dave would be instrumental in helping her secure a permanent job when she had qualified.

Liz watched in amusement and decided to add to the fun: "Yeah, that's why they hire professionals for the real exams in this school," she said. "They won't let us do it."

"Not after the last time," Dave said darkly.

Belle sniffed again and gave a small toss of her head.

Liz relented. "No, seriously, the kids don't even realise we're doing it," she said, "and it's only the year ten mocks, not the real GCSEs. Take no notice of Dave; he's winding you up."

Belle seemed mollified and Dave chuckled and stood up. "Come on, then. Phones on silent," he said. "Let's invigilate the fuck out of this exam."

Once the students had been installed in their seats and the exam had started, a purposeful silence settled on the hall, broken softly by the scratching of pens and the turning of pages. It was too early for students to begin asking for extra sheets of paper yet, but judging by the furrow of his brow and the occasional upturn of his mouth, Dave was devising some entertainment for his team. He tapped his phone a few times, pocketed it and looked around expectantly. After a second or two, every member of the English department, including Liz, looked at his or her phone. Dave had sent the message, *Game 1- stand by student. Wait for instruction ;)*

Smiles and stifled giggles proliferated as they waited for Dave's follow-up.

Shittest haircut.

Immediately, they made their various ways—not so eagerly as to arouse suspicion or cause disturbance—towards various students. Lucy, making an exception to her politically correct principles of not criticising anyone's appearance—on the grounds that he was vile—beat Liz and Serena to a boy with a bleached mullet and tramlines. On top of this, he had trained his fringe into a quiff, which exaggerated his forehead. His chin was likewise augmented by a pointed beard, also bleached. Lucy had chosen the only student whose appearance any of them felt comfortable criticising, so Liz and Serena had to make do with the unwashed and the overly product-laden. Dave, on the other hand, had no such compunctions and planted himself decisively next to a delightful boy with the misfortune of having suffered a bout of exam-induced alopecia, which had rendered him semi-bald. However, even Dave had to concede that Patchy Pete was no competition for Macaulay's impression of Banana Man. He texted the winner to the others: *Lucy*.

A few more rounds of *Stand By Student* followed, during which they judged best hair (Lauren), most obnoxious (a race to stand by Macaulay), and those most likely to succeed (Pete), serve time (Macaulay) or end up in rehab (also Macaulay). All of the movement by the teachers confirmed to the students that they were fulfilling their invigilatory obligations and even Belle did not seem to notice any unusual activity of which she might disapprove and have cause to complain. Twenty minutes into the exam, Dave texted again: *Get 5 sheets each but quick game of pacman till paper needed :)*

Accompanied by a few puzzled glances from the students, all four of them approached the stage at the front, to the pile of spare lined paper, and counted their sheets. Liz got five for Belle as well and went to give them to her, whispering, "Kids should start asking for more paper before long."

Belle accepted the paper, but did not take up a *Pac-Man* position, so the other four chose their places to stand before Dave gave the nod and became the eponymous character to the women's ghosts. Serena was ruthless, mercilessly herding Dave towards the other two until there was nowhere for him to go and she touched his chest, claiming the win and taking on the mantle of Pac-Man.

As soon the students started running out of paper, *Pac-Man* became too much of a nuisance and they switched to *Chicken*. Pairing off, they walked slowly towards each other along an aisle, each holding his or her nerve for as long as possible; the first to veer off and avoid a collision, being the loser. The paper race added jeopardy to this game; if a student wanted more paper, the teachers would need to decide which game they wanted to win more. Often, it was a decision based on proximity and Liz and Dave had both reasoned that the most able students, who were in Dave's top set, would write more and need more paper. They had, therefore, placed themselves at the far end of the hall. However, Serena and Lucy were right at the other end, reasoning that the least able would make the most mistakes, finish first and ask for paper for doodling.

Liz and Dave's reckoning turned out to be correct and, as they approached each other step by slow, unerring step, a hand went up—behind Dave. Liz now had to decide whether to forfeit *Chicken* in favour of *Paper Race*. She avoided alerting Dave to the movement he had not seen and waited until they had almost reached each other and then, feigning silent disappointment, she swerved to the right, leaving Dave to celebrate his victory, again, in silence. Liz seized her opportunity and speed-walked to the back of the hall to deliver the paper, but she must have given herself away because Dave wheeled round and sprang towards the bemused student with the raised hand, slamming it onto the table in front of him and narrowly escaping crashing to the floor by allowing his momentum to carry him to the back wall, breaking his fall, but almost dislocating his left shoulder, which he rubbed, shaking hysterically, whispering to Liz, "Double victory!"

It became clear that some of the students in Dave's top set were wise to these games and Liz noticed a couple of exchanged glances. The next hand to go up was right at the front of the hall and suddenly about a dozen of Dave's students' eyes were on them, ready to watch the race. They both started towards the student in need, gathering speed as they went, judging when to stretch an arm for the final slam.

They had reckoned without Belle, though; she calmly placed a sheet of paper on the student's desk and raised a triumphant eyebrow at them. It was difficult to calculate whether she was joining in or quashing the game and Liz was trying to weigh up the probability of each eventuality when her phone vibrated in her pocket. She looked at the screen. It was a message from Belle: *I win :)*

Liz nudged Dave and they looked over at Belle. She was delicately wiggling the fingers of both of her hands in the air. Her empty hands.

Later, in the office, Dave admitted Belle's tactical supremacy in winning *Paper Race*. "I can't deny it, Belle," he laughed; "you crushed us."

"Thank you, Dave. I always win at games," she crowed.

"I didn't even think you were playing," Dave said.

Belle batted her eyelashes. "I always do."

36: Summer

Summer established itself and the school year slouched its way towards the end of July—but Liz would not allow herself to think about that yet. Life became slower, days hotter.

One afternoon, as the thermometer in Liz's stifling room, empty of students since the exam classes had left, reached thirty-eight degrees, Liz tried, without success, to concentrate on planning for the following year. She wilted as trickles of sweat ran the length of her back and she tried to keep cool by flapping her clothes and spreading herself out as much as possible so as to avoid any contact between one part of her skin and another. In this attitude, she gazed listlessly out of the window.

A dead blackbird with a twisted neck and gaping beak was even more awkwardly splayed on one of the picnic tables in the shade outside the tuck shop. It looked as if it had flown into one of the windows and suffered an agonised death. Liz roused herself to dispose of the pitiful creature and, armed with some paper towels and a plastic carrier bag from the staffroom, she made her way towards it. As she approached, she noticed some movement in its chest. Its heart was still beating and its beak convulsed as it laboured to breathe. Perhaps this would be better dealt with by one of the science teachers; it would have to be euthanised and surely a biologist would be best equipped to perform the task. Liz turned towards the science block and, as she did, she heard gentle scrabbling. She turned back to see the blackbird get to its feet, blink at her and bob its tail before hopping to the next table and carefully, but misshapenly unfolding itself again in order to cool itself in the same grotesque parody of death as it had before.

Heartened and refreshed, she returned to her room. When she got there, Belle had arrived, face lively and animated as she concentrated on her tablet. Liz was mildly irritated; she wished Belle would put as much effort into her lesson planning as she did into her romantic encounters. No doubt she would be sloping off early to meet someone from Tinder. However, as Liz got within eyeshot of the screen, she saw that Belle was, in fact, working—and it looked pretty good. Liz admonished herself for being so judgmental and attempted to redress the balance by adopting something approaching motherly interest.

She opened with, "How's your love-life, Belle? Met anyone nice recently?"

Belle looked a bit surprised, but recovered herself and answered, "Oh, I'm not looking any more," she said and answered Liz's questioning expression with, "I'm focusing on passing my training and getting a job."

Liz felt almost proud; she was a pretty good kid really and, now Liz thought about it, she had not done anything to annoy her for a while; they'd been getting on fine and her teaching had always been sound. "Any good ones coming up?" She faltered. "Jobs, I mean."

Belle smiled and reddened. "Well, I've got an interview at a school in Exeter on Friday," she said, "I really want it. Dave said he'd give me a good reference."

"I bet he will," thought Liz, knowing Dave's opinion of Belle had always been stubbornly low, despite her recent improvement in attitude. She said, "Exeter's a long way away. Good luck though. Let me know if you want any help with the lesson you have to teach."

Belle spoke with enthusiasm. "I've got to teach a poetry lesson to a year seven class, so I thought I'd practise a few ideas on ours, if that's all right. I just want it to be perfect."

Liz didn't have to be asked twice to give the class to Belle a few times in the next week. "Of course," she said magnanimously. "Whatever it takes."

She and Belle worked companionably in the same room, the sultry heat in a quiet room being more conducive to productivity than the constant chatter and interruptions downstairs, where the air conditioning was. Suddenly, Belle squeaked, "Ooh, Bog Blog! I'd forgotten about that. My uni friend just sent me the latest link. Shall I read it out?"

Liz sat up, amused. Belle had still never put two and two together and realised that the water-closet gossip came from this very lavatory or that she had sometimes been its main subject.

"Here goes, then," said Belle and wriggled, settling herself comfortably, ready to read. "*Welcome to the washroom. Lulu Rolls here, your lady of the latrine with the next in—stall—ment of that to which I'm privy here in my watery world. Not all of the entrances and exits were as easily performed as in my first edition. One who paid me a visit overstayed her welcome; she secured my entrance too vigorously and the lock stuck tight, cloistering her in these living walls of toil*-et *(sorry, Donne)*—Not sure I get that. Funny, though, Lucy locked herself in the loo here, didn't she?" Belle said, still unsuspecting, before resuming her reading. "*—until a knight in shining armour attacked the door with his silver lance.* Hang on." The scales began to fall from Belle's eyes. "That sounds *a lot* like Lucy. Remember when Andy had to come and unscrew the lock and get her out and he still had all his hi vis on? Shining armour! His screwdriver could be the lance!"

The only sensible course of action available to Liz was to go along with Belle; she did not need to know it was her—yet, so when Belle asked, "Do you think someone here is writing Bog Blog?" Liz had to be seen to entertain the possibility.

"Well, maybe," she conceded, "but who?"

"Let's see what else it says," Belle said and carried on. "*That's not the only lavatorial mishap to pass into these hallowed walls. On an evening when parents were visiting, a mother brought with her a pungent reminder of her child. This mother's son neither mewled nor puked on his mother's knee, rather he deposited his offering upon her ravelled sleeve of care, but this too too solid was resolved into a dew—adieu—and rinsed down my porcelain's pipes. But it is my job: to witness the basest doings of man, the things rank and gross in nature, and to oversee their disposal.*" Belle stopped and looked at Liz triumphantly. "It *is* here. That was Lucy at parents' evening. It's too much of a coincidence otherwise."

Liz looked as if she was trying to remember.

"Remember?" Belle prompted. "She had to go and wash her sleeve when she realised."

"Oh yes, I remember," said Liz.

Belle's eyes widened. "Maybe it's her."

"Maybe," said Liz, "but it could be anyone who uses the English Block loo. That's any of us, DT, the site team or the caterers."

"Ah, but look at all the Shakespeare and poem references. It's got to be an English teacher." Belle was in detective mode now. "Right, let's see how it ends," she said, "Ready?"

Liz nodded, enjoying her last few moments of secrecy.

"*My last visitors never made it across my threshold. A secret assignation, thwarted by a spoilsport.*" Belle paused; the scenario seemed to be ringing a bell. "*Like Pyramus and Thisbe: he, with his long sword never drawn—which this lady could not abide—and she, never putting her lips to that cranny. There he waited by the entrance to this Ninus' Tomb, when she to him did appear, as if by chance—*" Belle paused again, pondering. "*—and this grisly beast appeared... like the lion in the story...and she...fled.*" Belle's voice slowed as she finished the blog and realisation dawned. "Hang on, that's me! That's what happened on parents' evening."

"Is it?"

"Yeah: remember, you came down to the loo and Ben was, er, just about to go in and then I came the other way, through the DT rooms," Belle said.

Liz recalled it perfectly. "Oh yes, I remember."

"Someone else must have seen what happened, then," said Belle. "They must have thought Ben and I were..." she trailed off. "Oh my God!" she squealed as the penny finally dropped.

Liz tried to look innocent.

"It was you! You're the grisly beast!"

"I... I..." Liz stammered.

Belle stared, wide-eyed and open-mouthed.

The two pillars of anonymity and entitlement that had borne up what, to Liz, had seemed like harmless fun, especially when Belle had been less agreeable, now crashed around her ears as the Samson of her guilt took hold of them and pushed with all his might. "Guilty. I'm sorry," she said simply.

In a wholly unselfconscious gesture, Belle threw her head back and howled with laughter. "No, this is brilliant. Wait till I tell my friend!" she screamed, but her expression soon became serious. "I need to tell you something, Liz."

Another bullet dodged and Liz felt a second surge of warmth towards Belle. "What's that?"

Belle looked towards the door and lowered her voice. "You can't tell Dave."

"Okay," said Liz, "as long as it's nothing criminal, I don't have to."

"Don't worry; it's not," Belle said and checked the door again. "You know I said I wasn't dating any more?"

Liz nodded.

"And I've got that interview?"

Liz was beginning to put two and two together now.

"Well, Ben's got an unconditional offer from Exeter." Four.

"We're a thing now," smiled Belle and accompanied her next sentence with digital inverted commas. "We're in a relationship—or will be once I've left here."

Liz smiled cautiously. Are you sure you want to tell me this?"

"Look," she said, "After New Year's, I was really worried and I kept out of Ben's way, but do you remember on World Book Day, we passed him on the stairs and we both knew there was still something there."

Liz pretended she had not noticed. "Oh?"

"I'm pretty sure you realised, Liz," she said. "Look, I know I was a massive bitch before, but this is the real thing with Ben. He's older than the others–he's only two years younger than me and he's made me grow up. I didn't even know he was a student when I met him—well, he wasn't; he came back after Christmas."

Liz was happy to agree this was true; she had always backed Belle on this in principle.

Belle continued, "Anyway, he's insisted we wait till I've finished here and he's already left school, so there'll be nothing to stop us soon." She stopped again. "But I really want that job near him and I really need that reference from Dave."

"I'm really happy for you, honestly," said Liz, "and I'll try and big you up to Dave."

"Thanks, Liz." Belle smiled and returned to her lesson planning.

Liz turned to her computer again. Dave had given her the responsibility of being in charge of the department's display material the following year and wanted her to start with making a set of mnemonic and inspirational posters that could be displayed in every English room and this seemed more appealing a task than the planning she had been trying to concentrate on before. The devil found work for her idle hands, however, and soon, she had mocked up some rough ideas and printed them out. Chuckling to herself, she went downstairs to Dave's room.

"Hey, Bish, you know those mnemonic posters you wanted me to do?" she said.

"Ja, Herr Goebbels," he replied, "vot heff you got for me?"

Liz started with a couple of slogans she knew she would not get past him. "How about *careful where you put your colon?*" she ventured.

"Nein."

"You're not going to like *squeeze in a semi*, then."

Dave laughed. "Is that all you've come up with today?" he asked. "Anyway, the second one was from the revision sesh. Call yourself Minister for Propaganda? Vee heff vays off making you do better."

Liz straightened and stamped her foot to attention. "Jawohl, mein Kapitän," she said. "Do you want to hear the rest? I've got a few mnemonics here."

"Hit me."

Liz started shrewdly. She knew there would be some bartering involved. "Okay, this one's for when the kids have to do their corrections," she began. "Directed Improvement and Reflection Time for You. This one's used in other schools nearby, Belle said; she's given me some great ideas she's been working on at uni. "

Dave's face contorted slightly as he tried to remember whether he'd come across the acronym in area training courses, so Liz helped him. "It's only the key words, so you wouldn't count 'and' and 'for'." She waited a second or two before supplying the answer: "Dirty."

"I love it but it's a no to that as well," he said. "From what I remember, other schools aren't adding a Y."

Liz shrugged. "Your loss. Can we have 'DIRT' though?"

Dave conceded that *dirt* had a ring to it and he thought the students would remember it. He asked her for her next offering.

"Well," said Liz, "bearing in mind we already had *flap* for transactional writing..." she tailed off, waiting for Dave's response.

He smiled, remembering the reaction this mnemonic always had on the GCSE students. "Ye—es," he agreed. "What was it again? Form, Language, Audience, Purpose."

"Yeah, some of us even added an S for 'structure', so we had *flaps*, which was more helpful," Liz said, glad of Dave's appreciative smirk. "I didn't think that was helpful *enough*, though, so I've come up with 'Plan, Interpret, Subject, Style, Form, Language, Audience, Purpose, Structure."

Dave was quicker on the uptake this time and his answer, though comically elongated and euphonious, was most decisively in the negative. "No-o-o."

"Okay, how about one for analysing language? There's so much they have to remember to get into each paragraph."

"I can't fucking wait for this." Dave was chortling in anticipation.

Liz took a breath and wrestled with the urge to giggle. "Viewpoint, Allusion, Justification, Analysis, Zoom-in, Zeitgeist, Link."

"Okay," said Dave slowly, "give me a minute." His eyeballs slid upwards as he tried to work it out. "No, say it again and I'll write it down."

Liz obliged and Dave wrote, realising relatively quickly what the acronym was.

"I appreciate a vajazzle as much as the next man," he said, "but it's hardly catchy, is it?"

Liz affected wounded indignation.

"It's not exactly going to be clear to the kids what the words mean, is it?" he said. "I mean, *allusion*?"

"Quotation," said Liz, "as in reference, so they back up their point—I mean *viewpoint*."

"I rest my case. Zeitgeist?"

"What people thought at the time the text was written," Liz replied. "Context."

"Is *vajazzle* one of Belle's?" Dave laughed. "I bet it is."

"God, no," Liz tried to steer her positive rebranding of Belle back to favourable waters, "she said it was too much and that you'd say it wasn't suitable." Suddenly uncertain, she added, "You do know I'm just having a laugh, though, don't you?"

"I know. Come on, what have you really got, then?" he asked, "What did she suggest instead?"

"This is really good, actually," said Liz. "Paquazzle: P-Q-A-Z-L."

"I like the sound of it," Dave said. "It's funny, but not too obvious. What does it stand for?"

"Point, Quotation, Analysis, Zoom-in, Link to task."

"Clever Belle," said Dave, impressed. "I take back everything I've ever said about her. Well, most things," he added with a wink.

Liz felt she had atoned somewhat and she'd have hours of fun explaining *Paquazzle* to next year's GCSE students. She bounded back up to her sticky room to get started on her poster designs before her next class arrived, subdued by heat exhaustion or frantic with it.

Rules were relaxed and in these dog days, students were permitted to undo collars, take off ties and even fill water bottles from the fountain in the playground during lesson time. Liz took smaller classes outside, to read under the cherry trees, eating the usually forbidden fruit while they did so. Other classes practised playlets in the playground, and the year tens sat at the picnic tables, preparing for the traditional post mock-exam speech-making assessments.

It was only two weeks before the end of term and all the written assessments were over, the syllabus had been completed and the reports had been written and sent home. Now, they could stop worrying about any key stage three books that hadn't been marked since last Easter because of all the exam marking that had besieged their every waking thought; all the scheduled exercise book checks had been carried out by senior management so now, no one ever needed to know. Now, students could be given projects that they could actually enjoy without having to fret about being assessed, projects that could be allowed to meander, organically, towards the end of term, whether they were teaching the curricularly prescribed skills or not. They were teaching valuable skills, though: independent learning; otherwise known as leaving Miss alone to make sure all her student data has been input, ready for next year's groupings; extending, redrafting and enriching or, to put it another way, enabling Miss to avoid planning another lesson, and, finally, perfecting the clarity and visual impact of work: providing Miss with new material for displays, ready for September.

Liz was just saving her last poster when Dave rushed in, clearly agitated.

"You all right, Bish?" Liz asked him.

"We've had the call."

"Shit! Not—"

Dave nodded grimly: "Ofsted. Tomorrow."

37: There's Only One F in Ofsted

A lead weight seemed to plummet from Liz's solar plexus to stomach. Her panicked heart felt as if it was squirming, searching for an escape route. Her blood galloped through her veins and arteries, rushing in her ears and reducing her brain activity to white noise. She tried to suppress the rising tsunami of nausea that burgeoned in her stomach.

"Breathe, Liz," said Dave. "It's fine. We're ready."

Liz's voice was shrill. "*I'm* not. I haven't marked my year seven or eight books since Easter; I haven't had time. They'll want to see the books."

"Don't worry." He patted her arm. "We've all got classes like that. Just hide the books and tell Ofsted the kids have taken them home 'cause it's the end of the year."

"Do you think they'll accept that?" Liz asked.

Dave was sanguine. "They'll have to. If they decide to come in two weeks before the the end of term, what do they expect? Next week's Activities Week and all the assessments are done; we're bound to have given kids their books back. Hopefully, it won't fuck up the arrangements for the leavers' ball."

Liz started to regain control of her physiological reactions.

"Anyway, got to go and spread the good news," said Dave. "There's an emergency staff meeting straight after school, so we'll see what Dildo has to say about it."

The meeting was held in the main staffroom, the site team having more important things to do than put chairs out and then put them away again half-an-hour later. Things like dealing with some of the more obvious graffiti: covering up especially conspicuous breasts; scouring the penises that were hardest to remove, and erasing the numerous persistent and derogatory Dildo-related declarations from classroom walls. Gordon hushed the clamour of anxious voices and stood, hands raised.

"Well, the day has come," he announced. "Better late than never, eh?"

Liz nudged Lucy, next to her, and whispered, "Was *never* an option?"

Gordon carried on. As head, his duty, like a general's before battle, was to fire up his staff, endow them with the confidence to be able perform at their best, and inspire in them the loyalty to want to.

"School will stay open till nine tonight and open at six-thirty in the morning, so there's no excuse for any untidy classrooms, unmarked books or out-of-date data," he warned, as if warnings were needed.

Almost every eye looked daggers at him—daggers that had been sharpened on the whetstone of mistrust and poisoned with the venom of threatened redundancy.

"I insist," he said stonily and jabbed his finger towards them, "that all lessons must have a PowerPoint and must be typed up on the standard *pre firma*,"—Chris flinched— "and that you adhese to the Learn From the Master training and use Rhys Owen's Paideia methods."

Gordon's expression contorted suddenly, twisting from the antagonistic glare he had just adopted into an ugly leer he seemed to imagine was a smile and he gave them one last piece of advice. "Data sheets, class improvement plans and seating plans must be printed for every lesson you teach for the next two days. That is a direct ord—instruction and anyone found to not be doing this will be dealt with severely by myself."

Having spat this last warning at them, Gordon marched out of the room, leaving the fire-hinged door to hiss in his wake. The moment it had stopped, signalling that the door was closed, outrage erupted.

"Way to inspire confidence," said Liz morosely.

Their collective displeasure was short-lived, however; they had about a week's work to do before the next day.

Back in her classroom, Liz emailed her inspirational posters to the rest of the department, before hastily printing them and pinning them up on a recently emptied display board. She also printed the most up-to-date data sheets and seating plans for each class she would teach over the next two days and laid them out on her desk, thankful that she only had half the classes to teach that she would have had until recently. The real work, however, had yet to begin. She still had to prepare those lessons and that was best achieved at home, where Jack and the boys would feed her and tolerate the tears to which she would, inevitably, have succumbed before bedtime—if she even managed to go to bed.

Once home, Liz shut herself in the study and, flooded again by panic, tried to plan her lessons. Food and drinks came and went on trays and by just before midnight, Liz had managed, with a brain like treacle-soaked cotton wool, to plan one lesson—and that was drivel. She crept into the kitchen to make another coffee. Jack was still up. "Christ, you look awful," he said. "What can I do?"

Liz shrugged helplessly. "Fuck knows."

"Right," said Jack. "Ten minute break." He poured her a glass of wine and pushed it towards her.

Liz sank into a chair and gulped before Jack took control again. "Okay, have you got one great generic lesson that you can use all day tomorrow?"

Liz conceded that she had. "But it won't be outstanding. Dildo says we've got to do his weird Paideia lessons," she said. "That's why it's taking so long. That and the brain-freeze."

"Look, you don't have to be outstanding," Jack said, sensibly. "You just have to be good enough."

Liz smiled and took another swig before Jack resumed his pep-talk. "You're always telling me that if you get an *outstanding*, it just gives you a load of aggro you don't need."

"Yeah, training other people, even more observations..." Liz trailed off, shuddering.

"Exactly! And what happens if you get *good?*"

Liz grinned. "Nobody bothers you," she said. "No observations, no extra training, no interference."

"There you go then," Jack said gently. "And you know you're good enough—just about." He smiled mischievously. "You must be; you've still got a job."

"That could all change after tomorrow," she said ruefully, "but, you're right. "Thanks, love."

Somewhat restored, Liz drained her wine and went back into the study where, a mere two hours later, she had found the one great lesson and copied and adapted it to suit each of tomorrow's classes. Dave had observed her teaching this one last year and had rated it *outstanding*—the one and only time she had ever had such an accolade—and she had kept it for exactly this purpose. What was it about the prospect of an inspection that had made her brain completely malfunction and fail to remember anything? Luckily, Jack's unflappable brain had functioned faultlessly. If only he had spoken four hours earlier, but she couldn't have everything. All she had to do now was fill in her lesson plan forms and she could go to bed and enjoy three hours' sleep.

Three hours' uneasy sleep, plagued by the usual nightmares. Losing teeth, hair and clothes along the way, Liz's sleep-self was beset by jeering inspectors, feral teenagers, and treacherous teaching assistants. She was sent to teach in ever more inaccessible destinations, ever more impossible to reach by the time the bell went. Her heart thumped as she half-woke and turned over, time after time, until her alarm clock put an abrupt end to the dreams' torture; now reality could take over.

When Liz arrived at work, an hour earlier than usual, the car park was already full and when she lurched into the English staffroom, the mood was frenetic as her colleagues rushed around, ashen-faced, formally dressed (despite the humid weather) and twitchy, muttering learning objectives and unearthing resources that had not seen the light of day since the last observation. The photocopier was in overdrive, the laminator was overheating and the guillotine screeched its way through piles of paper, creating sequencing activities that were far too much trouble to prepare for a ten-minute task at any other time.

"Anyone seen my thinking dice?" asked Serena, scrabbling through some drawers.

Lucy replied, "On my desk. Sorry!"

"Oi, Liz, can I borrow your Bloom's question stem laminates?" said Lucy.

"Yeah. Can I have some of your *Oral Feedback Given* stickers?" said Liz, too terrified even to notice that there was a punchline to be added.

Peggy bustled in with a bulging bag and upended it on the table. Chocolate bars, dozens of them, slithered and rustled out, ready to reward or reinvigorate whenever they were needed. "Well, there's the chocolate," she said. "Now, who wants some of my simile fingers?"

"No thanks, Peg," said Gareth. "You have got the yellow ones, this time, haven't you?"

Dave came in and did a final check that everyone had everything they needed. "Right, gang, let's make sure that if we're free, we're supporting anyone who isn't: lining kids up quietly, last-minute photocopying, removing naughties, anything like that," he said. They looked round at each other, nodding. The bell for registration was about to go, but Dave had one last thing to say before it did. "We can fucking do this!"

Another, unanticipated, advantage of the inspection's being the penultimate week of the school year was that, without years eleven and thirteen, the atmosphere around school was reasonably calm and the students moved around with more space and less hysteria than was usual and, by the third lesson, when Liz still had not been observed, she had started to feel slightly more at ease. However, by morning break, the humid air had intensified into gravid, leaden clouds, which emptied their loads, in a sudden, violent outpouring on the heads of the students in the playground, who all shrieked wildly, although only some, prudently, ran for cover. The rest, frenzied at the extreme change in the weather and highly strung, as a result of behaving themselves for two whole hours, turned their faces up to meet the torrent and splashed in the newly formed playground lakes, before the downpour stopped—almost as suddenly as it had started. A grim-faced inspector with a clipboard stood under the canopy that sheltered the picnic tables and watched.

Liz groaned. This could mean disaster. Hundreds of over-excited youngsters, all drenched to the skin, would be almost impossible to settle and control, even without the trivial fussing over soaked books, puddles on desks and bags full of water. She was in her classroom, setting up for the next lesson—even she did not make time for morning coffee when Ofsted was in—and, as soon as the bell went, she made sure she had plenty of paper towels to hand before stationing herself outside her room to welcome her year eights, relieved that no official-looking inspector had arrived with them, although that did not mean she was safe; there was still time.

The students dripped their sodden way in and, one eye on the door in case of a visit, Liz made sure that any wiping, drying or wringing was dealt with immediately so that they could embark on the creative writing lesson she had planned. She had organised the students into groups and they were designing characters for fiction, which they would flesh out and pretend to be for 'hot-seating', a question-and-answer activity, which would take place later in the lesson. While they were intent on doing this, Liz took a moment to calm herself and gazed out of the window again.

A glamorous inspector in elegant, impractical suede heels, ventured out through the main staffroom door and crossed the tarmac, towards their side of the playground, teetering past puddles as she went.

"Here we go," thought Liz and braced herself, heart beating more quickly now. She looked again, but the inspector was heading for the playing fields. Liz breathed out and turned back towards her class. The reprieve was short-lived, though; a squeal came from the back of the room, by the window.

"Miss, she just went to the edge of the field, looked at the mud, looked at her shoes and shook her head!" the girl at the back reported. "She's coming this way now."

"Right, everyone, keep working brilliantly, as you are," Liz said. "If she comes in, show her what you can do."

When, a minute later, Liz looked up from the group with whom she was working at the inspector in her doorway, her students were working enthusiastically on their characters. Liz smiled and strode towards her, picking up her paper-clipped sheaf of photocopied data—with shaking hands—on the way.

"Hi," she said, swallowing away her suddenly dry mouth, "come in."

The inspector held out her steady hand. "Mrs Fletcher?"

Liz exhaled and relaxed. "No, I'm Mrs Marshall. Mrs Fletcher's downstairs in room two," she said, before remembering her manners and adding, "Would you like one of the students to show you down there?"

"I'll be fine," the inspector replied, glancing at the learning objective and success criteria on the board and then at the class, many of whom were so intent on what they were doing that they did not even notice her. She left the classroom and paused to write something on her clipboard, before heading towards the stairs. Liz watched her, wishing there was a way to warn Peggy and Belle—whom Peggy was observing—that they were next in the firing line.

As soon as the inspector was out of earshot, those students who had realised she was there, bubbled up, excitedly, alerting the others that they had missed something noteworthy.

"Was that an Ofsted lady, Miss?"

"Why didn't she stay? The man one was in Mr McGee's lesson for ages."

Liz flopped into her chair and grinned. "I wish she had stayed," she told them; "you were fantastic: all working hard and enjoying yourselves. Well done."

She scribbled a note on an official *out-of-lesson* pass and gave it to a student to take down to Dave in room one. It read, *'Inspector in English block- Peggy's room.'* "Give this to Mr Bishop and come back past room two so you can tell me whether the lesson is going okay," she said.

After the lesson was over, Liz was free. She went down to Peggy's room to find out how she and Belle had got on, but the door was closed and Liz could see both Peggy and Belle talking to the inspector. It was not until lunch time that she was able to find out that the inspector was actually observing the quality of the training received by graduate trainees and had wanted to see whether Peggy's assessment of Belle's lesson had matched up with her own.

"I gave Belle a *good*, but with quite a lot of ticks in the *outstanding* boxes," Peggy told Liz. "I hope I haven't been too soft, though."

"Well, you'll be able to find out at the end of the day," said Liz and turned towards Belle. "How was it?"

"I think it went quite well," said Belle. "I hope so, anyway."

Liz reassured her. "It must have been fine. You practised that *Timothy Winters* poetry lesson on our year sevens, ready for your interview, and it was great," she said, "*and* now you know it works, you'll be fine on Friday."

By the end of the day, only two other English teachers had been seen and Belle, Peggy, Serena and Gareth went over to the main school to get their feedback from the inspector, while those who might still be seen the next day prepared what they needed for another night of lesson planning and when the four returned to the English staffroom, all smiling, the others were there, drinking coffee and waiting to hear the verdict.

"Two *outstanding*s and a *good*," said Gareth. "Mine was the *good*."

Peggy added, "They don't give my mentoring a rating individually, but they said I was a bit mean and bumped Belle up to *outstanding*."

Belle blushed and smiled and, like the girl in *Of Mice and Men*—except alive—all the bitterness and attention-seeking had disappeared from her face. She looked pretty and simple and sweet and young.

38: Tits Up

The next morning was calmer. Dave told them that the inspectors had confirmed they were satisfied with the key stage three lessons they had seen and would only need to focus on GCSE today, which meant year ten.

"So," he said, "If you've got any key stage three today, just make sure they're reasonably calm lessons, in case any inspectors walk past your rooms, but any year ten lessons could be watched, so same plan as yesterday."

The only lesson Liz needed to worry about today was year ten, then. Lively, noisy, chaotic and overrun by hormones, they were definitely not as biddable as her younger students and now the year elevens had left, they considered themselves to be the school's top dogs. These days, many of them had decided that registration was beneath them and sauntered into school late, often some time during the first lesson, and it was first lesson that Liz saw them today. She leaned out of her doorway and, at her invitation, the year tens straggled in, chatting animatedly, sat down and, as usual, ignored their exercise books and the whiteboard.

"Come on, you lot," said Liz, "don't forget, we might have an inspector in today, so open your books and write down the date, title and learning objective while I take the register and when you've got that down, have a go at the Spoken Language criteria word-search I've given out."

Only a handful of the severely depleted class actually followed her instruction and Liz started to feel panic rising. Her heart quickened and fluttered as she remembered that Ofsted like to see that the students are in a routine and this bore no resemblance to one of those. Many members of this class had resisted all her attempts to instil habits and still needed to be reminded every single lesson.

"Come on, everyone. Books open," she prompted before starting the register, glancing anxiously at the door between each name. "Chloe?"

"Yes, Miss."

"Kyle."

"Yeah."

"Lewis...Lewis?"

"On his way; I just saw him in the shop with Connor and Liam," Kyle said helpfully.

Liz squinted at the computer screen to check whether the three boys had been marked present at morning registration. They had not been, so Kyle was probably right.

She continued with the register. "Keira?" No answer. "Gemma?"

"Yes, Miss."

Just then, Liz heard someone come into the room—and the sound of stiletto heels, like nails being tapped into Liz's coffin, told her it was not one of the latecomers. Liz looked up from her register and blanched. As expected, the inspector from the previous day walked in.

"Hello again," she said. "Carry on; I'll find somewhere to sit."

The students, not as cowed by the intrusion as Liz was, gaped at her.

"Are you an Ofsted?" Kyle asked her. She just nodded.

"Sh, Kyle, I'm taking the register," said Liz, endeavouring to maintain a calm and orderly start to the lesson, despite feeling that it could only deteriorate from here. She carried on: "Lauren."

"Yes, Miss Marshall."

"Shall we write this down?" came Kyle's voice again.

This was what Liz had been dreading. "Yes, Kyle." She forced a smile and feigned patience and cordiality.

"Same every lesson. When you're done, start the word-search."

The inspector frowned and wrote something on her clipboard while Liz, trying to make the best of a bad job, finished the register as quickly as she could, took the obligatory bundle of papers over to her and returned to the desk to address the class again.

"Right," she started, her voice quavering, "um...remember, you're preparing talks about important inventions and you're going to give those talks next week. You've been doing lots of research on your inventions and today we're going to look at the marking criteria so you'll be able to make them as good as they can be, ready for the assessment."

Chloe put her hand up. "Is this for our GCSE, Miss?"

"Yes, Chloe," Liz answered. "Remember, we talked about this last lesson—"

"And the one before... and the one before that," said Lauren.

"I've slept since then, Miss," Chloe said cheerfully.

Liz was beginning to feel powerless. The inspector would never believe she had been doing her job properly if the students had no idea what they were doing. She took a slow, deep breath, aware the inspector was writing again. "Look back in your book, Chloe," she said. "That's it; you wrote it all down there. Just look at that if you forget again."

She started, again, to introduce the first activity of the lesson. "Now, in the middle of your tables, you'll see some laminates with the beginnings of questions on them and—"

She was cut off mid-sentence because the three anticipated late boys wandered in, hoods up, jostling and exuding a strong aroma of smoke.

"Morning, boys, sit yourselves down quickly and get the date, title and learning objective written into your books," Liz said hastily. This was not going to plan at all. She tried to keep the tremolo of mounting terror out of her voice. "Hoodies off, please. I was just explaining about the speeches you're preparing."

"Sick," said Liam and turned to Connor. "I'm doing cannab— "

"No," interrupted Liz, glancing at the inspector, who was regarding the scene expressionlessly. "We've talked about this."

Liam grinned. "Chill, Miss. It's banter."

Liam looked around to assess the effect his sophisticated repartee had had on the others and noticed the inspector for the first time.

"Oh!" he said. "Are you the Ofsted thingy?"

The inspector nodded and made a note on her clipboard.

"Is that about me?" Liam asked. She did not respond.

"Just write Miss Marshall's a legend," he advised before reassuring Liz, "Got your back, Miss."

"Um, thank you, Liam. Now, er..." said Liz, floundering, and tried again to start the lesson properly, hope for a reasonable verdict fading fast. "Right—your speeches. You've done lots of planning, so now you need to make sure you've explored your subject in enough depth so you can talk about it well and answer any questions you get asked," she said and gave them the task of using the increasingly sophisticated question ideas on the laminates to interrogate each other about their chosen inventions for ten minutes.

As soon as they were settled, Liz returned to the register to enter the latecomers, taking the opportunity to steady her breathing and have a sip of water before circulating round the class to refocus the inevitable 'off-task' students and ask open questions that would stretch and challenge them. Liz needed to get out from behind her desk and interact with the students if she was to create a better impression; the inspector had joined a group already and was clearly talking to them about the task and looking through exercise books. Liz glanced over again, panic-stricken once more. What if the penis that had been mysteriously scrawled on the front of Connor's book hadn't been removed as she had instructed? She'd forgotten to check.

Just as Liz was halfway towards one of the tables of students, Keira drifted in, ignoring Liz, sat down and started to tell them about the previous evening's activities.

"Keira," said Liz sternly, "What should you be doing?"

Keira tutted and rolled her eyes dramatically. "I haven't got my book, have I?"

Liz handed her a piece of paper. "There you go. And a pen." She put one down in front of her, shot a look towards the ever-watching inspector and mouthed 'coat'. Keira tutted loudly and shrugged off her coat.

"Thank you," said Liz, sitting next to her and added quietly. "You can tell me why you were so late at the end. Now, let's bring you up to speed."

Liz explained the task again and left Keira to join in the discussion on the table. She looked around; most of the students did seem to be doing what she had requested, but her attention was drawn to one group that was not, so she went over to them, ready to re-engage them with the activity. A glimpse of the inspector told her that she, also, had noticed them. Connor had raised his exercise book so that it stood, like a screen—a screen decorated with its graffiti so carefully scribbled-out, exactly over the lines, that it now looked like a furry phallus—on the table in front of him. This could signal many things: perhaps he was chewing gum, although he was not usually so shy about it. Maybe he was talking about something he should not have been discussing, but, again, he did not often censor his speech during lessons. The last possibility was that he was using his phone and if this was the case, Liz dreaded to consider the effect that would have on the inspector's appraisal of the lesson, not to mention the confrontation it could cause, which would put paid to any slim hopes she still had of receiving anything higher than *inadequate*. Liz's mouth, again, turned to dust and as she moved, unnoticed, behind him, she caught sight of his phone screen's blue light.

Desperately hoping she was not lighting a blue touch-paper, Liz reached out and picked up the phone as she passed him and deposited it on her desk.

"Oi, Miss!" said Connor. "I was researching my invention."

Liz laboured to keep her reaction light. "Sorry, Connor; you know the rules," she said. "You can have it back at the end."

Connor opened his mouth to object, but Liz swiftly changed the subject. "What was the best question you got asked, one that really made you give interesting detail about your invention?"

Distracted and pleased to be given centre stage, Connor told Liz what she wanted to know, all the time watched and noted by the inspector, and Liz congratulated him and his table for their excellent ideas before moving on to Lauren's table. Having bonded with Liz on her first day of term, Lauren was keen to support her in any way she could and when Liz sat down to work with the group, Lauren said quietly, "Don't forget to move us around to work with other people, Miss. Ofsted love that."

"Thanks, Lauren, that's coming up next," smiled Liz.

"And don't worry," she added. "When she asked me about homework, I said you never forget to give it. I even showed her some in my book."

"Bless you, Lauren," said Liz. "I'm not sure it'll help, though," she added gloomily.

Liz drew the activity to a close and directed each student to a different group where they would plan together how to include structural features and rhetorical devices into their talks. "Don't forget, they're are all up on the display boards, together with examples," she reminded them, prompting all eyes in the room, including the inspector's, to swivel towards the walls. At least she could not get marked down on that, not like last time.

Starting to calm down and resign herself to all the 'help and support', most likely from Colin, she would get next year to enable her to improve her appalling teaching—the inevitable result of a poor Ofsted rating—Liz looked around. The inspector was talking to Lewis about the displays, by the look of it. She was pointing to a photograph that Liz had had taken a few years previously for a school initiative designed to raise the profile of reading. Teachers and students had shared pictures of themselves reading in unusual places and ways. Contributions had included the head of PE, perusing *Fever Pitch* while playing football; Lucy, reading *Riders* on horseback, and a student reading *Cold Mountain* while skiing. Liz's photograph had simply been taken in the bath and was a close-up, showing only half of her face and part of an arm, which she had covered in bubbles. The rest of her face, chest and shoulders were masked by *The Book of Human Skin*, which she was reading. The picture had been intended to give the impression that she really had allowed someone to photograph her having a bath and some of the more cerebrally lacking students found it impossible to believe that the photograph was a deception, that she was, in fact, fully dressed, in an empty bath with some bubbles on her arm.

Lewis was one of these students and Liz could see by his gestures that he was telling the inspector all about it. On his final warning from the head of year, Lewis was making a huge effort to behave well and to treat people with respect and his report card for the last couple of weeks was testament to how well he was doing. Now, Liz moved closer, in an effort to eavesdrop.

"Not wanting to be rude," Lewis said to the inspector, the search for suitable language evident in his contorting face, "but you see she's holding a book in the photo?"

"Yes." The inspector nodded, narrowing her eyes.

"Um, I don't know how to say this without using a swear word." He struggled, visibly ransacking his vocabulary.

"Go on," pressed the inspector.

Lewis went on. "She was trying to hide her...um...um..." but faltered once again. Suddenly, inspiration struck. "I know!" he announced. "Tits."

Liz's throat constricted and her stomach tightened itself into a knot. The students on Lewis's table screamed with laughter. The inspector cocked a surprised eyebrow and bent over her clipboard, scribbling copiously.

"What?" said Lewis, clearly hurt that his efforts not to offend had gone unappreciated.

Liz carried on miserably. If only the inspector had come in yesterday. She would have seen teaching that was definitely *good*. There seemed little point in trying any more, but she soldiered on; she still had to teach this class in year eleven, so she couldn't let herself to crumble in front of them.

Eventually, the lesson came to an end. Liz dismissed the students and found herself alone with the inspector, who said, "Can I just clarify something with you before I go?"

Liz was free next and all she wanted to do was shut her door and have a well-earned cry, but she nodded wretchedly.

The inspector continued, frowning at her clipboard. "Those students who came in late. You didn't mention it to them. Is there a school policy about that?"

Liz had known she should have taken them to task. She felt cornered. "I probably should have said something to them," she said, "but I wanted them to use the lesson time to learn. I thought if I told them off, I would have been creating a confrontation that could stop them learning what they needed to. We're supposed to record the time they get here so the pastoral head can follow it up, so that's what I did."

"And that's Mrs Dillon, isn't it? I see," said the inspector, writing. "Thank you. You can come and get your feedback between three-thirty and four-thirty."

The need to weep having passed, Liz went downstairs to the staffroom to make a cup of coffee. Dave was there. He looked at her anxiously. "Well?" he asked. "How did it go?"

Liz didn't sugar-coat it. "Fucking abysmal."

39: Feedback

Liz groped her way through the rest of the day, avoiding contact with her colleagues, knowing that just one kind word from any of them would remove a finger from the dam that held back her tears. Thankful that her last lesson of the day was free, now her year elevens had left, she sloped home a few minutes early, evading the outgoing rush. Ofsted had done their two days and everyone would be elated now that it was all over; they had survived, but Liz had let them all down. The best she could hope for individually was a *requires improvement* rating. She might even get *inadequate* and bring the whole school's rating down. If King Richard's didn't achieve *outstanding*—or even *good*—it would be all her fault.

As she got into her car, Liz's phone vibrated. It was a text message from Dave: *Are you ok? We'll talk about your feedback tomorrow x.*

Liz replied, *Not getting fb- rather not know- going home x,* turned her phone off and started to drive, wanting only to be on her own.

By the time Jack got home too, Liz was halfway down her second glass of wine. Jack dropped his bag and jacket onto a chair and put his arm round her shoulders. "What happened?" he said. He rubbed her shoulders heartily, adopting the reassuring briskness of an Akela, and put the kettle on. "Come on. I'll make you a coffee and you can tell me all the gory details."

Sniffing, Liz outlined the disaster that had been the year ten lesson: the unreprimanded latecomers, the blatant misuse of a mobile phone and the ill-chosen reference to her breasts, an anecdote that temporarily distracted Jack from his role as consoler.

"So he was trying *not* to swear?" he asked.

Liz nodded miserably, but Jack was still puzzled. "What could he have called them that could have been worse?"

On any other occasion, this would have triggered a game of 'who can think of the most hilarious names for breasts?' and would have given them a good half hour's entertainment, but not on this occasion; on this occasion, Liz just sighed. "Fuck knows."

Jack shrugged and shook his head. His bemused expression showed that he didn't think it sounded too bad, but he worked in the real world, a place where many employers use common sense and kindness to get the most from their employees. He'd known Liz long enough to know that she worked under a black cloud of fear, which often almost disappeared—almost—but was always restored to its proper position, right above her head, at the slightest provocation. And the provocation of an Ofsted inspection was anything but slight.

"I'm sure it wasn't that bad," he said. "You gave her the data sheets and target grades and all that crap, didn't you?"

Liz nodded and stared into her coffee cup.

"Well, she'll know what those kids are like, so she won't expect perfection." He pushed the biscuit tin towards her. "Here, dunk one of those in it. It's probably not as bad as you think. Wait till you get your feedback and then deal with whatever it is."

"I'm not getting it," said Liz. "I don't want to know. I can't stand the humiliation of sitting there, being told how shit I am. And they'll be so sympathetic." She suddenly recoiled. "Oh God, Dildo and Magoo'll have a fucking field day," she said. "They'll be on my back all next year." She drained her glass and gulped unhappily.

Jack didn't push her. "Come on," he said, "I'm sure it won't be that bad and if it is and you do have to put up with those two watching you all year, you'll get through it."

Liz's horror did not abate. "I don't think I will. I don't think I can do it. It'll be so humiliating; everyone will know—even the kids." She swallowed again and panic started to flood her voice. "There'll be twice the amount of work—and I can't cope with what I've got now."

"What did Dave say?" Jack asked.

"He was fine, but he can't tell the inspector what rating to give me."

Jack tried again: "Give Dave a ring. He'll reassure you."

"I can't," Liz said. "It's so embarrassing. I hate him knowing how bloody useless I am."

"Why don't you switch your phone on?" Jack said, "He might have tried to ring you."

She did as Jack suggested. Two missed calls and a text from Dave: *Ring me back asap x.*

Liz put her head on her arms on the table in front of her and sighed raggedly. "Why didn't I just do it properly instead of thinking I knew better? Why did I think I could get away with no one finding out how shit I am?" she wailed. "I bet everyone else did Dildo's stupid Paideia lessons. Everyone else managed to mark all their bloody books. Everyone else can control their classes."

Jack smiled indulgently. "Come on; you know they didn't," he said. "You're just making yourself feel worse now. You need to relax and forget about it for a bit." He stood up, adopting an upbeat demeanour again. "Up you get; I'll run you a bath and order takeaway."

"Thanks, love," Liz snivelled. She picked up her wine glass and bottle and followed Jack upstairs. As she got undressed in the bedroom, she inhaled the scent of bubble bath, heard the harsh rasp of a match being struck and listened to the gush of the running water, secretly enjoying being cosseted now. "If I'm not down in an hour, I've just let myself slip under," she said.

A few minutes later, as Liz lay, stretched out in the bath, like a corpse in a coffin, she continued to reproach herself. In the flickering light of the candles Jack had lit, she sipped her wine and let her mascara-blackened tears slide into the water like tiny, unravelling threads. The flickering quickened as one of the candles stuttered, guttered and finally went out, the small spark on its wick disappearing and releasing a ribbon of gauzy grey, which meandered in a languid line heavenwards.

Soon she heard a muffled knock, a creak of the front door and muted voices as Jack accepted their take-away and she grudgingly hoisted herself from the cooling water and got ready to go downstairs and eat.

"Dave phoned again," said Jack. "I said you'd ring him back before we eat."

"I can't," said Liz.

Jack dialled for her. "Yes, you can."

When Dave answered, Jack shoved the phone into Liz's hand.

"Is that you, Liz?" It was Dave's voice. "What are you like, you massive drama queen?" he said sympathetically before continuing. "I went and got your feedback form and I talked to the inspector."

"Oh God," said Liz.

"You got a *good*, you twat," Dave said.

"Oh, thank God!" she yelped. "How?"

Dave laughed. "Because, despite what you think, you're not totally shit!"

Satisfied that Liz was reassured, Dave congratulated her and said he would see her the next day. "And I'll turn a blind eye to your hangover—again," he said, "you big lush."

The click of Dave's phone as he hung up was the starting pistol for Liz's squeal of relief. "Oh my God; I can't believe it!"

Jack beamed. "And you know what the best thing is?" he said. "Dildo and Magoo'll have to get off your back now."

"And for the whole of next year," Liz added.

The next morning, Dave gave Liz her feedback form and talked her through what the inspector had said—that, although there had been room for improvement, she was doing pretty well with some challenging students.

"She said you obviously have good relationships with them and they enjoyed the lesson," Dave told her, "and most of them were on task—most of the time."

Liz could not believe what Dave was telling her. "But there was so much that went wrong and so much I didn't pick them up on."

"She said she liked the way you picked your battles—and they *are* learning, most of them, don't forget," Dave said. "The data showed that."

Still incredulous, Liz asked, "But...what about the late boys?"

"Yes, she did mention that. You followed all the school and department procedures," he replied, "And she said that what happens further up the chain isn't down to you, so it sounds like they weren't happy with the way leadership deals with that stuff."

More convinced now, Liz had another question. "Didn't it matter that I didn't use the proper lesson structure?"

"They don't want any particular type of lesson," Dave told her. "She said classes are all different and so are teachers. They just want to see that they're learning."

"So she didn't want us to do Dildo's bloody Paideia lesson thing?"

Dave's voice took on a tone of triumph. "She said they weren't looking for that at all. She said it was old hat and all those educational gurus are being taken with a pinch of salt nowadays," he said. "Anyway, we'll find out more at the meeting after school. Dildo's going to announce the overall verdict."

Liz clutched her feedback form to her like a newborn baby and went upstairs to put it safely in her performance management folder. The door opened and Serena and Lucy came in.

"Bloody hell!" said Lucy. "Are you all right, you idiot? Fancy going home before your feedback!"

"You never think you can do it, but you're fine," Serena said, smiling and shaking her head. "Maybe this'll finally convince you."

Lucy perched on the desk and nudged Liz. "You could get a good Bog Blog out of this," she said. "By the way, Belle told me she knows about it. She took it well, didn't she?"

"That's another triumph for you," Serena added. "Belle's complete turnaround. I said you could do it."

"Well, I'm not sure it had much to do with me," Liz added mysteriously. The other three raised their eyebrows and waited for more, but Liz brushed them off. "I'll tell you—but not yet," she said.

"Spoilsport!" Serena moaned.

"Anyway," said Lucy, "she's on her interview today, but she said she hoped you were okay and that she'd let us know how she gets on."

After school, everyone piled into the staffroom, as they had three long days previously. The atmosphere of dread from forty-eight hours previously had been replaced by one of anticipation, but when Gordon came in, he stood, for a moment, in front of them, his former belligerence having given way to what looked like self-doubt.

"That doesn't look good," Liz murmured to Dave.

"I don't get it," said Dave; "he said everything was pointing to *good* at the meeting yesterday."

Gordon continued to look around the room, blinking and scratching the bald patch on the top of his head like a third-rate Stan Laurel.

When the hum of speculation had died, Gordon coughed and began to speak: "Firstly, I'd like to say thank you for your efforts over the past couple of days," he said. "The full report will be online soon, so you can read the details then, but I'll just give you the headlines for now."

The smile he forced onto his face seemed more diffident than it had been during his previous headmasterful addresses. "Right, well, it looks like we got a *good*," he said.

A clamorous exchange broke out as teachers turned to each other, smiling, their fears assuaged, palpably more relaxed than they had been a minute before.

"The judgement is separated into four main areas." His smile evaporated. "Firstly..." He froze for a moment before gabbling, "Leadership and management," and then hesitated for another microsecond before admitting in a rush, "*requires improvement*," and racing on to the next area: "Quality of education...*good with outstanding features*."

There was a gasp of shock at the first rating, which was quickly followed by a cheer at the second. Glyn Evans raised his hand. Gordon's look enabled rather than invited Glyn's comment: "*Requires improvement?*"

"Yes, Glyn; I'll go into it later. It's nothing to worry about though," Gordon replied hurriedly.

Glyn sat back, folded his arms and nodded, his expression, a thrown down gauntlet.

Gordon went back to his Ofsted areas. "Behaviour and attitudes...*good with outstanding features.* Personal development ...*good.*"

The teachers looked round at each other, nodding and expressing their pleasure and relief. "Finally, as I'm sure you know," Gordon broke in, "there are separate judgements on safeguarding and sixth form and, obviously, the recent unfortunate mishap in relation to a year seven student counted against us, but I stopped that before any real harm was done and I persuaded the inspectors that the requisitioned systems are now in place. Even so, we'll just have to take that *requires improvement* judgement on the chin."

"I? We?" whispered Liz.

"Now for the sixth form," he paused again, perhaps calculating how he could claim the triumph as his own. "We achieved *outstanding*, so I must be doing something right." He chuckled, glancing—with a micro-expression that could have been sheepishness—at Chris, who leapt on the opportunity afforded by the brief eye contact and responded in a gracious, measured tone that must have belied his attitude: "Yes, Gordon, our sixth form students and their teachers did extremely well."

Glyn was less gracious, however: "The sixth form always did well before you came, Gordon. I think it's the fifth *outstanding* since Chris has been head of sixth form," he added helpfully.

Gordon shot one of the looks he, by now, almost exclusively reserved for Glyn, a thorn in his side since the beginning of the year. "Thanks Glyn," he spat ungratefully and then continued. "I don't want to belittle Chris's achievements versus myself," he lied, "but it's easy to get *outstanding* when you're already outstanding."

"Well, if I remember correctly, it was Chris's first year as head of sixth form when it went from *needs improving* to *outstanding* all those *outstanding*s ago," Glyn pressed.

Chris, eschewing the credit he was too modest to accept individually, started to speak: "Well, it wasn't only my—" but his input was interrupted by Gordon, answering Glyn. Gordon's face turned stony, his voice to ice. "Believe it or not, I'm actually delighted that leadership requires improvement."

Nobody did believe it.

"It gives me something to work with," he explained.

Glyn would not let go. "So the fact that you've taken the leadership and management of this school from *good* to *requires improvement* is cause for celebration, then?"

Gordon grinned, his smile a sabre. "Exactly, Glyn."

"And better than five *outstanding*s in a row?"

Chris's forehead puckered and he looked at his hands.

Gordon was clearly agitated. "Look," he said with an appeasing laugh, "Let's not worry about all that. I don't want to waste everyone's time now. It's Friday and we all want to go home, but," his voice hardened to glass again, "if you want to continue this conversation in my office, we can do that, Glyn," he offered.

"I'd rather do it here," said Glyn dangerously.

"If that's the way you want it." Gordon's voice had suddenly risen in volume, the aggression shrill and undisguised. "When I got here, there were so many problems. The previous head left the finances in an absolute mess."

"Is that why Ofsted rated his management as consistently *good*?" Glyn was the only one with the stomach for this fight; the rest of the staff seemed to hold its breath.

The floodwater of Gordon's anger breached the levy of his professionalism and he strode towards Glyn, florid and shouting into his face now. "You think you know it all, but there's so much I haven't told you."

Glyn's head moved back in a gesture that was at once defensive and challenging and the rest of the staff shifted uncomfortably in their seats, at once attracted by the prospect of a satisfying comeuppance and repelled by the possibility of an embarrassingly public row.

Yvonne had got up, visibly angry, and now stood at Gordon's side, hands on hips, in front of Glyn. Gordon returned to his place at the front, but continued to speak forcefully, recklessly, a wounded bull at bay, Glyn's barbs almost visible in his reddened hide. "This place was in a financial and organisational mess. We were quite literally heading for a black hole. I mean, it was literally staggering, that hole we were heading for," Gordon shouted, to the whole room now.

Liz nudged Dave and they risked a glance at Chris, who, flinching at the malapropism, did not disappoint.

"And this Ofsted rating means I can start to sort it out."

"Now we're getting to it," said Glyn. "You're saying you deliberately got *requires improvement* to justify your changes and redundancies?"

Still standing in front of Glyn, Yvonne weighed in now. "You've always had it in for Gordon, haven't you? How can he be expected to run the school with jumped up little bullies like you getting in the way all the time?"

The whole staff gasped and turned to where Yvonne stood over Glyn. Glyn had paled, but did not respond; he simply looked round at the roomful of witnesses.

Gordon faltered, perhaps regretting, at last, the decision to appoint Yvonne. Suddenly, he smiled and stepped towards Glyn again, placing an arm round Yvonne's shoulders and steering her away. "Hey, let's not argue about it. We got *good*. Let's leave it at that."

Gordon stretched placatory hand out towards Glyn, ready to clasp his hand in resolution. Glyn's arms remained firmly folded as he met Gordon's eyes coldly.

40: Leavers' Ball

The next day was the last big celebration of the school year: the leavers' ball. This year, it could be enjoyed just as much by the teachers as by the students now that the spectre of Ofsted no longer hovered over them. However, there was the distinct possibility that it could be moderately uncomfortable; Bob Woodfield, the previous head, now retired, but still emotionally attached to students he had guided for up to six years of their school lives, had also been invited. The tradition at King Richard's was that the charity committee, this year, headed by Jake and Lana and helped by various other ex-sixth formers, would come back into school to organise the party, sell the tickets and decorate the hall. They were there, pinning up garlands, balloons and streamers, when Liz wandered in, during one of her would-have-been sixth form lessons, to see how the preparations were coming along.

"Hey, Miss," said Lana from behind a rapidly inflating pile of balloons, "are you coming tonight?"

"Yeah, definitely," Liz smiled.

Jake appeared from behind the same pile, put down his balloon pump and rummaged among the balloons, scattering them so that they puttered delicately around his and Lana's feet. "Here it is," he said, rattling a coin-filled bucket at her. "That's four quid."

Liz peered into her purse and found a five-pound-note. "There you go," she said and shook her head to refuse the proffered change, but took the ticket. "What's the charity this year?"

"St Anne's Women's Aid Refuge," he said. "Maisie from your form suggested it at the last form reps' meeting 'cause they helped Alfie and his mum so much."

So, the form rebel had found her cause. Liz peered into the bucket again. Among the coins were several five and ten pound notes. She took another fiver from her purse and put it in. "Well, since it's for Alfie... kind of," she said.

Just then, Gordon strutted into the hall and looked around, smugly. "Morning everyone," he said. "How's it all going?"

Jake went over with the bucket and tickets. "Good thanks, Sir. Have you bought your ticket yet?"

Gordon laughed. "I don't need one," he explained. "I'm master of ceremonials."

"Yeah, but everyone always buys tickets," Jake smiled patiently. "It's for a good cause."

Gordon's face darkened. "Do you have any idea how many of these things I have to go to?" he said. "I'd be bankrupt if I paid for them all."

Lana weighed in. "This is different, though; it's to raise money for the refuge Alfie Willis and his mum were at."

Liz busied herself with the balloon pump and a balloon, trying not to be noticed, not completely confident that she was totally out of Gordon's firing line yet.

Gordon did not seem to understand. "But I've *got* to be there. I don't *need* to pay."

"But it's for St. Anne's," Jake reminded him; "they really struggle with fundraising and we've got a real connection with them."

Concentration broken, Liz fumbled the balloon and it leapt from her hand and whizzed its wailing, farting way towards Gordon, who glanced briefly at Liz with an expression of undisguised annoyance. "I'm not paying." He ended the conversation by turning and leaving.

"Did that really just happen? What a—" Lana interrupted herself. "Sorry, Miss."

Liz retrieved the now flaccid balloon. "Don't stop on my account," she said. "I'm as gobsmacked as you are."

"And, according to Maisie, it was his wife whose fault it was Alfie had to leave the refuge in the first place," said Jake, shaking his head in disbelief. "God knows what Maisie'll think when she finds out. She'll probably organise a sit-in."

"She won't find out, though, will she?" Liz said. "Not before tonight. I don't want her getting into trouble—or causing any."

Lana became militant. "Right, we need to let the rest of the committee know, though. He's not coming in without a ticket."

"I'm not sure we can do that," said Jake. "He *is* the head."

"And you don't want to get into any trouble," Liz added.

"What trouble can we get into?" Lana said. "The exams are over. We've left. As long as we man the doors with only year thirteens, there'll be no come-back on anyone else."

Jake smiled broadly. "Brilliant! We might not be able to stop him, but we can embarrass him and make sure everyone else knows he was too stingy to pay."

Later, when Liz arrived for the ball, with Serena and Lucy, the school hall glittered with foil streamers, metallic confetti and mirror balls. Organza swags beautified the now invisible grey plastic of the chairs and paper lace cloths graced graffiti-daubed tables, hiding the obscenities beneath. The staff trickled in gradually, arriving well before any year eleven students so as not to steal the thunder of their various luxurious, curious and hilarious arrivals. Liz and the other two were standing, waiting for things to get going when they saw Gordon and Yvonne approach the door, which was being kept by Jimmy and Frankie, two of the most outspoken members of the charity committee, deliberately chosen for this eventuality.

"Hello, Mr and Mrs Dillon," Frankie said politely and clearly enough for everyone nearby to hear. "Can we have your tickets?"

Liz nudged the others; this would be worth watching. She hissed at the members of staff closest to her, including Dave and Gareth, and jerked her head towards the door.

"What's going on?" asked Dave, but Liz was trying to hear. "Sh! Just watch and listen," she said.

Gordon was clarifying for Frankie and Jimmy that, as head, he had not needed to buy a ticket. A small queue, comprising a few teachers and the preceding head—recognisable at a distance by his head of thick, wavy, grey hair—was forming behind Gordon and his wife.

"This is an exception, though, Sir," explained Frankie fearlessly. "It's for charity, so we always insist everyone has a ticket."

Gordon's forehead was developing a sheen and he puffed out his chest, as if primed for combat, and opened his mouth, beginning to object again. "But I—"

Whatever elucidation he was going to employ was truncated by Jimmy, who appealed to Yvonne now. "We're collecting for St Anne's women's refuge, this year," he said, looking her unswervingly in the eye, "and I'm sure *you* want to give it *your* support."

The emphasis on *you* and *your* was almost inaudible, but its weight was felt by all those who heard it, including the Dillons.

Lucy drew her breath in sharply and Serena raised an eloquent eyebrow.

"That's got to hurt," said Dave.

Yvonne reddened and looked first towards her flustered husband and then at their audience in the hall, all of whom had paid or they would not have been allowed in. By this time, other teachers were reaching round the ignominious pair, giving in tickets or money and walking past them, shaking their heads scathingly. Liz was even sure she heard a sibilant *Dildo* or two as people came past them, into the hall.

Frankie helped Gordon and Yvonne out. "Don't worry if you haven't got tickets; you can just pay now. It's five pounds each."

"Nicely done, Frankie," whispered Liz.

"It was four pounds earlier!" Gordon spluttered.

"That was for advance tickets," Frankie said, unwavering, her smile evaporating.

Bob Woodfield, the old head, stepped round Gordon and greeted Frankie and Jimmy warmly. "Giving Mr Dillon some grief, I see, you two," he boomed, jovially. "Well, I'm going to be a nuisance and pay on the door too."

Gareth nodded appreciatively from the safe distance of the main hall and put his hands in his pockets. "Exceptional timing, Woody."

Bob handed a twenty pound note to Jimmy, who offered a ten pound note in change, but Bob smiled and shook his head, gently pushing Jimmy's hand back. "I hear it's for a special cause, this year," he said before going into the hall and being greeted heartily by his former staff.

Visibly disgruntled, Gordon thrust a bad-tempered tenner towards Frankie and he and Yvonne slunk into the hall, where they stood, ungreeted, just inside the doors. Behind them, silhouetted in the doorway, Frankie and Jimmy's high-five expressed the triumph felt by all who had witnessed the exchange.

Having said *hello* and exchanged pleasantries with Bob, Liz and Dave sat down at a table and watched as he chatted amiably with his former employees, now and again shaking hands, hugging or exchanging cordial kisses on cheeks. On the other side of the hall, Gordon and Yvonne skulked unheeded for a few minutes until Bob caught sight of them and beckoned them over with a genial call and an expansive, inclusive arm gesture. Gordon obeyed hesitantly. A supplanter no match for the abdicator, he approached the group, whose bonds had been easily and immediately re-established. Janet, her arm looped through Bob's, was nodding up at him with a simpering smile and now noticed Gordon for the first time. Apparently conflicted, she released her former head's arm and turned her ingratiating smile towards her present one, who joined the group, lingering on its periphery. Janet turned immediately back to Bob.

"It's like a wildlife documentary or something, where the head lion goes off hunting," commented Dave, "and leaves his harem alone and another lion comes along and tries to take over."

Liz attempted the gentle vocal wisdom of a BBC nature documentary voice-over. "In the intense heat of the Serengeti, the battle-scarred, but still powerful alpha male returns after a lengthy hunt."

"Classic," sniggered Dave.

"The lionesses, unsatisfied by the young pretender, crowd around their former protector, nuzzling and purring, offering themselves to him," Liz continued.

"Like the sluts they are," Dave said, un-Attenborough-esque.

"Too much, Bish," scolded Liz, before Dave took up the reins again in more appropriate style. "The smaller, weaker lion arrives, attempting to win back the loyalty of the harem..."

"...but he is no match for the formidable older male, resplendent with magnificent mane and unquestioned authority," Liz continued, "Even though one of the older lionesses considers him, painfully aware she is past her prime, the inferior male fails to attract her back and slinks to the outer edges of the territory with just one low-ranking female, where he is ignored, and soon forgotten."

Dave snirtled into his drink and their mockery was abruptly curtailed by a beep from Liz's phone, immediately followed by one from Dave's.

"It's Belle," said Liz. "She's got that job."

"Fair play," said Dave. "That *outstanding* from Ofsted won't have done her any harm and I gave her a fucking good reference."

Liz sighed. "She turned out all right in the end, didn't she?"

Dave nodded his agreement. "We might even miss her next year."

"Are you mellowing, Bish?" Liz laughed. "Must be that romance. How long has it been going now?"

"A few months," he said, almost glowing. "Nothing like some good, hard loving to smooth off your rough edges."

Liz smiled enigmatically again. "That's what Belle said."

A sudden surge towards the front entrance of the school averted their attention and Dave's questioning look went unanswered. The first students were starting to arrive. Liz and Dave joined the others on the front steps and looked towards the gate where a black limousine was creeping under the wrought iron 'King Richard the Lionheart' arch. The car pulled up and six girls emerged, one by one, in a rustle and slide of silk and satin, hovering, for a moment— lustrous and vibrant as humming birds—to smooth creases out of and shake life into their skirts. After them, almost unnoticed, one dark-suited boy emerged from the depths of the limousine in a parody of Pandora's Box. One of the girls grabbed his hand and the seven of them went through the path created by teachers, who parted for the students this time, and into the hall, where the lights had been dimmed and the music started.

There followed a stream of students arriving in style, which caused traffic jams all along the main road. There were more limousines and several cars hired or borrowed for the occasion: stately old Rolls Royces, E type Jaguars and Aston Martins. Some of the more petrol-headed students arrived in Porsches or Ferraris, posing for photographs on the bonnets, their brand new suits gleaming almost as ostentatiously as the cars. Wisely side-stepping the conspicuous shows of wealth, some arrived comically on unicycles and stilts or in wheelbarrows and tractors. There was even a horse-drawn gypsy caravan, representing one student's generations-old heritage.

For that one night, the school hall became animated with glamour, as if a plain, wooden box had been opened to reveal a tumble of riches: jewels of every colour and cut, glowing and twinkling, enhanced by flickering (albeit simulated) candlelight. The tinkle of music, laughter and glasses augmented this impression and the teachers receded into the shadows at the back of the room, now and then approached by students who wanted photographs taken with them.

Tom and Ellie, followed by the rest of Liz's English class—Joe, Dan, Becky and the rest—grabbed her hands and forcibly pulled Liz towards the velvet curtains in front of the stage, the best spot for group photographs. Dave followed and spent a few minutes taking pictures—with and without bunny ears and pulled faces—with everyone's phone cameras.

"Don't get the penis graffiti in!" warned Liz, knowing he would definitely move back a step to ensure its inclusion.

Towards the end of the evening, a tall, willowy girl with glossy, ebony hair approached Liz and Dave, holding a phone set to camera, and beckoned her poised and ethereal-looking friend. Liz did not recognise these two, but held out her hand for the phone.

"Okay," she said, "stand over by the velvet curtain; that'll look good."

"No, we want you in it too," she said. "Come on, Frabe, hurry up!"

"Kayleigh!" said Liz. "Freya! Wow! I didn't recognise you!"

Kayleigh spoke to Dave now. "Come on, Sir, you too." The two girls made their tottering, cackling way to the curtain, angular arms linked at the elbow like badly fitting jigsaw pieces. Kayleigh held the phone at arm's length, adjusted the angle until she was happy and then took the photo.

"Thanks!" she said and showed them the picture: four people and—just within the frame—a felt tip phallus.

"That's going straight on Insta." Freya grabbed Kayleigh's phone and typed furiously with her thumbs for a few seconds. "There," she said. "Guess what the caption is."

"Go on," Liz urged.

Freya showed her the picture, now on Instagram, complete with its legend, 'so i managed to squeeze a semi in'.

41: The Summer Ramble

Finally, it was the last week of the summer term and King Richard's was, at long last, able to wind down for the summer holidays. The concluding activity of the year for the students who had not yet left was Friday's long-established final-morning walk on the Bremeldon hills or the *Summer Ramble*, as it was known. There was no chance of its being rained off, this year, thanks to the glorious sun, and it would be the first time Liz's form had taken part in the tradition, so she needed to explain to them all the routines and regulations to which they must adhere for their safety: they must let Liz have their phone numbers so she could keep a copy for herself and give a copy to Mrs Dillon; wear suitable shoes; carry water, sunscreen and a waterproof; always stay with at least one other student; follow the route printed on the *Summer Ramble* card; get the card stamped by the teachers manning each of the ten checkpoints, and at the end, go back into the school foyer and get signed out by Mrs Dillon and the year heads. After that, which was usually around lunch time, the students would be free to go home and start their summer holidays.

The day before the ramble, Liz opened her emails to find one that Gordon had sent to all the staff. Still defensive after his damning verdict from Ofsted, Gordon used a tone that was even more aggressively dictatorial than usual and expressed himself with even more abortive erudition. *It has been bought to my attention*, it read, *that some co-workers are in the habit of bringing their dogs on the Summer Ramble and also failing to completely finish the walk and derelicting their duty by choosing to attend one of the local public establishments instead. Either of these practises represent a safeguarding issue and will result in severe consequences by myself.* Apparently still smarting from the leavers' ball too, he ended his missive with, *My predecessor may of been satisfied with such lapsadaisical arrangements, but I am not.*

"Bloody killjoy," Liz thought and made her way down to the staffroom.

Chris, for whom Gordon's presentation of Ofsted's verdict on the sixth form had been the final straw that broke the back of his already plummeting respect, had totally given up keeping his opinion of Gordon professionally discreet—with the English department, anyway—had printed the email and was cheerfully dissecting every solecism and malapropism in Gordon's message. "When did the word *colleague* go out of fashion?" he asked and, "So, *derelict* is a verb now, is it?" He curled his lip and skimmed further on. "*Public establishments? Lapsadaisical?* Has this man actually got an academic degree?"

"And aside from all that," said Serena, "he's ruined my day. I always bring the dogs, take a short cut and dive into The Snowdrop with the doggy teachers. It's tradition."

The others nodded sympathetically. "Remember that time Woody caught us on the way out?" Gareth said. "He dragged us all back in for another one!"

"Fucking *lapsadaisical* of him," said Dave, shaking his head in mock disapproval.

"It's health and safety gone mad," added Liz. "Seriously, though, there are plenty of us with tutor groups, who have to supervise the whole route. There's no need for everyone to do it. Why can't they have a bit of fun?"

Even Peggy joined in. "And we all get our turn when our forms leave in year eleven."

Serena had been listening, part amused, part annoyed and now posed the question, "Who *brought it to his attention*, anyway?"

"I'll give you one guess." Liz screwed up her eyes and hunched her back and shoulders. "Zvngh...I think you'll find...fnh," she said, nasally.

Lucy was there like a shot. "Magoo!" she said. "Of course. Little snitch. He's talking about forcing the kids to walk in an *orderly crocodile* from the last checkpoint back into school as well. Talk about a spoilsport."

Later, Liz photocopied the list of her form's mobile numbers and put a copy in each of Yvonne and Barbara's pigeon holes. She also put Alfie and Maisie's numbers into her phone and sent Alfie's mother, Sarah, a text message so that she had Liz's number too—just in case. Next, she emailed Yvonne, copying Barbara in, to tell her about the extra measures she had taken with Alfie and reminded Yvonne, as tactfully as she could, of the need to be extra vigilant and to make sure that, when he had been signed out, Alfie went home with his mother, who would be picking him up after the walk. After parents' evening, she did not want to take any chances with Alfie's safety, even if that meant ruffling Yvonne's feathers.

Yvonne's curt reply came after only a couple of minutes: *Liz, I am well aware of my responsibilities regarding Alfie. Regards, Mrs Dillon.* Liz rolled her eyes. Another black mark against her, no doubt, but at least she had a 'paper' trail.

The next morning, as arranged, the few hundred students taking part in the ramble met at the bottom of the Bremeldon hills. Each form teacher registered his or her form and distributed the Summer Ramble cards, which had a map of the route on one side and a grid for the ten stamps they had to collect on their way round on the other. Peggy wore a bright yellow cap with a peak, blew a whistle from time to time and held aloft a flag, on which she had written 7MF.

"Morning, Peg," said Liz. "Nearly didn't notice you there."

Peggy was horrified. "Oh no! I thought my form wouldn't be able to miss me with all this."

Liz laughed. "I'm only joking; they won't have any trouble at all."

One or two local dog walkers scuttled round the outside of the ranked masses, having forgotten that this was the day King Richard's occupied the hills, and rushed ahead, probably planning alternative routes. Others had parked and begun to walk before they noticed the crowd, but turned back, repelled, and bundled their dogs back into their cars.

As soon as the students had registered and met the groups with whom they were walking, they were allowed to start rambling. First, came Maisie and Alfie, inseparable as ever, armed with notebook and camera in case of a scoop.

"Morning, you two," said Liz. "You're early. Now, remember what I told you: be careful and stick together."

"We will," they said. "Don't worry."

Liz gave them each a slip of paper with her mobile number on. "Now, this is just for emergencies," she said. "If you're worried about anything, just give me a call, or you can call school—the number's on your summer ramble card—or ask any teacher from King Richard's; we've all got our IDs on our lanyards, so you can recognise us."

Maisie laughed. "Chill, Miss; it's fine. We've got this."

Alfie smiled too. "Yeah, we've had the talk from our mums and her dad," he said, nodding his head towards Maisie, "so we know what to do. Thanks, though."

They strode towards the path up the hill. "See you later!"

Jordan and Emin were next, their penchants for both sporting activities and performance trainers appropriate today. They were among the first to start too and had charged off with their relative posses, eager to finish and sign out well before lunch, if possible. Ted's group was next. Sensibly kitted out in stout walking boots, bucket hats, daubed in sunscreen and hauling rucksacks full of provisions, they were going to get the most out of the walk. Liz even thought she had caught sight of a pair of binoculars and a birding book among their hiking accoutrements. Kate and her friends went off next, strolling and chatting about the ice cream van that was rumoured to be at checkpoint seven.

Liz looked around and saw Peggy, still holding her flag up to attract the last few latecomers. "Isn't your arm aching, Peggy?" she asked. "Haven't you put it down this whole time?"

Peggy smiled with pride that her superpower had been noticed. "No, I can do this for hours. Me and my sister used to have competitions to see who could keep their arm up the longest," she said. "I always won."

Liz, Peggy and Serena sent the remaining year sevens off and started the walk themselves, enjoying the warmth, the congenial atmosphere and the prospect of the six-week holiday, which was starting in just a few hours.

Dave was in charge of the first checkpoint and a small group of students was waiting to have their cards stamped before continuing to the next one. From a distance, Liz could see Dave standing up and it looked as if he was ministering to some sort of student facial problem, perhaps removing grit from an eye. However, as they watched, the student on whom he seemed to have been performing this delicate procedure moved away, another took his place and Dave repeated the process.

"What's Bish doing?" Liz wondered.

Peggy sped up. "Looks like my first aid kit might be needed," she said eagerly.

Serena shaded her eyes with her hand. "I think he's drawing something," she said. "Must be some new joke he's dreamt up this year."

When they arrived at the checkpoint, the last small student was just leaving, his face adorned by a felt tip beard and moustache.

"What are you doing to those poor kids?" Liz queried.

Dave sniggered. "I just thought it would liven up the day and freak Dildo and Lady M out when they get back to school," he said. "I told the kids they have to have facial hair drawn on so the other checkpoints can see who's been to mine."

"And they believed you?" Liz said.

"Proabably not, but they fucking love Mr Bishop's beards," he said. "They were all queueing up for them. Clamouring, they were."

Peggy rolled her eyes. "You daft bugger."

"That's not all," Dave said. "Lucy and a couple of others are on the last checkpoint, just before school, the same one Magoo's on. They're going to tell the kids they have to get individual selfies with Magoo for the school website."

Liz, Serena and Peggy looked at each other dubiously. "Why?"

Dave laughed. "Picture it. Magoo won't know what's going on," he said. "He's not a people person, so he'll hate all those kids getting close to him. And—" He paused dramatically. "—his evil plan to organise them into orderly pairs before they can go back into school will be foiled 'cause he'll be too distracted. He'll freak!"

Liz and the others carried on rambling, enjoying the peace and lack of animosity, and chatting about how most of the kids were pretty good really and it was nice to be reminded of that. The ramblers, not in school uniform today, adorned the hillside paths ahead of them like colourful paper garlands and it seemed the perfect way to end what had been a difficult year.

As they approached a path that led down to some bushes on their left, Liz noticed billows of smoke emanating from one of the shrubs, even though, like Moses's, the bush remained miraculously undamaged. Liz nudged Serena. The look that passed between them was a tacit agreement to turn a blind eye and distract Peggy until they got past. Liz grabbed Peggy's arm and pointed ahead and to the right. "What's that, Peggy?" she said loudly. "I think it might have been a little cat with a hurt paw."

Peggy rushed in the direction of Liz's finger, towards the undergrowth where she peered around branches and between leaves, trying to find the creature. Liz and Serena followed, but turned back and watched as, from out of the middle of the shrubbery behind them, appeared, not the angel of the Lord, but Connor, Lewis and Liam from Liz's year ten, stinking of cigarette smoke. They grinned sheepishly and walked up the path, greeting Liz and Serena, who feigned ignorance as they passed.

Emerging, catless, from the undergrowth Peggy hailed them. "Morning boys. Where did you spring from?" she said.

"Short cut," they explained, picking up their pace and coughing. "Have a good summer!"

"Silk cut, more like," Liz whispered to Serena.

The three had sauntered their way to the halfway point when Liz received a text. It was from Sarah Willis: *Just phoned Alfie but goes to voicemail. Is he ok? Phoned school but no answer so sent message- would have rung you but keeping it free in case they ring me.* Liz tried Alfie's number too, and then Maisie's—with the same result. She texted

Sarah: *Prob no signal- will keep trying and get others to as well. Will phone school and go back there now.*

Unsettled, Liz spoke rapidly to Serena and Peggy. "Look, it's probably nothing, but we can't get hold of Alfie. You two keep going and ask everyone when they last saw him and Maisie and let me know."

Serena and Peggy nodded. "Of course. He'll be fine, though; don't worry."

Liz jabbed at her phone, held it to her ear and then jabbed it again, sighing in frustration. "No one's answering the emergency numbers at school. I'm going to take the short cut back and make sure they know. They can start off a search or something if they need to."

Luckily, there was a steep path down the side of the hill, which led from where they were back to school in a fraction of the time it had taken them to get there and Liz launched herself down it, sliding and scrabbling along the dry bracken and dusty tree roots. When she arrived at the bottom, breathless and grimy, she was able to check her phone again. There was a message from Serena, which read, *Just got to cp7- A+M came through a little while ago. Will let you know at cp10.*

Liz replied, *Will let his mum know*, and sent Sarah a message too. Next she phoned Alfie. "Are you okay?" she asked. "We couldn't get hold of you. Your mum's worried."

"Yeah, we're fine," he replied cheerfully. "There was just a bit of the walk where there was no signal. Sorry we worried you. We're on our way back now."

"No probs," said Liz. "Phone your mum and let her know. I'll see you back at school soon."

Liz texted Serena and Peggy and, unwilling to go back to the ramble until she had seen Alfie with her own eyes, she set off the short distance back to school. As she passed The Snowdrop on the way, Gordon stepped out from the car park, where he had obviously occupying his time usefully by lying in wait for disobedient staff.

"What do you think you're doing?" he demanded and without waiting for an answer, continued. "Didn't you read my email yesterday?" he barked.

Liz was too harassed to curb her indignation and retorted instantly. "I've been looking for Alfie."

Gordon sucked in his breath, visibly frightened, perhaps not so much for Alfie as for himself.

"He's okay; we've found him now," Liz said, "but who was in charge of the emergency mobile? Who was manning the phone? No one answered them."

Gordon patted his pockets, crimson rising under his skin, from neck to hairline. "I—er—Yv—" he stuttered, appearing reluctant to admit responsibility, jumped into his car and sped back towards school, heedless of the hundreds of wandering students he could injure.

Mentally berating Gordon and Yvonne, Liz walked along the pavement that led to school. Some way up the road, a mother was holding a car door open for her young son and by the quick, angry animation of her head, Liz guessed at some sort of disagreement, whether he would sit in the back or front, probably. At any rate, the boy seemed to be resisting getting in—and the woman was pushing him now.

Something was not right. Liz's pace quickened and so did her heart. She recognised that boy. He twisted away from the woman and, as he turned round, Liz understood rationally what she had just felt in her gut.

It was Alfie.

And the woman with the car was not his mother.

42: The End of Another Year

"Alfie!" Liz sprinted towards the car, startling the woman, who let go of him and jumped into the driver's seat, speeding away in a scream of rubber and reaching over to slam the passenger door as she went.

Alfie ran towards Liz, clearly terrified. Liz grasped his shoulders and looked at him. "Are you okay? What happened?"

He was shaking now, his eyes brimming. "She—she just came out of the school doors and grabbed me and pulled me towards her car. I hadn't even signed out. They were just watching. Why did they let her?"

"Come on," said Liz gently; "let's get you back in and we'll wait for your mum."

She put a protective arm around him and began to guide him back to the school's foyer, where Liz could see Sarah, now. She must have gone in through the back door.

"There she is now," she told Alfie.

Before they got as far as the main doors, however, Sarah burst out of them, clearly frantic. Alfie sprang towards her and she fell to her knees, crying and hugged him fiercely. Liz hung back, but after a minute, Sarah looked up, bewildered.

"Mrs Marshall saved me," Alfie said.

Liz was embarrassed. "Well, I was just there at the right time," she explained. "I'm just glad you're all right."

"Thank God you *were* there; those two haven't got a clue," Sarah spat, jerking her head back to the foyer, where Gordon and Yvonne could be seen looking through the doors in confusion, presumably wondering why Alfie had two mothers and the second one had just run out in panic.

Liz, Sarah and Alfie went back into the school where Yvonne was already stammering that she could not have known the first woman was not Alfie's mother.

"But it was *Alfie*," Liz said. "You knew you had to be extra careful and you've already had one scare with him."

Barbara came over. "If you'd let me help with the signing out," she said to Yvonne, "or if you'd let me look after the phone, instead of sending me to supervise Sick Bay—"

"But you—you're not..." Yvonne trailed off.

"What?" said Barbara. "Not head of year any more?" She put her shoulders back and raised her chin, her demeanour taking on the steely dignity of the Duchess of Malfi in the face of death. "I am still head of year seven—until half past three, anyway."

Gordon, who had been bravely watching from a distance, stepped in and spoke to Sarah obsequiously. "Why don't you take a seat and we'll get you a cup of tea while we get to the bottom of this?" he said.

Liz turned to Yvonne. "*I'm* struggling to understand how this could have happened as well—especially after you assured me you were aware of your responsibilities with Alfie."

Clearly shaken, Yvonne tried to explain. "Well, she said she was coming to collect Alfie and I knew he couldn't go with his dad. What else was I supposed to think?"

"Where was Maisie? She'd have known that wasn't his mum," Liz said.

Alfie spoke now. "Maisie came back with me, but she just went straight round the back, to the library, so she didn't even see her."

"Why didn't *you* say anything, Alfie?" Liz asked.

"I didn't even go into school," he said. "I didn't get a chance to sign out. I was just coming along the path when she came out and grabbed me and—"

Yvonne cut in. Her face was scarlet. "I could see Alfie was just coming, so I told his mum I'd sign him out and she could go and get him."

"But it wasn't his mum, was it?" Liz pushed. "*This* is his mum." She pointed at Sarah.

Yvonne sounded like a petulant teenager when she retorted, "Well, I didn't know."

"Well you should have known. It was your job to know." Liz had dropped any pretence of diplomacy now. "And what about the voicemail Sarah Willis had to leave on the emergency mobile because it wasn't answered?" She turned towards Gordon again now. "What about when *I* tried to phone and no one answered then either?"

Gordon held up the phone and attempted a triumphant recovery. "Ah!" he said. "I've seen the messages now and he was okay, so that wasn't a problem, anyway."

Liz spoke with disdain now. "That's not the point. No one was checking or answering it. How many more calls could have been missed?"

Sarah had stood up again and re-joined them. "How do you know any other children aren't in danger?" Sarah added. "Thank God Mrs Marshall had the sense to put Alfie's number in her phone and swap numbers with me. If she hadn't, she wouldn't have come back to school and seen what was happening. He'd have been taken by that woman and God knows where he'd be now."

Yvonne's self-preservation overrode her morality again and she became defiant. "Well, if you're not happy with the safeguarding arrangements of the school, I suggest you take it up with the governors," she said, before stalking along the corridor to Gordon's office.

"I will," Sarah assured her.

"Well, Mrs Willis," Gordon said icily, "we should all be grateful that Alfie's safe. Have a pleasant summer," and followed his wife in the direction of his office.

There was over an hour until two o'clock, when the end of term staff buffet was due to start, and after Liz had seen Alfie and his mother safely off, she went over to the English block staffroom and, sighing heavily, slumped into a seat with a cup of coffee. When the others trickled back in, after a few minutes, having completed the ramble and their various duties, Liz filled them in on the excitement they had missed.

Dave had already found out about it from Glyn on his way back into school. Glyn had intimated that, as union representative, he had also been fielding a variety of complaints from staff about Gordon's recent handling of the Ofsted visit and the meeting after it as well as less recent issues, which were resurfacing now, thanks to that inspection. According to Dave, Glyn had been liaising quite intensely with the governors for the past week.

"Glyn said he can't advise this publicly, obviously," Dave said, "but if we're not happy with anything, we should all email the governors now. Parents too. Lots of people already have. Maisie and Alfie's parents have just started contacting everyone they know too."

"Well," said Liz. "I've definitely burnt my bridges with both of them, so I'd better stay out of it."

"I heard," said Dave. "Glyn said you were fucking magnificent."

"How did he know?" Liz pretended to be less gratified than she actually was.

"Barbara was there. And some of the other heads of year, remember," said Dave. "Apparently, you gave it to them with both barrels."

Liz put her head in her hands. "Shit! It was in front of everyone, too. I was just so angry," she wailed. "I should have bitten my tongue. My life won't be worth living now."

Just before two o'clock, Liz and the others crossed the vacant playground to the main staffroom for the buffet, the final event before they left for the summer. Liz skulked at the back of the group, loath to draw attention to herself. As they approached the door, Gordon and Yvonne came through it and stepped onto the tarmac in front of them. The pair glanced with stony contempt at them, their frowns confirming, for Liz, what she already knew: that she had earned their hostility and, far from making it through the year without antagonising the new head, she had stored up even more torment, not only with him, but with his wife as well. They would spend the holidays festering over her public condemnation of them and plotting their revenge. Next year would be intolerable.

Gordon and Yvonne readjusted their bags, pointedly turned their faces away and hastened in the direction of the car park.

"What's up with them?" Peggy asked? "Miserable pair."

Liz grimaced. "I think those faces were meant for me."

"Looks like they're taking their bags over to their car so they can make a quick getaway after the speeches," Serena said.

"That'd be right," snorted Dave. "Cowards."

They went into the staffroom and found a group of seats. The usual buzz of conversation was more excited than usual and Glyn looked about to burst.

Just then, Lucy and Gareth strode over and Lucy hailed them. "Oi, you lot!"

"You managed to get to the pub without Gordon catching you, then," Liz said.

"We managed to imbibe an ale or two, as it happens," Gareth smiled.

Lucy plonked herself down in a chair. "It was weird," she said. "We were just trying to sneak past Gordon's office so he wouldn't see us coming in late—"

"He was heading towards the car park a minute ago with a face like fucking thunder," said Dave. "Surprised you didn't see them."

Lucy's expression of wonder turned to one of revelation as she processed the evidence. "His door was wide open, there was nothing on his desk and it looked as if his office was empty." She paused. "Bloody hell!"

Hope leapt, new born, in Liz's heart. "You don't think..." but she smothered it, reluctant to worsen the inevitable disappointment she'd suffer when she found out the reality of the situation, which must be something mundane. "No."

As people digested the snippets they had heard and tried to piece them together, they turned to one another, ravenous for news. Then all eyes focused on Glyn, who gave a theatrical shrug, which clearly disclosed that he had been prohibited from telling rather than that he was uninformed. A brittle silence fell upon the room. The clock ticked. The oven's fan whirred as it heated the snacks for the buffet. In the playground, a gull gave its repetitive call, like the creak of a rusty swing.

The silence was broken by the sound of the staff room door opening and Janet came in, followed by Chris and Doug, the chair of governors. The teachers gasped and swivelled their heads towards one another again. This was unprecedented; Doug only ever appeared to the masses at Christmas, never at the end of the year, and something told them this was not a time to lay bets on the frequency of his hand-fly coordination.

Janet spoke first, her official retirement speech forgotten for now, and, pale of face, introduced Doug, who shuffled and coughed gently, far less imposing in his casual, summer chinos and short-sleeved shirt than his formal suit. It was as if he had been interrupted while pottering in the garden.

"Afternoon, everyone," Doug said. "No doubt, you're wondering what I'm doing here and I'm afraid I can't tell you very much because of confidentiality regulations and also the fear of prejudicing any possible future legal action, but you'll just have to trust me."

Nobody breathed. A cold tingle, somewhere between excitement and fear, spread from Liz's scalp to her chest. Legal action?

Doug carried on. "A number of issues have arisen recently, concerning the behaviour of the current leadership," he nodded towards Glyn, "about which the governors have met with Glyn, the unions and the local education authority, but, as I said, I'm not able to share the details of either the concerns or the meetings at the moment. Today, however, the second incident involving Alfie Willis in year seven necessitated an immediate response, particularly after Ofsted's findings about management and safeguarding, including the school's duty of care in relation to the recording of absentees, latecomers and 'at risk' students."

A ripple of speculative susurration followed before Doug continued.

"Sarah Willis, Alfie's mother, contacted the governors an hour ago about an incident in which, for the second time, her son was exposed to potential harm or abduction, this time by his father's girlfriend. Actually, we've been inundated with calls and emails from parents."

"Thanks to Maisie and her family," whispered Liz to Dave.

Doug continued, "Anyway, we called an emergency meeting with Mr and Mrs Dillon."

Once more, the talk in the staffroom proliferated and dwindled almost instantly when Doug opened his mouth again to speak.

"They have now been placed on suspension, pending an investigation into this and other irregularities, including some surrounding a breach in regulations regarding the appointment of Mrs Dillon. A number of emails have been sent to the governors concerning their conduct at the recent Oftsed verdict meeting too." Doug paused and turned towards Chris. "Mr Moran has agreed to take the position of acting head until all this is sorted out and I hope the heads of year will be good enough to continue their existing roles next year too; the governors have to assume Mr and Mrs Dillon will not be returning."

There was a second's absolute silence before the staffroom erupted in a thunderous cheer. Drinks were upturned as people leapt to their feet, fists punched the air and work-mates hugged each other. There was a loud pop as Glyn (prepared in advance by being in possession of the facts before most of the others) uncorked something effervescent and another cheer as it overflowed, soaking carpet and colleagues alike. The first drink was thrust into Barbara's hand and her tears, this time, were happy ones. Evidently, Glyn had not just brought one bottle, though, and soon, Doug, Chris and even Janet were picking their way through the crowded staffroom, filling glasses and handing out glasses and plastic cups of Prosecco, making ready for a toast.

When every glass was charged, Doug spoke again and lifted his glass. "To King Richard the Lionheart High School and better days to come."

A hundred cups were raised. "King Richard's."

When Liz finally got home, Jack was there already and handed Liz a glass of wine. "Well, you made it through another year." He beamed contentedly, pouring himself one too.

Liz grinned back and they chinked glasses before each took a gulp. "Wait till you hear about today," she said.

"I heard. The king is dead; long live King Richard's," he said and chinked her glass again.

"You couldn't make it up," she agreed. "Although..." her voice took on a speculative tone, "maybe I'll finally get round to starting my novel this summer. They say write about what you know and I think I've got an idea."

Liz kicked off her trainers and they made their way outside, onto the patio. The sun was still shining and the stone slabs were warm on the soles of her feet. Bumble bees lurched drunkenly from one bloom to another, their humming drone enriching the evening birdsong: the throaty comfort of the wood pigeon, the lyrical vivacity of the robin, the languid euphoria of the blackbird.

Acknowledgements

So many people have helped, supported and advised me in writing this and my thanks go to everyone who did: Scribblers writing group, which encouraged me, reined me in and gave invaluable structural advice, especially Melanie Dufty, Sarah Dukes, Olivia Levez, Eleanor Porter and Michael Woods; my mum, Jenni Hyatt, who was unerringly complimentary, as mums are supposed to be, and stopped me swearing too much, as mums are supposed to do, and my sons, Dan Knight, for reading, copy editing and letting me know what you can and can't make jokes about, and Alex Knight for the beautiful cover design.

Printed in Great Britain
by Amazon